A unique world treasure is held to ransom in a compelling
story with characters to love, fear and fear for – Anne Sikking
captures the beauty and significance of Granada's past, the
complexities of the political present, and the power of the
human heart to confront and overcome all manner of obstacles
in a complete page-turner.

J.G. Harlond
author of The Empress Emerald
www.jgharlond.name

A twenty-first century tale in a timeless monument. Granada's
Alhambra, throughout its long life, has been witness to every
type of event, from the worst of crimes to the most beautiful
of love stories, from terrible miscarriages of justice to the most
noble piety. Now, thanks to Anne Sikking's novel, we have a
drama, tense to the last page. SONG of GRANADA plunges us,
once again, into a fascination for this unique site, which crowns
the city of Granada.

Brígida Gallego Coín
author of Isabel de Solís. Soraya
twitter.com/BriGallegoCoin

A work of art that mixes reality with history... Taking place
over a Friday, Saturday and Sunday, the book races along with
an intensity that is breathtaking. Anne Sikking's poetic style
delivers us today's Granada with sensitivity yet a clarity of vision
that is both fragile and luxurious...

Juan de Dios Jerónimo
RADIO COPE
www.cope.es

Page One was so horrific, so gripping, that I did not know if I dared read on. Happily I did, and was rewarded with a tragic tale of tangled love, music and terror in Andalusia.
Fans of Lorca will thrill to this story.'

Pan Zador
author of ACT OF LOVE - published by Crimson Romance
www.crimsonromance.com

As the leading English-language newspaper in Andalucía, THE OLIVE PRESS is privileged to receive a great number of ex-pat books to review. But it is rare that we are lucky enough to to read one so clearly born of a love for the region, its people and its culture.
Anne Sikking's characters represent the diversity of Andalucia, yet in their interweaving narratives are held together as part of a complex whole. The story tackles a quite incredible range of topics, from homosexualtiy to the 'war on terror' to duende.
And at the centre of everything is the ever-changing, yet eternal, Alhambra Palace.
SONG OF GRANADA is a wonderful read, driven by an in-depth knowledge, admirable research and an almost tangible passion for Andalucia.
I loved the book and couldn't put it down.

Imogen Calderwood
THE OLIVE PRESS
www.the olivepress.es

A 'Granadino' cannot stop being one with a copy of SONG OF GRANADA in their hands. Before even talking about the literary value of the work, or the intensity of the drama, this first reaction is almost inevitable. The 'native' reader turns to each paragraph, examining it through his or her particular 'reality' filter, eager to verify its accuracy, to ensure the veracity of the places described, to check for the slightest error. I must say that Anne Sikking's book is beyond reproach. The descriptions of the urban areas of Granada are completely reliable, and this credibility enhances the narrative value of the book.

SONG OF GRANADA takes hold of you as you race through its pages with breathtaking speed. Each character brings his or her own angle to what marks the history of the city... its Arab past, its relationship with the Gypsy world, Lorca's murder... a death that still weighs heavily on Granadinos and Granada. The diversity of the characters in SONG OF GRANADA enriches the text and contributes to its almost dizzyingly frantic pace.

The Alhambra has been written about extensively throughout history. This Nazari monument has starred in countless stories, but we needed one closer to our own time. In this latest tale the Alhambra is more than just a scenario, it is a silent witness to its own "abduction".

It is often said that the Alhambra is a living monument; in SONG OF GRANADA it is so alive that it does not even need dialogue, it is as important as Rashida, Antonio, Mary, David, the children, as important as the entire cast of characters and varied human beings parading through its pages.

They offer us a glimpse into a kaleidoscope of life, each character a hue. Through them we are submerged in the human condition and meet people who, when faced with extreme situations, like those in SONG OF GRANADA, as in life itself, are neither good nor bad, neither angels nor demons, neither heroes nor villains.

Congratulations! I will give this book as presents and recommend it to everyone!
Aurelio Cappa
Programming Coordinator - CANAL SUR, Spain

Song of Granada

Anne Sikking

SQUAW PIES
YORK

Published in 2014 by
SQUAW PIES

First impression in 2014 by
SQUAW PIES
an imprint of

COLLAGE INTERNATIONAL LTD
4 9 6 5 3 8 2
15-17 Grape Lane
YORK
YO1 7HU
ENGLAND

printed in Italy

for more information about
COLLAGE INTERNATIONAL LTD
see
www.collage-international.com
information about
SONG of GRANADA & CANCIÓN de GRANADA
www.song-of-granada.com

ISBN - 978 0 9563980 2 4

For

José Antonio Domínguez Banderas
familia, amigos y colegas

in appreciation of a life's work

to the memory of

Federico
del Sagrado Corazón de Jesús
García Lorca

thank you

and for you,

that fireman

whose conversation I shared
during those long hours of delay in Philadelphia airport
whose name I may never know,
who I may never meet again,
and who gave so much.
I hope one day you may recognise yourself here
and believe I have done your story justice.
I salute you.

FRIDAY

Darro tiene prometido
al casarse con Genil
y le ha de llevar el dote
Plaza Nueva y Zacatín

Darro has promised to wed Genil
And the dowry agreed has been
The lovely Plaza Nueva and all of Zacatín

Trad.

dawn

La Alhambra, in *la plaza de armas*, Rashida Santiago reached into the warmest and the darkest place on earth. Her hand slid to meet the shoulder, the head well away. She didn't allow herself to hear the woman's cries. She simply tuned out everything but the feel of her hand.

At times like this, it was never Allah that she called upon. She called upon memory, her own and that of other women who had assisted her in Bolivia, in Mexico. Could she catch this one whole? Silently she looked at the woman and breathed, *help her, help her*.

The way was hard, and she punctured the sack with her fingers. The waters flooded out onto the bare earth, thick, murky and flowing over the pebbles with a putrefying stench. The child was rotten. She had to be quick. The birth canal would close and she would only have the unmoving arm. She began to pull on it.

She reached for her bag. Whatever their fancy names, in the end they were tools, inelegant metal objects to lever out, to wrest, to cut and slice. She loved and hated them. She took the meanest hook and passed it across the woman's eyes. Sometimes the sight was so fearful that the mother would receive a shock from the brain that engaged her in one last effort. There was a little effort now, but not enough. The woman was tired, too many days carrying dead meat.

The hook went in, past Rashida's hand, over the shoulder and thrust into the mouth. She dragged the carcass as far as she could but the womb was hard and would not yield. She took the arm off at the shoulder. It gave her space to turn, but not enough to take hold of the torso. She tried to catch it by the feet, but in the end took it in another two pieces, severing the head. The skin dropped off as she laid the three precious parts on the earth.

She never thought to look up. Later, when she remembered every moment, she realised it was just as well. The horror in the faces of her audience would have made her falter. Yet in some ways it was easy. For when the child is dead, there is only the mother to save, in whatever way you can.

But there was a small mercy. With the bulk gone, the woman revived and found a strength to push. The afterbirth came away quickly, and as one.

Above the Sierra Nevada David García had closed his eyes but was far from sleeping. This was the last leg. Madrid's Barajas airport was further behind than Granada airport was ahead. He had reviewed the files. As usual, a lot would depend on luck. Luck. Wasn't that what Commissioner O'Reilly had opened with?

"Well lucky you," he had said in his office, "it's gonna work in your favour again ain't it García?"

It had been both the Commissioner's greeting, and his farewell as he had cast the file of paperwork on the desk and left abruptly for another appointment. David had watched his disappearing back, then reached and picked up the heavy file. He opened it briefly, and then closed it when the commissioner's secretary said she needed the office. García doubted it – more likely she just wanted him out of it. Twenty years of O'Reilly always being meticulously polite did not fool García. The Commissioner had never been his greatest fan. Now, like everyone, he must hate him. Things could not go on as they were, nor could they get rid of him. This was an acceptable way to at least remove him.

Sat in the departure lounge at JFK, García had looked out at the dismal attempt at spring. The runway grey, the baggage handlers barely visible in a thin dawn with relentless drizzle. He had allowed himself to remember the last time he had travelled to Europe, three years before. Before. Before Richard had died. Before the twin towers had been razed to the ground. Before he'd opened his mouth and spoken a viewpoint no-one wanted to hear.

He and Richard had travelled to Europe for their last Christmas together, cramming what seemed like everywhere into two weeks, from Athens to Edinburgh. What he had seen of Spain he scarcely remembered. Of course the Alhambra, who could forget that? And of course the strong Spanish Andalusian accent, so foreign to his own Cuban. But anything else was blended in with Italy and Portugal, this mountain range and that coastal road, such that even he, a sharp observer, was hard pressed to distinguish one set of scenery from another.

And all the time Richard dying of thirst, begging for just one drop, and David desperate to get him to the UK where they could find a Chapter of AA that spoke English. First London, then Stratford, Bath, York, Edinburgh, the tourist trail, the only two days in the fourteen that David had himself had any peace or pleasure in the trip. And now here he was, set to go to Europe again, only this time on his own, all expenses paid, and not a pleasurable moment in sight.

He twiddled the ring on his little finger knowing that in a few short hours a new unknown awaited him.

Rashida sat back on her heels, hot with disappointment. She knew this heat. It was a very particular type of disappointment, one half-cut with shame. She remembered in Mexico, when the baby did not live, they used to lay the child on the birthing cloth which had been prepared to swaddle the living child. Instead the dead child would be placed on the cloth, left open and handed to the family. The baby catchers would look down to signal the shame at failure. Then whoever took it would put their free hand on the shoulder of the deliverer.

Rashida used to think that the hand on the shoulder was a way of indicating a common understanding: life is unpredictable, even capricious. In the hand on the shoulder there was a forgiveness of sorts, not a direct forgiveness, more an acceptance of life, of all it brings and all it takes. Then, after the hand left the shoulder, there was freedom to pass.

She never knew what happened next. People sometimes asked why she didn't know more about Mexican customs; was she not more curious? She thought the answer might be that she had been too close to birth for too long. She found she was comfortable with its mystery.

But with these raw parts on the earth she was sorry she had not more choices for their disposal. No-one was coming toward her with a cloth outstretched. No-one spoke to claim the death. There was no hand on her shoulder. Here, in the Alhambra in Granada, in the Andalucía of a modern Spain, Mexico seemed a long way away. There was only the fast retreat of dawn.

Slumped back on the stone, colour was returning to the woman's cheeks. Someone was holding her hands. Rashida looked up. She saw that everyone was looking, not at the woman, but at her. Their looks were not expectant, not blaming, nor even awed at witnessing a butcher at work. They were blank, she imagined not unlike her own.

She had no comfort to give. She looked at her hands and arms, smeared in blood and vernix. She had a moment's yearning for clear hot water. Then she heard a man say:

"Bury it."

Tiptoeing through the *generalife* in the Alhambra, Mary Stansfield noted the patterned pebble work, beautiful under her feet, as it dug up through the thin soles of her shoes. The cypress trees flanked her, the gentle sound of falling water caressed her ears. The promise of sun touched her back and shoulders. Except for the occasional rustle of her own feet, there was no human sound. Something in the unexpected peace seemed unnatural.

She had pondered on their journey as she lay on the cool sheets in the room at the *parador*, basking in the luxury of the famous government-run hotel within the Alhambra compound. The coach up from Málaga airport now seemed an aeon ago. The men had talked and guffawed and gibbered all the way until at last, full of beer and half ill with it, and with the heat and motion of the coach, she had told them enough was enough. It was time they saved their voices for the weekend's concert and enjoyed looking at the scenery or their newspapers. Someone had made a ribald remark about girls on page three, and Daniel Goddard, the only one of them near her age had met her glance, perhaps apologetic, then reached for his hip flask and taken a deep slug.

Pay-back had hit some of them hard when they each got into their hotel rooms. A third of them had virtually passed out with the combination of heat and drink, and maybe even childish excitement. Even Mary had missed dinner and she suspected others had too. Sounds across from her room suggested that a few of them had even vomited.

As dawn was breaking, a huge bang had made her toss and turn on her sheets. Whether thunder or the back-firing of a vehicle she could not have said. Then all had fallen quiet again. In the end it was the deathly quiet of the dawn which had fully awakened her. No staff had been about. No-one was in the bar, there was no smell of brewing coffee. Indeed, not even all of the choir were there, just ten of them, creeping from their rooms, white-faced and hungry. They had all left the *parador* together, then wordlessly separated, slipping stealthily along the paths, unsure why they should be so secretive, yet all feeling an instinctive wariness.

Despite the early hour, the sun was almost shining. She should have felt relief. The promise of dry warmth, the wrangles with the City of York for funding behind her, a well rehearsed repertoire of Andalusian folk songs for the event ahead ought to have made her carefree. Even their Granadino hosts could not fail to be pleased with the program highlighting works collected and transcribed by Granada's most famous son Federico García Lorca. But as she continued along the paths there was nothing to suggest a concert underway, no staff fussing with chairs or barriers. Nothing at all. Instead of relief, she had a creeping anxiety.

Toward the stage end of the *generalife* gardens the turnstiles to the Alhambra were closed. The wooden steps to the right, up toward the *archivo*, were barred. She made for the stage itself in the *generalife* where the *festivales* were scheduled to take place. Her anxiety was momentarily replaced by delight. It was a natural amphitheatre with curved stone seating. Already a sea of chairs reached back into the spray of fountains.

She saw her colleagues walking toward her and beckoned them. As if reading each other's minds the choristers forgot their disquiet and arranged themselves before an imaginary audience. Mary, thrilled to have the chance of a sound-check with no-one around, sounded a note on her tuning fork and raised her arms. On the upward stroke of her hand the men opened their mouths and sang. The noise filled the *generalife*.

Then they stopped, staring over her shoulder, and she turned and saw him for the first time.

He looked like death warmed up, and very, very angry.

Mario's in New York was always a perfect haven. Unable to sleep, Commissioner O'Reilly had left home in the dark and taken his usual booth. He drank long and deep of his coffee, pleased García was already far away. He hated David García, or rather Ángel David García. Ángel. What sort of a man was called angel?

"Lots of men," his daughter Colleen had once told him. "Lots of perfectly decent ordinary Hispanic men." And then she had added, "You are a pot calling the kettle black Daddy," referring to his own curse of being christened *Gabriel Edward*. But O'Reilly had dismissed her even handedness. Gabriel was nowhere nearly as bad as *Ángel*. No wonder García never used it.

The fact was, O'Reilly hated García. He hated him so deeply and with such conviction and devotion, that it had risen like bile in his throat and made him leave his bed to seek solace at Mario's before the sun came up. It was as if the Catholicism he shared with García had transmuted into a sort religious zeal such that O'Reilly longed to see García fail in some absolute and soul-damning way. That is not to say that O'Reilly was a bad man. But just that García excited in O'Reilly an emotional response so adverse, deep, dark and profound, that even O'Reilly at times was frightened by it. The bits of his hatred that he could label, he understood. He could even run through them like a sort of litany.

One, García was a faggot. And O'Reilly hated faggots. But he was not afraid of them. He was long acquainted with the amateur psychology of 'faggot fear', as he called it privately. The prevailing wisdom being that, somehow if a man hated faggots, he feared he might be one. O'Reilly was self-aware enough to know he was not, and honest enough to know he was grateful that neither he nor his sons were. Not because he hated faggots, although he did, but because what man would wish on himself, and what parent would wish on a child, a life in a largely heterosexual world filled with such faggot haters as himself?

He hated faggots because he believed that all of them were essentially afraid, and fear made them weak and malleable and unreliable. No policeman could want to put his life in the hands of a fellow officer whose common platform of belief could not be depended upon. He hated it that García was a policeman, and worse, until 9/11, a popular one.

Two, García was Hispanic. And O'Reilly hated Spics. But he was not afraid of them, either. By rights, O'Reilly, himself only a third-generation Irishman, should have felt camaraderie with García. God knows the Irish had suffered the indignities of immigrant communities the world over. Yet he hated it that unlike the Irish, Spics could hide in language which in turn had safeguarded their culture, whereas the Irish had pretty much lost theirs, with only their surnames, and seething Irish anger to distinguish them.

O'Reilly hated it that the modern approach to positive discrimination allowed Spics an easy entry to policing. No-one had given the Irish any quarter when they had arrived, and none had been effectively demanded. Yet Hispanics were given more representation, more civil rights, more advantage and more consideration just in virtue of being called Ortega or Rodriguez. O'Reilly knew that García had never asked for special consideration, nor been given it. O'Reilly hated the fact that García's high rank was due to merit alone. O'Reilly prided himself on his dispassionate evaluation of facts, on his logic, and knew he was being contrary in his analysis, and he hated that too.

Three, García was a Catholic. And O'Reilly definitely did not hate Catholics. Nor was he in the least afraid of them. But he did hate the David García type of Catholic. Colleen had once again challenged him on that. Those were the days when she had been friends with García's girl, Marilita. (This was another irritation; García had a daughter. It offended O'Reilly. Wasn't it enough that the man was a faggot? Must he fudge the edges of his identity by being a father as well?) Colleen had wanted to know what the difference could possibly be between one type of Catholic and another. O'Reilly had avoided answering her and moved on to another topic.

He did know the difference; he just didn't want to tell her because it sounded ridiculous. But the difference was colour. When he thought of his Catholicism, the Catholicism of an Irishman, he thought green and white. When he thought about the Catholicism of the Italians or the Hispanics the colours he could see were yellow, red and gold. That was the difference. His Catholicism was calm, controlled and pure. Theirs was running riot, full of flamboyance, lacking reserve, even irreverent. They danced freely, they fornicated at will. Look at the mob: they might be Italians, but the colour of their Catholicism was the same as Hispanics. They had, what O'Reilly could only think of as HEAT. And he hated HEAT.

Finally, the one thing in the litany that O'Reilly found hard to articulate was that García was smart. Not smart as in cracking open cases, delivering the goods to the prosecutors, although God knows he was smart enough on all of that. No, it was something more, García was quintessentially smart; saw, knew, 'got it', in a really unusual way. Until 9/11, that is, when he messed up big time. And that was what made it possible for O'Reilly to live with his hatred without it chewing him up from the inside. García had made a big mistake, and now he was having to pay for it.

As the aircraft descended García wondered idly how the local police and the army would receive him. He imagined, thanks to O'Reilly, that his reputation for both his 9/11 remarks and his lifestyle had gone before him. His favourite poet Lorca might have been from Granada, might have also been gay, but García knew that did not mean he himself would be any more welcome.

Observing, is what O'Reilly's memo had said, *Observing the Spanish authorities in their efforts*. Ever since 9/11 the US government always sent observers to any major terrorist activity, seeking any inter-connectivity between events that might lead to apprehending them more fully. *Observing* was an impotent role; at best a fact-finding mission. David was fairly certain that O'Reilly had manipulated events to ensure the name David García was put forward.

Arriving in Málaga at the crack of dawn had seemed a good idea since it guaranteed the lowest fares from Liverpool. But in his enthusiasm Jack Fisher had overlooked a few important facts. He and Paula had to be at the airport two hours before departure. It took two hours to get to Liverpool from York and parking cost a fortune, even for four days. As they got into their hire car at Málaga airport they were more than a little travel weary. Yet it didn't seem to diminish Paula's enthusiasm.

They were going on this particular weekend because their friend Carmen Romero, a Latina living in York, had insisted that the *festivales* in Andalucía were a sight worth seeing. And they were going to Spain because ever since the Festival of Angels three years before, when Jack and Carmen's families had grown close, he had become more interested in Hispanic life and culture.

Jack Fisher was also the policeman responsible for issuing licenses for the sale of alcohol in York. Changes in the law in the UK had created a crisis of confidence in how drinking would be managed. So he had a professional interest in Spain and in Spanish drinking culture. Carmen often said if only people would eat a little as they drank, their behaviour would improve.

"It's hunger Jack," she told him, "that's all. Booze stimulates the appetite. Then there's nothing to eat and it makes them cross."

He had thought to combine checking out her theory with a long overdue break without the kids. Then when he found that York's own Constantine Singers were going to be appearing in Granada as part of the *festivales* at the Alhambra it just seemed too good a chance to miss.

"When they come for him he comes out of the door into *calle angulo*. That's the first time we see him."

"Is he handcuffed?" the child looked wide-eyed at the old

man.

"No. He is not," Agustín replied and thought again how small the boy was for his age, with the look of being under-nourished. Agustín knew that by the time the nuns got hold of these orphans and could begin shovelling the food in, it was often too late. Thanks to the half-starved early years, Alberto was probably destined always to be small. "But," the old man added, continuing his story, "he is afraid."

"How do you know?" the boy asked.

"Of course he is afraid!" the girl interjected. "They are taking him away. He is always afraid. You know that. I don't know why you ask it every time." She glared at him and the boy kicked at the earth, still cool from the night, and scarcely visible in the dawn's first moves toward daylight.

"But how do you know?" the boy insisted, determined not to break the spell by responding to Lola.

"At first you cannot see it," said the old man. "Because he is well-dressed, you think: *here is a fine man, he is alright.*"

"He was always well-dressed," the old woman murmured from the shadows of the terrace, the steady hushed pop and then drop of shelling broad beans. "He took pride in his appearance."

"Pride," repeated the girl looking challengingly at the boy.

"His hair oiled and shining like an angel," the old woman went on. "Dark, and lustrous, like his eyes, and that widow's peak, like you Alberto. Like you."

"And like Agustín," trilled the girl

"And in the street it is so bright you are nearly blind," the old man went on, unperturbed. "Especially coming out from inside, from that cool, shady courtyard."

"And it is so hot, so hot. August hot. You could fry an egg on the pavement," the boy recited.

"Yes. Hot like that." The old man nodded in agreement. "Without relief." And the old woman stopped shelling beans and watched the children mouth the same words with him.

How long had it been since these two had been coming to their small-holding, the *finca*, dabbling with Agustín in the earth, with her in the kitchen? How many times had Agustín had them seated before him while he told the same story? And how long before the nuns would notice that these two were often absent from their beds during that magic hour between night and day? How long before someone found them, as she and Agustín had, prowling the slopes of the Alhambra that divided their *finca* from the great fortress? Rosario began to shell her beans again, secretly hoping that the nuns would never find out, thanking God that He had seen fit to bring these two into their old and fading lives.

"But the fear is there," Agustín went on. "You know because he just misses his footing on the curb, and when they shoot their hands out to save him, to break his fall, they can feel through his soft shirt that he is shaking. He looks up. He raises his great dark eyes up, up to the Alhambra, here, on the hill. Then he manages to say something over his shoulder, into the darkness in the house, something light, something simple..."

"...something with an edge of hope," the children chorused.

"And then of course there is the other fear."

"The other fear," the children repeated leaning forward.

"They are afraid. In some way, on some level, they know. For they have in their hands the Flower of Granada..."

"...the Flower of Granada," said Lola dreamily.

"And..." Agustín intoned.

"...and they know not what they will do..." the children joined in with the old man. Then they added in unison, "Viznar, Viznar, so near, so far..."

Agustín looked at them both, hearing their familiar chant. It was their own contribution to the story. Viznar. Agustín turned his head toward the horizon, prevented by hills from seeing the small village of Viznar whose infamy as an assassination site outstripped its fame for its eighteenth century palace.

He turned back and saw how the children's hair was now catching the early light, a tint of rose gold illuminating on each head, the sure sign it was time for them to go. He sensed rather than saw Rosario get to her feet. That was an advantage of a long marriage, verbal communication was minimal. Rosario too would have noted the coming of the light and would now move toward them and usher the children off toward Sacromonte.

He cleared his throat, knowing the story could not be told in its entirety today and would have to wait. They would not mind. They had heard the end many times. So he seized their final moments together and they all said as one,

"...or they know it, and the weight of regret is already upon them."

In the *comisaría* in Motril Manuel Pedraza spat sunflower seed shells onto the marble floor. Typical. If, in the teeth of this terrible crisis, the USA wanted to send in an observer then Spain had to be gracious and accept. *Yet again*, he thought, *tomado por culo*. The US press had poor appreciation of Spain. The Americans had short memories. They had conveniently forgotten the beginning of the Iraqi conflict where only the UK and Spain had been on their side. To make matters worse, the Americans couldn't even use the right fax number – and why a fax anyway? He snatched it up, put his coat on as he walked from his office, got in his car, gunned the engine and set off fast for the road up over the mountain to meet Antonio.

At the airport in Granada Antonio Marín was waiting, but not for either Manuel or the fax. The Americans had sent it to multiple

destinations. Antonio had picked his copy up from Granada a good hour before Manuel had his copy in Motril. He had been early and had sat for a while in the car, listening to the radio, clapping softly along with the Flamenco music that was in vogue again. He had smiled to himself that his typically Andalusian habit of automatically clapping out rhythms had reasserted itself so quickly. Despite a career on the Madrid force, he may as well have never left his home town on the *vega* of Granada.

Now he was in the arrivals hall as dawn receded. He looked with half closed eyes at the replica *Dama de Baza* in her glass case. The statue's muted colours, barely diminished by hundreds of years under the earth, always impressed him. He remembered the day construction workers in Baza, north of Granada, had found her. She was a reminder to him and to all Andalusians, how ancient their land was.

Antonio relaxed his shoulders under her scrutiny and dragged on his cigarette fairly confidently. The new laws to prohibit smoking in public places just didn't seem likely to catch on. Besides, it was way too early to worry about some security guard asking him to stop. Very likely any guard would himself be smoking somewhere not too far away. He looked toward the board for news of the gate that would discharge David García.

Antonio could have sent anyone to meet García. But why bother the younger staff? He had nothing better to do. His wife was dead, his children grown up, his own need for sleep was seemingly diminishing year on year. He decided he might as well meet García and make use of the time to bring him up to speed.

Information about García was impressive. The son of Cuban immigrants surviving the high seas to make a life in the US, he had made Captain in his thirties. He was an ace negotiator and had the valour citations to go with it. On top of that he was the father of another highly decorated young officer. And then there was the other thing: García was homosexual. O'Reilly had told him over the 'phone during their final confirming conversation.

"Not the sort of thing you can put in a file or an email these days," the commissioner had said.

So why say it at all? Antonio had wanted to ask.

O'Reilly's disclosure made Antonio wonder if the Commissioner wanted to scupper or support García's capacity to succeed in Granada. What did O'Reilly think? That Spain was so macho and backward as to be a nation of homophobics? Surely any commissioner would want one of his own to shine on such a mission?

Even so, if Antonio Marín was honest, García's homosexuality had probably made him want to check out just how 'homosexual', before adding that to the list of possible variables to manage. At the same time he also knew that García could not have had such a good career unless he was sound. Antonio had spent his life among men. He prided himself on being a good judge of character. He took one last pull on his cigarette, saw the arrivals board flicker, dropped his dog end and ground it into the marble floor.

García was easy to spot. In his early forties, handsome, lean and athletic with a slight African kink to his hair that many Cubans have. Scant baggage was a dead give-away. *Working policemen travel light*, thought Antonio as he advanced. The two men shook hands and left the airport building for the car.

Agustín and Rosario shuffled further forward, the storytelling with the children now an hour behind them. Rosario watched her husband and wondered what was wrong with him. He was old but he wasn't that old; he looked positively doddery. She caught his eye and he winked. She stopped short. It might have been twenty years since Agustín had winked at her.

A push from behind almost sent her off her feet and she resisted the impulse to protest. *History is repeating itself* was her only thought. Once again they were being marched along the same route they had trodden all those years ago, the only difference being instead of going up the hill as her parents had done, to be shot at the cemetery, they were being moved downhill into the Alhambra.

THEY, as she referred to them – for what other term could describe these shabby half-starved men? THEY had come for them within ten minutes of Alberto and Lola disappearing down *la cuesta de los chinos*, across the Darro and up through the Albaicín. THEY had no idea the children had been there. That much was obvious. THEY. *It seems as if all of history is punctuated by THEYs*, Rosario thought. Very likely these THEYs were the ideological descendants of the THEYs that had been at *calle angulo* in Agustín's story, on that hot, hot August so long ago. She wondered, if these THEYs set their hands on her arm as they had on His, the Flower of Granada, would they feel her trembling as Agustín always said He had? And now she and Agustín, like the Felangist cattle of her parents' day, were moving down *calle real*, the central street of the Alhambra.

Just ahead she could see that María Santos Moreno was already outside her fancy house opposite the marquetry workshops. Doña María did not look nearly so proud in her nightwear, without her make-up, stumbling toward the front doors of the *hotel america*. Rosario almost felt sorry for her, almost forgave her the decades of insults. María Santos Moreno, the last legitimate inhabitant of the Alhambra compound, the grand old dame of *calle real* now reduced to an equal mercy from hostile strangers. What would become of them all now?

In the quiet of his own small cave in Sacromonte, even as he dozed, Joaquin Montez ruminated, drifting in and out of consciousness. He never knew what he liked best, to lick the inside of a thigh, the lips, the breast or the sex mound itself. Hmmmmmm. He rolled back, half awake. The truth was, in Ana, he loved it all. He ran the back of his hand across his mouth and raised it absent-mindedly to his nose. The scent of a woman. No doubt about it.

Briefly he went up on one elbow and looked at her. She was sleeping, her mouth slightly open, little sighs from time to time puthering through her lips. He could see a nipple exposed above the line of the sheets and couldn't decide whether to pull the sheet down or up. Which was better, the sight of flesh or the promise of it? Instead he closed his eyes and breathed deeply, aiming for sleep, and slid his hand beneath the sheets, down her back, across her buttocks and between her legs. Warm and sticky, the evidence of him was slick under his fingers. Good stuff.

Having Ana here was a risk. He hoped lazily, between dozing and waking, that his cousin would never find out. Any of his cousins for that matter, other than of course the cousin beside him. What were the chances? He flicked his hair off his face and neck, too hot to have it down his back. Remote? No, unfortunately not; fairly likely in fact. These were secrets that could never be kept. In their neighbourhood there were secrets like this breaking out all the time.

The consequences? A fight? Probably. With Fernando? With his father? With Ana's father? Who knew? Maybe with them all. The outcome? The usual. As long as no fingers were broken. A smashed nose, maybe a split lip. Hey what the hell, this cousin, this hellcat of unbridled passion that had ridden him dry through the night? Hell, split lip, smashed nose? Yeah. Probably worth it. Broken fingers? Never. And then it would be business as usual.

He watched as she stirred, as if she had a built in alarm system and knew she should return to her marital bed before the sun was fully up. He pretended to sleep and watched as she slipped into her clothes and moved quietly to the door and then through it.

Moments later the sound of an explosion had brought Joaquin Montez upright in his bed like an arrow from a bow, making his guitar fall to the side, expelling a discordant reverb in the otherwise empty room.

He watched them unseen from beneath the shade of the largest cypress tree, almost unable to believe his bad luck. He felt too tired for fury, it was more like a lukewarm impotent rage that life could have dealt him yet another misfortune, and one so inconvenient. As if he didn't have enough to contend with, with the disabled old lady from next door to the *hotel america* and then the couple from the *finca*, the small-holding, just beyond the walls. Now there was a wretched choir of foreigners.

He ran his eyes over this new group with their uplifted faces and saw to his relief that they too were old, only one near his age. The only woman had her back to him and was directing them in her flowing clothes, her red hair down her back and her arms out-stretched, very likely a pensioner like the rest of them. But then she turned and looked him square in the eye; no pensioner at all.

Someone like her had never been part of the plan. Until that moment in the amphitheatre of the *generalife* everything had been clear. He had known, with absolute certainty, where this was going and he was pretty sure how it would all end.

For one, he and Jay had always put the women first. And the children. And that had made a difference, to them, to him, to them all. The dynamic had been defined from the start. His first demand to the authorities had been framed to meet their basic needs.

Now looking directly into her eyes, she stood everything on its head. She was bold as brass, unflinching, the red hair a halo of fire. As if that were not surprise enough, still more surprising to him, he thought laconically, was that he, Gerardo, was still here to see it.

morning

There is a sweetness about the plain of Granada, the *vega* as they call it. People write of its beauty, the ragged serrated mountains to the east, the majesty of the Alhambra, the Islamic jewel in the crown of civilisation, the rich fertile plain with its short downhill run to the Mediterranean. But few write of its sweetness.

Under the mantle of Catholic disguise, the blend of Rajistani gypsy and Arabic culture is undeniable. Cloaked in bogus folk traditions, the sway and thrust of life, the rhythm of breath, the deep penetration of human life into the very soil of the *vega* pulses beneath the veneer of modern life. Perhaps it is the mix of blood and time that brings the sweetness, a veritable psychic perfume to tantalise the senses.

Arriving from Motril to the south, the road crowns at Suspiro del Moro, the place where the last Islamic ruler in Spain stood and took one last backward glance. The sigh of regret? Resignation? For nearly eight hundred years the Caliph and his forbears had staved off the Christians. He was the last leader, of the last stronghold, of the world that might have been.

And there is a grief about the city. But for the treachery and brutality of the court of Isabel and Ferdinand, this Islamic world would have brought to Europeans the possibility of sanitation and clean running water, democracy and art, for all, three hundred years earlier. Perhaps the sorrow of unfulfilled promise is the sweetness...

The new southerly Motril route, paved and intermittently three lanes, is bordered by olives, new houses, red earth, and stark foothills with startling bursts of growth and colour. From the north, the most recent road from Madrid, via Jaen, is not long completed. The approach is less arid, more green, and then changes at the interface with the city, the vastness of the arable plain fanning before it.

Arriving from the west, time was, the traveller from Málaga or Antequera would have taken a good day to cross the mountains, even as recently as the 1980s. Now blasting has incised modern communications onto the stone and gullies. These snake-like scars quarried into the hillside make the *cañons* passable, and like all scars, there is a stronger, tougher quality to the change.

And with the roads have come all the trappings of modern life. Car graveyards heralded by old cars raised on platforms are visible for miles. Cranes stand stock still in the early morning, with wheelbarrows and cement mixers pendulous from them, out of the reach of thieves. Row upon row of low-level modern buildings house the goods and processes of moving from being a second world nation to a first.

So, perhaps against all of this, it is the quality of light that makes it sweet. The dawn comes upon the day swiftly, scything between the dark and light. And the skies, vast across the *vega* can, in one glance, be purple, sugar pink, ink blue, then grey to a molasses dun.

None of this beauty, nor its contradictions, was lost on David García.

"Those trees. What are they?" he asked, indicating a few sparse dark silhouettes topped with pink blossom.

"Almonds," said Antonio Marín answering his mobile phone at the same time. After a few words he rang off and said, "One of my men, telling me when you are arriving! Seems your arrival has been faxed to everyone. That's the trouble here I think sometimes. You either know everything, or nothing."

"Universal," said García. "Whatever police force," and then asked, "Sunflowers. When do they bloom?"

"Summer. And further to the south."

"And here? On the left? What are these?" García asked him, pointing at the sisal.

Antonio was beginning to wonder if García was ever going to ask him anything about why he was here. From his arrival García had been punching out his staccato questions. He seemed pleasant enough, but his verbal brevity and brusqueness made Antonio wonder if García was tired. Antonio had said as much to him as they left the airport, but instead of blaming a long flight, García had surprised him with a smile that transformed his face and had said,

"Not at all. I am happy. Happy to be here," and then he added, as if he felt an explanation might be necessary, "It's freezing in New York." He had spread his hands as though magic had occurred, "Now, here I am."

"*La vida es así*," Antonio had philosophised. His statement *life's like that* reminded David of what he had noticed when he had been in Andalucía before with Richard. It had seemed almost every conversation was taken as an opportunity to make some home-spun comment on life. At first he had been charmed by it, then he had been irritated. He wondered if on this trip he would get past irritation and find it charming again.

"Ah, and Fuente Vaqueros," García commented, nodding toward a road sign. "I have a fascination for it."

"Fuente Vaqueros?" Antonio Marín was surprised.

"I have always wanted to go. Since I was twenty," García said, and then added, "Federico García Lorca. I'm a fan. His birthplace."

"Well yes. I know."

García had eyed him then and said,

"Of course you do. I thought I'd let you know I did." When Marín said nothing García continued, "Not all Americans lack culture."

It was on the tip of Antonio's tongue to say,

And why would I think that? And anyway, aren't you Cuban? but instead was silent.

García was aggravated that he had allowed himself to care what Marín might think. Neither did he want to dignify with any caring what O'Reilly may have included in any communications.

37

Caring was something he didn't much want to engage in any more.

The fact was, he had been wrong-footed in his first meeting with Antonio Marín. The sight of the latest Federico García Lorca anthology uppermost on the front seat of Marín's car, amid the detritus of newspapers, cigarette packets and files, had taken him aback. After all, David García thought as Antonio had swept it all aside to make room for him, what senior policeman would ordinarily drive around with a book of poetry on the front seat?

A brief silence then fell. Antonio apparently felt no compunction to fill it. García was equally disinclined to indulge in some shallow exchanges about Lorca. Later Antonio would think back to this silence as being like a thick red line in their interaction, the boundary between not yet having the measure of him, and all the rest that followed.

García broke the silence and said,

"Why Rashida Santiago?"

Finally, Antonio thought, *game on*.

Rashida Santiago would ordinarily have agreed with any description of the beauty of her native city. But on this early morning she was crouched beneath the parapet of the city's most famous monument, hunkered well into the wall. There was sun, but not enough for her liking. And now that the adrenaline had subsided she was cold. She braced against the red concrete, shifted her weight and kicked at the gravel. The light was beginning to strengthen.

Today she was not the least interested in the view over the *vega* from the *alcazaba*, the old fortress tower. The plain stretched out from the foot of it to an even, unpuctured horizon. The two million tourists a year would have given anything to sit as she was, silent, alone, in the quiet, absorbing in complete solitude the sights of kings, queens and caliphs. All of this was within her vista. All she had to do was stand. She could not. She would not. She let her tired thoughts wander. She had got the picture gradually, over hours, only fully understanding as late as last night. The first she had heard was on the radio during the early evening.

ETA, they had said, had taken the Alhambra, eschewing all visitors and personnel. Then not long after there had been a spectacular explosion taking out the entrance between *puerta de la justicia* and *puerta del vino* where they bordered *el partal*. *So*, she had thought, *this time the Alhambra has been taken by physical force as in historic times, rather than the modern occupation by administrators and politicians*. Rashida's version of history was that Godless royals had driven out the Moors in the name of Catholicism and they had then broken every promise. Systematically waging a war of terror on the city, they had destroyed a civilisation, an agriculture and an entire system of government and belief. All of this after they had seized the Alhambra, which she considered to be the home of her ancestors.

She wondered how many times the Alhambra had been occupied since 1492. Only a few decades ago, during the Civil War, it had been occupied so as to fire down on the Albaicín. In peace it was occupied to generate tourism income. And now it was occupied again. It was extraordinary, bizarre, wild. The Alhambra, the greatest monument to Islam in Europe, arguably the greatest Islamic treasure anywhere, apparently in the hands of terrorists.

Everyone had been constantly tuned in to the radio. Televisions were on in every office. The authorities had appeared to be immobilised by the shock. News reports were only capable of conjecture. The TV had played and replayed the statement from the professor they had dragged in as an expert, until she thought she would be able to recite it as perfectly as the Holy Qur'an.

"We estimate there to be thirty people involved," the

professor had intoned. "All the signs are that this group is a break-away group from ETA and is committed to violent means. They are led by Joaquin Rafael." An old photo then came on the screen, a young man hand-cuffed to the front, taller than his captors, staring defiantly at the camera with piercing blue eyes. The professor went on, "Rafael was convicted in March 1990 for his part in the Barcelona Atrocities. Thirty-three people were killed in the Police Headquarters bombing in 1989. He escaped police custody in the same month and went to ground, although his signature is believed to be on many bombings since. If he is at the Alhambra this will be his first public action since his trial. It is our view that this group will simply destroy systematically every beautiful thing within the great Moorish palace, uproot every tree, trample every flower, in the gardens that have been planted and tended for nearly half a millennium." Then the professor had looked directly at the camera and folded his hands.

Other academics joined him and together they cast over the history of terrorism in Spain in the last twenty years, of this group's former involvement in ETA, of its break-away ten years before. The army and the *guardia civil* argued openly on TV as to how impenetrable or defensible the Alhambra was. They exchanged opposing views as to the ease with which the fortress could be taken from the west, the steepness of the river banks to the north, the ready access through the woods at the east, the gates to the south.

The media aired discussions every hour with every academic expert in the country about the motivation of attack. They laboured politics, commented on the deviation from human hostages to heritage hostages, remembered the car bombs of Valencia in 1993, drew connections with the Red Army Faction in Germany of the 1970s, drew more biographical pictures of the alleged perpetrators and guessed at the next moves. Finally even Rashida, removed as she was from ordinary political excitements, wanted to scream at the impotency of it all.

But the big question on everyone's mind was, *For what?* They made it clear they would blow up the building if their demands were not met. But there was a surprise. What they wanted, or what they wanted first, was her. Well, not her, herself, but a midwife. And they wanted one immediately. And then they said they would let the authorities know what they wanted next.

And to show that they meant it, from the *alcazaba*, the very fortress promontory where she now sat, they had lowered an entire plaster-fretted window from the *palacio de los colmares*. To underline their complete commitment, they had tied to the centre of it a bough from the oldest pomegranate tree in the *jardin de machuca*. The pomegranate, *granada* in Spanish, the symbol of the city, the source of the sweet red liquor grenadine, was lashed like an amputated limb to the masonry, and an affront to every Granadino.

Now, hours later, hunched down in the cold, Rashida was pretty sure that whoever was in charge, whatever they might think, the Alhambra was as likely to lay siege to them, as the other way round. The Alhambra was a miracle of survival. The Alhambra had seen it all. The Alhambra was unlikely to disappear.

Gerardo flexed his back and shoulder muscles and straightened up. He stopped and started, periodically wiping his arm across his brow. The dead baby was getting to him. *Silly,* he thought. There had been plenty before, but this one, butchered at his feet, this one was one too many. At the same time it underlined to him that they were doing the right thing here. The trees, the water, the softness under foot, all might have seduced a lesser man to mercy, but not this man.

The noise of people talking caught his ear. He raised his head toward *calle real*, saw his cousins and nodded recognition.

He stopped and sat on one of the low walls that was still standing after the charges had been set in *la puerta de la justicia* and caught his breath. He looked to his right and then to his left before deciding the direction to continue, and once again recited to himself the numbers and locations of the charges.

In the *reformatorio,* the reform school of San Miguel el Alto, they turned over in bed. First the one, and then the other. They seemed to settle for a while. Then the rustle of a cockroach dashing across the floor, or maybe the barking of a dog in the night, made them stir. And then one turned back the other way, and then the other.

Now that they were eight there was talk of separating them. The day would have to come. It could not go on forever, although in some ways, the nuns wanted it to. They had such an investment in the innocence of children. The boy had arrived when he was barely five. His grandparents were so old they had been unable to care for him and the child had taken to thieving and living rough. Then two months later, the little girl had been assigned by the court. An alcoholic father and a drug dependent mother had tried to pimp her to paedophiles and she had kicked and screamed her way into care. When the two children had seen each other for the first time they advanced on one another and joined hands, never to be separated again.

It was hardly surprising. The two children were the same age, had arrived within months of each other, both had curls and blue eyes, but for both to have red hair, this was something else entirely. Andalucía after all was a long way from the north, which everyone knew was the only place in Spain likely to have red-haired Spaniards. There was nothing whatsoever to suggest they were related, but as soon as they themselves had grasped the concept, they called themselves 'twins'.

If Lola or Alberto were in any confusion as to their identity, it didn't show. They behaved as classic twins. Until they were seven they spoke almost entirely to each other. They played as one, studied as one, ate and slept as one. They fought with no-one, neither each other, nor the Sisters, nor the other children, all of whom regarded Alberto and Lola with a barely surpressed awe. That isn't to say these two were the same. They were not. He was strong willed, determined, and focused, a starter-finisher of the first order. She, by contrast, was fey, gentle, accommodating and watchful. The nuns said, it wasn't that they did not trust adults, it was more that they just kept their distance.

Sleeping now, after the early hours of story-telling, their dreams were full. In colour and in slow motion, they dreamed of the day long ago when the city's most famous son, Federico García Lorca, poet, pianist, patriot, their Flower of Granada, stepped out into the heat of August, and in the narrow *calle angulo*, knew his freedom for the last time.

Rashida was aware that she was now a hostage herself. Since the baby's death she was suddenly focused on what that might actually mean. It occurred to her that, if she could not help them with the deliveries, she might not have much time. And time was deceptive. She was living proof of that. Less than twelve hours ago her world, her life, once so sheltered, so ordinary, so well organised, had been almost humdrum. Today, at the Alhambra, it had been like going back to Mexico where the life was rough, abrasive and uneven.

Only three hours ago she had arrived at the *palacio de carlos v*. The dawn sky had been soft-hued with a gentle rosy fluff and no hint of the savage wind that would whip up by mid-day. The *guardia civil* captain had taken her to *la puerta de los carros*, the main entrance to the Alhambra. Not the entrance where people bought tickets, but the entrance anyone, people, taxis, even dogs, was free to use. It was the way to the book store, the hotels, the souvenir shops. Yet today the enormous gates, normally opened flush with the walls, had been formidable before her and, but for a slim gap, almost closed. The captain had told her to pass through and wait. Someone would come for her.

Waiting was a natural requirement of her work but after five minutes Rashida had begun to feel self-conscious. She suspected she was being watched. Reluctant to look other than dignified she had examined the old iron cannons nonchalantly, and then the drinking fountain. She had cast her eye over the rubbish bins. Empty. She had studied the vast metal hoops hanging from the walls of the *palacio de carlos v*. All the time her ears had strained at the silence. There was no-one. Having worried at first about who would come, she had begun to worry that no-one would.

She also worried that she might not be equal to the task, whatever it was. She might be a good midwife, experienced at field deliveries, but she was not a surgeon, and this last year, since starting her PhD, she had taken few patients. Her recent focus had been on mastering English as an essential key to research. Her hope was that her thesis might help with the long slow climb to recognition for midwifery, and the work of midwives everywhere.

In the solitude of a silent dawn there was little comfort for her in her academic theories about the benefits that came to entire populations when mothers and babies were well cared for. Any ideals of care were unlikely to be in evidence here. Doubtless what was waiting for her would add little positive to her theories about fractious mothers in physical pain making a hell of family life. She wondered if her research about reducing sleepless nights, easing the strain of caring for any other children, minimising tissue damage which made for better sex, would have any relevance to the women she would meet. The prospect of barefoot midwifery, with only herself to rely on, made her theories seemed irrelevant, almost frivolous.

Involuntarily she shivered in the sharp morning air, drew her jacket round her and made herself relax into the midwife's waiting game she knew so well.

The *comisaría* in the centre of Granada is an imposing building draped in large flags that these days include that of the European Union. Antonio Marín strode forward, pushed past the press, nodded at the armed police flanking the entrance and ushered David García toward the stairs. The public areas on the ground floor were cold and in darkness. *Far too early to be taking pubic enquiries,* García silently supposed, *although*, he thought wryly, *just like the US, seemingly never too early for the reporters*.

The stairs led to a mezzanine. A few people were working. All seemed uncommonly calm given the magnitude of the crisis that was brewing. Wider corridors, bigger windows, and a general feeling of airiness presented García with a sense of freshness that was always missing in New York. Here one did not get the feeling that every breath one breathed had already pumped its way through someone else's lungs, or that, as in New York, every glass of water drunk had passed through eight other people before you. It felt strange, and yet, with the chatter of Spanish, also familiar.

Mary and the ten choristers were moved away from the *generalife*. Yet Mary wasn't afraid. She was more confused than anything. She had tried to explain, in a mixture of poor Spanish and English coupled with hand gestures, why they had been in the amphitheatre. He would have none of it. When the singers had come forward to assist with her attempts at communication he had simply jerked her by her arm and shouted. That was the first moment when she had some misgivings. Out of the corner of her eye she had seen that the men had all fallen back, even Daniel, usually the first with a quip or a challenge, especially when he had a drink in him. Then, when they began to talk among themselves, the man had turned on them and shouted again. Only when all was silent had he released his hold on her and motioned them all before him down the path and across a footbridge toward a collection of buildings.

She recognised the buildings of course. She had had months to prepare for this trip. She had been chipping away at learning Spanish and filling her flat with everything about the Alhambra for twelve months. Despite the circumstances, nothing could rob her of the thrill of seeing the buildings, as she later framed it, *in the flesh*.

Finally, into an almost ethereal silence a woman had come, small, dark, young and clearly within a month of giving birth.

"We need to see in your bag," she had stated, pushing Rashida gently to the left. A man took her other arm and led her forward.

"I'll open it for you," Rashida had said.

"No," the man spoke, "we will open it."

"This bag is not for you to rake through. It's not a bag of tools for a car mechanic. I can open it for you. You can look. You may not touch anything. Is that understood? If you touch anything I will not, I cannot, help. I will do nothing if the sterility of my tools is compromised. Tell that to your leader."

The man looked past her into the shadows beyond the trees and then back at her.

"All right."

And then she had opened the bag, named everything in it and closed it again.

"When are you due?" she had asked the woman.

"I'm not sure. Soon."

"Perhaps I should examine you. Is there anywhere we can go?"

"Oh!" she had smiled, putting her hand to her mouth. "It isn't me you're here for. It's Dolores."

"Dolores?"

"Yes, Dolores, and then there's Nita, there are three of us, nearly ready," she had sounded almost apologetic.

"Three?"

"Yes. Three. And we have lost so many. Now we are here, we need help. I'll take you to Dolores. We can talk on the way," she had nodded at the man and he had stood aside. "We've been on the move so long now, I can't remember even when it started."

"On the move?" Rashida repeated at the same time willing herself to sound less inane.

"Well yes. The struggle, if you like," she had paused. "And we move around a lot. We have lost many, many babies."

Rashida could not believe she was hearing this. This was the twenty-first century, they were talking Europe, not South America, where Allah alone knew, she had seen enough child-death to last two lifetimes. This was Spain, her country. This was Granada, her city. How could people choose this?

"But you don't have to live like this. You could...."

"What?" the woman had cut across her. "We could what? Give up? Be made into scapegoats for this society? So that everyone can get rid of us and feel better? We are committed."

Rashida could not fathom what on earth the woman was talking about and seized on the only thing that had relevance to her and said,

"And the babies? Are they committed too?"

The woman had then looked at her, not with contempt or with anger, but with a sort of infinite patience. Rashida had seen that look a thousand times. The imminent mother, the madonna, whom nature makes impervious to life's great questions so that she might get on with life's great work. And all the woman said was:

"You'll see."

And she had seen. In three hours she had seen. In the royal palaces they had built a make-shift central camp in the *palacio de los leones*. On one of the gravel quadrants the embers glowed from the fires of the evening before. Rashida had shuddered to think which priceless Islamic fretwork had fuelled it. The fountain above the lions trickled, and among the pillars to the sides, in the cloisters, there were the lumps and bumps of people sleeping under blankets and beginning to stretch and writhe to wakefulness.

"Dolores isn't here." Nita had said. "She doesn't sleep so well. She sleeps in the Hareem." Despite herself, Rashida had been amused.

"Why don't you all sleep in the *hotel america*? In the *parador*? You have it all don't you? The whole monument?"

"It is forbidden," the woman had said.

"By whom?" asked Rashida, but was ignored.

"This way. I'll show you fresh water. I expect you'll be needing it."

"My office," Antonio said opening a door.

Inside, at last, there was action, plenty of it. A young man came toward them. García felt himself jolt involuntarily. Tall, fair, with an air of youthful authority, he approached David and Antonio and hesitated in a slightly staged manner, a trace of *waiting to be introduced*.

"David García," said Antonio, "meet Raúl Sanchez. Raúl commands the army contingent on this."

García thought he might have heard regret or disdain in

Antonio's tone and made a mental note to revisit the notion. Banks of ringing phones, blinking computers, men gesticulating, or shouting, or both, stole Raúl's entrance. David had forgotten the noise level of Spain. Even for a New Yorker, even for a Cuban New Yorker, Spain was loud. Another young man came toward them hailing Antonio.

"More info," he shouted, waving a paper and rotating something in his mouth at the same time. "And this time I don't think you can have seen it already! Seems they've got hostages."

"David García, Manuel Pedraza," Antonio introduced them as they shook hands. García noticed that it was sunflower shells that were now discharging from Pedraza's mouth as Antonio went on, "Manuel's joined us from Motril," Antonio said to David, as if David had any idea where Motril might be. And then to Manuel, Antonio said, "What have you got?"

"There's been a call from..." Manuel referred to his paper,"... from the security guys who work for the *patronato*. Some guests from the *parador* are unaccounted for. They have sent a fax through listing names. It seems they are still in the Alhambra."

"I thought the hotels were evacuated," Antonio barked at him.

"I guess not all," said Manuel.

"What do they want? Any more ideas on that?"

"Nothing yet Sir," Raúl interjected and looked at García. David decided it was as good a moment as any to interrupt.

"OK. Catch me up here. *patronato*? *parador*? A hotel I presume. Missing people?" He caught Antonio's look of exasperation, understood it, and said, "I'm quick. All I need is five minutes. Maybe ten. Then I'm briefed. I'm good to go."

"OK." Antonio knew the time taken to brief García would be worth it. "Get David up to speed. No, not you Raúl. You Manuel. Raúl, take me through everything the army have done in the last two hours. Then you two," he said nodding to Manuel and García, "be back here in ten."

Rashida was alarmed at her own sense of exhaustion. *How could that be?* she thought. *I've barely been here two hours!* She re-ran the mental video of her morning in her mind.

She had been taken through the familiar *hall of the ambassadors*, grim and dreary for all its attempt at splendour. Exquisite fretwork and beautiful ceramics were overlaid with incongruous medieval works obscuring the daylight and preventing the lifting of the soul that the architects had intended. They had continued out into the gardens that stretched between the palaces and the fortress of the *alcazaba* where she was now huddled.

Such a short time ago they had almost strolled like visitors toward the edges of the fortified walls. But the smell of the air had changed as they had moved along. It became acrid and caught at Rashida's throat. It was the smell of smouldering masonry, wood, plaster and paint. They had rounded a corner and she had seen men laying what looked like fuses and charges in *el partal*. Any amusement she had felt in the *palacio de los leones* was gone. These people meant business.

The water source appeared good, clear and running. But it was too far from the *palacio de los leones* or the *hareem* if she needed it in an emergency. The still water in the pools was nearer but there was a danger of stagnation and therefore infection.

"What about the toilets?" she had asked.

"Nobody trusts them."

Again she felt like she was out of time.

"What do you mean?"

"We try to avoid processed water. We try to only drink mountain water. Wild water. Dolores lost the others drinking water."

"The others?"

"Her other children."

"I see," Rashida had paused, deciding to get as much of the medical history now as she could. "Has she had many?"

"Three. Maybe four."

"What happens?"

"I don't know. But when they come, they live a few days, and then that's it."

At the time Rashida had been puzzled. Even now, when the delivery was over, she was still puzzled. It could be anything from diabetes to rhesus. Without more information it was a waste of time to speculate.

What also interested her was the use of "we". The woman had talked the language of a tribe. They seemed to live in a tribe and seemed to live as one. Rashida knew tribal life. She had lived and worked among tribes, but they had always been cultural strangers. She had never known people from her own culture that lived like this. She had been instantly cynical. Gypsy life, hippie life. A dream that would sour.

"And you? How many have you?"

"This is my first," was the shy answer.

They had then ambled back through the *jardines de machuca*. The scar where the bough had been taken from the pomegranate tree and sent over the wall, now immortalised by yesterday's television cameras, shone white in the brightening sun. Rashida had stepped past it carefully.

Before her had been an older woman plaiting her hair. She had turned when hearing them and stared long and hard at Rashida, before turning away and continuing her braiding. Rashida had waited. There was an unnatural stillness about this woman. Perhaps so many births with no children had taken what would have been a bloom of expectancy from her demeanour. Perhaps fear cast a shadow on her animation. She did not look defeated, just still. Too still. After a while Dolores had said:

"I have pain."

"Where?"

"In my back. I have pain in my back." she had put her hand in the small of her back. "I have pain here. I have had pain here for many days."

As she spoke Rashida had been aware that the Spanish words, though perfectly accented, were not coming easily.

"May I?" Rashida had moved forward.

But Dolores had stepped back and continued to speak.

"I have had many babies. I always get this pain. Then the babies come. And then they go," she had made a movement with her hands and a noise through her lips as though dandelion seeds were being scattered on a wind. "Every time I think I will be lucky," Rashida knew that feeling of empty hope only too well and slid her hand to her own belly. "But every time I am wrong. I am not so young, the years go by, and I have no children. Children. They are the future. This is why we do what we do. We save the future. They say," she had paused and corrected herself, "it is said, we need you to bring this child safely in and keep it safely here so it can see the future."

Rashida had sensed that for Dolores this was a long speech and wondered how much of it was learned by rote and how much she understood what she was saying. The woman was certainly dignified, she didn't look simple, but she spoke as though she was, as though she was struggling to make herself coherent, using a voice not wholly her own.

"Where are you from?"

"Galicia," Dolores had answered. That explained the slow speech Rashida had thought. In the Galician region of northern Spain, next to the Portuguese border, they spoke Gallego, as distinct from Spanish as French or Italian. Rashida thought she saw tears in the woman's eyes. She had looked toward her bag and then thought better of it, *poco a poco – little by little*. She needed to gain Dolores's confidence and not over-face her with medicine and equipment. At least not yet.

When she had finished touching and listening to Dolores, Rashida had sat quietly. From the side she had seen blankets being folded quietly with the air of long practice. Another pregnant girl had come over and was introduced to her as Nita. She too had looked as if birth was imminent.

Rashida had excused herself to go and talk with Nita discretely and take whatever medical case she could. As they moved away from the group and walked slowly into a more private space, Rashida had noted the girl's grey pallor and discoloured nails, and this had added to her fears that something was very wrong. None of these fears was alleviated by the continual sight of the men, who kept their distance, but whose gait and silence was pregnant with a purpose of its own. Men, who, in their own angular way, were an eternal balance to the mysteries of women.

And then these same men had come for her. Dolores's time was upon her and two hours hard work by both of them was rendered a bloody mess. And now, dawn gone and the morning broken, she found herself against the wall raking her hands through her hair.

García watched Manuel Pedraza throwing pipas into his mouth, then cracking the shells between his teeth, extracting the sunflower kernel and discharging the stripy shell without his hands ever touching his face. The working of his jaw whilst speaking was at once both fascinating and mildly discourteous. García found himself involuntarily fixing his eyes on Pedraza's mouth, as he had once watched his wife, and then later their daughter Marilita, rotating pins in their lips whilst they sewed. He wondered if Pedraza would have behaved in the same way with a senior member of his own staff. García sensed resentment in Pedraza.

The *patronato*, according to Pedraza, was the committee charged with the care of the Alhambra. Unfortunately its director and the chief archaeologist were away at a conference in Australia. Not that there was there anything unusual in their absence. The Alhambra was a World Heritage Site. As such it received international money and had to represent itself on an international stage. While there were no end of protocols for imagined emergencies, Manuel laboured the point, they had never had an emergency quite like this one.

For fear of being seen as patronising David resisted saying what every senior office knew; no emergency was ever like the protocols, no emergency could ever be fully anticipated. Pedraza went on to explain that someone was going to come from the *patronato* as soon as possible. The chief of security was already in the *comisaría*.

To complicate things, Manuel elaborated, this year, as Easter was so late, the *festivales* were taking place. The annual event of music and dance was organised for the stage in the *generalife*, the summer palace with its beautiful gardens, Pedraza explained. Although he had forgotten the name of it, García could clearly remember it from his visit with Richard. The *generalife* was a place of relaxation for generations of royal Moors. Water, light, foliage, and one delightful, visual, verdant surprise after another.

It seemed that choirs and dance troops had come from all over, Manuel continued. One had come from the UK. Apparently they had arrived at the *parador* the night before. The *parador*, the state run hotel, was within the Alhambra walls. No, Manuel did not know why some were still there, and yes, all the other guests had been evacuated by the terrorists. It seemed that the ten or eleven unaccounted for were from the visiting English choir. García felt himself smile a small smile. *Ten or eleven*. So typical of Latinos he thought, so long under the thumb of some dictator or invader, they had never acquired the cold numeric efficiency of the northern European.

"Is it ten or eleven?" García wanted to know.

"I don't know." Pedraza shrugged.

"Shouldn't we find out?"

"It's not that easy." Pedraza was defensive. "It's a local thing."

"Say what?" García's New York vernacular seeped out.

"The *policía local*, they deal with that sort of stuff. We are having enough trouble with the *guardia civil*."

"OK," said García, raising his hands in mock surrender. "Back up. Who are *we*?"

"Special Task Force comprised of officers from the *policía nacional* and the *guardia civil*. Me, I'm *policia nacional*, that's drugs, murder, terrorism, that sort of thing. The *policía local* does domestic disputes, parking fines."

"And the *guardia civil*?"

"National roads, coasts and borders, the countryside."

"And so the trouble with the *guardia civil* would be.....?"

"The Alhambra is a national monument. More than that. As I said, it's a World Heritage Site. UNESCO would say it belongs to the world. The *guardia civil* take the view that as such its borders are more international than national. Although they have backed off a bit since Sanchez and his boys arrived."

"As they are the army right?"

"Yeah." Pedraza's apparent resentment at García seemed to melt a little into a resentment of the army. "The *guardia civil* still think they are in the army most of the time. Hence the jodhpurs and the jack-boots." He spat sunflower hulls on the floor.

"I see. Some co-ordination issues here," García said dryly, only too familiar with similar issues between NYPD and the FBI. "Why think anyone from the choir is in the Alhambra?"

"Because they haven't been seen outside it." Manuel struggled a little to hide his contempt.

"Fair enough."

"You must know something about the Alhambra right?" Manuel almost sneered.

"Ancient monument. Dates from the Islamic rule of Spain. Covers a fair amount of ground. Is on a hill above the city. Considered priceless. Have I missed anything?" And when Manuel didn't answer he added, "Tell me, are you this tetchy with all newcomers? Or is it just me?" He had almost inserted the word *gay* before *newcomers*.

Manuel was taken aback and muttered, "I just don't see why we need to draft in an American to help us with a very Spanish problem. Look, even now, at the time it is taking to tell you what is happening when we could be resolving it instead of briefing you."

"Fair point." David looked at him and remembered how it felt to be passionate about work, opinionated about management decisions. Manuel looked surprised at his response and García added, "Except I wasn't drafted in. This is government to government. I am an observer. Here to log one central issue: does this tie in with 9/11? I can offer some expertise," David shrugged, "if your boss asks for it. To be honest," García stopped, then started again, "my bosses wanted to get rid of me for a while."

This final comment threw Manuel and all he could think of to say was,

"I expect Antonio wants us now."

Without the hours spent in York pouring over her maps Mary could not have hoped to place them, but there were some signs visible as they were marched along. The words *la puerta de los*

siete suelos etched on marble indicated a tower to the left and this told her they were heading toward the centre of the complex. Rounding a corner she knew instantly *palacio de carlos v*, square and monstrous. She had spotted it from the coach the day before as it had driven past to deposit them at the archway into the *parador*. She had been too ill with the heat and the smell of drink to do much more than promise herself that she would see it the following day.

At first she thought they were to go inside. But they were pushed past, then right, and then crossed in front of it before taking steps down toward an older structure. The light was poor and they passed quickly through it, out into an enclosed courtyard. There, to her great surprise, was a group of mostly women engaged in what seemed to be almost domestic duties. The man indicated they were all to sit and threatened them with gestures and shouts until they did so.

Mary's confusion had grown at the sight before her. Fearing to speak, she sat quietly and watched. There was something almost stone-age about the tableau. The pallor of everyone was ash grey. Everyone seemed small and ill. It crossed her mind that they looked almost starved. Their camp was dull and make-shift. The only exception was the clothing of one woman who wore a brightly coloured scarf tied like a turban, jeans and loose jacket. Mary almost called out to her but the shadow of the man who had marched them from the *generalife* fell across her and instead she raised her eyes to him.

"May I speak?" she asked.

"*Háblame,*" he replied.

"I don't speak Spanish very well," she said to him in halting Spanish.

"Then you shouldn't be in Spain," he replied curtly in English.

"What's going on? Who are you? Who are these people?"

she began and then stuttered to a stop.

"There's nothing here you need to know," he said flatly and turned and walked away.

Mary didn't have red hair for nothing. She sprang up and caught at his arm.

"Yes there is. I am here at the invitation of the *ayuntamiento de granada*, a guest at the *festivales*," she was proud of the pronunciation she had been practising for her opening speech at the concert. "My colleagues and I," she swept her arm out across the men at the side, "were guests in the *parador*. Where is everyone?" and when he didn't answer she said, "Look, we were simply taking a dawn walk and wanted to see the Alhambra."

"Well now you have seen it."

"So now we can go then," she said more matter of factly than she felt.

"No. You can't. Unfortunately."

"What's going on?"

"What is going on is that you and your colleagues are going to sit against that wall without speaking until I tell you otherwise. Do you understand me?"

She met his look, eyeball for eyeball and said,

"Perfectly," and then, just as he turned to walk away she turned to the men, raised her arms and began to sing. He turned again in an instant, pulled her backwards against him clamping his hand over her mouth.

"*No te metas conmigo*," he whispered in her ear. And eight or nine of his companions came across. "In polite English, in case you are wondering, that means *don't mess with me*," and when there was no response, he said, "Do we understand each other?"

She nodded, looking toward her singers. Seeing their fear, for the first time she allowed some of her own to seep into her veins. Someone else approached and there was a rapid exchange of Spanish. Her captor let her go, and she stumbled briefly and watched as he went with the woman in the headscarf through another opening and out of sight.

Lola and Alberto joined the other children in the line and waited. The bus was overdue but nothing was running ordinarily now. The *reformatorio* in San Miguel el Alto had been closed for nearly an hour. They had packed their few precious items in one small case and stood hand in hand. Some of the children had fallen out of line and were jumping along the low wall, on and off, on and off. A few were seated at the kerbside. Despite the bright sun, it was cold. Most of the children were puzzled to be going away, some grew fractious. The nuns moved backwards and forwards along the lines, comforting and cajoling.

Alberto was not so puzzled as many of the others. He had known since yesterday that things were different in the Alhambra Palace. A tree here, a bush there. A child sees such things. Especially this child, whose solace had long been rolling in the ivy and working his way up to the walls and back on his belly. He knew every plant on every approach from the Albaicín and back. He knew where the water ran, which cats marked the territory, where the gardeners dropped their cigarette butts, who of the guards was snogging whom. Where, even when, there was consummation and the discard of used contraceptives, Alberto knew of that too.

Lola knew also, because Alberto told her. When, in her fey fashion, she appeared disinterested he made her look, insisted that she see what had moved, what was different, what was the same. And now they had been told they had to leave the *reformatorio*. It was not the leaving of the reform school building that Alberto cared about. It was leaving its proximity to the Alhambra that bothered him much more.

He cast his eyes across from the *reformatorio* over the

ravine that separated the walls of the Alhambra from the city below and ruminated on what he knew. He looked for evidence of Agustín and Rosario. If anyone knew anything, they would. Agustín, working his *finca* bent double, his gloves always hanging from his back pocket alongside a little string, (*just in case* he would always tell Alberto), Agustín would know. Or Rosario would, hobbling around with her bad knees, threading garlic, stringing peppers, shelling beans. Rosario, who always nodded smilingly as Agustín fed Alberto and Lola's hungry imaginations with more stories of the Alhambra, or told and retold the arrest of Federico García Lorca. Rosario would have an idea.

Someone had moved into the Alhambra, Alberto thought. Someone was making everyone else move out. Even children like them had to move, and Alberto knew that children, especially the children from the *reformatorio*, were considered a special case. Someone was there who should not be. He just needed to decide what to do about it. And then of course he had to convince Lola.

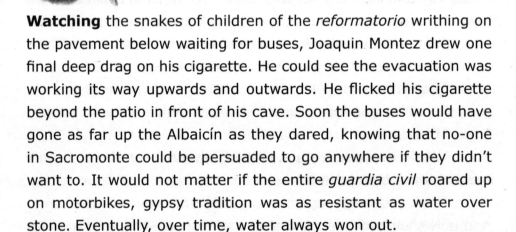

Watching the snakes of children of the *reformatorio* writhing on the pavement below waiting for buses, Joaquin Montez drew one final deep drag on his cigarette. He could see the evacuation was working its way upwards and outwards. He flicked his cigarette beyond the patio in front of his cave. Soon the buses would have gone as far up the Albaicín as they dared, knowing that no-one in Sacromonte could be persuaded to go anywhere if they didn't want to. It would not matter if the entire *guardia civil* roared up on motorbikes, gypsy tradition was as resistant as water over stone. Eventually, over time, water always won out.

"So what do you think?" His cousin Ana was at his side, reaching across his chest for the cigarettes visible in the pocket of his shirt.

"About this nonsense?" he said indicating the Alhambra and

clicking his lighter for her.

"About me, silly," she said, dragging on the cigarette and then evidently changing her mind and handing it to him.

"I think I'm going to get my nose broken is what I think," he said laughing. "And as for this," he swept his hand down towards the Alhambra, "I think it is going to be very interesting to see how it plays out."

"Fernando says we may have to go too."

"They can't make us."

"No. But it's not going to be simple to resist. Fernando says they have been there a day now and no-one has managed to figure it out," Joaquin managed not to interrupt with an exasperated *Fernando says this, Fernando says that*. Fernando was the husband after all, what did he expect? He heard Ana continue, "They say they have explosives. Then the army will come, or some other special force, and they will have explosives too and then, poooof" she shrugged her shoulders, "it will all tumble down."

"Tumble down," said Joaquin. "DOWN being the operative word. Whereas here in Sacromonte, we are 'up' from the Alhambra. It won't tumble up."

"Who do you think it is? What do you think they want?"

"Who knows?" It was his turn to shrug

"Don't you care?" she asked him.

"Yes," he nodded slowly. "Yes, I probably do."

"You don't sound so sure."

"Well I suppose it's just that it's always been there. I can't imagine it not being there."

"Well get imagining," she laughed. "It's our heritage."

"Na," Joaquin Montez shook his head smiling. "Na. The music is the heritage. Portable, insubstantial, impossible to steal or blow up. That's real heritage. Here. Inside," he tapped his chest and reached forward to tuck a lock of hair behind her ear.

"OK. Let's go through it again. WHAT and WHO. WHAT have we got?" Antonio Marín looked across at everyone in his office.

"The grid is out. We did that first," said Raúl. "No demands but the midwife. No threats, other than the damage at the beginning."

"No electric," nodded Antonio. "That usually ups the ante, puts a few stresses on. But they seem to have rolled with that punch. Am I right?"

"No reaction so far," said Manual

"Any news on the debris?" Antonio's eyes raked the room.

"They're working on it," Pedraza answered. "We can't get in close but we've got the sights on it. Raúl?"

"They're going over it under magnification, but it's hard at this distance. It's slow going. No sign of the detonator yet. We are a lot less advanced with the evacuation," Raúl went on.

García looked at Antonio and raised a quizzical eyebrow. "It's the end of *festivales*," Antonio said by way of an answer. "This is a big week in Granada. Thousands come for the processions."

"Processions?"

"The effigies of the Virgin are carried through the street," said Pedraza in a tone that suggested he was indulging David's ignorance. "Not as many as *semana santa*, Holy Week, but enough."

"So there are more people here than usual. Many more," Antonio emphasised.

"The army effort so far," said Raúl meaningfully, "apart from reconnaissance, has been focused on moving civilians from the immediate proximity. We intend to evacuate the city entirely. If the Alhambra blows up, the last thing we want is more casualties than we need. And anyway," Raúl Sanchez said impatiently, "civilians just get in the way."

David García wanted to ask Raúl Sanchez if then it might not be more convenient for him if civilians were blown up. But he had the wit to recognise that this brand of macabre humour could only be appreciated by people who knew him well, as had his own team in New York, in the good old days, before the fallout from 9/11. Instead he asked,

"How wide an area could be affected?"

"Last report, yesterday's explosion was felt about six miles away. On that basis we estimate about twenty kilos of explosives, minimum. We don't know how much they have, but that's not going to be all of it by any means."

"Anything else?" pressed Antonio.

"Nothing significant," Raúl replied. "I'll let you know."

"OK. Now WHO have we got?" Antonio looked across everyone again. Pedraza began,

"We've got Rashida Santiago, midwife, traveller, and," he paused, "scholar one supposes? Yes?"

"Yes," said Antonio. "She is a leading light in midwifery research. And she's a wife. Her husband's here in the city, waiting for news."

"Who else?"

"The residents."

"Residents?"

"There are private properties in the Alhambra compound. Some residents we can't account for."

"You're kidding me," said García flatly, knowing he wasn't. "Who?"

"An old woman who lives in *calle real*, next to the *huerta de santa maría*."

"Between the *hotel américa* and the *parador*," Antonio added for clarification. "She's pretty house-bound. And then maybe an elderly couple from the *finca*, they have the house just at the edge of the northern wall. Probably they are still there. Agustín Lopez and his wife Rosario."

"Christ," said García. "Who else?"

63

"Some choir from England."

"Those you mentioned?" García directed his remark at Manuel Pedraza. Manuel looked down at his notes and half read out,

"We know there were forty-one of them, thirty have been accounted for. That leaves eleven in the Alhambra. Ten men and one woman – she's the director. No Spanish speakers as far as we know. Just here to perform at the festival. I have faxed the UK to ask for any relevant information they have about their backgrounds, ex-army, police, anything like that."

"Wait," David put his hand up at face level, "wait. Where are they from?"

"England."

"Yeah, but where?"

Manuel consulted his papers again.

"York, it's in the north."

"Yes it is," said García and then more loudly, "yes it is. And I know someone there in the local force." He spun toward Antonio taking a card out of his wallet as he did so. "Can we try this number?"

"Sure," Antonio passed the card to one of the team.

"Anyone else?"

"Not that we know of," Manuel shook his head.

"And what's happening now up there?"

"Nothing. Nothing at all. Rashida Santiago went in at dawn. That's it."

"And explosions?"

"Just the one."

"Sir?"

"Yes?" Antonio answered one of the junior officers.

"We have that English number on the 'phone."

"Excuse me," said David to Antonio and walked over to the 'phone. "Hello, it's David García here. We met a couple of years ago when I was over..."

He was interrupted by a woman saying,

"This is Jack's sister Ange here..."

Antonio Marín watched García from across the room as he spoke into the telephone in English and saw a different man.

He couldn't believe it. Surely not. Surely, surely not. The only reason he had his mobile switched on was so his sister Ange could phone, but this was not Ange. It was Superintendant Michael Small. Jack Fisher had to stop himself answering the name on the liquid crystal display with *Hello Dinky,* the well known moniker within the force for his boss, and said instead,

"Fisher here." Paula looked at him sharply, knowing immediately that it could not be Ange. It was Jack's official telephone answering voice and she was instantly furious. She raised her eyebrows at her husband. Then there was a pause and he said, "Yes. I know who it is Sir. Superintendent Small," he said for Paula's benefit.

She watched as her husband listened, barely saying anything into the mouthpiece. Then he wrote down a phone number and hung up.

"Seems I have to go to work," he said.

"You're kidding me!"

"Nope."

"Jack this was to have been our first real holiday without kids since the twins were born!" and when he didn't say anything and just smiled she said, "you're enjoying this!" and when his smile became infectious she added, "Well they had better pay our fares, that's all I can say."

"You are never going to believe this."

"Try me."

"Listen."

Jack Fisher dialled the number he had written down into his mobile. After a minute he said,

"David García," then repeated the name more slowly and waited. "García," he said at last, "Jack Fisher here." After a pause Jack said, "No problem. We were in Granada yesterday just before the explosion. I noticed it then," Jack grinned a little ruefully at himself, how typical of a copper to notice the police station where any other tourist would see shops and museums. "We're at the beach now. It'll take about," Jack looked at his watch, "I don't know, maybe two hours to get there. I'll be bringing my wife."

"You are kidding me?" Paula's fury was being replaced by incredulity as her husband rang off.

"Look at it this way," he said grinning at her, "it's a working holiday and we'll see a side of Spain we never expected to see. And anyway, you said you liked Granada."

"Modern communication," said García to Antonio as he replaced the handset after talking to Jack Fisher. "A couple of years ago I was in England. On a trip. In York. I met a policeman there. I kept his card."

Antonio tried not to imagine why. Before he could stop himself he asked,

"What sort of trip? Business or pleasure?" and then silently chided himself for being judgmental. García eye-balled him and at first would not be drawn.

"Turns out he's right here. In Andalucía, on vacation," he threw Antonio a bone by adding, "with his wife."

But inwardly García cringed. The UK trip had been anything but pleasure. Hearing Jack's voice on the phone had reminded him of the one sane day in the entire fourteen of his whirlwind European trip with Richard. He and Richard had attended the AA meeting in that funny building right smack in The Quarter, the city centre of York. The Elim Church was a modern, red-brick edifice, strangely secular in a city stuffed full of spires, elegant stonework and carved gargoyles.

The meeting was the usual format, the *Hi, my name is bla bla bla and I am an alcoholic.* Christ how many times had he sat through the same rigmarole? After Richard had died, David had wondered if it was in that funny building in that medieval city that he had first come to realise that he had had enough.

Jack Fisher had been a part of the process. Jack with his steady grasp on the disease, and his apparent strength of character. Jack, who at that meeting had briefly stood and gone forward, and accepted his six-year sobriety medal. Six years. Richard was lucky to be sober for six months.

It turned out that the York group met weekly and then afterwards always went across the street to an odd little café. They had invited Richard and David to go along. He and Richard were each so fed up with the company of the other that they had readily agreed in unison.

He tried to remember what it was called: *La Guitarra? No, El Piano, that was it.* It had reminded David of *cantinas* he had visited in Honduras, all gaudy and disjointed yet a unified whole. They had ordered herb teas, a few bowls of curried lentils, some hummus and warm bread. It had been a type of heaven to sit there in the low lighting, relaxed at last, and listen to Jack talk to Richard, watch Richard's edges soften and see him finally lose that semi-permanent look of a man with an over-wound spring.

Later the owner had come, a South American woman. Jack had introduced them. Carmen had been her name, and she and David had had some fun exchanging pleasantries in Spanish, his Cuban accent and her mix of central and southern patois making them laugh together, low and sonorous in the dim orange-hued lighting. García had seen Jack look at her and wondered where the love for such a plain woman came from.

"Are you married?" David had asked him.

"Oh yes," he had replied warmly. "Very."

But evidently not to this woman.

"You spend a lot of time in here?"

"Just if I go to meetings. But Carmen and I go back a way," he said as if aware of David's unspoken question. "Our families are close."

And then they had talked of policing. A bit about drugs and drink. Some stuff about structures and hierarchies. It was the days before 9/11, a time when the world was different. It had been an urbane conversation about a common profession. Then they had exchanged cards. Jack had said to ring him if ever they were in town again. And then that had been that.

He and Richard had returned to the hotel. Eased by the company and the respite from travel, they had been briefly at peace with each other. David remembered the hotel room, the view of the ancient city walls from a window that framed a cold night sky and crisp bright stars. That night was the last time the love had been any good.

But all this time David had kept Jack's card in his wallet. Once Richard had seen it there and tried to make something more of it, as if David wanted to pursue something personal with Jack. Finally, goaded by Richard's constant jealousies, of which the keeping of Jack's card was only one, David had told him,

"I keep it to remind me of the man you might have been."

That had shut him up. But David had had plenty of time after Richard's death to reflect on the fact that such a statement, while true, was also cruel.

"I want your opinion," Antonio's voice brought him back to the present. "You may be an observer, but I want you fully on board with this. Look at the maps." David joined him at the table, and saw on the uppermost map the whole city of Granada. "What do you think?"

"Before we start," David said, nodding at the maps, relieved not to have to fight for involvement, "what's the accommodation?"

"Here. Cots upstairs."

"Fine. That includes me." He wanted Antonio, and all the rest of them, to know that he was one of them. If they disliked close quarters with a queer, too bad. He wasn't interested in challenging homophobia or in building morale, so much as letting them know he was going to be around the whole time, listening, watching, being tripped over if necessary. Now that Antonio had invited him to the table, this visit, whatever O'Reilly might have intended, was not going to be just some flimsy window-dressing.

"Of course," Antonio concurred, and then added lightly, "hardly five star."

David García smiled and returned to looking at the maps saying,

"So what do ETA want with the Alhambra?"

Antonio missed a beat, and David, keen respondent to people's covert and diverse communications, heard the small space between his question and Antonio's answer. It told him that the man was holding something back. He needed to talk to Antonio alone. And he needed to be subtle about it. Deftly he changed the subject saying,

"We need height," he stabbed at the map. Indicating the location of the *comisaría* relative to the Alhambra on its hill, he asked, "can we re-locate? Can we re-locate fast? Say, up to here? Can the infrastructure cope?" David pointed on the map to the high ground up to the north north west of the city and the Alhambra.

"It's done," Antonio replied. "There's a reform school that's been evacuated, at San Miguel el Alto, it's the highest place in Sacromonte. We are just waiting for the technical guys to do their stuff."

"No access past the Alhambra needed?" García said in his

brusque way.

"None," Antonio said.

David cast his eye over the group, some of whom were looking decidedly bleary eyed. He used the moment to engineer a chance to get rid of them,

"How long since these people had a break?" he asked.

Antonio picked up on his cue saying,

"How about everyone takes ten? It will give me a chance to go through the maps with Captain García."

"What's with the army?" García then asked as the last man left the room.

"Raúl has command of four hundred. Full SWAT capability. Here SWAT is part of the army, not police," Antonio explained.

"Sanchez seems a bit young. Who's in charge? Operationally."

"I am," Antonio replied. David found it hard to believe that such an operation would be placed in the hands of a local man. As if reading his thoughts Antonio went on, "I'm from the Madrid squad, anti-terrorism. They drafted me in. I just happen to come from Granada originally. From just outside, a village called Pinos Puente in fact. It was me your people contacted when the US said they were going to send someone."

"Disappointed?"

"No. On the contrary," Antonio half smiled, "I was afraid they would send me a general." Then Antonio took out a cigarette. García couldn't remember how long it had been since he had seen anyone smoke in an office, let alone a police station. Antonio tapped the end of it on the packet and lit up. "One wannabe general is enough."

So, thought García, *when you introduced Raúl, that was the source of your hesitation*.

"The younger men," Antonio continued, "may think their honour is at stake if they can't figure this out without help. Me?"

He shook his head. "Honour has nothing to do with it. If the Americans want to send someone, frankly, we could do with all the help we can get. Besides," he added, "I read about you in the New York Police Gazette. You don't think in straight lines."

David balked momentarily. First to find that Antonio read in English. Second because the Gazette was the first place his controversial views had been made known. Last because he wondered if by using the word 'straight' this was Antonio's clever way of letting David know that Antonio knew he wasn't. García was then annoyed with himself again. Surely to God he was old enough now not to care what people thought anymore? Surely to God.

Antonio went on,

"I don't know if we need a negotiator or a strategist."

At that David knew his instincts had been correct. There was something not right here. Alone they could speak more freely. Antonio was probably even grateful for it.

"Tell me more," García said to him.

"If we need a negotiator," Antonio continued, "I don't know if we need someone like you, someone different, who can create a connection that someone familiar cannot. Or, if we need to find a negotiator to match the profile of the perpetrator and validate them. We keep waiting for some psychological profiling."

"What's the hold up?"

"We still don't know for sure who this is."

"ETA, right?"

"We don't know."

"Come on," David's head snapped up and he stared at Antonio, fixing him with his dark eyes. "Islamic Jihad then?"

"We really don't know."

"It's a joke, right?"

"No. It's not."

"Wait a second, all this bullshit about Joaquin Rafael...?"

71

"…is bullshit."

"Why?"

"Because we don't have a clue. At the moment, our only hope is tracing the detonator. And that's a faint one at that." Antonio Marín sucked sharply on his cigarette. "We had to start with something, give people something. You've seen the press outside. You want to know about intelligence? There is none. There was none. This has been a total, I mean TOTAL, surprise."

"It's more than twenty-four hours," David looked at Antonio and shook his head. "You are truly caught. With your pants down…"

"…and on international TV," agreed Antonio, "and to cap it all," he said, taking his last drag before grinding the tab underfoot, "your dick is very small and your pubic hair is balding."

There was a pause, a small, but perfect, silence, and then David García threw back his head and laughed like a drain.

Daniel Goddard was hungry. And he was cold. And he was thirsty. And it wasn't water that he had in mind. What he had in mind was a little stronger. The thing was, Mary Stansfield was aggravating in the extreme, as indeed were all women, with the possible exception of his mother, and maybe Carmen Romero.

The thought of Carmen Romero made him long for El Piano in York and a jug of coffee. Actually, he longed for his mother too. But above all, if he couldn't have his mother, a coffee or a vodka, or maybe he could have that very cute little pregnant girl he had been watching out of the corner of his eye. *Little Nita, nothing sweeta*, he rhymed to himself and then promptly lost his train of thought.

As the fantasy faded, as they always did, he was aggravated again. All this sitting in silence was like school, and Mary with her quick darting glances and flame hair was hardly peaceful.

Everyone else was so plain and boring, even the few children were quiet and boring, and the woman with the bright headscarf, who seemed to command an authority, did not appear to be popular either. Where was that little Nita now?

Daniel began to hum. Mary glared at him and made a sign for him to shut up, so he hummed louder, and then louder. Two of the men returned and cast their shadows across him, and he hummed still louder. Then there was a dull thud as he was slapped on the jaw by one of them who then walked away.

Mary shuffled over to Daniel and reached out to touch his face but Daniel was angry and tearful all at once.

"For Christ sake get off me," he said pulling away. "What the hell is going on here?" His voice was petulant and full of self-pity.

"Daniel. Listen to me." Mary spoke softly. Then she looked at the others. "I don't know what's going on here. I can't understand much, the women hardly at all. She speaks English," Mary nodded toward Rashida. "We just have to wait this out a bit. Try and piece it together."

"How many men?" Reginald Coussins spoke up, a man not much under sixty.

"Hard to say," said Mary. "We just don't know enough yet. God I wish I had read the paper at the hotel. Can you remember seeing anything? Reading anything?"

"How long do you think they will keep us here?" Reggie asked.

"I don't know," said Mary. "Rats! We can't just sit and wait, knowing nothing," she got to her feet. "I'm going to find out."

Jack Fisher parked outside the *comisaría* and didn't care about whether it was legal. If they towed the hired car, they towed it. If it got clamped, David García could sort it out. He held the door for his wife and handed her out as if she were royalty.

    Yes, he thought, *I'm going to enjoy this*.

afternoon

Rashida refused the soup, preferring to take an orange from the trees in the patios. It wasn't that the food didn't look good. On the contrary, with the kitchens of the *parador* and the *hotel america* at their disposal this unhappy band could hardly have failed to create something presentable. It was mainly that she didn't want to eat with them, to enter into that almost holy estate of breaking bread that might impose personal obligations. Her professional obligations were enough. It looked like there would soon be another opportunity to prove them. Nita was restless, surely a sign of impending delivery. Maybe, Rashida thought, soup was a good idea after all. She might need her strength. She took a bowlful, sat apart, and tried to count them.

In South America the people of the forest had resisted being counted. *Never let them count you* they had told her in hushed whispers whenever there was a government official visiting, whether to fix prices, examine schools, or talk of better health care delivery. She had dismissed this as superstition, but now, trying to get an idea of the force of this tribe, she realised that knowing the numbers would give her power, that information was always power, and that was what her people of the forest had known and rightly been afraid of.

It was easy to mark the women. There must have been about thirty in all. The numbers of children were negligible, no more than seven or eight. But the men, that was a challenge. The man who had examined her bag when she arrived was often around. Then there was the man who had been so harsh about burying the baby, the same man who had brought the English people. But where she had waited outside, there had been silhouettes of men along all of the walls. If it were true that a circular walk of the Alhambra was about three kilometres, and if there was a man every twenty to thirty metres or so of the perimeter, then a crude estimate meant there could be as many as fifty to a hundred men. and if she was right, this was no casual invasion.

So far, she could not fathom their motivation. Nor could she see any evidence of the infamous Joaquin Rafael or indeed anyone who resembled a leader. The only indication that there might even be one was when they had tried to search her bag at the beginning and seemed to defer to someone in the shadows. The accents of some of the women, like Dolores, placed them as from Galicia. It didn't seem like an action from ETA. A background in research had ensured Rashida was slow to jump to conclusions. She tried to listen but nothing was coherent with any familiar political theme.

The English seemed as bewildered as she was. They sat quietly to the side, slurping on soup and speaking in snatched whispers. Except for the man they called Daniel and the red-haired woman, they were older people. She felt for them, cold and isolated in strange circumstances.

The lack of weapons nagged at her. She had seen a few hand grenades strapped to men's' waists, but little else. Perhaps the place was mined? She heard a few people arguing about rope and someone barking on about silos, but otherwise there were no clues. Weapons seemed to consist more of axes and saws than anything state of the art.

As she saw more and more ancient timbers being assigned to piles ready to ignite. She realised that this seemed to be a rule of terror by policies of 'burnt earth' rather than technological havoc. It made her surprisingly angry to recognise fretwork, the contents of the marquetry shop on *calle real*, some carved panels from God knows which palace, all being assembled for destruction. This was history beyond price, these were the artefacts of a civilisation that had outstripped anything that had followed. What were they doing? And why?

Had Jack Fisher not arrived David García was sure he would have flagged. Jet lag was pernicious and creeping up on him and the muddle of information was using up his energy in frustration. He sensed Antonio felt the same.

"We are wading through treacle here," Antonio had cried out at one particularly frustrating interaction with the chief of security of the *patronato*. "Treacle for God's sake! Let's start again. I know that the Alhambra is an impossible site to secure. I know this because I am from Granada and I am totally familiar with the number of people who go in and out. So how, I ask you Sir, since this is an impossible site to secure, how do you think, that this group of terrorists has managed to get hold of it?"

As if these types of futile exchanges weren't enough, Manuel Pedraza's defensiveness, whilst momentarily pierced by David's frankness, nonetheless had re-asserted itself and certainly seemed to be preventing García from getting a firmer grip on anything remotely resembling hard facts. Raúl with his army colleagues remained goldenly aloof. And when García caught his eye there was always a question in it.

García's overall impression was that the police personnel were running around like chickens with their heads cut off, whilst those of the army were standing back and biding their time. García had an odd sense of foreboding that Raúl was secretly waiting for them to fail. He wondered what was going on behind his cool, self-possessed exterior. García found himself oscillating between longing to see Fisher come through the door and genuine concern as to whether it might be just one more cook spoiling the broth.

One thing Manuel Pedraza had managed to do effectively, however, was to get some statements issued to placate the press, now camped in force outside the *comisaría*. After a brief discussion, Antonio had decided to release the information concerning the terrorist demand for a midwife and to use Rashida's photograph in a news bulletin.

There were two good reasons for doing so, Antonio had

told them. First, if she was going to die in the attempt, apart from her family having a hero's recognition for it, the nation, in any aftermath of panic, might be able to hang on to a hero as an anchor. David admired the subtlety and the foresight. Second, Antonio proposed, it might set up a wider reaction, cause a response from someone, if only from her jailers. For without any further demands, he reluctantly remarked, it could only be assumed that Rashida Santiago was also now a hostage.

"Jack Fisher is here Sir," said one of the young officers behind him, and Antonio turned to see Fisher and, he presumed, his wife, entering the room.

"David García, my wife Paula," said Fisher, clearly pleased to see a face he knew. They all shook hands.

David motioned to Antonio as he came over,

"Antonio Marín, Jack Fisher from York."

"My pleasure," said Antonio in accented English.

"So, what have we got going on?" asked Fisher

"A siege of the Alhambra. Almost no information."

"The English?"

"Eleven of them," confirmed Antontio. "Any information you can hurry through from England would be good. Who might be among them and any residual skills."

"No problem. Aims and objectives?" asked Fisher

"You mean are we saving people or things?" clarified Antonio.

"Yep. What's the policy for outcomes?"

"The monument is priority," said Antonio, choosing not to meet anyone's eyes.

There was a silence.

"Is that official?" asked Fisher.

"At the highest level," confirmed Antonio.

"Very well." Fisher eyed Paula into silence. "Paula can start 'phoning and see what we can get through from York. I don't want to slow anyone down."

"You can't. We couldn't go much slower if we tried," said Antonio beckoning to a colleague. "Take Señora Fisher to a desk and 'phone," he told the youngster, and then to Jack Fisher he said, "Indulge us. Look over the problem with us."

"Over here," Agustín called to her, finding it hard to believe that he would ever have hailed María Santos. Ever. Thirty years of never speaking and now he was trying to get her to come and sit with them. The world was mad.

"Over here!" called Rosario when María Santos looked confused, scanning the room for the source of Agustín's voice. "Over here!" repeated Rosario and made space next to her. "Come. Sit with us. Over here." And then Rosario said, "We'll keep her with us Rashida."

What they had said was that the monument was at risk and that a midwife had been demanded. Officially Rashida supposed she had offered, but on balance, given the *comisaría* had rung the university, it was as much commandeered as volunteered.

Listening to Antonio Marín in his offices before dawn, there was no mention of Islam, but that didn't mean it wasn't there. These days any terrorist activity was instantly thought to belong either to ETA or to Islam. But when she met with the Brain of Madrid, as the local officers had scathingly referred to Antonio while she was waiting outside his office, even he had been closed about who was involved. Lack of candour put her off. Until he mentioned that there was an observer coming from New York.

"The US are watching all of this. They are concerned. After 9/11 they watch every terrorist situation."

"Shame they weren't watching when the trains were

bombed in Madrid," Rashida had said dryly. Antonio had ignored her.

"They are sending a policeman who has worked in hostage and terrorist situations before. He is well known for his abilities. In fact, he's on his way now."

"Well, the Americans are nothing if not fast."

"Look Ms Santiago, I can appreciate this is not an easy situation for you, or for your husband. Everyone will understand if you pass on this."

"I didn't see a queue of volunteers outside," she had said tartly. "I just think it is naïve to imagine that some policeman from New York is going to contribute much to this."

"As I say, Ms Santiago, no-one will blame you for walking from this," and he turned from her as if the interview were over. So she had said casually, not really interested in the answer,

"What's his name?"

"Who?"

"The guy from the States."

"Ángel David García."

"Ángel David García?" she had said.

"Cubano." Marín had said. "Well New Yorker, but his family originated from Cuba."

Marín had been wrong to think that it was García's origins that had caught her interest. It was the name itself. She almost let her jaw drop. Ángel David García.

One of last things her mother had ever said to her was to always be ready for the help of angels. She had told Rashida as she lay dying, that angels could come in any form. That they were as common in Islam as in Christianity and their message was always the same.

"It is simple *hija*," she had said seriously, "it is merely this: *assistance in dark times.*"

"In any form *Mamá*?"

"In any form."

And Rashida had looked around her and through the window and seen their Scottish neighbour watering the plants on his balcony, and to lighten the mood referred to him and said,

"Even David?" she had smiled at her mother and the older woman had gripped her daughter's hand, pulled her toward her and said, almost harshly,

"Nowhere is it written Rashida that there can be no Ángel David."

In all the years since Rashida had met many men called Ángel such-and-such, or such-and-such Ángel. Never had she come across Ángel and David in the same name. It was that, and that alone, that had decided her.

She was surprised that the authorities also agreed. It was no secret that Rashida and her family had been a part of the new conversions from Christianity to Islam. They surely also knew that she was married to Mustafa, who was well known for describing the move to Islam by many young Granadinos as *reversion* not *conversion*.

But Antonio Marín had appeared not the least interested in her religion. He seemed just grateful. Neither the army nor the police had midwives, and even if they did, it would have been hard to find one ready to go at zero notice. There was no time, with more explosions being threatened, artefacts being torn up and dangled from parapets. He had simply stamped the paperwork for her to continue through a short briefing and then to the Alhambra.

So maybe in the rush no-one had considered that if this attack on the Alhambra was a religiously motivated attack, they might use her or abuse her. She adjusted her head scarf. *Enshallah* she whispered, *as God wills it*, and then she added, *let there be assistance in dark times from Ángel David García*.

When they counted the children onto the bus they were all there. When the bus arrived in Ronda where beds had been allocated to accommodate them, they were sure everyone went in for lunch. At siesta they counted them again, and two were missing.

In bed again Ana sat up suddenly at the sound of the radio, Joaquin's head and tongue still between her legs.

"Good God!"

With his neck slightly cricked Joaquin Montez threw off the sheet,

"What?"

She swung her leg across his head and leapt from the bed, moving toward the television and snapped it on.

"I don't believe it!"

Joaquin was at her side watching, a photo subtitled *Rashida Santiago* was on the screen.

"You know her?" Joaquin asked.

"Yes. She's my midwife."

O'Reilly was surprised to see her. It wasn't her end of town. At first he thought it was by chance. But then he figured, what sort of Latina would venture into an Irish bar? Least of all a curvaceous Latina, and alone. But when she came straight over to him he knew she had come expressly to see him. He had time to have a good look at her as she walked over.

She had been a beautiful young woman. He had often looked at her sideways in the many years their lives had run parallel, before their girls had grown up, before he was Commissioner, before 9/11. He saw that the years had been kind to her. She certainly looked better than at the funeral. That had been a hideous day. Even though he hated García, he could not have missed it.

Apart from supporting his own daughter Colleen in her distress, the loss of everyone in the twin towers had been a call to arms, to forget the local differences and to stand as one. García's girl Marilita had been among the fallen. That was that. Shoulder to shoulder was the only response. And now here was Marilita's mother, García's ex-wife.

"María."

"Eddie," she reached up and pecked his cheek. Hardly anyone called him Eddie anymore.

"Let me get you a drink."

"Gin and tonic with a twist."

"Haven't seen you for a while."

"Well no. Why would you?"

Why indeed? Marilita dead, and María many years divorced from García, the years of their paths crossing in the Force were long gone. No police functions where they might meet, no giggling daughters in common to chauffeur or chaperone. And anyway, María and David were younger than he and his wife. Colleen was their youngest child whilst Marilita was the first child of a young marriage. He knew she had married again, had a couple of boys by all accounts. He thought maybe he had heard she was divorced again. Funny Catholic that. Divorcing.

The Irish weren't doing divorcing. Not yet, at least. Well not in droves anyway. Although God knew he would not have minded ditching Colleen's mother, which was how he always referred to her. Naming her might give her personality, and in his eyes that was long gone. It went the day he found her fornicating with the delivery boy. When challenged she had flown at him screaming after him like a banshee as he stormed from the apartment. He could still remember the string of insults: his dick smelled like a bull, he was built like a bull and he had the rhythm of a bull. Christ, she talked like a bitch on heat. And since he was a

Catholic he stayed with her, and since he hated HEAT, he denied her everything but a marriage in name.

"Children OK?"

"Yeah. The boys are fine. They seem to cope," she twiddled with her drink. "First Marilita, then Matt. I don't know Eddie, it's been a tough few years."

Then he remembered. After García she'd married a cop, of course. Matt Fry from the south side. Nice guy. Regular WASP but pleasant enough. Got wiped out in some minor arrest that went wrong. Not divorced. Widowed, that was it.

"You come to see me?"

"Yeah."

"How come?"

"It's about David."

"What about him?"

"He told me you sent him to Spain to work on this Alhambra thing."

"Yeah."

"Why'd you do that?"

"Why do you care?"

"No-one ever got me and David," she said into her gin.

"What's to get. The guy's a faggot."

"You're lucky I don't throw this drink all over you Eddie O'Reilly," she said, glaring at him. "You're lucky I don't waste good gin on your miserable face."

He saw her toss her head at him and carefully put her drink on the bar.

In those two actions the years rolled back. He remembered how she used to toss her head when she was telling Marilita and Colleen they were to come straight home, that they were not to get in boys' cars, not to accept alcoholic drinks, and then she would carefully close the door of the car.

Then he remembered how she would toss her hair at the

Christmas dance when she and García were still married, and then carefully take García's arm. Christ, he had forgotten that he had noticed her even then, before he had any idea a man could be a faggot and be married, be a faggot and be a father.

O'Reilly then looked at her again and saw something else. The care that she had always used to accompany rushes of emotion was perhaps more raw than it used to be, mottled somewhat by what? By ageing? Or was the control just a habit, and now something beneath had given way. Perhaps too much death and loss had robbed María at last of balancing emotion with control. He put his drink equally as carefully on the bar and then said to her softly,

"You wanna have sex with me María?"

"San Miguel el Alto is here," Antonio was pointing to the *reformatorio* on the map. "It's on a par with the *deposito*, the pumping station over here," he stabbed at the hills to the north of the Alhambra. It's higher than anything else for miles, and it was evacuated this morning. I've just had word that it now has infrastructure to support computers, 'phones and satellite."

"OK. Let's go." García was suddenly typically American in his response.

"Why relocate?" Fisher was peering over David's shoulder.

"We need better visual on the site," Antonio replied. "Hotels are plenty, and many with good elevation, but nothing that takes us enough above the boundary with a good panoramic view. We may not see much, even with all the technology, but we have the sweep of the walls."

"You've got a bloody fortress on your hands, haven't you?" Fisher said.

"That's about the size of it," said Antonio. "An ancient fortress, but still a fortress."

"I've got a list here." Paula Fisher interrupted and pushed papers across the table. "Everything they could think of about everybody."

Jack picked it up and ran his eye over it and said,

"Couple of ex-military but in their seventies. Ah, here's one I know slightly, Reginald Coussins. Plays cricket in my club. Civil engineer, also retired. No cops. No medics. Choir director speaks a little Spanish. Oh Christ," Fisher groaned, his eye running further down the list. "An old school mate of mine, Daniel Goddard, one of our local York drunks. Christ, what bloody rotten luck to have him here."

"Carmen's Daniel?" asked Paula at his elbow.

"The very same." Then he looked at García and said, "You remember El Piano? Where we went after the AA meeting. Carmen Romero? This guy is her chap."

His tone was disapproving. Fisher couldn't help it, like reformed smokers who hate anyone puffing on a cigarette, he had no time for drunks. None at all.

"There's been some response to the news." Miguél Pedraza pushed forward, returning from his breakfast and wiping crumbs from his mouth.

"What then?"

"Some people claiming to be part of Islamic Jihad."

"Proof?"

"Nothing substantial."

"Anything else?"

There was a commotion from the 'phone centre. Everyone turned. Raúl was talking excitedly, his blond head steady but bent into the phone. He hung up and turned, saying,

"There are some fires burning."

"Where?"

"Near the *palacio de carlos v*."

"Can you be sure?"

88

"Aerial says it's confirmed."

"Any demands? Any contact? News?"

"Not so far."

"Anything else from Aerial?"

"Nets."

"Nets?"

"Seems there are nets," he rolled his eyes and shrugged his shoulders as if to say, *search me* or *go figure*.

"Where?" Antonio went to the table and demanded again, "Where?" Raúl approached. "For Christ sake Raúl, where?" Antonio repeated.

"Here," he pointed to the long strip running alongside *la torre del agua* on the southern side. "And here, all along the *medina* pathway, before *calle real*. The thing is," he said half annoyed to hear himself sounding apologetic, "this is something we haven't come across before. ETA have never used nets before. But with so much open space here, between the outer walls and *calle real*, well..." he shrugged his shoulders again.

"Nets to stop a drop? Nets to stop aerial descent? Am I right?" García asked the assembled group.

"Possibly," Raúl agreed reluctantly.

"Any other ideas?" Antonio Marín asked for proposals. David waited and idly watched Raúl trace the line on the map with lean brown hands, then heard Antonio's voice low in his ear,

"He's too young for you."

García started, the combination of the voice so low and near and unexpected, and the shock of being *seen*. Christ. How he hated being *seen* almost more than anything. Had he been looking at Raúl with lust or longing? Had he? He was pretty sure he was just observing a beautiful young man tracing lines on a map. Was it that working through Spanish he had let his guard down? That somehow without the filter of English he was more visible? He turned and looked at Antonio, but the older man was

89

looking at Raúl himself and nodding in agreement with him.

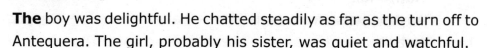

The boy was delightful. He chatted steadily as far as the turn off to Antequera. The girl, probably his sister, was quiet and watchful.

"This is as far as I go," said the trucker. "I'll leave you up there," he pointed to a gas station. "Lots of trucks stop there before the climb. You'll get a lift. No danger." They had both got out, she with a small suitcase. "And you be careful. Just take a truck. Don't mess with cars."

The truck pulled out leaving a spray of gravel.

"What did he mean *don't mess with cars*?" Lola asked.

"He meant stick with the trucks, they'll get us back faster."

"But they're slower."

"Yes but they mean business, they don't bugger about," Alberto said with finality.

Joaquin Montez took up his guitar, played for a few minutes, set it down and reached for a cigarette. He could hear Ana laughing across the shared courtyard between the caves. Laughing, for Chrissake. He picked up his guitar again, regretted it didn't have steel strings so he could stick his cigarette butt into the string end and carry on playing. Nylon just didn't do it. So instead he dragged on it, tossed his hair aside and tried to make sense of what had happened.

"Midwife?" he had said, "What do you mean midwife?"

"I mean she's my midwife."

"You've never had a baby."

"No, but I'm going to."

"One day I suppose."

"No, Joaquin. Not one day. In about 185 days."

He had gone quiet then. And so had she.

"A baby."

"Yep."

He had wanted to ask, *whose baby?* but pride stopped him. Fernando was his cousin. Ana was his cousin. The whole of Sacromonte was his cousin. Jesus, any baby was going to be his baby, one way or another.

"Finished watching?" he had asked, meaning the television.

"I'll never finish watching you."

He had put his hand up then as if to stop her, ward her off, a shaft of pain darting through his heart. And she had come toward him, taken his hand and lowered it to her belly and said,

"Your baby silly. You always worry too much about Fernando. I love Fernando. I love him like a brother. But he isn't interested. Believe me. He never has been."

And he had looked at her then and seen love for the first time.

It wasn't love. That wasn't possible. Not now. Not at their age. What had got into him? Other than his dick of course. *As good as it gets* would be how he would describe it to himself for days. At his desk he would find it hard not to touch himself remembering her. It was like being a kid again but without the guilt. Where had the guilt gone? Christ, he was a married Catholic, an Irish Catholic at that, rutting with a gorgeous round-assed Spic.

Was that what made it so good? That it was forbidden and that he hated Spics? But then he'd had plenty of women. Whores were easy picking for a man like him. Always had been. Sex was hard currency in his line of work. Lately, as Commissioner, with a public profile to maintain, and, he assumed, ageing, his desire had reduced. He had once heard it said that the trouble with having a prick is that a man is more or less shackled to an idiot for the greater part of his life. These past years he had rejoiced in a sense of freedom from sexual urge. But now it was upon him again and he was astounded at how it delighted him.

She had come to talk to him about García, and they never did have the conversation. He popped the question from nowhere and she had quite simply put her hand right on his crotch. No more direct answer than that. Two fornications later in the nearest cheap hotel their bodies had slipped apart, slipped into clothes, and slipped out the door. A very slippery business altogether. Should he call her? No contest.

"María?" he said into the 'phone.

"Sí."

Christ, one syllable and he was rock hard.

"It's Ed O'Reilly."

"I know who it is."

"I thought you might like to have lunch with me."

"I don't think so Eddie."

"I owe you lunch."

"You don't owe me anything."

"You wanted to ask about David. Maybe I owe you that conversation? Shall we have lunch?" He thought he heard her hesitate. "Just lunch mind," he said, as if to reassure her.

It only took an hour to locate and set up in the *reformatorio* which surprised everyone. Some sort of efficiency had kicked in. Antonio Marín, David García and Jack Fisher had travelled together in a spacious unmarked car toward the top of Sacromonte.

As they climbed the hill from the city centre toward the hermitage the road narrowed and twisted. García felt the car change gear, the pull of the incline, and momentarily gave himself up to the surroundings and to Lorca's own recollection of observing the ascent toward San Miguel. He turned to Antonio and said,

"Shame there are no mules and no sunflowers."

"Ah," said Antonio, beginning to recite the ending the Lorca poem García was referring to... but then stopped short. García knew in a heartbeat why and turned his face to the car window.

Fisher, unable to follow the Spanish, nonetheless sensed the atmosphere change from cordial to uncomfortable. He was glad when the car drew to a halt by a large white building high up on the hill opposite the Alhambra. They all got out and stood looking across at it.

"This is more like it," García said.

The red of the walls of the Alhambra deepened as the sun changed its position. He moved his eyes from the right to the left and back. The entire northern flank of the fortress was before him. He could see figures along the walls, some moving, others still. This was infinitely better than simply being on the end of a 'phone surrounded by tall buildings in a city centre. And infinitely better than the last part of the car journey.

Saint Michael, *san miguel*, patron saint of homosexuals, or, more subtly, those who cannot form heterosexual relationships, was presented by Lorca as the King of all party balloons and of all uneven numbers. Anyone who studied Lorca knew what all uneven numbers referred to, and there were plenty of ribald interpretations for *globos*. It was pretty clear to García that in quoting Lorca's poem Antonio Marín was engaged in some sort of top-dogging. David might have expertise in negotiation, and he might be a US observer, but nonetheless Antonio was making it clear that he was the senior officer in every regard. First the remark about Raúl and now this.

David realised that he needed to watch his step. Granada was not New York, and even in New York, where virtually anything was permissible, he was smart enough to be on his guard against the subtle – and not so subtle – reactions to being a gay cop.

93

Granada was a provincial city in the middle of a macho heartland. Just because they spoke Spanish in Granada and reflected a culture closer to his own, he should not be led into assuming acceptance here either. There was a job to be done, he told himself, and that was what he would focus on. He twisted the ring on his little finger and decided to wipe Antonio's opinions from his mind.

The move from the *comisaría* allowed a series of subtle changes to take place. Marín had been set up in an office, separate from the others. It was small and almost entirely a table. Paula had a desk with the other uniforms in a huge adjacent space, not unlike an institutional dining room. Jack organised a photo gallery on the longest wall, drew lines between them and added key words about each one of them. He might now be a licensing officer tied to a desk, but he still knew how to organise an incident room. The entire effect was one of a centre of international operations at last.

García walked over to Fisher's display and stared at the photos. Rashida Santiago, wearing some sort of colourful flowing dress, and staring into the camera. She looked young and somehow vulnerable. The angle of her head and her wide-eyed look at the camera gave her the air of someone half surprised. García reached out and touched the face, thinking of Marilita. His only child. She would not have been much younger than this woman had she lived. How surprised had Marilita been in those split seconds after the plane had hit? He dropped his hand.

Then there was a photo of Joaquin Rafael as last photographed after the atrocities in Barcelona, wild eyed and defiant. There was a photo of the elderly occupant of the house just up from the *hotel america,* and a faded image of the elderly couple who must have been Agustín and Rosario from the *finca*. Eleven poor quality digital images of the English, which had come over the Internet, were posted up side by side.

In Antonio's office, on the massive table in the table room, was the map of the Alhambra. Manuel Pedraza had detailed the points of damage in red. A few shards of sunflower seeds lay scattered over his markings that indicated where *la puerta de la justicia* had once been. The descent path of the pomegranate tree attached to its exquisite fretwork was marked. The location of the bonfires, as described by the aerial reconnaissance, was criss-crossed in red.

García looked from the map across to the monument and seeing the smoke, felt a sudden pang of recognition. No buildings could be more different than the ancient Alhambra and the modern twin towers. Few cities less similar than New York and Granada. Yet destruction; that was universal.

"You OK David?" Antonio was beside him. David glanced around at him.

"Yes. Yes. Certainly."

What a lie. Christ, what a goddamn lie. He was never going to be OK again. He had known Marilita was gone. He had known it within seconds of seeing the planes on his TV screen plunge into the towers. That was it. Gone.

They had all answered the call. It had seemed as if everyone he had ever known had been there. Officers he hadn't seen in years, officers he had thought were dead or retired. They were all there. If not in the action, then surrounding it, buffering it.

Then there were the firemen, many he had worked with a score of times or more. Men who had 'held the blanket' while he had tried, and sometimes failed, to talk someone off a ledge. Men who had watched him gentle the suicidal along a roof, draw them with words away from open windows.

When it came to negotiating with jumpers, the truth was that no-one was really bothered if the poor bastards lived or died. Mostly people cared about the clean up and trying to avoid it. It was a pain in the ass mopping up the blood, bone and brain matter of jumpers. The most love a junior negotiator ever got was from the street cleaners. Few jumpers had anyone who cared about them enough to say thank you, or they probably wouldn't have been in the position of jumping in the first place. And the jumpers themselves, those who were talked out of it, they pretty much hated you.

If he hadn't been the first on the scene at the raid on the City Central Bank, two years before 9/11, and saved the proverbial day, (at least that was how it had been reported), he would probably never have been elevated to the position of senior negotiator.

Some excellent training had followed, and then the glorious two years at the top of the tree. Richard was jealous as hell as usual, angry at anything that stole attention from him. But Marilita was proud. She had been the one person that made life worth living.

Standing near the smoke and dust at what would later be called ground zero, he had inhaled over and over, thinking that some part of her was in the air. If he just breathed deep enough, fast enough, for long enough, something of her would live in him. The tears had simply poured down his face.

It was much later that he realised that María had been looking as much for him as for their daughter. María had taken him with her and then in some alley, some dark place, he still had no idea where, surrounded by the sea of grief of other strangers, they fell upon each other and wept until they had nothing left.

"David?"

He turned and saw both Fisher and Marín looking at him.

"Hey," he said, shaking his head as if to clear water from his ears, "I'm going to get a coffee. Maybe close my eyes for fifteen. Jet lag is catching up with me. Call me if anything breaks."

"David hasn't been himself since María died. Then Richard. I think it has been too much." María pushed her lasaña around on the plate.

"Tell me if I've got this wrong," said O'Reilly leaning forward. "You were married to David. You had Marilita. You got divorced and he went homo."

"David was always gay." she said.

"Don't make me laugh. Gay men don't have kids."

"Eddie, they have them all the time," she smiled gently at him.

Of course O'Reilly knew that, he just felt the need to say something extreme. He wanted to somehow flush out her feelings. He probed further,

"And you still care about him?"

"Of course."

"I don't get that. I'll never get that."

"You care about your wife don't you?"

"What's that got to do with anything?"

"Well, what was it we were doing yesterday?"

"That's different."

"Not really. I imagine you feel loyalty to your wife, you have your children together, you've seen good and bad times, maybe ugly ones. I guess you like what we did in bed, or rather on the bed," she paused, not for effect or agreement but to let it sink in, and he felt himself harden again. "But you would do whatever you had to do to support your wife. Am I right?"

"Maybe."

"David is my second cousin. Our parents were cousins. Our family came from Cuba looking for something better. He and I more or less grew up together. We always knew we would get married. Everyone knew it. So when we were eighteen we did. We had Marilita within a year. But I knew before he did that it wasn't for him. He hated that I knew. He hated himself. We kept going for a few years, but it was pretty hopeless." She looked at O'Reilly, willing him to understand. "Then he met Richard. The cat was out of the bag. Our parents went crazy. I insisted we tell them that we simply weren't compatible. They were hard to convince. If David and I are anything, we are compatible. Same values, same family, same culture."

"So what happened?"

"His father found out and that was that. He was cut off, considered dead. No, more than that. It was as if he had never been born. We weren't even allowed to mention his name. I took Marilita to see him regularly but never told anyone. David was excruciatingly grateful. I think of all the hurts I suffered, him being grateful to me for allowing him to see his own child was the most painful."

"Coffee?"

"Look Eddie, I don't expect you to understand. I wish you would, but I don't expect you to."

"Is that why you had sex with me, so I would understand?"

"No, I had sex with you because you are not a stranger. You are attractive. I needed it." She paused and then added finally, "I know you."

"Thank you." O'Reilly felt unaccustomedly humble, and thought for the first time that María was more than just physically attractive.

"And I came to talk to you because David was a wonderful father and has always been my great friend, and I think he's in trouble."

"On the take?"

"No, nothing like that. I think he's in trouble on the inside. In his heart, in his spirit. I think he's in real trouble."

"We're in real trouble," Mary sat close to Reginald Coussins, pulling her blanket around them both. "I spoke to the woman with the headscarf turban. She's a midwife. She isn't with them. She got called in," Mary's voice trailed off. Then she said absently. "The sun's going down, we're all getting cold. I don't know why we can't use the hotels, the *parador*, the *hotel america*. I don't know Reggie. I can't work out why we're here. What they want. What's going on. I'm going to have to go figure something, go find someone."

"You be careful Mary. It'll be dark soon and who knows what will happen."

"We can't just sit here and wait," she bit out. "I don't know where I am going or when I'll be back. Just say I've gone for a wee if they notice."

At first Gerardo was convinced he was saddled with the English and the old Spaniards. If he let anyone go there was the danger they would talk about what was going on. They might have noticed the numbers of explosives. They might talk, not so much about how many men they were, but worse, the state of them all.

But talking it through with Jay it became clear that many hostages, especially foreign ones, might be a gift. And given their history, English ones were the very best. International press would have caught it by now, and since the British were to blame for their sickness, on balance it was good, if such events could be described as good.

And then there was her of course. Would Jay understand?

Rashida noticed at once that Mary had moved away. She saw her shuffle almost noiselessly along the marble floor of the *palacio de los leones*. Rashida had thought she might be the only one with the wit and strength to do anything. The other women were half-dead with whatever ailed them, Mary's companions were just plain old, but Mary herself seemed to have plenty of wit and strength. And a fair bit of stealth too. Where could she be going? Rashida retreated into the shadows, gathering a blanket around her shoulders and then quietly followed her.

She saw Mary keep to the walls of the palaces, slip up the steps beside the *palacio de carlos v* and grope her way along the circular wall, up toward *calle real*. Someone was advancing and Mary turned sharp left before the Arab bathhouse and ducked down. Rashida was caught standing.

"What are you doing here?" A man stopped her.

"Nita's time is near. I need to clear my mind. I don't want a repeat of this morning."

"Clear your mind inside."

"No." Rashida was defiant. "No. I know what I need to do to be a good midwife. Leave me alone. I have no weapon, no phone, I'm just walking to clear my mind. You need to stand aside and let me pass. I know my way back and I'm not leaving my patient. Your leader won't be pleased if I don't do a good job."

"We have no leader."

"I think we both know to whom I am referring," stated Rashida flatly. It was a risk, but a calculated one. There had to be someone who had asked for her services. Possibly it was the person in the shadows, to whom they had deferred briefly when she had stood her ground about her kit. Maybe it was the man who had told them to bury the baby. The man seemed convinced and glared at her. And then he let her pass.

She wanted to call out to Mary but was afraid that, if not this man, then some other might hear her. So she walked leisurely up, past the cannons and toward the *parador* where the fires were still smoking, most of their fuel spent. There, at the side, she saw Mary crouched, warming herself beside the embers. And suddenly Rashida remembered.

David García remembered. He lay back on his cot, closed his eyes. He was unable to stop himself. Raúl with his blond beauty had struck at the core of García and all day David had set it to one side, refused to think of him, disciplined himself to discard any impact that the sight of Raúl may have had on him. But now, tired from the day, from the newness of the environment, from the flight, he allowed himself to recall.

He could see Marilita as an infant so vulnerable, so tender, and María so happy with the baby in her arms. All their parents had been so proud. It had been a good life. Nothing was wrong with it. María was happy, she had a husband, a baby and status. OK, so he had felt a little restless, but he had put it down to pressure. He had felt restless for years. This was nothing new, nothing to worry about. It would pass. Maybe he needed to join a gym or a football team he had thought, engage in something physically exhausting.

He remembered as clearly as any glass the first time he had seen Richard. It was at the gym. Richard was tall, lithe, fair, almost English in appearance. Cultured and well-spoken, he was *in antiques* as he would always say, and he oozed privilege. They played tennis a few times, then basket-ball. Richard had asked David about his family, invited them to a barbecue at the Hamptons where he stayed in the summer, chatted amiably to María, and dangled the baby Marilita on his knee. Occasionally the men met for a drink after work. In those days David was still in blues and Richard jokingly told David he enjoyed being seen drinking with a man in uniform. At the time David thought little of the remark.

Richard had asked him about poetry and when David said he was ignorant of it, Richard had lent him a few volumes, some Keats, some Robert Frost, and then one day some Federico García Lorca.

"You will like it." he had told him. "I got it for you in the original. Spanish. And there's the English, here," he had leaned across him and pointed, "running along the side in the margins."

David read as if the words would disappear off the page if he didn't read them fast enough. He read both languages together and set up in his memory a duality of Lorca. He read Lorca's plays until he could recite great tracts from it all. He read about Lorca, about Dali, about Granada, about Fuente Vaqueros, and Richard vowed one day they would visit it. And when that day came, all those many years later on the European trip of a lifetime, Richard had a headache and a longing for a drink and refused to go. The sign whizzed past them as they made the descent to Málaga airport, just as a similar sign had tantalisingly pointed the way to Fuente Vaqueros this morning.

María had asked him about the reading, about the gym, about Richard. David had answered it all truthfully, with an innocence that was entirely genuine. At the same time he was aware that something about him, about him and María, was wrong. He loved her, but he couldn't find in the love anything he recognised from the poems. He couldn't find the intensity, only the affection, the familiarity. He couldn't map the Lorca onto the life.

And then, one day, as dusk fell, he was stood at the window of the gym looking out over the basketball court and turned against the aluminium frame that held the glass, twisting away from the view. The aluminium edge ran almost up the centre of his back and he felt some deep longing for something he could not name.

Richard came toward him in his suit, kit bag in hand, came right up to him, dropped his bag, put one hand on his face, fingers across his cheek and round his ear and then moved his head in for a kiss. With his other hand he reached down to David's penis and David felt himself leap in Richard's hand, like a wand, and he had self-knowledge for the first time.

After that, for a long time, the rest, except for Marilita, was easy.

It was easy. Nothing to it. They were in Granada. Dusk had barely fallen. They waved the last truck away. Safe and sound.

"What next?" asked Lola.

"We do this next," said Rashida to Mary. "Like this." And she plunged the blanket from her shoulders into the running water from the aqueduct and along the open channel at the side of *calle real*.

"I'd say that was where it was coming from. Yes, *calle real* Sir," said Manuel Pedraza straining at the binoculars.

"Get García," was all Antonio said, and passed the binoculars to Fisher.

"What is it?" García was at their side.

"Look," Antonio gave him another set of binoculars.

"Really?" said García, hoping against hope to make out the smoke in the failing light. "Smoke signals?" he looked first at Antonio and then Fisher.

"Looks that way," said Fisher.

"Well," said García, putting the binoculars to his eyes again. "Let's hope it isn't Comanche."

"Let's hope it's Morse," said Antonio

"Hang on," said Fisher, "I think it is Morse. Here." He put his binoculars down. "Sing it out and I'll take it down."

"Take it down stone by stone, is what I heard," Ana said over the meal. "I listened to the news. They're saying it's only a matter of time. They say they have hostages, and they are burning it up slowly and the rest they are going to blow sky high."

"But no-one knows why," said Fernando

"No. No-one does," his father agreed.

"Don't you think it's weird that no-one is doing anything? I mean, like the army or the government or something?"

"Pass the salt."

"They'll be afraid of damaging the building."

"And the hostages?"

"They won't give a toss."

Where did you learn this?" Mary asked as they crouched by the fire and Rashida instructed her to rise and sink in time with her own efforts, covering and exposing the fire with the wet blanket with a steady and choreographed rhythm.

"Mexico."

"You lived there?"

"Yes. For a few years. Smoke signals are not just the domain of the cowboy films you know. Peoples have used them to communicate over vast distances for years."

"Will they see them? Will they know what they mean?"

"Maybe they will see them. And if they have a boy scout among them, they will know. It's Morse. SOS to start, then the message, then SOS to finish."

"You know Morse too?"

"Yes," Rashida smiled ruefully. "Morse too. We were taught it as part of our survival training before we went into field medicine. In remote areas it's still used."

"Well it's exhausting," said Mary, rising and falling in time with Rashida. "Shouldn't we wait until dark? Won't THEY see us?"

"I hope they don't see the smoke." said Rashida. "As far as I can judge all our guards are looking at out, at the horizon beyond the walls. But you can bet every policeman and his dog is looking at the Alhambra from somewhere. They should see the smoke. If we wait 'til night falls nobody will see smoke at all.

"Bloody hell, this is hard on the knees," said Mary.

Rashida grinned at her across the fire,

"Isn't it just!"

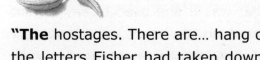

"The hostages. There are... hang on," Raúl hesitated deciphering the letters Fisher had taken down, spelling out Spanish words, none of which meant anything to the Englishman, "There are maybe fifty."

"Fifty!" reported Antonio in English for Jack's benefit.

"Hang on, hang fire," Raúl raised his hand, looking carefully over Fisher's shoulder at his scribbles.

"Fifty what?" asked Pedraza

"Men I suppose," said Raúl

"That's it?" asked García

"Takes a lot of Morse to say that," said Fisher looking at his sheet of dots and dashes.

"Antonio?" David deferred.

"Aerial and amplification," he answered swiftly. "Can it be done?" he said to Raúl.

"Well we can hover high enough not get shot at," the young man replied.

"Such weaponry?" García asked sharply. "Do they have it?"

"Well I'm not about to risk it to find out," Raúl replied tartly. "Someone needs to draft the message," then he added, "and our terms. Since they are not telling us what they want, it's time we told them."

"Manuel," said Antonio, "can you get to it?"

"And our signaller?" asked David García, "Who do we reckon?"

"Rashida Santiago," Antonio said without hesitation. "Has

to be. Like her file says, natives in South America and all that. Smoke signals. Stands to reason. If she didn't get caught, then I reckon we can expect more when the light's up."

Once again David thought of Marilita – she had always had pluck and determination. How else could she have advanced so far in the force, so young? What was it she used to say to him when he cautioned her about working too hard? *You should talk Papá – look how hard you work. Anyway,* she would toss her thick dark hair just like her mother and add, *you know what they say?* And he would laugh, knowing exactly what was coming next. *You can sleep when you're dead*.

"What about signalling back?" asked someone from the depths of the incident room.

"It's not that easy," Antonio shook his head. "Even if we could get it right. Fire and smoke. The right cloth. The right size and moisture. It's a long shot," he paused, then added, "and we would be seen. Maybe no-one in the Alhambra has noticed them. But if we start doing the same from up here? Everyone there will see." then he turned and asked, "Anything else? Are you sure there are no demands?"

"None," Raúl was quick to answer.

Maybe too quick, thought David.

"Nothing," said Pedraza. "Silence."

Silence greeted Rashida and Mary as they walked back. Brazen, Mary announced she'd been for a wee, and Rashida thought she even gave a small flounce. The quiet was unnerving and then Rashida knew why. Nature's profound silence in anticipation was the reason. For Nita's time was upon her. Rashida moved to her side.

Silence, for David García, was the thing that didn't add up: no demands. One thing he knew for sure was that whether cool and calculating, or hot and fiery, the egocentricity of hostage takers was universal. Their motivations might differ, as might their methods, but they were always, always, metaphorically jumping up and down, pushing themselves into the middle of any picture. This terrorist activity was different.

At her side Alberto said definitely,

"We're going to the *comisaría*."

"What for?"

"To tell them what we know."

"We don't know anything."

"We do. We know about the Alhambra," said Alberto defensively. "And we know what happens when the people in charge make mistakes."

Lola looked at him wide eyed. Yes, she thought, they did know. Her parents, who had been in charge, had made loads of mistakes. And if anyone thought she was too young to remember, they were wrong. Besides, Agustín was always telling them stories of how people in charge could come at any time and take people away who had done nothing wrong; how people in charge could come and take the Alhambra away if they wanted to, just like they had taken the Flower of Granada into the hot August sun. Maybe they could even take Alberto away she thought.

"But why would they talk to us? Even if we went, why would they see us?"

"Because they need us," he said flatly.

"David is the best we have."

"You hate David."

O'Reilly was surprised by María's reply. If it was that obvious it saved him a lie.

"I do."

"So are you telling me you sent him for his own good?"

"In a way." She looked at him with her penetrating gaze. So he added, "David made a mistake after 9/11. Everyone was sorry about Marilita, sorry for him and people were prepared to make allowances. But he went too far."

"And now you've sent him to Granada for God's sake, to do a job he can't possibly do well. Jesus Eddie, it's the last thing he should be doing."

"Relax María, relax," O'Reilly said in almost honeyed tones. "He likes Spain. Everyone knows that. He will have been happy to go. If nothing else it will give him an excuse to keep on with his reading. You know what he's like whenever he's on a job, whenever the action cools. After all," said O'Reilly lightly, "even wannabe assassins have to sleep sometime. Then David's always got his nose in a book."

"I know," said María. "That's the problem. The *wannabe assassins*, as you call them, might rest, but not David. I used to think the reason he was such a successful negotiator was because he barely slept. While they are sleeping he is reading. The reading is the problem. More and more he is living through books, more and more that's where his reality lies."

"The job is stressful María, all the guys have their foibles."

"I know it's stressful," she said putting her hand on his. "I know that. And I know you know that, but he immerses himself. What if he never comes out the other side?"

"You seem to know a lot about him and his current life?" O'Reilly questioned, seeing in his mind's eye García's good looks, his lack of affectation, and feeling an unexpected tingling of the green-eyed monster.

"He came a lot after Marilita," she raised a shoulder in a

gesture of despair and defeat. O'Reilly watched and waited until she continued. "He was great when Matt was killed, and the boys love him. Then Richard died, and well..." she trailed off and then said, "It's as if every time I see him he's letting go more."

"Letting go?"

"Yes, of the here and now. And these books he reads?" she raised her eyes to his. "They're always the same. Lorca Lorca Lorca."

"Who he?" O'Reilly mocked in a New York slang, shrugging and raising open palms toward her.

"Federico García Lorca. Spain's greatest contemporary poet. Came from Granada. Well, just outside," she said and then fixed him with her eyes, "and here's the rub. Just like David, Lorca was gay, like David, he spoke out against the perceived wisdom of the day, he was David's age, they even have the same name."

"Jesus María. So how many Spics in New York are NOT called García? Please!"

"Hear me out Eddie. Lorca was assassinated."

"And so?"

"After Marilita's funeral David came back with me and the boys. That evening, we sat for a long time in silence after the boys went to bed and then he started quoting Lorca at me. Lorca had been to New York and wrote a whole set of poems about his time here. David had fixed on one and sat with his elbows on his knees, looking down at the floor and reciting.

"The thing is Eddie, I am afraid. I am worried David is going to do something foolish."

"He's a Catholic María. We don't generally kill ourselves if that is what you are worried about."

"But what if he throws his life away?"

"María. Listen to me. David has to work. What would you have him do? Retire? Can you imagine David García retired? Christ you say he lost Marilita and," he not could bring himself to say

Richard's name, "and, what's his face, and now you want him to lose his job?"

María smiled at him.

"I thought you hated him."

O'Reilly paused and then he said,

"Let's skip coffee. Come have sex with me."

"Come have sex with me," whispered Daniel Goddard to Mary Stansfield.

"Not on your life mate."

"Come on Mary. We might be dead tomorrow. Besides, that Nita girl isn't interested in me and I can't sleep."

"Nita is about to give birth Daniel, she is hardly going to be interested in much else. And you can't sleep because it's too early, that's why."

"Aw come on. What if we all die?"

"Well then you are going to die a virgin Daniel, and an insomniac."

"You're such a bitch," he said good-naturedly.

"I know I know," she grinned. "Anyway, Reggie's on a promise."

"Oh, P L E A S E," drawled Daniel.

"Don't be so age-ist Daniel. Reggie's got plenty of poke I reckon."

"Poke being the right word."

"Don't be jealous now," she teased.

"To tell the truth. I'm just plain scared."

"Well don't be. That woman Rashida and I, well, we've sent a message."

"You have your mobile?"

"No. They took it."

"So what gives?"

"We figured something out."

"*We figured something out*," he mimicked.

"Piss off Daniel. Why not dream of a gin and tonic?"

Mary turned from him and leaned her head against the wall. Then she saw him standing about fifty yards away, looking directly at her. She knew it was him from the way his clothes hung on him. It was as if his shoulders were a coat hanger, and everything fell from their breadth in loose folds. She refused to lower her eyes and at last he turned and walked away.

"**I'll** find out more and call you tomorrow," he heard himself say, and knew he meant it.

"Thanks Eddie," she said and she slipped through the door. He turned into the pillow and smiled a deep, wide, sensuous smile. There was nothing to beat it; sex in the afternoon.

"**Sex** in the afternoon is one thing, a baby is another altogether."

"Christ Joaquin, you're scaring me."

"What? You think this is a joke. This is a baby. We can't carry on as if this isn't happening. Fernando will know."

"He'll know I am having a baby. Of course he will know it isn't his. But that doesn't mean he will know it's yours."

"Christ."

"Listen to me. You guys have to play together. And Dad and *Tio* and *Tia* and all the *primos*," she referred to her uncle, aunt and cousins. "Soon it will be summer. Loads of tourists. You just have to get on with it. To be honest Fernando is going to be grateful. It gets him off the hook."

Joaquin had blanched at that.

"What's this? I'm the cousin who impregnates you in order to get Fernando off the hook? Jesus, Ana, listen to yourself!"

"Look," she replied. "You are the most beautiful thing I have ever seen. I have loved you all my life and I get weak at the sight of you. But I'm not married to you. I'm married to him. And that's the reality."

"The reality is," Antonio said fixing David with a look across the table, "we have no idea who they are. No intelligence. No demands. In the absence of anything else, we are stumped."

evening

Antonio Marín sat back in the office's only chair and smoked. It gave him a temporary relief from the pressure and a moment to review. Raúl, for all his military expertise, seemed unexpectedly devoid of ideas. García's official capacity was only as an observer. He might be among the best negotiators in his field but as yet there was still was no-one to negotiate with.

He could see Fisher and García through the large glass partition separating his office from the incident room. They were talking in front of the photos. Fisher was pointing at some of the English, and García seemed to be nodding in agreement. Antonio thought how García seemed almost unnaturally unstoppable. Except for the brief rest he had taken earlier, he was as fresh as he had been from the flight. Fisher seemed to be a match for him, allthough with the rest of the men Fisher was handicapped by language.

Antonio stubbed out his cigarette hoping he was equal to managing such a varied team. He knew he had been chosen to head up the operation because of his army background. It had to be a police-led operation, yet the army also had to be involved. Policing in Spain was riven with differences, too many organisations all vying for, and protecting, their own patches. If soldiers like Raúl were going to follow orders, it was only going to happen if they came from the mouth of someone with an exemplary military career. In Antonio, his superiors had assured him, they had both.

Added to that there was little that Antonio did not know of terrorism in Spain. And there was plenty to know. Of all European countries, Spain was the best-qualified in unbroken terrorist activity. ETA had been around at the time of the German Red Army Faction, had continued on after the demise of Andrea Baader and Ulrika Meinhoff, and was still going strong. An unenviable qualification, he knew.

He had used a long career to heighten and broaden his

understanding of what made such people tick. He was a people watcher, an *amateur psychologist*, as his daughters called him. It was the key to his ability to tread between the lines dividing the military from the police, and he valued it highly. Of course he had also been chosen because he knew the Alhambra. He stood up, discarding his cigarette butt, and cast his eye again over the maps.

He loved the monument. In his childhood he had played there, and after his career took him to Madrid he had made his wife return with him probably more than a hundred times over the years. They had eaten sandwiches in the shade of the cypress trees, shared cigarettes in the full sun of spring and read Lorca to the sounds of rushing autumn water. And although Lorca didn't refer that much to the Alhambra, what Granadino could not be sensitised by it, growing up in the light and shadow of such a marvel? To lead this task force would have been near impossible for someone who had no idea what the monument was like.

For that reason, in the quiet of the afternoon, Antonio had taken a long time to go through the geography of the Alhambra with García and Fisher. He had set out for them the fact that it was a complex; not one single monument or museum, but an entire community. He had explained that it consisted of a fortress, a set of palaces, gardens and a now ruined village.

He had pointed out that *la torre de la vela* in the *alcazaba* to the front, overlooking the entire city of Granada, was the dominant part of the fortress. He had taken pains to describe how the walls surrounded the palaces and were linked all along by towers and bastions. He told them that the inside of the walls could easily be walked along and varied in height as much as a hundred meters.

He talked about the *medina*, where the netting was now strung across the trees connecting the outer walls to *calle real*. He referred to the *medina,* once an extensive village accommodating the camp followers of the royal houses and where now little remained other than an exposed archaeological dig.

He had trouble not going overboard about the *generalife*, the fountains, the oleander, the oranges, the scent of rosemary, the coral of the pomegranate flowers, the delicacy of the jacaranda, the overwhelming peace.

When it came to the palaces themselves he was careful not to overstate their exquisite beauty. He tried to ensure he kept Fisher and Garcia's interest by not waxing too poetical about the timeless nature of the ceramics, the smooth tiles, cool to the touch, the extraordinary vaulted ceilings, the majesty and antiquity of this great Islamic world treasure. And he was aware of how carefully García was listening and was appreciative of his unwavering attention. What had García said to him?

"You love it don't you?"

"Like a woman," he had answered instantly, and he thought he saw García wince.

Now, Antonio could see them looking at the cross-hatching Manuel had added to the map to indicate the netting. It extended right across the *medina*, from the boundary walls, over the tallest of the cypress trees to the sidewall of the *parador* and all the buildings on the descent along *calle real*. It was a hell of a lot of netting. Basic technology. Keeping out any aerial assault. Very clever. How had they got them into the complex in the first place, never mind set them up so wide and so high? The fires must have been set in the larger space at the bottom of *calle real*, at the side of the *palacio de carlos v*, or the nets would have burned. Such a wide space was easily overseen, easily secured, if not from the *palacio de carlos v* itself, then easily from the perimeter of the *alcazaba* to the front.

Added to that, when Aerial had done their last surveillance sweep, they had reported the existence of pillars in the open spaces between the front of the *palacio de carlos v* and the *alcazaba*. More basic technology. To him these pillars smacked of lessons learned

117

from World War II. Antonio was old enough to have heard first-hand from old soldiers the detail of such history. To get in close enough to drop men, but not so close as to risk being shot at, a descent would have to be by parachute. The best defence against parachutists is to set up stakes to catch them on and then shoot them like dogs as they dangle from their tangled chutes. Antonio had a terrible foreboding that these pillars had been pillaged from the *palacio de colmares* or the *palacio de los leones* by chopping the stone supports out from beneath the fretted plasterwork and then standing them upright like bloody spikes.

"Antonio?" a uniformed officer spoke from the general office holding a cordless telephone..

"Sí."

"It's for you."

García held the door open. Antonio took the receiver hoping it was the voice that had demanded a midwife two days ago. He was disappointed. He looked at García and said,

"My boy," and then bent his head to the voice on the line.

Antonio listened while his son talked. He knew he was after a scoop. Working for the regional press in Andalucía the young man often tried to prise prime Madrid police news stories from his father. Antonio listed patiently, knowing he was not going to tell him anything, yet allowing the younger man the run of him. And he also listened to García and Fisher at the same time.

"This guy Goddard," he heard Fisher telling García, pointing at a photo of a young fair man. "He's a drunk. One of our better drunks, but drunk nonetheless. More a liability than an asset. As I was telling you, during the crisis we had three years ago at the Festival of Angels when the entire event was hijacked by drugs and child snatching, he was almost another liability. And now, here, he's the only young man among them. I can't imagine how he is getting on without a drink."

"He'll find a way," said García grimly. "The two hotels have bars. Tell me," he said looking at Fisher. "How did you do it?"

"Give it up you mean?"

"Yeah, that. And keep giving it up."

"Dare I say, *one day at a time*?"

"Like I never heard that before," García said with a grim smile.

"So how is Richard?" Antonio heard Fisher question García.

"He died."

"I'm sorry."

"Well you know what they say?" said García. Fisher did know, but he hardly felt it was his place to speak it out loud. The last time he had said it had been to Carmen, after the Festival of Angels, about Daniel Goddard in fact. García then said it for him,

"You live sober or you die drunk."

"Don't I know it." Fisher grinned ruefully. "But I'm sorry."

García wanted to say, *me too*, but it would have been a lie, or, rather, not the whole truth. He was sorry, but most of all he was angry and he had been angry with Richard for a long time. The full realisation had only hit when he had returned early from work one day and found Richard strung up on the beam of their loft apartment, surrounded by beautiful antiques, twitching and still alive. The chair had been kicked out from under him and David had cried out, rushed forward, grabbed his legs, knocked almost sideways by the stench of defecation mingled with the alcohol fumes, and lifted Richard toward the ceiling. Then, still holding Richard, he had looked for anything to support him and dragged the chair toward them, trying and failing two or three times to set it up with his foot and leg. All the while he bore the weight of Richard with his arms clasped around his legs, until at last the chair was upright. But by then Richard was dead.

He rang the police, left the body hanging and touched nothing more. He sat and waited. The liquid from Richard's bowel that had seeped through the dead man's trousers was smashed onto David's chest. Two homicide detectives he knew came. Some blues. The coroner.

There was a suicide note. It was an open and shut case. He could see the detectives felt sorry for him. He could scarcely bear their sympathy, clouded as it was by a residual disgust, if not for the stench on his shirt then for the life he led. They asked him if they should call anyone. Marilita was six months dead.

"My wife. My ex-wife. María Fry. Here's the number." He had reached into his wallet and an hour later she had arrived. And by the time she came, a deep unabated smouldering anger had set in.

"David?" Fisher's voice cut across his thoughts.

"Yes. Sorry. What were we saying?"

"Richard."

"Yes," said David bleakly. "He died as they all do. He died drunk."

Antonio replaced the receiver, having left his son empty-handed and walked toward Fisher and García. He looked closely at García and saw then, through the energy of the man and his fitness, a deeper fatigue, and said,

"You guys get some rest."

"And you?" García asked him.

"Raúl will relieve me shortly."

"I'll lie down then – alone," Daniel Goddard said exaggeratedly, and looked balefully at Mary, who decided the best policy was to ignore him. She remained seated and looked long and hard across the embers into the gathering darkness, certain he was out there, watching them. She stood up quietly and set off toward the deepest shadows.

García was quite clear that he should ignore Raúl, who had been at pains to point out his bunk in the living quarters to the back of the building. García had long had a rule: *don't shit where you eat*. He tried to sleep but couldn't. The way Raúl had looked at him had been an invitation. But it was one that could wait. If there was anything to pursue then it wasn't going to happen during this operation. Nor after it, very likely.

Besides, García wasn't a man for the one-night stand. *Too Catholic* he used to think wryly. And whenever he thought about embarking on a new relationship, about the sharing of history, learning all over again how someone likes their coffee, their shirts folding, their appetites satisfying, it almost made him more weary than excited. He heard the gentle snoring of other men. Raúl's blond hair reflected the moon through the window. García rolled away to his other side.

His internal clock was a mess and his thoughts of Marilita, María, of Richard, of his whole life, kept entering and re-entering his consciousness. Together with any thoughts about Raúl he felt a stab of doubt, as if he might be unable to concentrate on the job in hand. He had a sudden fear that he might be losing it, losing the last thing he felt able to do. What had Antonio said? That he didn't think in straight lines? Right now he felt he was only thinking in broken lines. A full moon. It would illuminate the Alhambra. He threw off the covers, noted Raúl was no longer in his cot, pulled on his trousers, tucked in his shirt, tossed his sweater across his shoulders and headed for the office.

It seemed deserted. So much for Raúl relieving Antonio. So much for professionalism. David García was grateful none of it was his responsibility. He bent over the maps on the table and followed the outline of the Alhambra, imagining the walk along the boundary. He recalled how, just before Antonio had taken the earlier call from his son, Fisher had commented to them both on how similar the Alhambra was to York, the walls surrounding each being about the same distance in length.

"We too value our monuments more than people," Fisher had said to both Antonio and David a few hours earlier. "If I were being cynical I would say that the revenue York generates from visitors to our ancient sites would be considered more valuable than a few lives."

Antonio had said nothing but marked in his own mind that Fisher clearly had no idea of David García's family history. Equally clearly, David García, Antonio noted, was not about to enlighten him.

"Things being more important than people?" David had interjected casually.

"It doesn't surprise me in the least that you have been instructed to save the building above the hostages. Although," Fisher added, "I would be very cautious about that view being leaked to the press. We do so love to maintain a double standard," he finished with a wan smile.

David had caught the irony, and it reminded him of what drew him to Fisher. Now, remembering the exchange, García found himself glad the Englishman was a part of it all. Someone else who didn't quite think in straight lines. García pulled his sweater back up tight over his shoulders.

Deep in a corner of the incident room, Raúl was talking on his mobile. His voice was low and he barely moved in the dark. Raúl was aware of García in the next room and twisted away from the sight of him through the glass. The movement of his blond head caught the corner of García's peripheral vision. García realised that Raúl was indeed on watch after all. The younger man was concentrating on his conversation and using more of a brick than a cell phone. García was surprised; Raúl struck him as the sort of man who would have only the latest and the best of everything.

He was probably talking to his lover, thought García with a small sting of emotion that he could not quite place. Jealousy? Loneliness? Simple sexual hunger? He discarded the possibilities as fast as they entered his mind. It was a mental discipline he was long used to: *keep focused on the job in hand*.

So, instead he concentrated on being pleased to find that someone was in fact awake. Perhaps the caller was the one they longed to hear from. Almost as a reflex David looked out at the Alhambra. Nothing. He left Antonio's office, passing Raúl with a brief nod and went out into the night.

Jack Fisher was restless, which he considered a health hazard. He always referred to himself privately as an *artificial sober* as opposed to the *natural drunk* he knew himself to be. He had long ago determined that restlessness went with the condition of being an *artificial sober*. In the years he had allowed himself to be a *natural drunk* he had never been restless. It was the only part of being a drunk that he missed. And when he missed it badly enough, he was restless as hell.

In the early part of recovery he had trodden the straight and narrow with painstaking care, avoiding every drinking venue, every drinking companion and every accompanying pastime. Football, pubs, good friends and cigarettes had all been assigned to the list of forbidden activities. In recent years, however, he had allowed himself an occasional cigarette. His twin sister Ange had never given it up, despite many attempts, and since he had never given her up, he was from time to time in close proximity to the glorious temptations of tobacco. He considered it a small vice, and an occasional compensation for restlessness.

Something about this situation at the Alhambra smacked of the Festival of Angels. He remembered how he and Carmen Romero, grey with cold and exhaustion, had sunk to the pavement on that York winter night. Beside her had been her boy Chico, with his wide, knowing, street-wise face, and their friend Johnny Wing. Johnny had rolled Fisher a cigarette and Fisher had taken it and inhaled with gratitude and relief.

And here again he was in the eye of a storm. A false peace infused their operations centre. A terrible unknown loomed over it. These twin sensations in some ways were worse than any eventual outcome. Once the facts were before them, they could make decisions. Until then, the limbo was almost excrutiating.

"Not quite what you had in mind?" Antonio smiled at Fisher some ten minutes later, passing the cigarette the Englishman had asked for.

"You could say that," Fisher replied, taking the light offered and inhaling deeply. "I sometimes wonder if marriage and policing go together at all." And then as if to explain further he added, "This wasn't just any old holiday. It was to have been our first holiday since our twin sons were born."

"Well, I am sorry about your holiday, but I am glad you are here." Then he said, "Do you want the packet? I have more," and added regretfully, "many more."

Fisher laughed.

"Like that, hey?"

"Yep," Antonio grinned ruefully. "Addicted. But tell me," he questioned, "how do you know García?"

"I don't really," and Fisher related the tale in brief.

"Yet he kept your card?" remarked Antonio.

"Yes. But then there is nothing unusual in that I suppose," Fisher inhaled his tobacco again. "When I turn my wallet out, about once every ten years," he laughed self-deprecatingly, "sometimes I am surprised at the junk I have kept. To be honest, it's good to see him. Unusual."

"He is unusual."

Fisher had meant the circumstances were unusual not that he found García in himself unusual. Although now that Antonio Marín had mentioned it, he had to agree, David García was not your average policeman, or your average American for that matter.

"I suppose," he thought out loud, remembering his friend Carmen Romero, also Hispanic and also living in what she herself referred to as a WASP culture, "García originally being Cuban has made a difference."

"It has," García himself said joining them and waving away the smoke. "Good God. It's a wonder you can breathe!"

"My fault," laughed Fisher. "I had a tobacco moment. I'm a non-smoker you see." He held up his fingers to make inverted commas around *non-smoker*. "I think I disturbed Antonio's catnap, although he assures me he was intending to wake himself anyway."

"The waiting getting to you?" García asked Fisher.

"A bit. You?"

"I'm used to it. Negotiating is 99% waiting," David García shrugged and then said. "Although this unnerves even me," García swept his arm toward the monument on their horizon.

"I'm probably out of practice," said Fisher, half apologetic. "Desk jockey now."

"Ah," said Antonio, "the joys of paper shuffling," and stubbed out his cigarette. "It may look like paper shuffling but things are not always what they seem."

Things are not always what they seem, was the part of the conversation with Antonio and Fisher that stayed with García as he had excused himself from their tobacco fug.

In the cleaner air of the office he looked at the map's perimeter and followed Manuel's markings. The Alhambra was the key to the whole incident. The terrorists, if indeed that was who they were, weren't interested in hostages, in human hostages, or they would have started trading by now.

He realised with a jolt that perhaps it was the Alhambra they had hostage. They were smart enough to know that the Alhambra was the prize and that the authorities would choose it over any number of hostages. García could have slapped himself for being so dense. Antonio had told them, for Chrissake, hours before. He had told them the directive had come from the highest level. It was the Alhambra that was to be saved. Not the people. Fisher had been first, saying *property is more valuable than people* and now Antonio's remark, *things are not always as they seem*.

García looked again at the map. It was the Alhambra they needed to know about. *Not the people*, he repeated to himself. It was the Alhambra that was in the middle of the picture, not the English, not the midwife, not the elderly residents, arguably not even their captors. Fisher putting all the photos of people up was a waste of time. None of them mattered. Then he caught himself in the mistake of choosing one thing over another. Whereas it was the interplay of people and place that they needed to fully explore and understand. The WHO and the WHERE in a balanced harmony would describe the options available to them in trying to end the crisis.

He heard a noise and was vaguely aware of Raúl leaving the next room. He allowed an undisciplined thought that briefly framed a feeling that was a combination of disappointment and relief. He pulled himself back to the job. What he needed to convince Antonio to do, was to think of the monument itself as a person, as a creature in its own right. They needed to consider what shaped it, how it lived and breathed, what affected it, what and where its strengths and weaknesses were. They needed to think beyond just bricks and mortar toward something approaching animation. They needed to determine the site's own rhythm. He felt a type of inspiration move in him, the first time for a long, long time.

Antonio watched García through the glass. He watched him focus on the table, moving his hands in great sweeps across the maps. He saw García discard the sweater from his shoulders and stretch toward the furthest point across the table and appear to mark the map. Then he watched him stand and stare for a long time across the table, through the window, toward the Alhambra across the ravine.

Across the ravine from the Alhambra, Ana and Joaquin's cousin Fernando was picking his teeth.

"They've moved the police into the *reformatorio*," he said. "José told me," he said, referring to yet another cousin. "You can see all the lights blazing. Look."

"It's the right place for them," his father replied and spat on the floor. "Pigs. But they should leave the church out of it," he said referring to the church at the side. "You know what they are like. They'll ruin it. Next year when we go for the party the place will have been trashed. It won't be fit for anything once they've moved in and left. It'll ruin the best *fiesta* in Granada."

"The wildest you mean," corrected Joaquin.

El día de San Miguel, celebrating the saint day at the end of September, was one of the best parties going. At the highest point above the city, the lights could be seen and the music heard for miles around. The acoustics were phenomenal. He and Ana had certainly had some wild times last September.

"Well, whatever," his uncle replied, ever sanguine. "Time we tried putting those numbers together again." He reached for his guitar. "We have to get this sorted. I know I know," he raised his hand in mock resistance, "the Alhambra is closed and we won't be performing there tonight, but we will be one day so let's get practising. They always want Flamenco but I agree with you both, you're young, you know what people like now. Let's give them something varied on the old themes. Something unexpected."

"Something unexpected, Sir."

"What?" Antonio had been interrupted from watching García by his mobile ringing in his pocket. Only his own children and the *comisaría* had his mobile number.

"Gomez here." Antonio did not recognise the voice or the name, but recognised the policeman tone. 'We have some children here."

"What children?"

"They say they're from the *reformatorio*."

"What do they want?"

"They say they have some information for you. Shall I put them on?"

Antonio looked at his watch. Almost midnight. Children from the *reformatorio*, in the *comisaría*? Surely they had all been evacuated... What the hell, there was nothing else going on, he may as well ask them what they knew.

"Put them on."

"My name is Alberto," Antonio heard a boy of maybe ten. "I am with Lola. We are twins. We are from the *reformatorio*. We know some stuff. We need to talk to you."

"We need to talk to you," Mary had finally found him. He had turned with that now familiar piercing look. She stopped herself from reaching out to touch him.

"What's your name?" she asked almost involuntarily. When he said nothing she ran on, "I was afraid when I heard the helicopter that there was going to be an assault by the army."

"Not yet," he said staring at her. "Not yet."

"You don't guard us very well."

Surely he must know that at first, when she had tried to move with the choristers to a more sheltered position, they had been stopped. He must also know that soon afterwards their captors had disappeared, leaving them on their own, able to take shelter wherever they chose. The guarding of them seemed to blow hot and cold. Their gaolers were amateurs, or there was something still more sinister going on and the guarding of them no longer mattered. Perhaps because they themselves no longer mattered.

"Are you complaining?" he asked, confronting her.

"No. It's just that the men are old. They need to be somewhere warm. Why can't we use the hotels?"

"I can't watch you in the hotels."

"You don't watch us anyway!" she exclaimed.

"What do you know what we do?" he could hardly tell her that all of his calls to the authorities were being ignored. That his requests had yet to be processed, that time was the enemy and was wearing him down – wearing all of them down. He had relayed his anxieties to Jay but Jay was, as usual, calm, sanguine, even phlegmatic, very different from his own position. He could not even say that he was frustrated any more. At this moment he was too exhausted to be doing anything other than standing up. If she but knew, it was only the sight of her, causing the blood to course through him, that had him standing at all.

"They're old," she repeated. "They're hardly going to go anywhere. They need to rest properly."

"I'll consider it."

Mary had decided before approaching anyone that she would keep it simple. Short sentences. Single issue demands. Nothing emotive, nothing complicated. She looked at him. She tried to fathom who he was, what he might do. She wondered if there was a way to touch his feelings, get him to relate to them.

"I'm sorry about the baby," she said.

He was silent. Then he asked.

"What do you know about the baby?"

"Rashida told me."

"There will be other babies," he said.

She reached for him and touched his arm and he started as if shot.

He started as if shot when Antonio spoke.

"Sorry," Antonio said, putting his hand on García's shoulder. "I didn't mean to make you jump."

García gave him an unfathomable look and then said,

"I've been thinking."

"Thank God someone has," Antonio said. "This lack of demands, this total silence is unnerving everyone."

"As I said. I'm used to it. It's normal," said García.

"Don't you get bored?" asked Antonio.

"I read," García replied succinctly.

"But not here," Antonio stated the obvious.

"No," García agreed, "not here. Waiting is no good. We need a new tactic," García realised that this flew in the face of all he knew about managing delicate situations, about not forcing the moment. Yet he knew instinctively it was right. He went on, "instead of react; act."

"Yet you don't want to send in the army?"

"I don't. Hear me out."

"I'm all ears."

"It's this," and García began his list of characteristic short sentences. "What is the Alhambra? It is a hostage. Stop thinking about people. Focus on the monument. List everything as if it were human. I want us to come up with questions. WHY and WHAT and WHO? But with the Alhambra in the middle."

"Such as?"

"Why has this monument lasted so long? Who knows it inside out? What makes it different? Indeed is it different? Is it hard to secure? Why this monument? Why not some other monument?"

"What changes within it season by season?" added Antonio.

"Yes," García looked at Antonio. "Questions about its special nature. Above all," he hesitated, wondering how what he had to say would be received, and then repeated for emphasis, "above all," there was another pause. "Avoid the army."

Antonio gave no reaction to the last sentence but asked, "And when you have your list of questions?"

"We need answers," replied David.

"From whom?"

"We will know when we have the questions."

"Why are we dying?" said Nita.

Rashida wiped her brow. She had never known a woman talk so much during a labour and a delivery. God knows Nita wasn't finding it easy. It was a typical first delivery. Everything was really tight and compact, the muscles all working hard and bearing down on the infant that was showing no signs of moving. Rashida could see its head on the runway, Nita was fully dilated, but everything seemed to have gone into arrest.

Rashida hated evening deliveries. Women were always more tired. So was she for that matter. Nita had chattered now for over three hours. Rashida had managed to get Mary to plead successfully to have Nita moved into the *hotel america*, but the bedrooms were all up a twisting staircase. In the end she felt that a rough passage to the first floor wasn't worth it and so she made them bring a mattress down.

The floor was cold, the tiles antique, chipped and ragged. There was little light. With the grid out and electricity unavailable she struggled to see, and had to let her hands do the work. She soaped them thoroughly to the elbows and tried to slide them in. Human forceps. She knew the technique worked. She'd seen it many times in Mexico, then later in Chile.

She knew from her research that it was a technique used long ago by midwives in France, before men had decided that birthing was powerful and therefore desirable to control. But their hands were too big, and they loved machines, even back then. So metal forceps were invented, to replace the soft small hands of practised women. Metal on tender flesh instead of flesh on tender flesh, metal tearing and ripping at women's insides to drag out a bruised child by any part of its body they could clamp.

She felt past the head and moved her hands to see if there was any rotation. But the head was wedged. She felt for the fontanel at the crown to check if it was pulsating. There was something. She pushed past trying to find a handhold on each side of the head. Then Nita gave a great push and the baby shot forward onto the bedding, and abnormally rapidly, within seconds, the afterbirth came away. There was a puny cry and Rashida reached to take him and place him with his mother. But before she could help put him to the breast, he was dead.

García was even more certain that sending in the army would be a disaster. As far as he could see the majority of those inside the Alhambra were civilians. An army was only very rarely a plausible response in civilian situations. As they still had no idea who they were dealing with, the best use of the army now was simply their being overtly present at the scene. It indicated to the terrorists that they were ready to be sent in, and to the nation that there was a strike force if needed.

So far, the behaviour of the terrorists was at odds with the norm. For as long there were no demands, Antonio and the rest of them were staggering in the dark. Therefore an assault could be a huge public relations mistake. Moreover he still couldn't shake off Fisher's remark *things are not always what they seem*. There was little hope of any forensic evidence from the explosion. It was unfortunate that no-one with any expertise had actually seen the explosion take place.

García was certain that until they knew more it was essential to remain inert. He had learned long ago that while any hostage situation had to come to a head, it should not be contrived, or worse, speeded up. If they were to act, rather than to *react*, whatever the action, it needed not to force a climax.

And they needed to remember that they had Rashida Santiago on the inside, who had already shown herself able. She might be as effective a weapon as any sudden onslaught from Raúl and his men. Even if there was silence from the perpetrators, at least they had some communication coming through her. For now, in the absence of any contact with them, García was going to follow his instincts and put some faith in her.

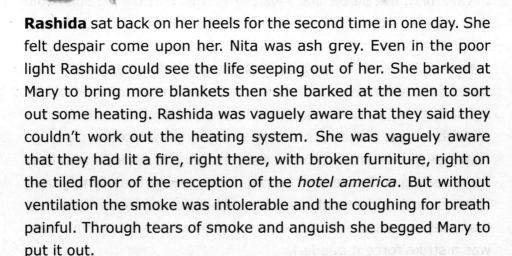

Rashida sat back on her heels for the second time in one day. She felt despair come upon her. Nita was ash grey. Even in the poor light Rashida could see the life seeping out of her. She barked at Mary to bring more blankets then she barked at the men to sort out some heating. Rashida was vaguely aware that they said they couldn't work out the heating system. She was vaguely aware that they had lit a fire, right there, with broken furniture, right on the tiled floor of the reception of the *hotel america*. But without ventilation the smoke was intolerable and the coughing for breath painful. Through tears of smoke and anguish she begged Mary to put it out.

Finally she held Nita's hand and spoke to her over and over, feeling with her other hand as the pulse dropped. She checked for bleeding. There was nothing out of the ordinary. She wiped Nita's brow and talked and talked into the silence. Nita's breathing grew more shallow. At last it stopped.

"Wait. Let's just wait a second," García said to Antonio, looking through the binoculars. Then the smoke began to rise again.

"Someone get Fisher," said Antonio. "Ah there you are. Are you ready?"

Jack Fisher looked with them for evidence in the smoke of dots and dashes. Raúl watched over his shoulder.

"Nothing," said Fisher. "Just a regular fire I guess."

"We'll send Aerial across," said Raúl, "See what we can see."

"Good," said Antonio. "Keep me informed," he said to Raúl's back as he left.

"Well, I guess it was a long shot," said Fisher, clarifying his remark with, "hoping Rashida Santiago manage more signalling. Well," he sighed, "never mind. I guess we will have to wait."

"Yes," García bit out. "Wait."

"He said they are coming for us," Alberto told Lola gravely. "He just said to wait."

"All we can do is wait," said Mary to her choristers. "Wait and not lose hope." She moved among them, trying to help them get comfortable, and trying to just be glad that for the moment at least, all was well.

"Well?" questioned Raúl again, wanting a response as to how long before the army could move. But he was cut off by Manuel shouting,

"Antonio!"

"Sí."

Manuel was beside him.

"The children are here."

"The children are here. I can't," María pushed O'Reilly on his chest to release herself.

"When then?"

"Tomorrow," she smiled at him and stroked the flowers.

"I'll do it," the words were out before he had time to think. She looked at him quizzically so he added, "when David finally gets in touch, I'll tell them to let him have some time out."

"He'll never ask for it. You know what he's like."

"I'll find a way to make it palatable."

"Thank you. And thank you for the flowers."

"You have thanked me," he said in a way that made her colour deepen. "More than once."

"More than once. I have done it loads of times," Alberto pushed his chest out and Lola moved to his side, their little white faces looking pinched after a long day.

"What's he saying?" Jack asked García in a low voice.

"He's says he can get in," García translated. "He says he often goes to the Alhambra. He never pays. In fact," David sounded amused, "he knows a few ways to get in for free."

Fisher looked at the child and at his sister. They had red hair, but other than that they hardly looked alike. Being a twin himself, and living with his own twin sons, he was fairly adept at seeking what didn't resemble one twin in the other. Apart from the colour of their hair and eyes, these two could have been strangers.

"Who are they?"

"Seems they are the true residents of this very establishment. They were evacuated yesterday."

"Boarding school?"

"You could say that," said García. "It's a reform school. Children with behavioural problems."

"He reminds me of someone."

"Well, you know what they say. All delinquents look the same." García joked.

"No," said Fisher. "It's not that. He has that look, that street-wise look." Fisher kept his gaze on the child and then said, "Yeah I know. I know who he reminds me of. Chico. Chico Romero."

"Chico Romero?"

"Yeah. This kid in York. You met his mother. Remember? Carmen Romero, the woman who owns El Piano. Chico is a canny kid. Sharp as a razor. This kid here," Fisher nodded toward Alberto, "he reminds me of him. The thing is," he said to García, "kids see stuff. I learned that from Chico," *and*, he nearly added, *from my sister Ange*. "They see loads more than we adults realise or ever give them credit for. You should listen to him."

García glanced at Fisher and then moved in beside Antonio.

"Hi," he said and put out his hand. "My name is David García. Alberto took his hand gravely.

"You sound weird," chipped in Lola.

"My family was from Cuba."

"Pretty warm in Cuba, huh?" said Alberto

"Yes. Now I live in New York."

"Pretty cold there, huh?" said Alberto. "Colder than here, yeah?"

Antonio watched David García move into the chameleon mode so characteristic of all good negotiators. He noticed how his speech lost its choppy broken quality, how the man relaxed when he was in his element, when he was lost in his work, saying and doing what he knew to be true.

"Yeah. Bit cold in the Alhambra today," García regarded Alberto closely, closed his hands into fists and blew into them. "So you guys can get into the Alhambra? Without paying?"

"We gonna get in trouble?" Alberto looked from side to side.

"I don't think so. No-one's here from the *patronato*," said García.

"Well they should be," said Alberto as if offended.

"How come?"

"They know stuff."

"Yeah. Unfortunately the head honcho is in Australia. At a conference."

"Pretty warm in Australia, huh?"

"Yeah. It's their summer I think," said García

"I think so," agreed Alberto.

"What's a *head honcho*?" asked Lola.

"*El director*," supplied Alberto to her.

"*El director* doesn't know anything," said Lola.

"Does anyone from the *patronato* know anything?" asked García carefully.

"Sure," said Alberto.

"OK," García dropped to a squat and to eye level with Alberto. "Who do we need to ask?"

"The gardeners," said Alberto, "They know everything."

"Any particular gardener?"

"Javi and Agustín. Agustín knows everything."

"Agustín?"

"Yes, he lives there. Have you found him? Is he here?" García thought he could detect a shred of panic in the child's voice.

"I don't know where he is," García answered truthfully. "Maybe in the Alhambra. We are still looking for people."

"Maybe he is hiding," Alberto said thinly. And as Lola listened to him she thought that he spoke like Agustín had described Lorca speaking; when Lorca stepped into *calle angulo*. She thought, *he is speaking with an edge of hope.*

"Maybe he is hiding," said García, aware that Alberto's Agustín and the presumed hostage Agustín were likely one and the same. Then he switched instead to enquiring about the other name.

"Javi? Does he know stuff?"

"Yeah. Javi knows everything too."

"Does Javi work in the Alhambra?" asked David.

"Yes. Every day."

"Do we have a last name or an address for Javi?"

Alberto looked at him blankly.

"No. He's usually in the gardens."

"OK Alberto. Thanks." García stood.

"Let's get Javi," said Antonio looking heavenward.

"Can we go to bed now?" Lola asked García, looking at him, her eyes now two dark circles in a still whiter face.

"Sure," said García, "Tell me your name again."

"Lola."

And David García heard Antonio next to him murmur softly García Lorca's poem mentioning a Lola.

"It seems, Lola," said García smiling at her, "that Captain Marín knows his Lorca. You, Lola, are in many of his poems."

"I know," said Lola. "He is the children's poet. He is the Flower of Granada."

David García rocked back. So Lorca was the children's poet now, was he? Not the gay's poet, nor the New York poet, nor the gypsy poet, nor, according to this child, was he the poet of any of the many other claimants he had heard over the years. Here was this little girl, claiming Federico García Lorca for her own. Surely even Lorca himself would have been touched to have been so definitely owned, and to have been named the Flower of his city.

"Manuel," Antonio then called to Pedraza, "can someone show these guys where they can sleep?"

"We're OK," said Alberto picking up their case and taking Lola's hand. García watched, noting how vulnerable he looked. His overwhelming appearance was one of a pair of large boots with a small boy in them. They moved toward the door and Lola sang out over her shoulder,

"We know the way."

"We know the way to play this *Papá*. We've played it a thousand times. Listen." Fernando was a little tetchy.

"Lighten up," Joaquin said. He knew if Fernando got too cross it would be counter-productive. "Lighten up. Listen *Tio*. Listen." And he played it out in rhythm and then in counter rhythm.

"But *hijo*, it's not *flamenco*!"

I know *Papá*," it was Joaquin's turn to be on the defensive. "I know. Not exactly. But listen. Listen up. One more time. Here we go." He played and then said, "Rhythm." Then he played again. "Counter-rhythm. You know why? So we can have more than one player, so we can really make a noise. So we don't have to amplify. Listen again."

"OK," his father said, picking up the dropped thirds.

Joaquin grinned at him,

"*Pappy*. That's it! Now, Fernando, you take the counter rhythm. Ana, are you ready? Now, one, two..." Joaquin looked at his uncle. The older man said,

"I see. I see."

"But *Tio*, can you hear it?"

"Yes," his uncle answered. "Yes. More volume without

having to abandon the tradition."

"So listen, *Papá*, *Tio*, I can get my voice over it and under it. *Cante jondo* lives!" Joaquin was triumphant, referring to the deep wavering song of *flamenco*. "The *flamenco* is still there, underneath, watch Ana's feet – all that is the same, she's taking the same turns, exactly. You and *Tio*, come on, you follow me *Tio*, *Pappy*, follow *primo*, Ana, go for it... ready, one, two..."

"One...two...three," on the down stroke of Mary's arm, the English began to sing it. Even though it was in English, it was obviously a lament.

The people from the palaces pressed forward and circled the silo as the men lowered Nita's body, wrapped tight in blankets and tied with string. The tears of the bereaved fell shamelessly, and the English choir, moved by the sight of so many young people in grief, felt united with them and let their old eyes fill. Then the young men lowered the small parcel of the baby, and Rashida felt her own tears. The bundle swung from side to side into the silo in the *medina*; deep and dark and out of sight.

dusk

García could no longer make out the walls of the Alhambra. He could hear people in the incident room just behind him, roused now from rest and eager to go again. He could see people on the 'phones ringing what must have been Australia, given the amount of broken English in use. Others appeared to be taking abuse from secretaries who were none too pleased to be rattled out of bed in the dead of night with a question about a man with only a first name, the gardener Alberto had called 'Javi.'

García stretched and reached across one shoulder and then the other to give each a rub. As he had headed out for some air, he had picked up his sweater as he went. It was cold and he put it on. For all his acquaintance with the life of Lorca, he had never quite taken on board the fact that nights were cold in Granada, even in the spring. The moon was in and out of the clouds and from the elevation of Sacramonte he turned away from the Alhambra and looked up toward the Sierra Nevada with the snow caps in plain view, almost luminous when the moon peeped through. A scent of pines lay in the air.

He leaned against the building and allowed himself to subside momentarily into the darkness and the silence. Occasionally he could make out the sound of the nightly waste collection. He remembered that about Spain; the refuse being gathered up in the cool darkness of the night. The start-stop of the heavy vehicles as they worked their way through the streets, the occasional shout of the men as they leapt and swung off the back of the wagons.

Focus. He said to himself. It was now time to make the lists, he admonished himself, not indulge in nostalgia. Time to give the Alhambra personality. The children had been a bit of a diversion. But at least they had given him an idea of who he might be framing the questions for.

Then, he heard it. Voices. Far away voices, but voices nonetheless, singing. Eerie and ethereal. He pushed off the wall and strained to hear. He rotated himself away from the view of the mountains back to the now familiar gaze across the ravine. The sound seemed to be coming from the Alhambra itself. Bizarre.

But he had no sooner adjusted his mind to the fact, when far nearer, and at far greater volume, he heard other music, different music, to the left, lower, where lights were burning among the caves in the hillside. He heard pulsating rhythmic stamping, singing, and what he imagined were guitars, strong and vibrant into the night. He recalled his Lorca to himself. He could clearly imagine six gypsies dressed in white dancing in the night. The noise went through him like electricity and he resisted it by turning sharply back toward the *reformatorio*.

And then, as he stepped across the threshold, an enormous explosion rocked the night. García spun round to look behind him, and up to the left he saw the plumes of dust.

"*El mirador romántico*," said Antonio dully to his left.

A second explosion tore into the falling light.

"*La torre del cabo*," said Raúl. "Christ."

"*No me digas!*" cried Manuel.

"I'm not kidding," said Antonio, his eyes fixed on the horizon. "They're both gone."

SATURDAY

Dale limosna, mujer,
que no hay en la vida nada
como la pena de ser ciego en Granada

Give alms to the beggar, woman,
for there is nothing worse in this life
than to be blind in Granada

Francisco A. de Icaza

dawn

Some mornings García found harder than others. That was all he could say about it. Except for the huge fading moon, Lorca's *luna, luna, luna*, this soft, still, dawn was like so many others. He slept little at the best of times. Once he had counted this as a gift. All those hours he had extra to most people. In his work it meant he had time to sit out his adversary and stay alert. Above all, it meant time to read, read and read. But since the deaths of Marilita and Richard he would have preferred less time being conscious in the world.

Most days he awoke feeling hollowed out. On bad days it hurt. On good days there was a numbness with a residual ache. Years ago, he had read a treatise on sense and meaning. Lately he had ruminated on the differences between the two. Richard's death made sense, for all that it was hard at times to bear. But he could make no sense of Marilita's death, nor could he give it meaning. If it had meaning, then perhaps that would help him lay it to rest.

He had avoided relatives of the victims of 9/11 in the same way he had avoided all forms of therapy. He met people in the course of his work, or just in virtue of living in New York, who had been bereaved by 9/11. He never made his own loss known to them. His sense of privacy held him back. But that was not the whole truth. It was also a fear that if ever he began to open up to what went on inside, he would struggle to differentiate between the ropes of anger twisted at his core.

There was a universal anger against an impersonal world and a group of anonymous people that had taken the life of his child. Then there was a specific personal anger against Richard that had been smouldering for years; an anger due to Richard's inability to overcome alcoholism. If they fused together and were allowed to course freely, he foresaw a corrosive flow of sulphuric grief. So he kept his distance, and instead read everything he could lay his hands on about the relatives of victims of 9/11 and their reactions.

Eventually he believed he had become desensitised by the seemingly limitless outpourings of other people's feelings. A resultant superficial lack of emotion had settled upon him. This had allowed him a dispassionate study of Islam, of the Holy Qur'an, of Arab culture, of anything that might give shape or form to *al-Qaeda*. *Understand your enemy* had always been a core training motto for the negotiator, followed by, *and then let them think they understand you*. He had been taught to collude, to find common ground, or at least to conjure up the mirage of common ground.

He tried to tie terrorism irrevocably into what was peddled as the Muslim worldview. Instead, in Islam, he found an intelligent set of coherent beliefs with a core integrity. There was a sophisticated social system, with carefully structured obligations and duty. He found that the position of women, so often represented as restricted and second class, was the reverse. Of all the world's major religions, in Islam, and only in Islam, was it actually written that women had rights; rights of ownership, of decision, of domestic power. The power of their position, unlike any other religion he had encountered, was enshrined in the very essence of Islam. And in Islam he also found a comfort in the initial duty of a Muslim: to question faith before accepting it. It was the antithesis of his Catholicism, drilled in and unyielding from the day he was born. It was the antithesis of Judaism, where male Jews began each day with prayers of thanks to God that they had not been born women. No wonder Islam was fearsome, for in its true form it had a profound social intelligence at its root.

In the end he decided that *al-Qaeda* had about as much in common with Islam as the IRA had with Christianity. Each group simply super-imposed their own values onto the prevailing system of belief. IRA Catholics invoked the word of God, and Osama bin Laden and his followers invoked the word of Allah. Yet each was just a bunch of men clutching at any rationale to lend support their own desires for power. García knew that as a Catholic he would not want to be judged by the values of the IRA, nor he imagined would Muslims wish to be judged by the actions of *al-Qaeda*. Finally he concluded that focus on Islam was merely a red herring.

He thought describing *al-Qaeda* always as *terrorists* might have been a fatal political error. It created a new genus of activist in people's minds, and as such, falsely required some new analysis or response from government. Whereas, in García's mind, terrorists were no different than any bunch of bandits from any time in history. In his view, the real focus should be instead on theories of war: *Understand your enemy and then let them think they understand you,* or, *Keep your friends close but keep your enemies closer*. As far as he was concerned it was a case of according them what you are free to give, luring them in and then taking the upper hand. It was just like having a wayward dog. Any negotiator knew you couldn't knock tar out of a dog if you couldn't catch it. And you could never catch a dog with threats.

Joaquin Montez didn't *do* dawn. Never had. That is, he never got up at dawn. None of them did. Instead they pushed through *until* dawn, a totally different thing altogether.

On this night of pushing through, as the dark met the light, he had even begun to try to adapt an old *cante jondo* version of his father's to accommodate Lorca's poem, *alba* – dawn. He had run through it a few times, trying to take the piano accompaniment set down by Lorca for some of the folk songs the great man had gathered, and tease it out into guitar strains that would best show off the lyric.

It was a long shot and Montez knew he would draw criticism, but if he could just get the two to work together, what would be more engaging than taking the old traditional tunes and setting them with the modern poems in a type of counter rhythm?

He put his guitar down and flexed his fingers, listening to the silence. Thank God in the last few years they had stopped the daily ringing of the infernal *vela*, the great bell at the top of the tower of the *alcazaba* within the Alhambra fortress. When he was a boy they had rung it morning, noon and night. And thank God the newly built mosque had not won the right to broadcast the call to prayer.

Dawn was still safe.

Safety did not cross Agustín's mind much. He was old enough to count each day he lived as, if not as a surprise, then at least as not to be taken for granted. Rosario was still curled tight where she had slept tucked into him. He thought he heard her stir but it must have been one of the English. Maybe even María Santos Moreno, who had slept on the other side of him. Oh she of royal blood! *Delicious* thought Agustín with a small smile on his face, *she had come to this, bedding down with the likes of him*.

After the baby and the woman had been lowered into the silo maybe their captors hadn't the will to fight the demands of the English woman with the red hair anymore. And once the hotel had been used for the birthing and the dying, maybe THEY couldn't see the point anymore of denying the old people some comfort. He and the others were now all piled together in the ground floor reception area of the *hotel america*, one mattress next to another, but at least under shelter.

He looked up toward the entrance to the inner courtyard to judge the time. It could not be much before dawn and it had been years since he had slept beyond it. THEY wanted something. The THEYs of this world always did. He rolled onto his back with his head on his arm and stared at the ceiling. THEY. It seemed as if his whole life he had been of aware of THEY and powerless to influence how THEY might act. His only sense of triumph lately was that he and Rosario had managed to hold onto the *finca* in the teeth of the steady advancement of the Alhambra itself. Their children couldn't have it. The lawyers had seen to that. But then none of them wanted it really, what with their careers in Motril and Sevilla. When he and Rosario were gone the *finca* would just get absorbed into the land mass around the Alhambra that already belonged to it. Gone. Generations of his family living off that land, an entire way of life, destined, doubtless, to become some sort of walkway for foreign tourists.

The thought of his own children made him think again of Alberto and Lola. Maybe if he got out of this mess he would enquire with the nuns to see if the children could spend more time with them. Try to make it more official. Less of the creeping around in the early hours, less sliding on their bottoms down the hill from the *reformatorio* so as not to be seen slipping out of *siesta*. The nuns could hardly be classified as THEY, although they had done precious little to stand up to all the years of... well, he sighed, best not go down that road again.

He rolled onto his side and inhaled deeply. The nuns would probably say they were too old. They might even think he and Rosario were a bad influence. Maybe they would be right. Maybe he, more than Rosario, had been poisoned merely by living too long, seeing too much, and therefore losing all faith in *buena gente*. *Good people* were as likely, maybe more likely, to break your heart than the out and out scoundrels of this world. *Good people* had taken Lorca after all. The Rosales brothers were *good people* for all that they were Felangists. They had loved Federico and were harbouring him in their home for safe keeping from the very same forces. *Good people*. It was all Agustín could do not to spit.

Nonetheless he knew that the nuns would be concerned about some of the stories he told the children. He had even thought lately of letting up a bit on the Lorca tale. He had noticed how entranced Alberto and Lola were with it. Agustín knew that those who suffer injustice find where it lives in others and are drawn in. Something about Lorca's fate resonated in those two children and they had somehow knitted it onto their own lives. When he next saw Alberto and Lola, maybe he would talk to them about it.

Raúl had suspected all along that he was a pro. This last explosion confirmed it. And at the same time, the terrorists had made possibly their first mistake. Two explosions. The first had drawn all eyes to the monument, including Raúl's. So he had been paying very close attention when the second explosion occurred. He had watched the side of *la torre del cabo* blow out, just at the bottom corner. Neat and tidy. And then the rest had simply fallen, almost in a straight line, with a cloud of dust, in a linear and elegant collapse.

His observations from the explosion told Raúl that the charges had been set on the valley side, low down, at the base of the tower, not at the shallow end, within the walls. There was no way they could have set the charges since the occupation. No way. His men had kept the perimeter under watch ever since the alarm had been raised. There had been no activity. None at all.

Besides, with the grid shut down, how could they have pulled electricity to drill into the brickwork in order to sink the charges? It had all been done well in advance. As soon as the light was up he would have to take a really good look. And with luck, he would see what was going to blow next, and maybe, just maybe, be able to pick out the stalk of the detonator from the new wreckage.

Raúl rolled onto his back and stared up. It had taken him a while to arrive at the conclusion but now he would have to tell Antonio. That they were up against a shot-firer, and he was good.

And he had been there a long time before Friday.

Friday seemed a long time ago to David García. Despite the strangeness of the narrow cots designed for the lean young bodies of children, he was again in a place that was all too familiar. Just one more situation where someone thought they were not getting what they wanted, were not living in the world they believed they deserved, and so they were going to jump up and down for attention.

Some of the people he had negotiated with had reminded him of Marilita as a child, during her short-lived tantrum phase. Except these people had never grown out of it. García laced his hands across his chest and stared at the institutional ceiling. Marilita who had become such a calm person, with such a measured commitment to her work, and, García often thought, a more stable person even than her father...

He twisted his ring and remembered the day she had slipped it off her finger and given it to him. *Keep it Papá* she had said, *until I make Captain. Then I'll have it back.* To which he had teased: *And if you don't make Captain?* It still hurt to remember her reply: *Then you give it to someone who you think is worthy, Someone who is a captain in life, if not in The Job!* She was always like that. A combination of carefree and steady. She lacked his continued torment of self-knowledge that even after all these years, he would have still preferred was otherwise.

On the rational surface, being gay was not a problem. Nor emotionally did it cause him any trouble. Certainly in the early years, Richard had wholly engaged his heart. And physically he had enjoyed the freedom to be as he was, to give himself up to the sheer corporal pleasure of man on man. But where being gay met his spirit, that part of him remained stubbornly and forever Catholic, and it rankled him. If he left it aside, followed his intellectual pleasures, took comfort from his emotional successes, initially with Richard, always with Marilita and generally even with her mother, he was fine. But death had exposed his spirit and a nagging hunger that could not be fed by his faith. Gay and Catholic simply did not square. His throat constricted and he turned his face to the side.

He swallowed a few times to re-assert his equilibrium and thought that the irony was that most people saw him as calm too. Hadn't Marín said the same of Rashida Santiago? Hadn't he said that was why he had selected her? Young, calm, competent. Antonio had said that she was perfect for it. *Compassionate and able*, he had said. He told García he had sensed her capacity to meet crises and retain focus.

García would have described Marilita in exactly the same way. And it had cost Marilita her life. Would Rashida Santiago have to pay the same price? García's eyes lit upon the final fading of the moon and he found himself feeling a sudden and unexpected primal connection with Rashida Santiago. He muttered an avowal: *not if I have anything to do with it*.

Mary was adamant. "It's the one way we can keep our spirits up. Come on!" she cajoled her choristers in whispers from under her blankets. "Come on, it worked last night. Running through a few numbers did us good. A little singsong is what we can do to help ourselves! We have to keep our hopes up. Getting depressed is the one thing that will do us down."

"No," Daniel whispered back vehemently. "What will do us down is staying here and getting killed."

Getting killed had crossed Rashida's mind. She was not afraid. Perhaps if she had children, it would be different. Had her parents been alive, maybe that would have made her feel compelled to outlive them. For if there was one thing she knew for sure then it was that there was no pain greater than to have a child pre-decease you. She had watched women bear that, and to a lesser extent, through miscarriage, had borne it herself.

She could remember her father. Then when she was scarcely a woman herself, her mother had died. Had they lived, she thought, her father would be well into his eighties by now. She was a miracle baby, her parents had been more the age of grandparents than parents. And that was not the only miracle. They had been able to care for her even though her father had been blind and her mother, although fifteen years his junior, had been severely beaten during the Civil War and was virtually crippled by arthritis.

Miracles. What did Mustafa say? *Miracles my love, they happen all the time*. And then he would give her that look that could melt stone.

The right to life occupied Gerardo's thoughts and had done for a very long time. He felt his sore skin over his shoulder blades abrade on the hard earth. Yet he preferred the ground to any bed. It was the one place in every day where he felt peace. There was something about laying flat on the cool earth that penetrated him.

He could not see the sky but he knew morning was breaking. The pale light of a new day was striking the water of the *palacio de los colmares* and although the water was still, it was playing a little shimmering dance across the pool.

A new dawn meant another punishing day of decisions and maybe even more destruction. Taking out parts of *el partal* as a first gambit was well done. They had their midwife, not that she had made any difference. Two babies dead as posts. And Nita too.

But taking out both the *el mirador romántico* and *la torre del cabo* had been good.

His own communications to the outside were getting them nowhere. If only they could get rid of all the English who were yet more people to feed and toilet and watch. On the other hand Jay still thought that the presence of foreigners might strengthen their case. Not that much news time was being given over to it on the radio. And the radio was all they had now that the power had been cut.

He was so tired he just kept going over it in his mind, a well worn rut of thought, taking less energy than any new ideas. Yes, the English needed watching, but they were mostly old men. Only the woman and the drunk had any real physical strength. And as long as the drunk had his bottle he was hardly a threat.

It was the drunk that had alerted Gerardo to the need to empty the bars at the *hotel america* and the *parador*. It reminded him, just in time, that the English were a nation of drunks. He had seen them in action in the days when he himself had had the strength to go to football.

As for HER. He rolled over onto his stomach. As for HER, he thought again. What hope that?

Fisher had woken to thoughts of The Constantine Singers in the Alhambra and how they might be faring. Many of them on a normal Saturday would be sat at home watching some sporting event on television. Perhaps the more keen and fit among them out there somewhere, watching or even playing.

If he were home this weekend then he would have been with the twins watching them play football in an Easter friendly for the under eights on the York Knavesmire. They would be exhausting themselves before returning home to a roast dinner and an afternoon of tormenting their sister Gabby.

He glanced across at Paula, still asleep but beginning to stir. He bet she had organised his sister Ange to take the boys to the match anyway. Carmen Romero's street-wise son Chico, who Alberto had so reminded him of, would be there too. He and Gabby would have planned how many sweets they would take with them to help off-set the boredom of having to watch.

Jack would prefer to steer his boys toward cricket. That had been his own game, and so of course he favoured it. And the cricket crowd, unlike the football crowd, had no *religious* commitment to drunkenness before, during and after the game. For all that he had been sober more than ten years, Jack still found it an effort to be encircled by the false bonhomie of booze. There was a fundamental unpredictable quality to the dedicated drunk.

Just like the unpredictable nature of their current predicament, he thought. The stress of not knowing the outcome must be taking its toll on the choir, both those on the inside and the twenty-nine on the outside. Hoping against hope was a torment. For the eleven Yorkies in the Alhambra there was also the strain of the conditions. Not, he thought, that anyone had much idea what the conditions were like. To have so little information feeding into an operation was at best uncomfortable.

Uncomfortable beds were a part of life, he thought, as he watched the moon recede from view. Alberto rolled on his mattress and Lola rolled with him.

He had a small regret that they never did get to sleep in the beds that had been made up for them in Ronda. If they had only stayed there instead of making the journey back maybe they could have enjoyed the softness and the warmth.

In fact everything had seemed a great deal more luxurious in Ronda than in the *reformatorio*. And, he could not help but notice, a great deal warmer. None of this sitting around with heaters under tables covered in floor-length cloths hoping to keep private parts warm while the rest of you froze. The whole building in Ronda was warm. Perhaps one day he might have control over the cold and the warmth in his life.

He was worried about Agustín. He imagined that Rosario would be alright. She had Agustín to keep her warm. But what about Agustín? For there was little doubt now in Alberto's mind that THEY had got hold of the Alhambra. All those big men in the big room with the big maps and the big worry hanging over them, it was pretty obvious that even those big men knew that THEY were in control.

And Alberto knew only too well that THEY could never be trusted to make the right decisions. Agustín was always telling them that the decisions that you make affect everything, forever. He had to get into the Alhambra somehow. He had to make sure it was OK, of course, but most of all, he had to make sure Agustín was OK.

What if they blow the whole lot? thought Antonio Marín to himself. What was it they said to him after his wife had died? *Life goes on*. He propped himself up on his cot and reached for the cigarettes. The adage *life goes on* would not save his career, although of course people were right. He swung himself from reclined to seated. *Life goes on* was what people always said. Today, he imagined, whatever happened, the same would be true. He lit up and drew on his cigarette. And doubtless, in the ruin of it all, there would be no end of help offered, national, private, international.

People loved to respond to a crisis AFTER the event. No-one had been there to help in all the months Maribel had been eaten by cancer from the inside out. But afterwards, help had been forthcoming from everyone. It had been almost too much, all the women in his family in and out of the flat all the time, if not his sisters, then his daughters. His son insisting they meet for a beer, when before he only wanted to tap up his father for either a loan or some news scoop. Marín pulled on his clothes, stood and stretched. He had felt a guilty relief when at last, as the months passed, all the people who had gathered in support when Maribel died, had finally fallen away and, at last, mercifully, he had been left to his own devices.

He could not let his own devices fail him now. He needed to retain a semblance of decisiveness and control. The men looked to him for that, and he sensed that if he was not careful, control could easily slide from him to García, whose strength of character was already apparent. Raúl Sanchez would resist such a power shift. Sanchez had made it plain that he disliked or distrusted the Cuban, doubtless, thought Antonio, with some wisdom, a sort of reverse attraction at work.

God he hated working in an environment that was sexually charged. Then he relented. It wasn't exactly sexually charged, it was just that García and Sanchez provided yet another complication that was usually absent in an all male team. It was clear to Antonio that García knew, as he himself did, that Raúl was gay. If operational control moved more toward García then the focus could move from the job in hand to internal squabbles.

Antonio needed to ensure this didn't happen. For that was the trouble with all teams, with all operations: in the end you were down to just plain humanity, the failings and flaws of individuals. You were always left with just trusting that enough of the strengths and weaknesses in your team would line up, like planets in a portentious pattern, and that people could see past themselves to the bigger picture, could do the analysis, and do it fast.

The weight of the future pressed down on his shoulders,

and the sure knowledge that the outcome of the next few days would determine history.

He finished his first cigarette of the day. *Screw getting a shave and a shower*, he thought. He would do that after he checked in with the night watch. He picked up his cigarettes and lighter and moved toward the office and a good strong cup of coffee.

Next to coffee in the morning, a cigarette was Carmen Romero's favourite thing. Not that she smoked many. But this morning she could not resist filching one of Ange's while she slept.

She crept toward her cold York kitchen so as not to wake the children. It was good having Jack's family around for the weekend. Good they were headed for football and plenty of boisterous activity. It helped her not to dwell on Daniel Goddard and what might be happening to him within the Alhambra; Daniel, to whom she had barely spoken in two years.

The trouble was, she thought, inhaling deeply, the curse of crossed star-lovers meant that instead of love allowing you to live in its light, it dogged every day with its poor reflection. Furthermore it was invisible. The lover, and only the lover, knew that they were alone. Love lived in a different time and space, Carmen called it *angeltime*. So she did not expect anyone to communicate with her directly about Daniel after the passage of two years in what she thought of as *realtime*.

She drew gratefully on the tobacco, hoped Jack would telephone again, and mouthed a silent Ave María.

María woke to the sounds of her sons watching early morning Easter TV. She turned in her covers and wondered if she had imagined Eddie looking at her with more than the usual lust; if she had imagined some connection of heart and mind. Maybe, and so what if not? What harm was there in self-delusion? What harm was there in taking comfort where one could?

There was a lick of life in sex, whether casual, anonymous, or even cruel. Since Matt's death the wick of a penis always had the ability to jump-start her efforts to carry on. There were two boys to raise. She could not fail them. At the moment, the feel of Eddie inside her propelled her from one day into the next.

The fact that he had known Marilita, that he knew David, that he had even met Matt, all brought María a sense of unity. Somehow, in the act of sex with Eddie, there was a comfort that all of these losses were coherent within her long acquaintance with him. So what if these were all desperate imaginings? At the moment, they were a set of imaginings she was more than happy to live with.

morning

Gravely, Raúl presented the information. He ended with,

"No phone contact whatsoever," and then, as if on cue his mobile rang. He apologised, took out a Space-Age model from his jacket, flipped it open, pressed it into silence and returned it to his pocket.

"Thoughts?" said Antonio

"Finding the detonators?" questioned García, and then added, "It's a long shot," followed by, "No pun intended."

"A better idea?" Raúl asked slightly caustic.

"Three explosions. What has been reported missing?" replied García, avoiding his eye. "You say commercial charges." Then he looked directly at Raúl. "Not military."

"I didn't say it wasn't military." Raúl crossed him in an acid tone. "What I said was that I don't think *the shot-firer* is military."

García ignored the tone and said,

"Look outside the Alhambra. Not inside. Look for an MER." And he jabbed toward a pile of documents on the table.

Jack Fisher was watching the exchange, unable to understand the words. He knew they were talking about explosives, that much was clear. Then he saw the letters M E R on the uppermost paper of the stack. MER must be international, he thought. Missing Explosives Report. Of course. This was Spain. An MER was essential in Spain as it was in the UK. Thanks to ETA and the IRA these two nations were uniquely distinguished in the European Union by the need to keep track of any and all explosives. If some had gone missing, there would be an MER somewhere.

"Why not military?" Antonio cut across.

"I hate to say it," Raúl faced Antonio, "but he's too good. Too accurate. Too tidy. So I doubt he will have access to military stock. It will probably be commercial. But I am only saying probably."

"What difference does that make?" asked Antonio.

"Longevity, right?" García said to Raúl.

"Right," said Raúl, concealing his surprise. This Cubano knew his stuff. "No preservatives," he masked a brief admiration with attempted humour. "Military explosives are bought and stored, stockpiled for any future eventuality. Commercial explosives are for immediate use. There's no need to make them long lasting. They've got a six to nine month shelf life in ideal conditions. They need to be kept cool and dry."

"Not much chance of ideal conditions up there," said Antonio nodding toward the Alhambra.

"But, no MER?" García persisted. "What was it? Twenty kilos more or less per blast? Three detonators used? At least two..."

Manuel came into the room, cutting across García,

"The images are loading. Look."

They all turned toward the wide screen. Raúl barked,

"Enhance bottom slice."

The lower quarter of the screen appeared four times larger.

"As I said," he leaned forward. "There, along the walls. See, *gallinas, cadi, cautiva, infantas.*"

"The names of the towers along the perimeter," Antonio said *sotto voce* to García as they all looked hard at the screen. Raúl stepped up to it.

"Here," he said, running his finger horizontally along the sides of the walls. "It's easy to see if you know what you are looking for. Primaflex. Rust coloured."

"Primaflex?" asked one of the junior policemen.

"Fuse wire," said Raúl flatly. "Or more properly, detonating cord. High explosives wrapped in a plastic sheath. It connects the detonator to the charges. Comes in just about any colour you like. Included, it seems, a shade of Alhambra red," he smiled grimly. "With this, we are talking detonation in the region of seven thousand metres per second."

"What?" said García looking at him hard. "What? Cord already in position? Connected to the charges? Charges drilled in?"

"Like I said," Raúl Sanchez raised his shoulders.

"No. You said the explosions that have already happened were set up in advance."

Raúl and Antonio each noticed this was an unusually long sentence for García.

"And now I am saying there are a load more," Raúl said with finality.

Mary Stansfield had found a sheltered corner, set back from the ruins in *el partal*. The slow running water had gathered into a shallow pool before cascading forward, where it had once fallen into a lotus shaped basin. The basin was now in shards among the dust. She had tried to go into the hotels to bathe but there were men everywhere. Last night she had been able to walk anywhere. Now, suddenly, there were restrictions on entry into all the buildings.

There was no continuity. Take the alcohol for example. This morning at the *parador* they had been unloading beer from a trolley. Earlier they had been throwing all the alcohol away. Take the surveillance as another example: yesterday they had been watched like hawks until dark. Then, she and Rashida had virtually had the run of the monument. Now, whenever they approached a building, they were all over them like a rash. Doubtless HE would be as caught up with it all as the rest of them.

She shed her skirt and blouse, put a stone from the wreckage on them to prevent them from moving with the breeze, and tied her scarf around one of the pomegranate trees. She stepped into the pool, removed her cotton cami top and immersed it in the cold water, and slowly, in only her knickers, she squeezed the cold water from the camisole over her shoulders.

The water slid over her front and back, and despite the cold she felt better, refreshed. She was even mildly amused at how a day before she would never have contemplated taking her clothes off in a public place, she would never have imagined being refreshed by the running of cold and probably dirty water over her skin. Life was full of surprises. Wasn't one of Lorca's *canciones* they were going to perform all about that?

"Back to whole screen then," said Antonio relieved to have something concrete for everyone to focus on.

"These are the shots from last night," said Manuel.

"It's just the fires burning from earlier," Raúl said. "But we can take a really close look," he indicated the computer screen. "If you look here, in the *secano*, the *medina* area, you can see two bundles. I would say bodies. Probably mother and infant. When we flew over this morning, they were gone."

García felt something constrict in his stomach. Rashida Santiago wasn't having a very successful time of it if she had a dead baby on her hands. If the baby didn't survive, then there was no need to keep the midwife alive. She would know too much. They would just rub her out, pitch her off the walls maybe, throw her into a fire perhaps. He felt his imagination running away with him. He smelled again the wretched New York perfume of ground zero.

"Hang on," said Antonio, "what's this?" and he pointed to squiggles in the earth toward the bottom right of the photo. "What's this?" he said again with excitement. "Enhance it."

There was a tapping on the keyboard and the image filled the screen. Manuel turned to Antonio and said,

"Arabic Sir?"

"What does it say?"

170

"No idea."

No idea seemed to come to Alberto, hard though he tried. The nuns were always telling him to think harder. But all it ever did was make him screw his nose up until his face ached. He stared at the Alhambra in the morning light, trying to think of how they might get in and what they might do there if they could.

When they come for him, he comes out of the door into calle angulo. That's the first time we see him. Alberto could hear Agustín's voice in his head. Agustín always started the story this way.Is that what had happened to Agustín? Had THEY come for him? And what would become of him now? The very thought made Alberto fight back the tears. The story Agustín told always ended the same way. *That was history*, he would say. *It doesn't matter how many ways or times you tell it, because it is in the past, the end is always the same.*

Then at last, an idea began to dawn.

Dawn felt like a long time ago. Mohammed Iqbal felt tired and rubbed his eyes. They had woken him hours before, and all he could do after all this time was shake his head.

"I mean I know what it says, but," he shook his head again, and looked up apologetically at Marín and García. "What it means? It's anyone's guess."

"Well you must have some idea," Antonio said. "You are the best Arabic scholar at the University. There must be something here in these photos to indicate some information. Are you sure?"

"The first part, over here, in this corner of the shot, is from one of the Hadiz. *If you fear tomorrow is judgement day, then plant a fruit tree.* The second part says, *of what we long for, three*

171

were possible, two are gone, one left to go. And then these," he pointed further toward the edges of the image, "these are all quotes from the Holy Qur'an. All from the Sura."

"Meaning?"

"Verses," Iqbal peered over his glasses at García. "As in the Bible. These are all the first lines of verses."

"OK. What do they say?"

"Well, this one says, *And remember We divided the Sea for you and saved you and drowned Pharaoh's people within your very sight.* And this one says, *Behold! How they invent a lie against God! But that by itself is a manifest sin!* And this one says, *The companions of the fire will call to the Companions of the Garden.* And then finally this one here says, *those who are really weak and oppressed, men women and children, who have no means in their power.*"

"Alright. Mohammed," Antonio patted him on the back with a sense of resignation. "Thank you for coming in and trying." He walked over to Manuel and said, "Any more ideas?"

"This won't do you or them any good," Gerardo spat to Rashida as he scuffed up the Arabic script that she had taken such care to write. It had been painstaking effort to do it in the falling light of the night before when she had laid out both Nita and her baby, each wrapped in blankets, on the red earth of the *medina*.

"It gave me some comfort," she said, watching him erase the holy words by kicking over them.

"Not much comfort for them though was it?" he bit out.

"Out of time, again!" Joaquin Montez was tired and impatient, with his fellow musicians, with Ana, with the world. He rested his guitar on his knee and looked at them all. "Look. The counter-rhythm is important. It's what drives it. It's what makes a very boring little traditional tune something special. If the timing isn't right the words don't fit. If the words don't fit, it won't work. It's going to be hard enough to pull this off, but if we don't get the rhythm right we're screwed. Listen." He began to clap, one hand on one knee and then to drum his guitar with the other hand. "This hand," he said raising the one above the knee, "is the music, and this one," he said with his other hand lingering over the guitar, "is Lorca."

"Sing it," his uncle said. "I think I've got it. I'll thrash it out."

"OK, listen," said Joaquin and threw back his head. From deep in his gullet, from way down under the diaphragm, the words of Lorca reached up through him and bucked against his uncle's tune. It was more than a song, it was anthemic, it was primeval, it was, at its most essential, a call.

"Call him," Ange said to Carmen. "Ask him what he knows."

"He will be busy. He'll let us know when he knows."

"Yes all that is true, but call him, Carmen, if it will make you feel better. I'll call him."

"No Ange. Really," said Carmen definitely. Ange was right. If Jack had anything to say he would call. And she also knew that no matter what was happening, even if he had the resources of all the mobile phone networks in Spain, Daniel would never call.

"It had better be a good excuse." María laughed into the phone at O'Reilly. "Calling me at this time."

"Do I need one?" he asked, his voice slightly provocative.

173

She had merely undressed in the open air, rinsed her body and then stepped back into damp and dirty clothes.

From where he was standing it was shocking for being so unexpected.

It was shocking for him how little effect it had on him.

It was shocking for him how which he longed for it to.

"It is in Arabic. Why?" David asked aloud.

"I imagine it's because Rashida wrote it," said Antonio.

"You're kidding me," García said quietly as truth began to dawn.

"She's Muslim?" Raúl too turned to Antonio "We've got a Muslim in there? Christ Antonio. Christ! Who authorised that!"

"I did."

"What in God's name for?"

"They demanded a midwife. Rashida Santiago is the best we have. She volunteered."

"Well isn't that convenient," Raúl almost sneered. "A bloody Muslim. Now we know we are dealing with Islamic Jihad or some other mad religious fanatics."

David García felt a wave of nausea wash over him.

"How do we know this?" he asked, dangerously quiet.

"She's a Muslim for Chrissake," barked Raúl with flint-hard eyes.

García almost recoiled. He knew that look, that set of assumptions, he'd met them a thousand times. Worse in a closet queer than any man in a dress.

"Definitely," he heard himself saying, "definitely Raúl. Rashida Santiago is a Muslim. So, without doubt, mad. A religious fanatic. A terrorist. Take me for instance. Hey I'm gay. I love to sodomise little boys at the weekends."

There was total silence. Even Manuel Pedraza stopped

masticating his sunflower seeds.

"Well," said Antonio finally. "Perhaps someone would like to suggest if and how these three Arabic phrases could be connected?"

Manuel Pedraza leaned lazily on the doorjamb of the *carmen* in the Albaicín, discarding some pipas shells on the doorstep. The city below was strangely quiet. The evacuation was having an effect. He had never known a Saturday morning so devoid of sound. It had been wonderful to drive here so quickly in almost no traffic.

Antonio had been right. He had rung and the guy was at home. He was bound to be. He was hardly going to leave, was he? What with all the uncertainties about his wife, what man would? Anyway, living in a *carmen*, one of the little jewels of the Abaicín, all whitewashed high walls on the outside, looking like a half deserted ruin, and then, on the inside the gardens, fountains and trees. *If I lived in a carmen*, Manuel thought, *I would never go out*.

It was a blessing to get out, get away from the *reformatorio* and all the tension. That was for sure. Sanchez and García were really at it, hammer and tongs. In Antonio's place he would have banged both their heads together and sent them packing.

He guessed it was not exactly possible to ship off the US government observer, but then Rashida Santiago being a Muslim was a bit of a surprise and even more of a surprise was the fact that Antonio Marín didn't think it was that big of a deal.

Manuel rubbed his neck. A lot of all this was going over his head. He figured the chances of him ever making captain were fairly remote. He couldn't see the shades of grey. And after the stresses of the last few days he was almost glad not to.

There was a slight movement and Manuel turned toward

the man in traditional Islamic dress who came to the door. After a brief conversation the two of them got into a car together.

With *you I feel connected*, Gerardo had wanted to tell her. *For the first time since the tiredness really got me in its teeth, for the very first time, I actually want to have the energy to do something other than just the bare minimum.*

"With your help we might be able to figure this out," Antonio said, greeting Mustafa with a handshake as Manuel Pedraza ushered him into the room.

García was surprised at Mustafa's calm. He had expected the man to be more concerned for his wife's safety. Was he hiding something? David watched him carefully as Antonio began to explain where the images on the screen were in relation to the building, and what they suspected had happened. Antonio thought it might be better to start with the whole picture, in case there was something in the image in its entirety that Mustafa might find significant but which they had missed.

"A dead baby and probably a dead mother," said Mustafa looking at the images.

Antonio didn't want to seem callous, but he could not care less. This was mere detail. Couldn't Mustafa give him something else? García's suspicions about Mustafa, however, were trumped by his worst fears possibly being confirmed. If the mother and child were dead, why bother keeping Rashida alive?

"And the writing?"

"It's too small."

"Enhance," said Antonio needlessly as the image was changed instantly by the technician, and the Arabic was writ large on the screen.

"*If you fear tomorrow is judgement day, then plant a fruit tree*," said Mustafa out loud and then looked at them all. "It's Rashida. She's telling me to have faith. This is what we say to each other if things are bad." Again his tone was flat and calm.

Antonio was disappointed but tried not to show it. After all, the woman had a right to communicate with her husband. And García thought, *I hope to God this is not her way of saying goodbye*. His only comfort when Marilita had been killed was that it had to have been instant. It had to have been. It was. He affirmed it to himself, for the umpteenth time.

"What about, *of what we long for, three were possible, two are gone, one left to go*?" asked Antonio.

"That's easy. What Rashida and I long for are children," then he pointed to the words, "I imagine this part means, two of the babies she went to deliver are dead, one therefore must still be viable. Maybe alive, maybe not yet born," he shrugged, and then, maybe feeling it was worth an explanation, looked up with sad eyes and said, "We haven't been able to have children so far. Rashida has had three miscarriages." García wanted to say something inane like *I'm sorry* but Mustafa continued, in his calm and still way. "But there is still time. *Enshallah*."

Then García got it. Mustafa wasn't calm or still or hiding anything. He was, instead, quite simply, a believer. *Enshallah*. That was the key. Whatever God willed, he would live with it, and he knew Rashida would too. This blind faith, which had all but disappeared in mainstream western Christianity, was still very alive and well in Islam. García remembered it in his mother, in many of the people who came in that wave of immigration from Cuba. *Sufficient unto the day...* wasn't that what his mother had often said? Something he had never understood precisely but which was said as a comfort mantra when they had worried how they would pay the bills, or get to school or find their way in the sprawling urban jungle of New York.

"Professor Mohammed Iqbal was here earlier. He says these are verses from the Sura," García continued kindly. "Does it mean anything? Does she mean anything by it?"

"*And remember We divided the Sea for you and saved you and drowned Pharaoh's people within your very sight.*" Mustafa read aloud and then, "*Behold! How they invent a lie against God! But that by itself is a manifest sin!*" followed by "*The companions of the fire will call to the Companions of the Garden.*"

"We know what they say," said Antonio patiently. "But what do they mean?"

"I don't know," said Mustafa looking up at them. "I don't know. They aren't particular to us. These are not verses Rashida and I have ever looked closely at."

"Yet Rashida knows them?"

"Of course. Of course. We are Muslims. We learn the Holy Qur'an off by heart. I can recite it all. So can Rashida."

Wow, García thought. He knew most of Lorca's poems, but the Holy Qur'an, in its entirety? He knew the Imam could recite the Holy Qur'an, it was a Muslim leader's duty, but ordinary people able to recite it? That was impressive.

"What about this one then," asked Antonio, pointing at, *those who are really weak and oppressed, men women and children, who have no means in their power*.

"Again, I don't know," Mustafa suddenly looked near break point. "I don't know what she means. She wants us to have faith, she is talking about the children. I am sure of that. But the rest..."

"OK. Thanks." García sensed Mustafa's frustration, bordering on despair and patted him on the shoulder. "Tell me. Anything else you say to each other often?"

"Such as?" Mustafa looked at him.

"I don't know. Like planting fruit trees?"
Mustafa thought for a minute and then smiled an ironic smile.

"Yes, she often says to me I should study harder and sleep less, especially when I say I want to *siesta* in the winter, when it's not that hot." García nodded, interested to find that Rashida, like him, was not big on sleep. And then Mustafa continued, "She often says to me, *you can sleep when you're dead.*" It was exactly what Marilita had used to say to him. David García had to muster all the control he had not to gasp aloud.

Vomit dripped from Rashida's teeth. She wiped her mouth on the back of her hand in bewilderment. Was she sickening for the same symptoms as the rest of them? Nausea had swept over her and she had clutched herself with one hand and a pomegranate tree with the other, before giving up to earth the small breakfast she had scavenged from the *parador*. Then, as suddenly, the ill feeling left her.

"Are you OK?" Mary was at her side, her hand on her back.

"I think so," Rashida straightened up.

"Are you getting sick like them?" Mary asked worried.

"You've noticed they're not right then," said Rashida.

"It's hard not to. The leader..."

"Who can't take his eyes off of you," Rashida said matter-of-factly. "I saw him watching you bathe."

"No! He saw me?" Mary burned crimson.

"No harm in that," said Rashida calmly. "A man can look. Hard for him not to when you take all your clothes off."

"I just had to wash, they wouldn't let me in the hotel. I felt so..."

"Shhh Mary. I'm just teasing. Why shouldn't you wash? Why shouldn't he look? I'm surprised he didn't come and talk to you."

"He does leave us all alone," Mary looked at her closely.

179

"Doesn't that strike you as odd?"

"Meaning?"

"I may be wrong. But I think, I am pretty sure he..."

"Could have you if he wanted to?" Mary flushed at her words. Rashida continued, "I think if any of them wanted any of us they could. Yet they don't." She looked at Mary quizzically making Mary wish she had never started the conversation. "And you? Do you want him?" Rashida looked at her directly. "No need to be shy. It happens. People get thrown together in high pressure situations like this. The dividing lines get blurred."

"Don't be absurd."

"Mary, listen to me. These people are sick. I think they may be dying. Three in less than two days. You would have to be a monster not to feel sympathy for them. For him. He's in over his head, and he probably knows it. If there is a connection between you, follow it, use it even, it may save us all. But be careful."

"Arabic. It's obvious," said García, thinking aloud and wondering if they had let Mustafa and Iqbal go prematurely. "The deaths were a chance. She got to write something near the bodies. She knew there were helicopters. Aerial pics. She can't risk Spanish. Arabic is a good option. Except what if one of THEM can read it? She can't risk it. It's double code. Right?" He said looking around him at the others.

"Go on," said Antonio.

"Write in Arabic. The first code. The second, write something inoffensive. A few Holy words. Easily explained away. The Hadiz so we get Mustafa. A reference to their personal lives: numbers of babies. Then more Holy scripture. But why these verses?" García looked up into the middle distance. "Numbers of children," he repeated. "Numbers," then he almost shouted, "get Mustafa on the 'phone!"

Mary knew he was never far away. There had to be some way past him. Rashida was right. Over time most hostages and captors became more united with each other than with any group on the outside. He was watching her. Maybe Rashida was right, he wanted her. If so perhaps she could get his goodwill. It was a just a case of seeking him out.

Maybe she should start with an offer of something practical. Feeding such a large group wasn't proving easy, and no-one seemed to be doing much about it. Perhaps she should cook? They'd managed to get organised enough to throw all the alcohol away, although, it seemed to Mary, if they were prepared to blow up the Alhambra, what difference did a bit of booze make? But they weren't so organised about food preparation.

She walked from the *hotel america* up the short incline to the *parador*. They were now as deserted as they had been intensively guarded earlier. She completed her quick reconnoitre of both hotels. There were plenty of tinned and dried supplies at each. Some sort of paper-wrapped sausages occupied shelf after shelf in the *parador*. She picked one up and sniffed it. Marzipan. It was a long time until Christmas she thought, they were evidently stocking up early. Some potatoes, onions, a good-sized fruit bowl at the *parador*, olives, nuts and the inevitable lentils. Soup the day before had been fairly grim. Now that she had seen for herself the extent of the larder she knew she could improve on it.

The she went to look for her colleagues. Daniel was gone, God alone knew where. He seemed to have taken it for granted that if Mary could wander around, so could he. She thought they must have figured him for a drunk and that was why they weren't that concerned, but how he was staying so drunk was a mystery to her. Knowing Daniel, he had his secret stash. He should have been an asset in this situation she thought, half grinding her teeth, not a bloody liability. Earlier when he had sat slumped sullenly at the side, nursing his hip flask she had chivvied him to try and get him to join in.

But he had just looked at her with a lopsided grin and slurred his words rhyming,

"Little Nita, who will greet her at the Pearly Gates," humming his own little accompaniment.

Before trying to find HIM to try and establish some sort of rapport, she thought she had better leave something to occupy them all. A few of the men had found spots away from the wind and in the path of the full rays of the sun. She went across to the group where Reggie Coussins was testing people in a general knowledge quiz of his own devising.

"I am going to look for the main guy," she said to them. "When this is over, we probably will still be invited to perform." Probably not, she thought, but never mind, "so while I am gone I think it would be a good idea to keep rehearsing all the Spanish lyrics so you remember them. The Lorca is really important, and, let's face it, they aren't too long and they repeat a lot. Think about the last two numbers we were going to perform and really concentrate on these verses."

"These verses that she quotes," García questioned down the phone. "Are they numbered? Like in the Bible?"

"I don't know about the Bible," Mustafa's voice came back, "but yes, they are numbered."

"What are the numbers? Do you know?"

"Yes," he said slowly. "Yes. I looked them up when I got home. Three are all number 50 in various Sura. But the fourth, the last one, is number 98 in Sura 4, Section 14. I'm quite certain. But she has left some words out. It should say *except those who are really weak and oppressed, men women and children, who have no means in their power **nor a guide** to direct their way.*"

"50 and 98. What does it mean?" García said aloud. "What

does it mean?" he repeated again to no-one in particular. "Tell me, Mustafa. When Muslims pray, they face Mecca. Yes?"

"Well yes, best guestimate."

García fancied he could hear him smile down the phone.

"How would Rashida pray in the Alhambra?"

"Easy. The Alhambra is orientated toward Mecca," then Mustafa hesitated and said, "thinking again about the photographs, I can't be sure, but I think the bodies are placed in the right orientation for Mecca." then he paused.

"Anything else Mustafa?" David García's ear was well tuned to pregnant pauses.

"Yes, well it may mean nothing," Mustafa cleared his throat, "but, at the head, is where she wrote the Hadiz. At the feet is her message to me about children, and then on the right were all the verses that have the number 50. On the left, was the one verse numbered 98. It was on its own. Is that helpful?" he asked.

García hesitated as an idea dawned and then he was astounded. Rashida was brilliant. Brilliant.

Brilliant sunshine beamed like lasers into the cold air of Sacromonte but did little to alleviate the chill. After dawn, morning was Joaquin Montez's least best time. He flexed his fingers and cleared his throat, tired from so much singing early in the day.

It was disappointing that the musical events at the Alhambra were being cancelled or postponed. Especially when they had such a good set prepared. Now better than ever. He looked toward the part of the bed Ana preferred on the snatched occasions when he could persuade her to let him take her there.

No tumbled sheets, no indent on the pillow. He threw himself onto his back and sighed. He should have made her say something to them all last night when everyone was there.

Everyone was there, including Alberto and Lola. Raúl was impatient.

"There's no point in waiting any longer. These people aren't talking. There's nothing they want."

"People always want something," David García said quietly.

"Not these people," countered Raúl. "They're monsters."

"No," said García quietly. "They are not. They want something. We just have to figure out what. Then decide if we are going to give it."

"You're making a mistake," Raúl said to García but looking at Antonio. "He doesn't understand. These people are never going to stop."

"They will stop," García said quietly again. "We just have to figure it out."

"OK wise guy," Raúl glared at him, allowing himself to be rude, knowing that as a military man he was probably beyond Antonio's reach and certainly beyond García's. "Any words of wisdom this morning?"

"Raúl," Antonio began warningly but García cut across him.

"Yes. Don't make the first mistake," said García.

"Which is?" challenged Raúl.

"Demonise the enemy. It's lazy," García had their attention. "It permits extreme thought. Then you take an extreme action." He paused and then went on, "Here's an analogy. Your car goes into a skid. Your instinct is to wrench the wheel. It intensifies the problem. You have to drive INTO the skid to get OUT of it." He cleared his throat. "People are complex. Realise that and they become very simple. Forget that, you're in trouble. Figuring this stuff out Raúl," he said meeting the blond man's eyes, "is creative, not reactive. Acting. Not reacting. It's about *becoming* them."

Antonio thought, *go David go*.

184

"Antonio?" Raúl looked at him with a challenge in his eye.

"What do we need to do?" Antonio looked past him to García.

"Back to the map. Back to the questions. Back to the one thing that's in the middle of the picture."

"The Alhambra," sang out Alberto. And David could not resist a smile.

A smile played at the edges of his mouth. Mary saw it and looked past him to what he saw. The smouldering ruins beyond the *generalife* gardens had made him happy.

"Why are you happy to see that destroyed?"

"*El mirador romántico*? Who needs it?"

And he turned on his heel and walked away.

"Away over here," pointed Alberto, standing on a chair so he could both see across the table and down onto the map. "This is the old tunnel."

"Which old tunnel?" asked García.

"I think maybe it took the water once from here," the boy pointed to the river Darro, you know, before they built the new system. Up here," he said pointing higher. "Over there," he said now pointing out of the window and over the hillside to the left of the Alhambra, above it and toward the scrubby woods, "that's the *deposito*, the new place where all the water rushes."

"The pumping station?" asked Antonio.

"Maybe. I don't know. It's like a big building with no windows, but you can hear the water rushing. Then it goes along here," he reverted back to the map, and it comes in, here." He pointed to *el mirador romántico*, or rather to where, until the night before, *el mirador romántico* used to be.

"And the tunnel, how big is it?" asked Antonio.

"I don't know."

"Can you stand in it?"

"Yes. Most of the time. Sometimes I bend."

"What about me? Can I fit?"

Alberto smiled and shook his head.

"No, I don't think so."

"You walk along all this way," García traced the side of the hill toward the *generalife*, "underground?"

"Well not always under the ground," Lola piped up. You can see out of the holes sometimes."

"What holes?"

"You know, where they dug for the gold."

"Dug for the gold?" García heard his own voice and knew it sounded almost exasperated. He felt Antonio's hand on his arm.

"That's right," Antonio said to the children. "That's right. There were mines there. Lots of mines. There's still gold up there. But mining was outlawed, I think in my father's time. So," Antonio continued the questioning, "you can go all this way, more or less under the ground, mostly standing, with the occasional view out." He looked at the children and then simplified what he had to say, "mostly standing, and sometimes you can see out the side through some holes."

"Yeah," said Alberto nodding. Lola nodded too.

"How long does that take you?"

"To get to the end?"

"I don't know. About four carrots."

"The time it takes you to eat four carrots?"

"Yeah about that."

"But he's a fast eater," added Lola. "He needs them to see."

García looked lost, but Jack Fisher grinned as Antonio, also amused, translated it to him. García had obviously not heard the one about why carrots are good for sight. The age old joke must not have arrived in New York. *After all*, Alberto would have told them, *have you ever seen a rabbit wearing glasses*?

"And then when you get to *el mirador romántico*, what happens?"

"We don't get to *el mirador romántico*."

"I thought you said..." now Antonio was growing weary of it.

"You just pointed here right?" García was back in the saddle. "Here near *el mirador romántico*, right?"

"Yeah. You see, you can't get out there because there's a wall at the end of the tunnel. Stones and things. We tried taking it down but it's very thick. There's nowhere to put anything if you pull it out. The stones just get in the way."

"So how do you get out of the tunnel?"

"We go through this window, this window in the floor, it's a bit before the wall."

"A manhole cover?"

"Yeah. And then we are in the *generalife*."

"All right." García straightened up. "All right!"

"Antonio?" It was Paula Fisher.

"Sí."

"It's Manuel on the 'phone."

García watched Antonio take the call and saw his slow smile.

"Javi," he said to them all as he replaced the receiver. "Alberto's gardener. He's on his way."

"His way is different. He sees where the world is headed and he knows something must be done."

"But this isn't going to achieve anything. This won't get him what he wants."

"You have no idea what he wants."

"Then tell me Dolores. Tell me!" Rashida almost pleaded.

"He wants us to have a home, a village, to have children, children that live. He wants the world to see how bad things have gone. Everywhere they are saving things, but they are not saving the things that count. Things like this place. What good is this place," she swept her eyes across the ancient walls, "if there's no-one left to see it?" Dolores sank back in the bed exhausted.

Rashida stood up and went to the window. It was no use pressing Dolores. Whatever she might know it was probably only half a tale. The whole thing was half a tale. And where were the bloody authorities? Where was Ángel David García? Where was her husband? Surely Mustafa must be demanding to know what was going on by now? Why was she still here? The next baby could be today or next week. How long was it going on for? How long would they have enough food? If they didn't run out of food then surely they were going to run out of things to blow up.

And sooner or later they would catch her. If not at her smoke signals, then at her Arabic or whatever else she could think of. She pulled her coat around her and shivered. Even inside it was cold. She looked out of the window. The sky was clear, but it looked like it could even snow. She took one last look at Dolores, now asleep, and decided to go and find Mary.

García believed that the latest communications from Rashida confirmed her earlier Morse message. It gave García a sense of triumph to dance his reckoning before them.

"Fifty is the number. Fifty men."

"How do you get that?" Raúl asked warily, still smarting from Antonio preferring García's approach. But García ignored him.

"Using the Hadiz was clever. It made us get Mustafa.

Only he could have understood. *Of what we long for, three were possible two are gone, one left to go*. Then that sets us up to follow numbers," he said stabbing at the verses in front of him

"All prime numbers," said Antonio.

"Or, the first three numbers," added Manuel.

"True. But I don't think either matter," said García cautiously. Then he shook his head. "It's always a problem." He gave a shallow sigh, "When to complicate things. When to keep it simple. She wants to convey number. Using the number of a verse."

"Three times? So it would be one hundred and fifty then?" someone chirped.

"I don't think so." García shook his head, now looking at Raúl, "She gave us fifty in smoke. Now it is written. The repetition is for emphasis. And it's on the RIGHT side, i.e. FACTS, but here, on the LEFT, this may be feelings..."

"Keep it simple you say!" barked Manuel. "This is just psycho-babble."

"Maybe. I don't know," replied García. "Maybe I'm reaching here. Seeing beyond what's there..."

Antonio interrupted.

"You said that Mustafa said there was a phrase missing."

"Yes," García nodded slowly and consulted his notes. "*nor a guide to direct their way*," he quoted.

"If they each know the Holy Qur'an off by heart, why would she leave that out?" Antonio said aloud.

García fixed him with his gaze and said,

"Maybe they have no leader?"

"Great," interjected Raúl, sarcastic. "No leader, no weapons, just enough charges to blow everything sky high."

"But worth considering," García had said looking up at him from under his brows, "wouldn't you say?"

Antonio had marvelled at David García's leaps of thought. Rashida Santiago wouldn't use prime numbers or a simple one, two, three. García was right: she wasn't that sort of a girl. How, without even meeting her, did García figure that out? Albeit, the woman was a scientist, but David seemed to have had no trouble in understanding that she was a *social* scientist, and therefore at the centre of her science was people.

A message from her would be about people and the codes she would use would be humanistic. If it was true they had a number now, and if it were true there was no real force behind this number, then the whole operation might conclude more easily than he had feared.

García, however, looked across Antonio, straight at Raúl and had the distinct impression that the army officer was standing down.

David García was wrong.

Mary had an instinct about him heightened by her conversation with Rashida. She had an inkling that he might like to get rid of a problem or two.

"I think you should let Rashida and me sort out the domestics," she said and he raised an eyebrow at her. "We're not sick, or tired, and I think you have enough to be thinking about."

"You think too much," he said.

"No I don't really," she said airily, half English, half broken Spanish, "I probably don't think enough or I would have said to do this yesterday." He looked at her, incredulous. "Rashida," she plunged on, terrified he might see through her, "is not a bad cook and I can help. Although with the amount of marzipan in the stores, it may end up being nut stew."

He stared at her.

"Nut stew?"

Yes," she said blithely. "But it may not come to that."

"What nuts?"

"All that marzipan they have in the *parador*. You know, almond paste."

When he said nothing, she thought she may as well be hung for a sheep as a lamb.

"So don't worry any more about it," she reached up and pecked him on the cheek and he jumped as if she'd burned him.

Mary walked briskly away thinking it was true that if you ever want to unnerve someone and get the upper hand, just treat them exactly the opposite to what they might expect.

She felt his eyes burn into her back, then turned and looked at him. He did not drop his gaze until she turned away.

"They expect me to be bitter. They expect me to agree. To support the war. Well they did expect it. They don't anymore," García was talking to Antonio over his disposable coffee cup, waiting outside for the gardener Javi to arrive with his police escort.

"I know. I read about it."

"Why do you read that awful publication?" García asked him.

"The NYPD gazette?" Antonio laughed. "I don't know. Something to do on the Internet in the evenings I suppose. Keeps my English dusted off. Let's me feel grateful I work in Madrid and not New York."

"For sure," David agreed with a touch of irony.

"So what happened? Why did you say that stuff?" Antonio asked.

"About the twin towers?"

"Yes," then Antonio hesitated, not knowing how hard to tread. "After all," he said euphemistically, "you had your own losses."

"Lots of people have losses. Take Rashida Santiago. She has as much right to be bitter as the next person. Parents, you told me, slow casualties of the Civil War," he shrugged.

"Still..." Antonio ventured.

"Look. It's not very complicated. I just have a good memory. No, better than that – an accurate one," García cleared his throat. "Marilita, my daughter. She was on the force. Less than a year. Her mother and I," he hesitated and then said, "María and I. We were divorced. A long time ago. We were always close. We still are. We are cousins. We married when we were kids. We had Marilita. I was eighteen. Hard to imagine. Eighteen and raising a kid. The Hispanic way." García punched out the last sentence as though it were in quotes. "I bet you were the same huh?"

Antonio nodded. "All of us in our family."

"She made the force. We were pleased for her." David continued. "Marilita was the apple of my eye. Always." Then García scrunched up his cup, stopped for a minute and went on, "I was at home. Just pulled four nights in a row. In that funny turnaround stage. You know. Trying to get straight in time for doing days again. I saw the planes hit. I knew. Then and there. I knew she was gone. I put my clothes on. I went straight down town. Flashed my badge. And you know what? My first thought was *I am right. She's gone.* I was butted right up close to it. My face was right in it. My next thought? *I would not wish this on my worst enemy.* The days followed on. I can't much remember what we did or said. But I never forgot that second thought. I had many other thoughts. Anger, of course." García shrugged. "Christ, I hardly need tell you. But that first thought. That first sensation. After the certainty she was gone. *I would not wish this on my worst enemy.* I always remembered it."

"And then you..."

"And then I opened my big mouth," he smiled wanly across at Antonio. "I said we could do better than go to war. I said other responses were worth examining. And then well...."

"It wasn't the right time for new ideas?" suggested

Antonio.

"No. It wasn't. Not when the old ideas work so well," García said with bitter irony. "And of course it was..." He gave a short rueful laugh. "It was very un-American. When did that happen I wonder?" he continued as if speaking to himself. "When did questioning government become wrong?"

"What would you have had them do?"

García switched to English. He still smarted at the thought of the response to his declared 'heresy'. Antonio had read about it but he may as well protect himself from anyone who might be listening. He may as well avoid falling foul of the Spanish police force as well.

"The government? Maybe ask *what's your complaint? You have 24 hours to make one. Then we're going to bomb the life out of you*. Rather than, *we don't negotiate with terror.* You know Antonio," he said fixing him with his eyes, "if history teaches us anything, it is this," he paused, "in the end, everyone does have to negotiate. It comes down to numbers. How many people. How many places. How much is destroyed before that negotiation takes place."

"And it comes down to careers." Fisher's voice cut in as he joined them.

"Careers?" repeated Antonio thinking it was cynical of the Englishman to imagine that policemen might put their careers before safety.

"Yes," said Fisher. "I never worked on anti-terrorism but a lot of my colleagues have. Especially when I was working in London. The problem with terror is that terrorists themselves can't give it up. And not for political reasons or because of conviction."

"What do you mean?" García asked.

"The longer people work in the terror business, the more investment they have in the activity. It becomes their job, their career. What we found during all the years of trying to advance peace in Northern Ireland is that there was a whole generation of men who knew nothing else. Their 'work' defined them. They were no more able to give up their job, their expertise, than any other man. They simply did not know anything else. Over twenty years or so, they had become, in effect, career terrorists."

"And so...?" Antonio posed.

"So nothing really. Just that whoever is up there," he nodded toward the Alhambra, "this is what they do. But there is a danger it may have become who they are. The situation is then different. Instead of being an acute situation needing an acute response, it becomes a chronic one."

"Needing a chronic response?" suggested Antonio with a half amused smile.

"Something more subtle than a military assault I suppose is what I mean."

"So in this situation?" it was García's turn to ask a question.

"Alberto's gardener Javi is as good as any place to start."

"To start with, Fernando will never agree and neither will *Papá* or *Tio*. Or anyone in the family."

"We can ask."

"Joaquin!"

"We should ask Ana. You want to live a lie forever?"

"Sometimes the truth costs too much."

"People die for the truth Ana."

"Like I say," she said with her characteristic shrug of the shoulders, "sometimes the truth costs too much."

"It's all we have."

"You always say stuff like that."

"What we have inside, Ana. I am talking about what you know about yourself. It's the only thing you can be sure of."

"You can be sure of me."

"Then ask him. Ask Fernando. Then I can be sure of you.
Or tell him. Or let me."

"Let me see." Javi was bent over the table. "Yes, the kid's right.
It comes out, here, just below the *el mirador romántico*."

"I want to just ask you a few things about the Alhambra."
García began.

"Sure."

Javi was nervous, García could see that. An older, smallish,
strong man with weather-beaten skin and deep-set lively eyes,
he probably felt out of his depth with all the big brass of the army
and police. He had grown up under Franco, maybe wasn't that
comfortable with authority, probably hadn't had a great education.
García could tell that he was a bit thrown by the Cuban accent as
well, had his head cocked from time to time obviously finding it
hard to follow everything García was saying.

Antonio had wanted David to do the questioning. Maybe for
that very reason. Or maybe so that he and Raúl could watch the
effect of the questions. David tried to modify the Cuban twang.

"There's a lot goes on in the Alhambra day to day. Right?"

Javi nodded.

"What sorts of things? What important things keep the
place going?"

"Well ticket sales. We need those. That's what pays for
things."

"Sure. And what else?" David nodded, knowing only too
well that ticket sales alone would not be meeting the costs of
maintaining the huge edifice. "What things come in and go out?
Besides money and people?"

"Well, there are deliveries to the hotels, most days stuff
gets delivered, beer, butter, bread. You know, regular stuff."

"Chemicals?" asked David.

"No. Well, some. Not a lot."

"Weed killers and things?" he pressed.

"Naw. We're the weed killers." Javi tried a joke.

"OK. How many of you are there?" asked David, aware of Raúl behind him, staring a hole in his back.

"Well, about thirty. There's about eight of us on staff, last year eleven."

"So how do you get to thirty?"

"We get contractors in."

Antonio made a mental note to see if there was a connection between contractors, explosives and netting. That was likely how it had all been brought on site.

"Any other contractors work on site?"

"Sure. Construction guys, you know, those new guys that were building the amphitheatre for this year's *festivales*. They were there until a month ago. I guess that's not happening now right?"

"Well, not unless we can get this cleared up in a few days," murmured Manuel with a touch of sarcasm.

"Others?" continued García.

"Let's see. Ticket staff, no, they're employees, so are the *patronato* staff, the *archivo* staff. We have some restoration guys in for the aqueducts and the drains. Security. They're all contractors."

Antonio raised his eyes heavenward. Contracted-out security for Chrissake. For Chrissake!

"What sort of tools do you keep?"

"On site?"

"Yeah. On site."

"Everything."

"Can you be more specific?"

"Rotovators, um, shears, lawn mowers..."

"Petrol?" interrupted Manuel.

"Sure. Meths, turps, and, I don't know, all the stuff you need."

"Saws?"

"Sure."

"This stuff locked up?" interrupted Antonio.

"Yeah."

"What sort of lock?"

"Padlock. Usual sort."

García thought this was getting them nowhere. Javi was half scared to death and, to be honest, who gave a shit about methylated spirits or petrol when they had Primaflex and detonators?

"I was thinking about the Alhambra," David cut across Antonio and said to Javi, "as though it were a living breathing real live creature."

Javi turned and looked at him and said,

"It is."

"What do you think then? What is the most important thing about it?"

"That makes it live and breathe?"

"Yeah. You know, the heartbeat."

"Other than the people?"

"Yeah, other than the people," agreed García.

"Other than the plants and the trees?"

García could see that this was going to go into a game of elimination and he was more than happy to play.

"Other than the plants and trees."

"More than the birds and the cats?"

"Yeah more than them," García agreed. "The special thing. The thing that sets it apart," García probed and then added, "In your opinion, Javi."

"Well that's easy."

"Cool. What then?"

"It's the water."

It's the water that's killing them, maybe? It's a possibility," Rashida confided to Mary. "It's the only thing that makes sense. It's been poisoning them."

"It's not possible," said Mary. "They've lived in too many places, I know it. Dolores talks of Galicia, Nita was from there too, you said the news talked about them having been part of the atrocities in Barcelona."

Rashida shook her head.

"I don't think so. I don't think these guys are involved in that stuff. On the news they also talked about Rafael. I've seen his photo scores of times. But I don't think Rafael is here or we would have seen him by now. I wonder if they just made that up to tell people, to give people something to satisfy them."

"Where are they all anyway?" Mary asked noticing the paucity of men prowling.

"Well I think when you told them we'd take care of domestics they believed us."

"It's weird, isn't it, how they've just left us to get on with it?" murmured Mary.

"What else can they do?" Rashida looked around her. "I don't think they know what they are doing any more."

"If they ever did," Mary assented.

"I think these guys are sick. Even the men. Really sick."

"So why aren't we? Why isn't my choir?"

"Poisoning is cumulative. Well, some poisoning I mean." Rashida chewed her lip thoughtfully. "Slow poisoning I'd say. Any poisons they have ingested they probably ingested a long time ago and over a long time too. Very likely this entire environment is entirely healthy."

"But not for them," said Mary

"Hard to say. But I would say they are in a bad way. I wonder how long they've got. I would guess not long."

"What makes you think so?"

"Still births," said Rashida. "Dreadful skin colour, ridges on the fingernails, bad gums, lack of concentration."

"But enough concentration to blow stuff up."

"A concentration fuelled more by will power than anything else. It takes a long time to die from chronic poisoning. But I would say they were nearly there."

"How long does it take?" asked Mary.

"Years."

"Years from now people will look at this weekend and we will be judged by it," Raúl was steaming.

"Well let's hope not," said Manuel spitting out some *pipas* shells.

García looked from one to the other. There was something typically public official about both of them he thought. Unimaginative. That was always the trouble about public officials in situations like this. Someone gave an order. And inevitably someone followed it.

He looked past them toward Antonio. He was in the incident room on the phone yet again, a cigarette on the go as always. García was struck again by his patience, his measured approach and felt fortunate that he was leading the operation. In the hands of a lesser man it would have already gone badly wrong. It might still, but García thought there was a chance, a slim one, that there might be a surprise ending.

As far as García could see there might be enough wild cards in the deck that the conclusion was still not foregone. Alberto and Lola and Javi were all bunched near the window with their heads together. García looked at the three of them. They were wild cards if anything was. And so by God, with her smoke signals and her Arabic, was Rashida Santiago.

"Well," said Antonio joining him. "The 'head honcho', as you call him, David, is on his way. His flight got into Barajas from Sydney two hours ago, he's a short hop away."

"Good news," said García.

"Yeah. However it seems we have a few problems more locally," said Antonio in English for Fisher's benefit.

"Surprise me," replied García

"You can see for yourself. Look."

Jack and David followed his pointing finger and looked through the window to the right, toward the town centre.

"What am I looking for?" asked Fisher.

"Traffic."

"Traffic?"

"Yep. Traffic. Seems like everyone in Spain is coming to watch the bonfire."

"Assuming there will be one."

"Well we haven't disappointed them so far, have we?" said Antonio with tart sarcasm. "Jack, I am wondering if you might want to go and be with the rest of the choir who are all still in town and get them on a flight out. There is nothing they can do here for those left in the Alhambra."

"Absolutely. Can we get a car into the city?"

Antonio beckoned to Manuel to instruct him. Then he put his hand on García's shoulder in a typically demonstrative Spanish gesture. "Back to the map my friend," he said encouragingly as García moved away from under his hand.

"And to the three of them," García said, indicating Alberto, Lola and Javi. "In this operation I am thinking of them as our wild cards.

"Wild cards in life are what make it worth living. David has always said that." María was propped on one elbow, watching O'Reilly's profile. "He says they are the things you can never predict and that make life interesting. I think you are a wild card for me," she said tracing her fingers across his chest.

O'Reilly found it incredible that he was lying in bed with this woman and listening to her talk lovingly about a man he hated. A man who represented a lifestyle he abhorred, and yet at the same time, through her, he was coming to, if not like, then at least know.

He was surprised he didn't mind listening to her talk about David García. The truth was, he hadn't felt this good in years. He probably wouldn't have minded what she talked about. María was delightful. Delightful was the word he had kept turning around over and over in his head. She was beautiful, and mysterious, and plain speaking, and, for his jaded police palate, entirely refreshing. And if she had HEAT, well, it was a heat that warmed him, even made him hot. He felt his groin stirring again. Unbelievable.

On the other hand, through her, this virtual proximity to García made O'Reilly uncomfortable. He liked hating García. It had long been a fixture in his life, something from which he took his bearings. If his perceptions were shifting then he felt something that he could best describe as a feeling of being at sea. And, on top of all that he was just plain apprehensive. García was away. What would happen when García came back? What would happen when his own wife found out? Or more likely his daughter Colleen, or his boys? Or even María's boys? Already he was trying to second-guess the future. Perhaps he should adopt a 'wild card' belief. Certainly life had dealt him María. Maybe it would deal him something else unexpected, like a solution?

"Have you heard from him?" he asked her, surprised to find that he was genuinely interested to know.

"No. He won't call."

"How come?"

"He never calls anyone when he's on a job. He says he has to concentrate, become someone else in order to get into the mind of other people. When he worked on that job at City Central Bank, you remember, he was gone for four days non-stop. Everyone knew he was working on it and Marilita and I were scared to death. But he never checked in with anyone." she paused. "That was always a big problem between him and Richard."

"Did you mind about Richard?" he asked softly.

"Yes and no," she twisted off her elbow and lay back on the bed, staring at the ceiling. "In some ways I was too young to really know at first what was going on. Then by the time I figured it out I could see it was much worse for David. Harder to *be* David than to be married to him.

"I had known David all my life. Played with him from birth. You can't just cut that off. I think that was why it was OK. Because I never doubted that he loved me, it was just that he didn't love me like that.

"But I did mind about Richard in that I didn't like him much toward the end. I mean I met him right at the beginning and at the time I thought he was OK. But then, with hindsight, I'm not so sure."

"You met him at the beginning? Really? How?"

"He invited us all over a few times."

"Whilst screwing your husband? Jesus."

"No. It wasn't like that. It was quite innocent. Well for David it was. Maybe Richard was always keen on him. Probably," she said. "David wasn't very experienced then. We were both virgins when we married. Obviously."

O'Reilly couldn't quite accede to the *obviously* part. He had lost his virginity when he was fourteen and then had been at it pretty much every opportunity until he married. After the wedding he was faithful in a determined Irish Catholic manner

202

until finding his wife fornicating with the delivery boy. Then O'Reilly resurrected his ability to perform often and quickly, and across a wide populace.

"So what was he like, Richard?"

"Self-possessed. Rich. Good-looking. Educated. Fair, aristocratic English type. Everything we were not."

"Don't sell yourself short."

She smiled at him.

"Whatever polish I have now, believe me, it was non-existent when I was nineteen and twenty," she laughed. "Now, looking back, I see that David must have appealed, so dark and with his lean young body. I see now that he was probably any gay man's fantasy. But then I was too stupid to see it."

"You are anything but stupid María."

"You know what I mean," she turned toward him. "And I think that's why I came not to like Richard. From the beginning he was insincere. He played on my stupidity, and on David's innocence. Don't get me wrong Eddie. David was gay. He was always going to find that out and that was always going to impact us. I have no illusions about that. But I don't think Richard was ever a very loving person, obviously not to me, and not to Marilita either, and I felt he should have been to Marilita. She was lovely Eddie," her voice broke.

"I know she was," O'Reilly put his arm around her. "She was always a great kid. You should be proud of her. I know Colleen misses her."

"Me too. Me too," María turned into his shoulder and was quiet for a while. Then she said, "Richard should have been loving toward Marilita, out of respect for David, if nothing else. But most of all, he should have been loving to David. David deserved better."

"So why did they stay together?"

"David's very loyal. And David loved Richard. And in the

end, you don't choose love. Love, if you are lucky, chooses you, don't you think?"

"Don't you think it's time we went in?"

"Very likely," Antonio replied to Raúl reluctantly, "Although, what interests me," he said turning to an older man at the table, "is how all these charges got laid. That might help us with our options."

Dr Jesús Garrido Lopez rolled up his sleeves and stepped forward. Little Alberto stepped forward with him. As Director of the *patronato* of the Alhambra, Jesús had overall cognisance of the entire monument. He stood tall and lean with an aesthetic authority. He rubbed his eyes, clearly a little jet-lagged from a long flight, adjusted his glasses, and cleared his throat to say,

"This is a grave day for the Alhambra," and he looked toward the monument, to the holes in its side, the ruins of *el mirador romántico* and *la torre del cabo*.

García's heart sank. *Oh no*, he thought, *a negative pompous functionary. Not a practical atom in his body. Doom.*

Dr Jesús continued, "But we have withstood worse than this. There isn't a lot we have not withstood over the centuries," he spoke as if he, personally, had lived at the Alhambra since the Romans. "Don't worry people. She has her secrets, and I know some them, and together she shall be delivered."

Fantastic, García revised his thoughts immediately, *Another wild card in the deck.*

"Can you help us with any information about the laying of the charges, along here Sir?" Raúl was painstakingly polite.

Jesús Garrido Lopez peered at the photos before him with the Primaflex cord overwritten in pink highlighter pen.

"Along here?" he asked.

"Yes. Has there been drilling along here? You mentioned

that there had been construction in the amphitheatre of the *generalife*. Have you had work done here?"

"**A** small tour of the city is out of the question," Fisher told them all. "The best you can do to be helpful is go home. Your return flights are booked for tomorrow."

"But what are we to do while we are waiting?" a querulous voice asked.

God save me from my countrymen thought Fisher, and then said aloud, "There is nothing to be done here. Any developments concerning your fellow singers in the Alhambra will be notified to the consulate and then to the Home Office. You are free of course to come and go from the hotel, but tourist activity has been suspended and tourists are being discouraged from coming."

That's a masterpiece of understatement, thought Paula, and then added to her husband's small speech.

"They're trying to close the roads, there are so many people flocking toward Granada. If anything happens between now and your flights tomorrow then obviously Jack or I will let you know."

Someone from the British press stepped forward, thrust a microphone under Fisher's nose and asked,

"PC Fisher, you and your wife were here on holiday. How does it feel to be at the centre of this huge event?"

"Well," said Fisher laconically, "I think the people inside the Alhambra are probably the ones at the centre of the event."

"But you were here as a private citizen," the reporter pressed on, "you must have some feelings about being drafted in. I mean it's not your field after all."

"Helping to run an incident room is pretty much within the gift of most policemen. Nothing special there." Jack was pleasantly dismissive.

"So how would you describe your experience PC Fisher?"

Another reporter had pressed forward.

"I suppose you could say I was in the right place at the right time."

"I suppose you could say I was in the right place at the right time."

The picture changed on the screen and the TV newsreader said,

"That was Lisa Collins reporting live from Granada where the hostage situation of the York Constantine Singers in the Alhambra continues. We will bring you more updates as the evening goes on. And now, Manchester United's shock tactics..."

Carmen Romero stood up and switched off the TV.

"Typical Jack," Ange Fisher said from her perch next to the children on the sofa. "Only Jack could describe an interrupted holiday and taking responsibility for trying to sort out an awful terrorist siege as being *in the right place at the right time*.

"How are the families taking it?" Carmen asked, aware that Ange, as a former police officer would have some inside knowledge.

"They're worried. There's no news from the Spanish authorities. Like Paula said yesterday, it's a lot of waiting."

"I wonder if The Constantine Singers will ever want to perform again," mused Carmen.

"They will," Chico affirmed on his way with the other children to raid the kitchen.

"No news of Daniel though," Ange ventured.

"I know," said Carmen quietly. "They must be bored," said Ange, "with so much time on their hands."

Chico spoke up from the kitchen, ears on stalks as usual.

"They're probably singing, *Mamá*," he said.

afternoon

"He said he had found a secret stash." Reggie verified Mary's fears when she returned without Daniel and enquired if anyone had seen him. "He thinks it will tide him over." Reggie rolled his eyes at her.

"That's all we need," said Mary and set off once again for the *parador.* If there was any booze left it would be there, and so would Daniel.

Alberto was clear: Agustín and Rosario had always been there when Alberto and Lola needed them. Now they needed him. Alberto decided that he and Lola would have to go to them, even if the walls were very steep. As if reading his mind Dr Jesús was shaking his head and saying,

"The walls here are very steep," then he added, "And the walls are also double." Dr Jesús drew his finger along the entire north face. "We haven't had to do any repairs here for a long time. Not since I have been in post, certainly. There have been some erosion problems in the past. I think there were some works done about twenty years ago to line the channel here. You can see that down here there is a gully at the foot of the walls, the water runs along here."

"What water?"

"The water that is left over, the discard, after the fountains, gardens and everything have had their requirements. It runs under the ground from the main channel, then under the walls here and here, and then out where it forms this stream that runs alongside *la cuesta de los chinos* all the way down into town and then rejoins the River Darro. Then," he continued, "you follow this on the inside. Here, at the top level of the walls, here are some of the public walkways, and here," he said pointing to spaces where there appeared to be no trees, "here are the paths to and from the palaces. Look." He pointed out the gardens and pathways that García vaguely remembered from his visit with Richard. "But between this outer wall, where these towers are, here," he stabbed at the map with his finger.

"Destroyed," Manuel reminded them.

"Then just along here is *la torre de las infantas*, then you have *la torre de la cautiva*, followed by, here, *la torre del cadi*, right up to *la puerta del arrabal*."

"But they're all wired to blow," Manuel persisted.

"What is the extent of our options?" asked Antonio.

"What about Alberto?" fired García. "What tunnel systems exist? Or is Alberto's tunnel the only one?"

"Between these towers, which connect the outer wall, and these upper pathways, there is a deep ravine, a walkway."

"I know that. I've walked along there, well, we both have," said Alberto.

"You have?" asked Dr Jesús.

"Yes."

"How did you get there?" Dr Jesús looked from Alberto to García and Antonio. "This deep ravine here," he said shaking his head, "it's not open to the public, well not now at least. It hasn't been for years."

"We shimmied in."

"Shimmied in?"

"Yes, we slid down this part. Where the water runs."

"Ah!" said Dr Jesús admiringly. "You followed the discard chute here? Under the ground, and then across this channel, yes?"

"Yes."

"And then what?" Dr Jesús asked the boy. "It's too narrow here to get under the wall."

"It used to be, but now they are digging."

"You're right." Dr Jesús nodded. "He's right, isn't he Javi?"

"Yes Sir. It's that time of year again."

210

"What time of year?" asked Antonio.

"Every year," answered Javi, "We have to do a routine clearance of all the drainage channels. Especially those that interface with the outside. Things get caught in them, leaves, sticks and branches, dead animals."

"And every year, the channels get bigger?" García guessed.

"A bit. Yes," said Javi. "That would be fair to say. And as they don't form part of the archaeological heritage of the Alhambra...

"The erosion as such, well," Dr Jesús interrupted, "it's not an issue really. These channels are for effluence only and at the perimeter."

"What was this deep gorge between the walls used for then?"

"Alberto's right, it is like a walkway, more than a ravine. It was mainly to provide extra fortification, to double the walls, so if the outer were breached then there was another wall, and from that inner wall it was easy to kill the intruders who were then caught in this space in between."

"And then finally where does it lead to?"

"Well it used to lead right into the *alcazaba*, here on the right of *la torre de la vela*, but it's hard to say now since the explosion. I've looked through the binoculars. I can't see how much of the stonework is gone or where it has fallen. I imagine that the blast will have cut off this walkway from the palaces."

"The gullies," said García flatly. "Who has been clearing them?"

"To be honest I don't know. I would have to consult the records."

"Would it be contracted staff or in-house staff?" Antonio pressed.

"Contracted. Almost certainly. Usually it would be the gardeners."

"So," García said quietly, "not the engineers? The guys working on the amphitheatre?"

"I don't think so. To be honest, I don't know. I don't walk the site everyday."

"Does anyone?" asked Raúl, slightly aggressive.

"Drilling? Any drilling?" García continued.

"No." Dr Jesús now seemed flustered. "I mean I don't know. Maybe. There's a lot going on in a monument this size."

"OK." David straightened up and pulled at his shoulders. "OK."

"May I suggest we break? Five or ten minutes?" Antonio proposed.

"Yeah, that's fine by me," nodded Raúl. "I'll get some food organised. Manuel?"

"I'm going outside for a smoke," Antonio said by way of agreement. "Coming?" he added to García.

Joaquin Montez reached for his cigarettes and narrowed his eyes against the sun. There was the illusion of a fine day. A spring sun was like smoke giving the illusion of heat.

He looked at the narrow spiral he was generating from his own tobacco. Smoke wasn't the only illusion in his life. Maybe Ana was too. Maybe this staying in Sacromonte, following the family tradition of music and performance was just as much an illusion.

In the end, if she was not going to stand up with him for their child, then what was love? What did he need to do to prove to her, that he was the man she needed him to be? All she could think of was her small world, and how change of any sort would disrupt her and her life. But surely that was what a life was all about? Change. Disruption. He cast his eyes toward the sky.

See, he said to himself, *even the sun is an illusion today, there's a storm brewing or I'm not a gypsy.*

"A gypsy once told me something when my wife and I were here at the Alhambra on holidays. She was working the steps outside the Alhambra, you know, pressing bouquets of rosemary into people's hands and then begging alms." Antonio was talking and dragging on his cigarette at the same time, half watching García out of the corner of his eye, aware that the Cuban at last was tiring a little. "And she said, *here is a blessing for you and your wife – you have to live your life, losses and gains, the whole lot – but always remember, that's what it is to have a life.* I thought about that a lot when my wife died."

García noted the homespun philosophy again, cringed inwardly and said nothing. Then Antonio said,

"Tell me about Richard?"

David García usually hedged the question. Although, if Antonio had been in any doubt, thanks to García's own outburst, he now knew he was gay.

"We lived together," he answered succinctly and then when Antonio made no response David added, "I'm not much for talking. Not about my private life."

"Except when it comes to your weekend preferences for little boys," Antonio said dryly.

"Ah yes," García laughed. "That. I was annoyed."

"Evidently."

A desire to explain suddenly filled García and he said,

"Don't think I am ashamed. I'm not. I got over that years ago." *Not quite*, thought Antonio, *not quite*. "But," García continued, "there was Marilita. My daughter," he added in case Antonio was in any doubt. "Children are cruel. A queer dad? Not pretty. I wanted to protect her. And then, there was Richard. Richard's social set was different. Art galleries, antiques, interior design..."

"Rich," Antonio supplied for him.

"Yes," García agreed. "Friends more interested in your money. They don't much care who you sleep with."

"Whereas policemen on the other hand," interjected Antonio, "unless they are taking bribes, know exactly how much money each other has and," he paused with a smile, "if it is the same in New York, are eternally interested in who people sleep with."

Antonio had hit the nail on the head. David had always felt he could handle any abuse from colleagues, but he didn't see why Richard, on the pretext of a social gathering, should have to be exposed to any unpleasantness or innuendo. But since the deaths of Marilita and Richard, there didn't seem anything left to protect.

"Yeah," he nodded slowly at Antonio. "Something like that."

"Did you live with him a long time?"

"Eighteen years."

"A marriage then."

García looked at him.

"Yes," he said slowly, twisting his ring. "I suppose you could say that."

"Do you miss him?"

García was quiet for a moment and then said,

"I have become accustomed to myself."

There was a pause and then Antonio changed the subject by asking,

"What do you reckon to Alberto and his escapades?"

"He's a clever kid."

"Seems the Alhambra is penetrable by water wouldn't you say?"

Rashida was astonished to hear the call to prayer rise up over the city from the new mosque. The chaos caused by the crisis at the Alhambra must be allowing other misdemeanours to be

overlooked. It had been a condition of the planning permission for the new mosque that they were not allowed to call for prayer five times a day. In a city as noisy as Granada the call going out seemed a trivial inconvenience among the dogs, the motor bikes and constant din of humanity. But, as she had once pointed out to Mustafa, it was evidence that his so-called reversion still had a long way to go.

She went and found a quiet corner under the vaulted ceiling at the side of *la plaza de los colmares*, unwound her scarf to make a prayer mat and began her ritual. She found it hard to concentrate despite reciting the familiar words. The beauty of the Alhambra palaces was distraction enough, but she couldn't help but wonder if Mustafa was also at prayer, hearing the same call, and somehow connecting with her.

She fixed her eyes on the Arabic words all around her, allowed them to feast on the beauty of the blue and green ceramic tiles below, and then cast her glance up toward the marquetry ceiling above. If Allah lived in silence and in space, then Allah could not be far away. *Enshallah*.

Barely a few metres away in the *sala de los dos hermanos*, next *el palacio de los leones*, Dolores was taking her seat on one of the leather slung chairs, helped into position by Mary Stansfield. A *mirador* toward the outer edge overlooked the Albaicín and allowed the sun through in patches, the sky clouding here and there. Dolores had begged Mary to take her there for prayers, saying it was her favourite place.

Mary at first was surprised to have been asked. Surely Dolores could find one of her own to assist? But then Mary had looked around her. They were a lacklustre crowd, struggling most days just to dress themselves and fold blankets. Who other than Rashida was there to help? Mary had seen Rashida following her own prayer rituals when she had peeped at her through the portico of the *la plaza los colmares*.

"I think we should have prayers," Dolores had said. "Someone should lead prayers. It is Easter after all."

Then she had solicited Mary's help. Leaning into the Englishwoman the two of them had made a slow journey from the *hotel america*. Mary hoped it had not been too much and that the utterance of words she found holy would renew her strength.

Dolores turned to Mary, who nodded, saying,

"Go on. The women need to hear words of comfort."

Mary closed her eyes and heard Dolores begin to speak, praying for Nita, for Nita's soul, for Nita's baby and then at last for her own dead child. All the dead children. Then she asked for a sign that they were on the right path, asking for children, asking God to forgive them their transgressions and show them his mercy with children. She ended, her face heavenward, her hands clasped together, all the other woman in the same madonna-like position all saying together,

"Please Lord, please, send us children."

"Children!" was Manuel's answer to Antonio's question about the racket in the courtyard of San Miguel el Alto.

"Children!" cried Alberto and Lola in unison, and then jumped up to run out into the cold sun.

Antonio and Manuel followed. Antonio, seeing Lola running and shouting a welcome to the children as they disgorged from the coach, clapped his hand on Alberto's shoulder and said,

"Not so fast my little lad. What's going on then?"

"These are the kids from the *reformatorio*."

"And..."

Alberto wriggled in his grasp and said,

"And they've come back."

"Now, why might that be?" asked Antonio and when Alberto didn't answer he said, "OK. Let's talk to the driver shall we?"

He marched Alberto over to the driver. Lola came and stood beside them.

"You have brought me a coachload of children I understand," Antonio told the driver, asking him for ID at the same time. The man handed it over along with a faxed document. Antonio read it and then passed it to David García. García read it, looked at Antonio and then at Alberto.

"Look Alberto," said David almost conversationally, "It says this on *comisaría* headed paper," García read out, "*the children of the reformatorio de San Miguel el Alto should be returned to the reformatorio at the earliest convenience*. Earliest convenience," repeated García. "Very big words. I wonder who wrote this?"

Alberto said nothing and kicked at a stone.

"Actually I did," said Lola. "It's my best writing."

"But," said Alberto, not to be outdone, "I faxed it. I got the number from Ronda and then last night I snuck in here and just sent it. I'd watched people sending them all day. It was easy," he ended.

The competitiveness of the two children reminded García of Lorca's poem about Paquiro and his brother in El Café de Chinitas... García wasn't sure which of these two was the more brave, although he was pretty sure neither was a bullfighter nor, with their mops of red curly hair, gypsy either. He reviewed the letter again. It was such a childish hand that García couldn't believe that it had been taken at face value. But then he remembered, there were plenty of older Spaniards who wrote poorly. Pre-democracy not much store had been put by education.

"Very nice writing indeed," García said to Lola indulgently, and then, "was there some reason to invite everyone back?"

"Back to York. That's the best thing for them all." Fisher was talking to Paula as they rechecked the flight timings. "Dinky," he said, referring to his boss, Michael Small, "thinks we should stay on until it's over, although he's worried we've run up quite a bill. He'll be relieved when I tell him we've been sleeping in a reform school."

"Have you checked with Ange?"

"Yep. She and Carmen have it covered."

"Until it's over." Paula chewed her lip thoughtfully. "That sounds a bit final. Do you think they will get out?"

Jack Fisher had been waiting for this question from Paula for a day. And now she had asked it.

"I think García and Marín are going at it steadily. I think this whole thing is in good hands."

"And the army? And prioritising the building over the hostages?"

"Neither García nor Marín are hotheads Paula."

"No. But they aren't really in charge either," she said. When Fisher was silent she pressed, "You haven't answered my question. Do you think they will survive?"

Fisher looked at his wife and tried to square in his own mind his determination never to lie to her and his desire to offer comfort.

"I don't know," he said at last. "On the surface I would say it doesn't look good."

"I was afraid of that," Paula replied in a small voice.

"But I have always been big on hope," Jack continued. "What worries me about the whole thing, is also what gives me hope."

"Which is?"

"The fact that there have been no demands. The fact that we have no idea who they are, or what they are doing, or why they are doing it. Since there are still so many variables, it has meant that the response has been slow, jumbled and, dare I say, Quixotic... You know," he smiled at her, "when I started The Job I thought I could control things, make society better. Put the bad guys away and keep the good guys safe. But the longer I work in the Job the more I think, not only can you not actually get to the bad guys very often, you can't put them away either. Even when you do, more often than not they get off and are back on the streets. Until people change how they think, we are never going to get much further."

"So it's all hopeless?" Paula asked

"No," he said, and then, "Maybe. Hell I don't know. I suppose all I am saying is that since the Festival of Angels I have grown up a bit."

"Why?"

"Why? Well I suppose because we were at the mercy of other people whose motives were so hidden and so complicated. I still wonder if even they had begun to lose track of why and what they were doing. Policing can control actions to a limited extent. But we have no control over what people think. And that's what makes people act."

"Maybe you are in the wrong job," Paula quipped. "Perhaps you should have been a politician."

"You know," Jack continued, waving her teasing away with a smile, "we were talking last night, just before the explosions, Antonio and García and I. I was remembering the Festival of Angels. They asked me about it. I didn't know where to begin to tell them what it was like. Mostly I just wanted them to know that somehow this and that are similar."

"You and David García are similar too."

"No!" Fisher exclaimed instantly.

"You are. Not on the surface. He's much more controlled than you are. And his way of speaking with all those short sharp sentences is brusque and he's..."

"So much more handsome, I know, Latin looks..." it was Jack's turn to tease.

219

"Well yes, there is that," Paula conceded. "But you are similar. Both men of principle. I like him. I like Antonio too."

"And Raúl?" asked Jack.

"Hard to know. I don't instantly warm to him," Paula replied. "But then I haven't spent as much time with him. But if pressed? Rather than be negative, probably I would say he was trying too hard."

"Hands down!" Manuel's voice rang out stridently. He felt exasperation at the prospect of answering the questions of a coachload of children. All he wanted to know was who to ask for when he rang Ronda. He wanted to get the nuns to come back and to take care of this sorry lot. That little red-haired monkey was going to be in trouble, big time. What on earth had got into him to instruct all these kids to be returned?

"It's never a problem." Dr Jesús indicated the *secano* and adjusted his glasses. "Of course we have dry years," he said waving his hand across the maps. "I mean this year has been a challenge, yes, Javi?"

"More than most," said Javi. "We didn't get the storms in September or October that we should have had. The water table is very low. Although," he said looking at the sky, "I think we might be in for some rain soon."

"So how do you compensate for a dry season?"

"Well we have the rights to draw water off the River Darro. It's the Alhambra's water. As you saw, it comes into the *generalife*, but then it goes into the main compound."

"Right, where the excess water drains off halfway through, yes?" asked Antonio.

"Not exactly," Dr Jesús said. "It's a bit more complicated

than that. Did you say the gates at *la torre del agua* had been secured?"

He was referring to the main entrance to the compound after the ticket barrier, between the pathway to the *generalife* and the *archivo*.

"Yes. Those gates are closed."

"God knows how they managed that," said Dr Jesús to Javi. "They are a real bastard to get closed." The profanity, delivered so genteelly, surprised and amused García. "But," Dr Jesús continued, "Maybe all this dry weather has made them fit together better."

"And the new gates at the *la puerta de los carros*, they're closed too," García added.

"Really?" Dr Jesús seemed impressed. "I really fought for those gates to be replaced," he said looking around him and speaking to everyone as though he was giving a lecture. "There had been gates there in the 1800s but then they fell apart finally. We had drawings of them and a few terrible photographs. The stone hinges had remained. And the big metal clasp where the latches slotted through? The clasp is thin, but still in working order, so when we got that last big grant through from the Museums' Trust we spent some on new gates. And now they're being used to keep you out. Well I never!" Dr Jesús seemed delighted that his new addition to the monument was proving to be of worth.

"Well I'm glad you're pleased Sir," said Raúl, somewhat caustically, "but we don't seem much further forward."

"On the contrary. I think the compound is quite secure. The gates and the walls are doing their job well."

"We don't quite see it like that Sir."

"No, well you wouldn't, of course," Dr Jesús replied to Raúl, "but if the compound is secure then you know what you're up against and what you need to do."

"And that would be?" asked Antonio.

"Well you're up against a fixed structure," he said looking

221

over his glasses at them, and you need to think about what is fluid: namely the water and where it crosses the Alhambra."

"Back to water," García said out loud.

Then he thought morosely, of Lorca and his description of a cross in the distance, how it was reflected in the water like mere dots, somehow suspended. People were 83% water he remembered being told once. Where people crossed each other, where their lives crossed, where the Cross of Christ featured, where the water crossed into the Alhambra; which interpretation of the cross mattered? For Lorca was right. There was always the end, some distant dot, refracted in any moving channel of water, just some dot dancing on the surface. Marilita was very likely 83% water, and she had just been a dot. Suspended, he supposed, for a nanosecond, between here, now, and the end of her road. A voice cut across his thoughts.

"We need that boy back I think," said Dr Jesús.

"If Jesus has any love for us he will bring us through this," Mary was appalled to hear Reggie say. She might have been moved to see Dolores with her clasped hands praying for children. Lord knows she had cause. But God help her if born again Christians were now burrowing their way out of the woodwork. Another extremist was just what they needed! She excused herself to go and find Rashida. At the very least they would need to raid the *parador* again if they were going to get a hot meal organised today.

She marvelled again at the freedom she now had to move around the entire monument. No-one seemed to notice, never mind stop her. She allowed herself to deviate a couple of times, once toward *la puerta de los carros*, hoping that she might slip through, but the gates, twenty feet high at the very least, were shut fast. Similarly the gates at *la torre del agua*, the main thoroughfare from the Alhambra palaces to the gardens of the *generalife*, were also closed.

She saw Rashida wandering below her on the terraces by the *palacio yusef III*, winding her scarf around her head and pulling her jacket down. She whistled at her and Rashida looked up, putting her finger across her lips while she continued along the terrace behind the *hotel america* and *patronato* buildings until she dropped out of sight. Mary wondered if she was trying to take a back route to the *parador* and cut out *calle real* altogether.

The light was fading, and it was becoming overcast. Rashida might be trying to find her way to the *generalife*, back to *el mirador romántico,* to try to get more smoke signals going. Mary wanted to tell Rashida that *la torre del agua* had been shut off since the night before, with the same tall thick wooden gates as the *la puerta de los carros* and that there was no way she was going to get up into the *generalife*.

Through his binoculars he could see her now. She walked as if she were floating. In fact the insubstantial quality of her appearance had characterised her from the start. Her hair, like some orange mist around her face, her scarf, usually around her shoulders but trailing nonetheless, her white skin, her huge eyes. A wraith, a witch, an angel.

Yet she was far from insubstantial. Her touch on his arm had told him that. And, when Nita's baby had been wrapped in rags and string, he had watched her helping the midwife, each move long and lingering on the infant's body, like a caress, and he had felt a jolt of energy shoot through him. The first time he had felt energy of any sort in a very long time.

The thing was, everything seemed insubstantial, that was the truth of it. But her version was luminous. The light shone, almost as she moved. Substance and light.

He wiped a grubby hand across his forehead. He must be losing it, he thought, and so must Jay... She was just a foreigner, and an enemy at that. He had to stamp these feelings out. He needed to focus on the frustrations of no response from the outside.

Maybe even that was her fault? Maybe she was why there was nothing coming back the other way? Maybe the English were at the root of this like they were at the root of so much.

Perhaps he might head her off at the *parador* and let her know who was boss.

At the *parador* there was no sign of Rashida. As for Daniel, who knew where he had got to? Maybe he was getting booze from his secret stash. Once again Mary Stansfield went into the deserted hotel. The electric doors had been propped open for so long now that leaves had blown in from the trees outside and were in piles along the carpet. Daniel was nowhere to be seen. Nor was HE.

She checked the kitchens. The store cupboard doors were open. Everything was as it had been in the morning except for one thing: the marzipan was gone. All of it. How strange.

Mary set back down *calle real* with a sinking sense of disappointment and took a sharp right, into the compound of the *patronato,* and skirted round the outside wall close to the boundary and ravine. At last at *la torre del cadi* she saw that Rashida was tucked in against the red brickwork. What was she doing? Mary crept nearer and although it was quite a distance, her line of sight was unbroken and she tried to get Rashida's attention.

"I think we should just stay here and see what she does next, don't you?" purred a voice in her ear, putting a hand over her mouth and pulling her back against him.

And to her horror Mary watched while Rashida seemed to empty her pockets and crouch over what was rapidly obvious as a small fire.

"Ah, the poor little Musselman is cold," she heard him say behind her. "We'll have to try and warm her up." Mary did the only thing she could think might work and relaxed against him. Almost immediately she felt him lose tension. Then she gave a thrusting dig behind her with her elbow, bit hard on the fleshy mound of his palm and pushed backwards.

For a split second she thought he had the better of her, then he lost balance, fought to regain it and in so doing released her. The commotion made Rashida look up and then back at her fire, spreading her hands in front of it as if innocently warming her hands. But he caught Mary easily enough and pulled her back toward the palaces by her hair.

As they all undertook a review García was stood next to Raúl Sanchez. Antonio was clear that he wanted a further delay on sending in any troops until they had more information. The hair on Raúl Sanchez's neck didn't quite stand on end, but García could feel his resentment toward him and almost felt the repulsion through his clothes.

García was pretty sure the resentment wasn't professional. A young man like Raúl might kick against the chain of command, but he was not so young never to have encountered it. Sanchez had a high enough command of his own to indicate he was no stranger to years of structure.

So if the resentment wasn't professional, then it was personal. It was the age old, *you're a fag, I'm a fag. We're connected.* As if sharing the same sexual preference was reason enough to create a special bond. García had come across this many times on the job, particularly with Hispanics. They would make an instant assumption when they met him, *we're the same, because we have the same cultural background,* when often nothing could

225

be further from the truth.

The fact that García had made no move toward Raúl, not a joke, a raised eyebrow or a shared smile, nothing to personally acknowledge that he knew they were both gay, would have aggravated Raúl. Raúl would have felt cheated, if not of a shag, then cheated of not being singled out and made to feel important. And he felt his jaw clench as he listened once again as Antonio tried to summarise their position.

Then García tuned Antonio out. He had already heard it before. He twisted his ring. He thought instead about his own approach in any operation. Faced with a hostage situation he would try to fill in all the spaces around the central question, in the hope that the important parts would become clearer.

If Rashida's messages were right, then fifty could easily be taken by force. But these fifty were also capable of causing great structural damage. Moreover there was still no overt political agenda. Dead mothers and babies suggested disease. Perhaps they were sick, although how sick was impossible to gauge. But most of all, *what did they want?* thought García.

"What do they want?" Dr Jesús spoke García's thoughts out loud. Looking around, David could see that everyone except possibly Raúl was perplexed by this key question. Raúl was evidently either too caught up in his own sexual tensions and resentments to be interested, or simply fixated on moving his men into the Alhambra and taking it by force. There had to be another way. As Antonio drew to an end, David spun around and butting up closely to Antonio's concluding remarks said,

"Get Alberto!"

"Manuel went for him a while ago. They're looking for him." Antonio said calmly.

"I've got him," Manuel said, crashing through the door limbs flailing from under his arm. "And her. They're here." And he deposited Alberto onto a chair and Lola on top of him. "Now sit still," he barked at them both.

"Can you get through here?" García shouted at them and stabbed at *la torre del agua* on the map. And when the children didn't move he said, "You don't have to sit still anymore. Come here. Look. Can you get through?"

"No," said Alberto looking at the map.

"Here?" García indicated the effluence pipe at the side of the building.

"Sometimes."

"Today?"

"I don't think so."

"Why?"

"It's too high and the water is coming out too fast I think. I can get out that way, but not in."

Raúl shouldered his way past García and focused hard on the map. Dr Jesús came slowly across and said,

"But what about here?" the academic pointed again to *la torre del agua*. "I don't mean the tower. I mean here. At the side, the aqueduct."

"Yeah, I think so."

"Aqueduct?" said García, thinking again of Lorca's aqueduct and his suspended dots. "What's it like?"

"Open water," said Jesús, "a stone channel. It's the main entry for the water to the palaces."

"I thought that was here," said Antonio, his finger on the the point they had all looked at before, where the water went underground and then under the walls before joining a stream and then the River Darro.

"Well," Dr Jesús explained, "the water comes in here, at *la torre del agua*, then it forks you see. All this," he drew a wavy line with a pencil, "goes sideways and down toward the palaces, feeds the fountains and all the plants on its way. Then," he drew over the marks from earlier and made them darker, "what's left over comes out here, under the walls, like we said. But this here," he went back again to *la torre del agua*, "this branch of the water just carries on straight. It goes through the filtering system, which is all stones, and then this part is the drinking water and also the water that supplies everything on *calle real*. Straight down to the *alcazaba*."

It was already dark. The silhouette of the *hotel america* was only just visible. He could only wonder whose strength would give out first, and hope it would be hers. His heart was in his mouth not that anyone would have guessed it by the thrust of his chin and the grip of his fist around her hair. He expected her to pull and writhe, to whimper or scream. He at least expected she might talk. Not a bit of it. She just matched him, long stride for long stride, completely unaware of the effort it cost him to set such a pace.

"A pace between each, you think?" García asked, closely focused on the map. "One manhole cover here. Then here and here," his fingers trotted evenly along the map of the cedar walk.

"Yes. Maybe two paces," Dr Jesús said.

"But here, this aqueduct is open all the way?"

"Yes, at the beginning, but then, as you say, it goes under the ground along the cypress walk, here with manhole covers all the way down the walk."

"And loads of grates," said Alberto knowingly.

"Well actually no, not at the moment," said Javi. "We've taken them all out and sent them to the foundry."

"I didn't know that!" Dr Jesús looked concerned.

"It's just a maintenance thing Sir. Every ten years or so, we just get them re-cast. It comes out of the standard maintenance budget," Javi added hastily. "The thing is," he said addressing García, "the acid rain now wears the metal faster than it used to, and well, we just send them, saves doing drawings or measuring anything."

"So Javi, there are no grates, the whole route?"

"Sorry Sir, not at the moment."

And García felt that they had just caught their first real break.

Their first real break in years had turned out to be a bit of a busman's holiday, Jack had to admit. Yet he hardly regretted it. Paula had quite enjoyed herself too, he knew. And so had he. He was enjoying being so close to a foreign police force – two if you counted García as representing the US.

This level of work was something Jack would never ordinarily have been invited to do. He knew his superintendent Michael Small was pleased or he would not have authorised their continued presence. Jack felt it was Small's way of showing solidarity with the York people and their families. A few days' wages for Jack was nothing in the scheme of things. Superficially he supposed he wished they were there at a different time of the year. He had heard Manuel Pedraza refer to the furnace of August and the oven-heat that virtually immobilised the city. Just his luck, he thought, not to have been there for some hot sun.

For all that it was a crisis, there were long hours of not much, and what little there was, he found hard to follow. There was a boredom about a hostage situation that he could never have imagined. Films and TV always portrayed such situations as high drama and intrigue, when most of the time in this real life situation, it seemed to Fisher that little could be further from the truth.

He admired David García for his energy and his native

genius, and also Antonio, who was the steadier man. He marvelled at Antonio's ability to manage so many people from apparently conflicting disciplines. He was fascinated to see that some of his management technique was physical as well as intellectual. He could not help but notice how much more the men laid hands on one another, whether back slapping or an arm over the shoulder or the daily handshake. It contrasted sharply with his own northern European 'hands-off' culture.

He had developed more than a passing affection for Alberto and Lola, who were not much older than his own children. He wondered how he was going to adjust to 63 Woodthorpe Avenue and the life of a licensing officer after living in the bubble of the last two days. He hoped that things would work out. He did not want to be the bearer of bad news.

Why was there no news coming the other way? He had the 'phone. Since they had turned off the electric, he had been careful to conserve the battery, ringing only the pre-arranged number, and then for less than two minutes. Each time he had spoken with someone he had used the same opening ID.

He had been careful to go to the *generalife*. He did not mind the others knowing he was making the calls. He reported them faithfully. However he did not want them to see the effect it was having on him; the delays, the double speak, his inability to manage the timetable. The same voice on the other end, smooth and calm, always saying more time was needed. He was so weary of trying to say the right thing. Up here in the relative peace, he could speak without an audience. And Jay's only remark was that anything he said was the right thing.

No-one would follow him, and if they did, they could not get past the aqueduct. And who among them was up to working the route out, or, if having worked it out, who would want to risk immersing themselves in water? Water, after all, was now seen by most of them as the enemy, or at least the first enemy.

As for attack from outside, they had put paid to that when they had set off the two explosions last night. The army wouldn't dare. If they were going to attack, it was going to be full-blown, all or nothing. Jay had made that clear. They would be aware that anything piecemeal would mean more explosions.

But he was growing afraid. Mary's offer to organise the food had been a mixed blessing. A godsend on the one hand, but he feared that she had seen how near to breaking point they were and, if she hadn't been when she made the offer, then she must have sensed his relief when he had agreed.

The almond paste. That had been a close call and had cost them more effort. They had had to move it all. Again. The kitchens in the *parador* had been the ideal place. Cool and dry. Hell, he should have got ammonium nitrate-based product that didn't smell of almonds. As if he could have chosen. He had taken what he could get.

So what if he had managed to drag her down from the ruins of *la torre del cadi*? Big deal. Hardly a great feat. But even if she hadn't noted his waning strength, the fact was, he noted it. And that was just his physical strength. There was the mental and emotional strength he needed to pull this whole thing off. He knew that was waning too.

When he had finished his last 'phone call he had wandered over toward *el mirador romántico*, the cascades of water down each side of the stairs still running, the dust and smuts of the early morning long gone. To one side some of the water had been escaping through the damaged staircase, and he had stood over a still pool trapped in the earth.

Reflected back at him was a face; thin, patchily stubbled and pinched. He hardly knew himself. There, with no-one to <u>see</u> him and only the gentle running of the water to be heard, he had kicked and kicked at the mud and then finally turned with hatred toward the few recognisable parts of the building. Yet even he knew the strength of his hatred was akin to love.

To love your enemy was supposed to be a Christian duty, Agustín thought as he helped María Santos Moreno raise her aged bony self from the floor on to her feet. And therefore, as he later told Rosario, all this assistance that he had given their neighbour with whom they had not spoken for more than thirty years, meant he was destined for sainthood. Not that the bag of aristocratic bones now leaning on his arm was a trial. Thanks be to God she was not an overweight sow and indeed she was even quite pleasant in manner.

So why had they stopped speaking? Sure her brothers had been Felangists. In those days had not everyone been, in some way, associated with the goings on? If not directly involved, then they were cooking the meals, or cleaning the houses, or driving the vehicles of the murderous assassins. Looking at María now, her wrinkled skin and faded blue eyes, he could barely see the beauty that had been renowned in Granada. In the end hadn't they just all been young and at the mercy of the old? Hadn't they just been victims too?

What did he think she should have done? Thrown herself in front of all those trucks that roared up the hill past her house to the cemetery? Rushed up the hill after them and placed herself in the line of fire as one body fell after another? Did he really imagine that at less than sixteen this woman, any more than he, could have altered the course of that terrible history?

The thought was only a modulation of the theme that he pondered every day of his life. If he had done something himself, anything at all different, might that not have changed the course of events? And then might that not then have touched the outcome

232

for Don Federico?

What if THEY had come for Federico García Lorca earlier? Or what if he had come out of the door into *calle angulo* a day later? What if, when Agustín had seen him, that last time, it had not been on that hot hot August day? What if Agustín had not been in the narrow *calle angulo* taking deliveries but had been instead with all his brothers, jostling and bickering for dominance? Would there have been a different outcome?

He would always wonder if the story might have changed. He would always ask himself if the Rosales boy would have relinquished his hold on the great man to exchange words with Agustín and his brothers? Maybe the older boys would have paused for a cigarette. After all, both families had known each other forever. Maybe if Agustín's older brothers had been there and the Rosales boy had stopped, in stopping for that moment, he would have taken time to think just for a minute about what was being done.

Instead, Agustín remembered with piercing clarity that the Rosales boy had called to Agustín, crying *stay back molino, stay back*. And at the mention of the word *molino* García Lorca had raised his great dark eyes and looked at Agustín. Seeing the boy's pronounced *molino*, the widow's peak, so like his own, Lorca had smiled at him, lost his footing for a moment on the curb, and then disappeared amid the body of men surrounding him. It may even have been his last smile.

Agustín shuddered, and then was aware of María Santos Moreno looking up at him, concerned. He smiled down at her and patted her arm absently and reassuringly. Then he raised his head and sniffed the air. It smelled like rain to him. *Wash the earth* he thought. *Wash it clean. Take the old blood and take the new, for sure as eggs is eggs nothing shall be learned and we shall see more blood before this is done. Nothing can truly erase them, not even the sweet fall of rain*.

"The water channel is exposed in *calle real* at the moment Sir."

Antonio and García looked from Javi to Dr Jesús.

"Yes," Dr Jesús said thoughtfully, "you're absolutely right." Then he turned once again to the others and to the map and said, "This channel here, below *calle real*, runs absolutely straight down. No bends at all, and hardly any sudden dropping in height either. This is partly the original channel that once drained into the great reservoir here." He pointed to the massive *plaza* between *la torre de la vela* and the *palacio de carlos V* where the vandalised poles had been all set up to catch would-be parachutes. "The reservoir is massive, under *la plaza*. It was used probably up until the 1930s to provide water to these fountains," and he indicated the fountains on the road descending into the city. People would come and take a drink here, with the option of a little anise added in. It was a favourite of Lorca, don't you know." He looked at García over his glasses and said as an aside, "Lorca was a very famous poet in Spain."

"In New York as well Dr Jesús," said García dryly.

"Ah good. Glad to hear it! Anyway, the reservoir isn't used now, but this channel here, just along in front of the *hotel america*, and running along, is exposed in some places. The original channel is being repaired. We're putting in pipes, plastic pipes."

"Instead of?" queried García.

"Well nothing, instead of nothing, it's the same square stone structure it's always been. But we need to reduce the evaporation. So many more houses being built these days, so much more demand for water. And the summers are getting hotter, the rainy season shorter."

"So, here's what you're telling me. There is an entire square channel of stone tunnel? Along this entire route here? Exposed in places. Underground in others?"

"An aqueduct," Dr Jesús confirmed.

"But without water in it, it's a tunnel right?"

"Yes, you could say that."

"And it's big enough for a boy to get through," pressed García.

"Yes."

"Or a girl," said Lola.

"Do we drain the water Sir?" asked Javi.

"I'm not sure. Give me a minute here. Antonio. A word?" García led Antonio aside.

"What's your thinking?"

"OK, we've got tunnels. We've got small bodies. No, no, hear me out." David raised his hands to Antonio. "I know. They're kids. But the monument comes first. Right? Highest priority. Yes?"

"Whoa, David. Whoa."

"They can get out easily." García overrode him. "The effluence channel here. Alberto has said so. They use it all the time. The water is high. They will just shoot out. Two things will happen. They will detach the Primaflex from the charges. They will let it be known we can get in and get out."

"I don't think children constitute 'we' David." Antonio's tone held a warning note. "You can't send in kids to an unsecured situation. The press will have a field day. You're running on smoke signals man, that may or may not be from Santiago, and Arabic writing in the dirt. Any of this could be from the very people who are just waiting for any excuse to blow up the next tower."

"Listen to me." García raised his voice and the others, even though they were at a distance, seemed to almost step back. There was a sense in the room that David and Antonio facing each other down was like a meeting of the Titans. "You forget. The missing piece. *What do they want?* Antonio, without it you're screwed. You are treating symptoms. That's why using force would be mad. If you can't answer WHY..." García paused. The length of his tirade was costing him. "These guys aren't talking. We have to figure it out. Why a midwife? Why? I'll tell you why. So she can

235

deliver babies."

"And all the charges?"

"Quite," García retorted. "We don't know. My point entirely. What do we know? What has happened? We know one baby has died. We saw the body."

"We saw what we think was a body," corrected Antonio.

García ignored him.

"They want babies," he went on. "If these children go in..." García lowered his voice on a sigh. "They are not going to harm them."

"Well they won't harm fifty of us will they?" said Alberto sliding in between them, Lola and Raúl not far behind him.

"Fifty?" García said looking down at him.

"Yeah, well they'll have to catch us first," he said cheekily.

"Fifty?" repeated Antonio.

"Yeah," said Alberto, "There's fifty of us. We thought we'd all go."

García looked at the child. He wasn't just a mixed up kid, he was a strategist. García suddenly realised that Alberto had orchestrated the return of his fellow inhabitants, not for fun, or for mischief, but because he was going to take action and he needed his own people around him. The child was hatching a plan. And all this time all the adults had just been thinking that at best they were cute and at worst they were a naughty irritant.

Alberto and García's eyes met and García saw in him what Fisher had seen: the kid was street-wise. And then he saw something else. He saw himself as a boy leaving Cuba for the great unknown, risking life and all his family to take to the waves because there was the promise of something that might be better. And he remembered that the complex, and perhaps even foolhardy, acts of seeking freedom had been taken, just like Alberto, one small step after another.

"Fifty children can't crawl through those tunnels and not

be heard. Besides it will take too long," said Raúl, at the same time appalled at himself for even dignifying Alberto's idea with a reply.

"We don't want to crawl," said Lola. "We want to float."

A slow grin spread across García's features and he said, "The child's a genius."

"**Don't** laugh." Joaquin said. "It's a good reason. If the child *is* a genius shouldn't he or she know who their parents are?"

"Oh Joaquin," she signed. "It's no use."

"Genius is always a possibility. Any child of ours will be special, genius or not. How could they fail, conceived in the aftermath of the *fiesta* of San Miguel? Remember the sunflowers Ana? Born in Sacromonte, music in his blood, direct descendent of the peoples who were here before the Romans, even before the Moors of the Alhambra, ..."

"There isn't going to be an Alhambra soon," she said glumly. "Don't you ever listen to the news?"

"The Alhambra will live forever Ana."

"It won't if people blow it up!"

"They won't."

"How can you be so sure?"

"**I am sure.** It's not happening David," Antonio was firm. "It's too half-baked."

"What happened to not thinking in straight lines?"

Antonio looked at him and shrugged his shoulders and reached for his jacket as if to indicate that the conversation and the meeting were over. Some of the men drifted out of the room, happy to escape the charged atmosphere.

"There are just some things you can't do. The losses..."

Antonio's voice trailed off.

"The gypsy told you, remember?" David went on, relentless, "Losses and gains. That's what it is to have a life." He knew he was out of line, referring to a personal conversation in front of the few who were left. But he felt desperate to get Antonio to think sideways, to turn fully away from the other options, to decide to really entertain that there might be a different way through this.

"But you can't play that game with other people's lives," was all Antonio said.

"Shit Antonio. You're a police officer. You can't tell me you don't do it all the time," García glared at him. "It's all about choices. This life over that one. This risk instead of that one."

"David," said Antonio Marín raising his palms as if to halt García in his tracks.

"People die all the time," finished García.

"But not on my watch," snapped Marín.

"Oh come on," David exhaled exasperation. "Madrid for God's sake."

"Don't even go there," Antonio advanced on him. "Who do you think was at that ground zero, pulling those corpses free, comforting the dying? Who do you think carries those images around in head and heart?" Antonio made a fist and beat on his own chest above his heart. "Do you think that New York has the corner on that market? Do you think that any twisted dismembered body whether in and amongst the rail tracks, the carriages, the upholstery for Chrissake, the girders, the concrete, the dust, in any city, with any nationality, is any different, has any less impact, bereaves fewer, bleeds more shallowly? Do you? Do you?"

García wanted to roll back the clock, only five minutes. That would do it. Anything to be as they were. What had got into them? Where was the seasoned NYPD negotiator? Who was this fired-up Cubano spouting the words of a hot-head from his mouth? And where was the measured, steadfast Antonio? He looked back at Antonio, felt himself wind down, consciously pressed down his emotional storm.

"You're right," he said in a steady voice and raised his own hands in surrender.

"Enough," Antonio was sharp and García thought he saw the shadow of a smile play on Raúl's lips as he too left the room. "Not kids David." Antonio softened his tone. "I'm sorry," he said putting on the jacket. "I'm just not authorising it. It's too wild."

Too wild was how they had always described him in the days when he had been schooled by nuns. But they were fooled. Beneath that wildness an attention to detail was Joaquin Montez's real gift. Not his guitar playing, although that was good in itself, not even his magnificent moments of *cante jondo*, but it was the focus of his practice that was notable, the determination of his ever-improving repetitions.

On the outside, with his long hair, compelling eyes and *gitano* strut, he was every inch the casual, sexy, romantic gypsy of any storybook fantasy. But this stood only to conceal his deep commitment to his art and all that it stood for. He looked long and hard at the Alhambra and felt is if the loss of it might break his heart.

David García was pretty sure he could withstand anything the emotion called love could throw at him. He was well armoured. But fury or rage was something else. He had to protect himself from that. He felt it beginning to rise in him again as Antonio crossed the room to leave. He wanted to punch Antonio and drop him in one blow, he wanted to grasp him with both his hands and make him see what he, García, could see, and he wanted to seize him and... and what?

"What's this?" Javi, the only one left in the room, had asked pointing at the cross-hatching on the map.

Glad of a diversion, García said,

"It's where Manuel marked up the position of the nets."

"Nets? What nets?"

"They've put nets across from the northern wall to *calle real*. Loads of them."

"That's funny. We had a lot of nets delivered over the last little while," said Javi.

And with that Antonio did a volte-face.

Javi was not the same as Augustín, thought Alberto. He had been glad to see Javi. There was no doubt about it. But he would never have run to him like he would have to run to Augustín if he had been there.

He didn't know the smell of Javi, and he did know the smell of Augustín. Every whiff of him. The scent of stale cigarettes on his breath, of warm earth, even the fragrance of his sweat was like perfume. He longed to bury his head in the old man's chest.

There was a real chance now that they could make a difference. He knew they could get past anyone if they just put their minds to it. They were going to be asked. The Cuban was already asking. They had been chosen.

Like perfume on his clothes O'Reilly could smell María on his body for hours afterwards. When he moved in his chair, reached for the 'phone, stood to open the door, the scent of her moved up between his chest and his shirt and filled his nostrils. He wondered how García was getting on.

On a sombre day Agustín would talk of Viznar. The children always recited their self-composed mantra, *Viznar, Viznar, so near and so far*, and then sat very still for Agustín.

"He goes to Viznar, Federico does. We know this because there were others who remembered and told. No, I am wrong, he does not go. That is not correct. He is taken. It is up there," and Agustín would point above the *reformatorio* of San Miguel. "And up there, he is waiting through the night. He tells some tales and some jokes. Maybe he recites some poetry or even has some new poetry that has come to him that he never writes down.

"He smokes. He smokes a lot you know. We did in those days. I still do," and Agustín would puff on his pipe. "He is scared now. People, you know, are like animals, much more than people ever like to admit. And like animals, they can smell death. Someone comes and asks him for his confession but he refuses.

"Then, he changes his mind. But the priest is gone now and he cannot remember the words. The young guard helps him. Soon, very soon, they take him. They take them all. And not so very deep in the forest, with at least three others, they shoot him. Viznar," Agustín would always say. "Viznar. So small, so utterly insignificant a village. Viznar. Who would ever have thought it?"

Looking across from the Alhambra toward the distant pines above Sacromonte, Agustín wondered. Without the hill which always blocked his view from the *finca*, he wondered if it were Viznar he would see.

García had had them focus on detail and on personality. And compelling though García was when he was angry, Antonio now thought David was wrong and Raúl was right. There was a campaign to mount.

His change of heart and his sense of certainty had come because of yet another explosion. This latest explosion, just

241

moments ago, should have been wholly expected. And he was livid. He was more furious with himself than with anyone else. What had he been thinking about? He should have foreseen it. Christ. Raúl Sanchez could not have been more precise. He had shown them the rust-coloured Primaflex, he had proven beyond doubt that all the towers were wired for detonation. It had been obvious even to an idiot that more would be blown up. Christ. He cupped his hand around the flame and lit his cigarette.

Antonio heard his own sigh as he exhaled. These people were going to get their way through destruction, one way or another. *Military action*. He inhaled and snorted all at once. He had been distracted from ordering what any sane commanding officer should have sanctioned a day ago. Distracted by García's theories to an extent, and by the lack of any real intelligence, but also, he knew, by his awareness of history. In the low sierra at his back were the gulleys of graves from the Civil War. Infamous Viznar itself was almost only a walk away. Antonio found it hard to imagine that Lorca, less than a lifetime ago, had been walking where he, Antonio, now stood.

As hard to imagine were the events of 1936, very likely within the lifetime of the old *finca* dwellers, Agustín Lopez and his wife. These two old people were now captive in the hands of new madmen, whereas seventy years before, other madmen, military men, had taken the high ground up on the *alcazaba* in the Alhambra. And those upright military men had sent their message to the Albaicín bearing down in bullets and bombs on the people.

He knew, with a sinking heart, that force could only ever be a last resort. And he knew that last resort was dangerously near.

The blast that Antonio heard had rocked García, but it had rocked his confidence rather than his body. He too had taken a break from the others. He too observed no obvious gash in the side of the Alhambra, but plenty of dust. Although the noise was definitely not a gunshot, he wondered if this might mark the end of Santiago. Thinking of the loss of Santiago somehow made Marilita seem nearer. He remembered one of her secret visits to him in her childhood when she had picked up the Lorca edition that Richard had given him and asked him to read to her.

"This one *Papá*," and she had pointed.

"No my sweet. Let's read another."

But she had insisted. So he began to read the familar words of a balcony, children eating oranges below, the reapers in the fields and above all the evocative plea that in death a window be left open.

"What does it mean *Papá*?"

"Why do you ask me to read in Spanish then?"

"You sound so big and grand," she had told him."What does it mean?"

"He says he sees a little boy eating oranges from the balcony, that the reaper is harvesting the wheat. Most of all he says that if I die you must open the balcony window."

"That's very sad *Papá*. If I die, will you leave the balcony window open?" And she looked at him with her great brown eyes.

"You won't die for a long, long time," he had told her.

"But will you leave it open for me if I leave it open for you?"

"Yes," and he had held her close and kissed her. "Yes my lovely. We can do that for each other."

Who would open the balcony for Rashida Santiago if it were necessary? In trying to persuade Antonio to look at other solutions was that what he was trying to do? Was he trying to be there for Rashida in a way that he could not have been for his child? Was he trying to influence how this situation was resolved so as to avoid sending in the army?

It was a mark of Antonio's generosity that he allowed García to express an opinion at all, let alone allow him to fight his corner on it. Even if he didn't think he could wholeheartedly support an attack, then at the very least David thought, he should apologise to Antonio.

Alberto and Lola were in a corner talking, their heads close together. Eventually, unnoticed, they slipped away.

"What's up García? You look grim. Something happened?" Fisher called out in the corridor.

"I'm looking for Raúl."

"I just saw Raúl," replied Fisher. "He says they are drafting in more forces. The explosion was small. What's happened? Have there been casualties?" Jack fired off one question after another.

"No." García waved an arm dismissively.

"Look man," said Fisher, halting before him. "I sometimes think you Americans suffer, if that's the right word, from too little exposure on this. In the UK we have been living with terror and terrorists for a long time. The IRA has been wandering around our country for decades blowing people and things up. Antonio is very experienced. Long before 9/11 this country was raking up the remains of car bomb debris on city streets. Look..." he held up his hands in mock surrender at García's expression, "...look. I am not trying to say this makes things less serious. I am just saying Antonio knows a thing or two..."

García cut across him at that and bit out,

"And so do I."

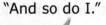

"We have had to bring in another five hundred men," Raúl stated, eyeballing García as if daring him to interrupt.

"What for?" asked Antonio, only too aware of Raúl's Sanchez's sense of triumph. Sanchez should have learned by now, Antonio thought. A career in the army should have taught him, good men back down when they believe they are wrong, and they don't have to be pushed to do so. There were no points to score.

Even if Raúl could not have known that García had already made his peace with Antonio moments before this briefing, and done it easily, clearly, manfully, Raúl should have been able to see that his case would not be strengthened by attacking García.

"There are other problems that are not of the army's making, nor can we resolve them other than by bringing in more men," he went on, now pointing blame at the civilian authorities. "We are struggling with the evacuation. With this latest explosion it is more imperative than ever that we get people moved as soon as possible." Raúl cleared his throat. "I have to say, people aren't exactly happy with the results so far," he added in a slightly acidic tone and turned on his heel.

Antonio watched him leave and then looked at García.

"Thoughts?" he asked him.

"You've had them," stated García flatly.

García was right. He had told Antonio exactly what he thought. After speaking to Fisher, David had come and found him in the hallway between the incident room and the toilets. Antonio had thought García looked to be in the grip of some profound emotion but before Antonio could say anything García had said,

"I was out of line."

"Yes you were," Antonio had replied, impressed that García's lack of discretion went both ways. In referring to Antonio's conversation about his wife and the gypsies García might have been more personal than was appropriate, but at least that was balanced by being prepared to humiliate himself in front of any passing colleague in a corridor.

"I will keep to an observer's role."

"Please don't," Antonio had said, and then clapped García on the back and snorted with amusement leading him along the corridor. "One, you won't be able to. Two, we should not promise what we can't deliver." *Another homespun maxim* thought García. "And three, we need everyone's ideas if we are going to finally do what is right."

"Right?" García had shot back.

"Yes. Right," he had looked at García and had said, "Come on David, you think there is a right decision or you wouldn't have given me such a rough ride earlier. Spit it out man."

"OK," García said slowly. "OK. An armed attack will destroy the monument. I am beginning to wonder if Raúl wants that. If he wants that because your government does." García had paused, as if considering whether he would say the next thing and then had added, "Or indeed if mine does."

Antonio had stopped then in his tracks.

"What do you mean?"

García had been suddenly mindful that he may have over-stepped a boundary that even a man like Antonio would find unacceptable.

"Well don't stop now man, for Chrissake," Antonio had said. "It's not as if I haven't read your – what did they call it – *treasonable ideas* in the Gazette. Come on."

"A world-sized catastrophe. The Alhambra blown sky high. What do you think Antonio? Do you think your average first world Westerner is going to do the analysis? Do you think Joe Blow, John Doe or María García will ask? Do you think anyone will care if something else could have been done? Should have been done?

"No. They won't," García answered his own question. "It will all get wrapped up neatly in the terrorism parcel." He had paused for breath and then added, "Don't get me wrong. It's shit. Terror, freedom fighters. Whatever they want to call themselves.

All the havoc they wreak on the rest of us," García had felt his voice break and side-stepped Antonio's arm as it came toward him to steady him, "it's shit," he had continued, regaining control. "It's especially shit for anyone caught in the middle. But our policy in the US, maybe all western policy, is now predicated on terror. We need something big like the Alhambra to blow sky high. It justifies everything. Weapons expenditure. Invasions of other nations. Protective tariffs. Keeping out immigrants. It keeps fear at the helm. Let Raúl loose and fear wins the day." Antonio had been silent so David had pressed on. "Raúl will not think through alternatives. This is the death of choice. People start talking of 'no options'. This nullifies decision making. That is the death of democracy. Democracy, for Chrissake. Isn't that what all protective action is supposed to be about...?" García swept his hand across an imaginary horizon, pausing for breath. "History defines us," he went on. "Our own history. That of our nation. And all this history? Where does it come from? It comes from people. You, me, Raúl and," he had scrabbled for words, "well, and, Rashida Santiago. God help her. From the choices that we all make. Ultimately we have to live with that. Without what might have been. Conflict is always there." He had waved a hand over his head. "All the time. It can't be avoided. It always needs resolving. The question is, how?" He had looked at Antonio. "What I see is this. We try to solve each new conflict as though we were fighting the last one. Old tools for new events."

Antonio had been amazed. This man of short punched sentences had been in the grip of oratory as he had been when talking with the children. When David García knew what he knew, the words flowed.

"And you know what Antonio?" García had continued, "You know what I think? I think you are right to shy away from using the children. You are right. They could get shot. They could be blown up. Even drowned. They could," he had nodded at Antonio.

"But that kid. That mere boy Alberto. He has more intuition in his little finger than many men in uniform. He gets it. He gets that we are all front line soldiers in this life. All of us. All that crap about gypsies and losses. This is what it is to have a life," he had stabbed his finger toward Antonio. "The solutions to these problems that we all face? I say to you that women and children are as likely to solve our problems these days as men and tanks. If those kids want to float their way into the Alhambra..."

"Like a boy might float across to the US from Cuba, David?" Antonio had said softly.

David had stopped moving.

"I don't think we should get confused here Antonio," García had said in a warning tone.

"I'm not confused," Antonio replied. "Your life experience has given you a position on risk and survival that is different from most of your fellow first-world citizens. That's why you can do the job you do. But it's also why your call on this is way out in left field."

And with that García had fallen back and had let Antonio go into the briefing alone before following on.

Yet García's remarks still remained with Antonio. Choice. History. Outcomes. He was not about to adopt them as his own, but they shone brightly in his mind. As Raúl left and García would not be moved to repeat any of his ideas, Antonio turned to Pedraza and said,

"Manuel? Your thoughts?"

"There's a lot of puzzles. I mean, take the nets for example. Keeping the gangway clear from anything we might drop in..."

"To be honest," Javi interrupted him, "when I first saw them all, I thought it might have been for protecting the trees from something," he was uncomfortable under the eagle-eyed gaze of so many policemen. "The thing is," he said nervously, "We don't do the big trees. Contractors do those. Since Dutch Elm Disease destroyed so many trees in northern Europe we decided to use specialists... Hmm. Lots of nets."

"Yeah," Manuel nodded in agreement, throwing a few more sunflower seeds into the hopper of his mouth. "We can't figure out how they managed to get it all covered so fast."

"Shouldn't think casting nets this far and wide would be that much of a problem," said Javi looking at the area and scratching his head, "for a fisherman."

evening

The children went to bed in their clothes. Alberto was warm. He had never been warm in bed before. Hot in summer. Cold in winter. But never just plain, unadulterated, warm. He snuggled himself down and thought it was a shame he would not be able to enjoy it for long.

Antonio Marín stood on the *terraza* of the *reformatorio* of San Miguel and smoked. García was tough. The moments of confrontation had not quite been at meltdown, but not far from it. Did David really think that they could just flush a few children through the Alhambra without any thought for their safety? Was he insane? Had his childhood escape from Cuba and the events at the twin towers made him lose perspective?

On the other hand, the man was a genius. He could turn and twist and connect dots as well as anyone Antonio had ever worked with. Maybe even better. And the diatribe on history and choice, well that had been quite something. In a perfect world maybe it would be worth hanging on and trying to make some choices rather than react. But that was a luxury encased in time.

And they were running out of time. Apart from the obvious exhaustion of the hostages, especially the elderly among the English who, unlike Agustín and Rosario and the old lady from *calle real*, would be unused to the conditions, the pressure from government was building. Not only did the Spanish government want a fast result, Antonio was pretty sure that, reading between the lines from his superiors, international pressure was also mounting.

Although they were not exactly running out of ideas, the ideas they did have were unpalatable to say the least. Did a fast solution mean a military one? Was García right that a military solution was what the politicians wanted, except no-one was prepared to say so? Was Fisher right in suggesting that property was always viewed as more valuable than people?

The onslaught of darkness served to underline how quickly the days went. He shifted his gaze and his thoughts to the night. It was falling, swiftly, as it always did in Granada. The light had started to change in the afternoon from the bright, merciless, cold sun, to clouded shadow. Now it was a livid purple and a rage of orange darkened before him across a horizon that seemed almost wider than the sky.

He remembered the evenings of his childhood, in Pinos Puente, not far from Lorca's birthplace at Fuente Vaqueros, the object of David García's self-confessed fascinations. The exquisite skies, the sunsets and sunrises and the storms that had arced across them had made them feel small and insignificant in a drama of god-like proportions.

He remembered the scorching sun of the summers, the heat beating down on his head, wandering along the irrigation channels, the stench of the drains, the odour of the olive oil mills, the occasional waft of drying tomatoes, the stacks upon stacks of yellowing tobacco leaves. He remembered the timelessness of it, the seemingly endless days and nights for exploring, for digging, for hiding, he and his friends scratching on the earth, on walls, behind trees.

From the *terraza* he fancied he could almost see Pinos Puente, or at least the beginnings of the Cordoba road that would take him there. How long since he had visited his cousins? The children must have been very young. Maribel had always preferred to be visited than to visit. She liked the control, was happy to trade the work of having visitors for the power of being in her own home. Besides she was from Madrid and Madrid was, as she had frequently told everyone, the centre of the universe.

Antonio shifted slightly and closed his eyes for another cat nap. He wondered why he didn't miss her more. He wondered if single life, at first so painful and uncomfortable, had now become more than a habit. Perhaps now it was instead a refuge. He now had a life where not only physical things such as, pencils, plates, keys, clothes were always exactly where he had left them, but the internal objects of his life were also stable. His feelings, once placed in position, remained there with nothing and no-one to knock them off their axis. What was it that García had said? *I have become accustomed to myself*. He thought, perhaps, being a widower had made him a better person. Without the volatile nature of marriage, or at least the volatile nature of marriage to Maribel, he had been free to develop his natural patience. There had been a time when he would not have handled a man like García well at all. Something about not having a wife kept him more contained, more able to withstand the emotional unsteadiness of others.

Perhaps that was why he didn't seek the company of women. He was not a man for whom casual sex appealed, and he had no wish to embark on marriage. He felt that as a result he was more effective than ever. His men respected him and this was nourishment enough. His children provided a sufficient personal life to give him the necessary social trading cards. News of their lives provided all the necessary parts of superficial conversation in the course of daily life. It gave him the currency of interaction. Perhaps Fisher's remarks about property over people were more true than Fisher realised. Antonio wondered if he himself had not arrived at a stage where this was true for him. People were more important to him than things, that much was certain, but if he were truly honest? He would have to say that things probably gave him more pleasure now than people.

And of course, he had his reading. Poetry was high on the list, but also biography, watered down philosophy and, to his wry amusement, the occasional American detective novel. He was as likely to tuck himself into a chair with a book and a smoke as he was to watch the inane television. He followed the paper of course. If nothing else Antonio felt it was his duty to comment on

what he had enjoyed about his son's reports.

And then there was the Internet. To the horror of his daughters he could be found in his flat surfing sites, spending hours at the small screen absorbing trivia. That was how he had found the Gazette after all. Not a bad outcome for the waste of time his girls often accused him of. What did they expect him to do with his time? Be crime-busting every minute?

It had been an education to watch García trawl information. Antonio was amazed at how García seemed to put two and two together, get five, and then divide five by two and get two again. It was as if there was some sort of sleight of hand going on with logical function. He had to hand it to him, he was doing what Antonio had hoped: he wasn't thinking in straight lines. But Antonio now feared that García was well outside the margins.

Watching him over the past hours, Antonio had wondered a few times if the strain was proving too much. Not the strain of the journey, or the newness of the environment he found himself in. On the contrary, García seemed quite at home. He seemed to have developed an immediate rapport with everyone, he even seemed to manage the scratchy moments with Manuel and Raúl quite well. And he had demonstrated a connectivity to the place, most especially the Alhambra itself. Not, Antonio reminded himself, that that was so very difficult. Millions came every year and declared its beauty and uniqueness.

Antonio was too much a parent and too much a leader of men not to be aware that at times García seemed distracted – even abstracted. Antonio had seen García fade out more than once. He remembered the whiteness of the man's knuckles on otherwise brown hands, crushing the plastic coffee cup when talking about the bombing of the twin towers.

In addition to the loss of his daughter, Antonio sensed a desolation in García about his relationship with the lover Richard. It was as if, unlike Antonio, García had arrived near the approach of middle age with none of its satisfactions, no sense of having had the life that most people hope for and partly achieve. Something in García gave Antonio the uneasy feeling that this was a man whose tremendous capacity to spark from one unrelated cluster of ideas to the next, his ability to be almost chameleon in his approach to people, had been bought at a terrible price.

If to have a life was to suffer loss and gain, in equal measure, then maybe García had not had this type of life. Maybe the losses had far outweighed the gains, or, that what had been gained through loss was the almost terrifying insight that García had for the heart of a dilemma.

Across from the *terraza*, David García could see Antonio. At first García had meant to call out, but in truth was too tired to engage in conversation, wanting to save himself for what lay ahead. He couldn't abide distraction when he was working. His anger with, and at, Antonio, his more personal conversations with Antonio had meant that he had taken his eye off the proverbial ball. They led him into thoughts and memories he didn't want to visit. He didn't think he was capable of anything more than leaning back, closing his eyes, and blanking his mind. Had Fisher been around, as he had been the evening before, García would have readily made himself known. Three people on the *terraza* would have reduced the intensity. But Fisher had long excused himself, and he and his wife had taken a room in town along with the free choristers.

Occasionally, now that night was upon them, as the clouds scudded across the sky, García noted that the moonlight broke through an aperture. Lorca had loved the moon and often wrote of it. David imagined the cruelty of the moonless sky on the night of Lorca's death at Viznar. No-one knew precisely when he had been shot, with whom or by whom. No-one knew where he fell, what became of the flesh and bones. The obscurity of the death

was only illuminated by the cruelty of the anonymous rumour that the assassins' hatred of his homosexuality had made them shoot him repeatedly in the arse. David found this an act so filled with its own small meanness of spirit that it served only to make of Lorca a giant of all that art stood for. It was fitting that there had been no moon.

David saw the intensifying of the red circle as Antonio dragged on the tobacco, the little straight blasts of smoke as he exhaled, the twists of smoke that worked their way heavenwards when the cigarette dangled at rest at Antonio's side. He sensed Antonio had peace; that whatever lay behind or before him, whether the outcome at the Alhambra was positive or a disaster, Antonio would remain unshaken. Except probably for María, García knew most people also saw him as unshakeable. For in all the aftermath of the twin towers, of the deaths of Marilita and Richard, it was María who had been his rock. He had not had enough reserves of his own to see him through. It seemed to him that she had always given him much more than he had given her. His mother had been the same.

They had floated across from Cuba, Antonio had been right about that. David was the eldest of a slew of kids arriving with their mother and an abusive father. All they had done was trade rural poverty for an urban poverty that only New York could deliver quite so absolutely. Yet his mother had always found time to sing to them, to praise them, to rejoice in their successes. Typical of many immigrants, they were clean and tidy for school and for church, hair washed and slicked back, first with water and then with the inevitable spit.

Before his wedding it seemed the usual dramatic thing a Cuban mother might say to her eldest son. Only later, after he had met Richard, after his mother had died, only then did it take on more meaning.

"Listen *hijo*. María, she is a good girl," she had said. "You are a good boy. You try *hijo*." And she had looked so hard at him before adding, "Whatever you do, Ángel, *mi ángel*, you are always my son."

Whereas his father was different. Even as old and weakened without his vicious punch, before drink killed him, he never lost his vicious tongue. Hearing from María that his father was dying he had gone to see him. All his father could say to him was that he thanked God everyday that David's sainted mother had died before ever seeing the life he was leading. It was all David could do not to tell his father that his mother had known where David was headed all along.

The fact was, the generosity of women had always astounded García. And now no distance away in the Alhambra, Rashida was another woman giving of herself. By contrast, the meanness of Richard was stark. It was odd having Jack Fisher around, a reminder of that day in York. Richard had followed the Viking, Roman and medieval trails and David had followed him. Richard had pontificated on the marvels of a city built on layer upon layer of civilisation. Yet apparently he had no understanding of the history of his own life, or the lives of others. He loved antiques and antiquities quite possibly because they were by their very nature removed from him. David had come to accept this. Equally he had come to accept that Richard, through no fault of his own, was cursed with the disease of alcoholism, and had to bear it. David, good Catholic that he was, never questioned but that he should bear it too.

And then they had met Jack Fisher. In one evening in that little *cantina* in northern Europe García had glimpsed another possibility, that there was *life after drink*. That if Richard could just do what Fisher had done, their life together would turn around. And so he had faced *muerto de amor*, death of love, like Lorca's poem of the same name. Richard had died, but even before that death, so had love. Ultimately, to David, it was this death of love

that had acted as Richard's legacy. Richard's bequest had long been seen by David García as a withering of his own heart.

García knew that tomorrow the Raúls of this world would take over, and the troops would move in. He knew that some deaths would result and very likely the ancient walls would come tumbling down. Dr Jesús could insist that everything could be re-built, and perhaps he was right. But it was so sodding wasteful, when, if you knew what people longed for, the negotiation was easy.

Then across his thoughts came the faint sounds of a guitar, or maybe guitars, similar to those he had heard the night before. It was evocative of the timelessness of the place. He strained to hear them, realising they must be coming from the same hillside as before. He heard a great voice drifting up toward him. *Cante jondo.* He recognised snatches of Lorca's work.

He fancied he saw some flames from an open fire on the lower slopes further down Sacromonte. Then they stopped and he heard the voices and laughter of children. How wonderful it must be, he thought, to be without care, to have music course through one, to be on the outside of all this.

He thought of the three elderly people caught up somehow on the inside. The love Alberto had for Agustín had brought the old man to life for García. He wondered if any of them could hear the music and if it brought them comfort. He thought of Mary Stansfield and her choristers as well as Rashida Santiago.

He remembered the photos of the people still hung impotently along the long wall of the incident room Jack had created. This operation didn't have to be a disaster. Antonio needed to trust himself, to trust his own instincts. Surely he would see that they didn't need to have yet another bombing, yet more people arriving on the scene trying to inhale the ether of the dead. They needed to try a different way. He crossed over to the terrace.

"Antonio."

"Sí."

"I've been thinking," said García

"*Lo veo*. I see that," he said softly.

And García realised that, quite apart from being disturbed at possibly being observed, Antonio had been aware of him all along.

"All along you knew this was possible," Joaquin Montez told her, catching her face in his hands and making her look at him. "Ana, look at me," his hands slid to her belly. "All along you knew this."

Antonio was as near apoplectic as he had ever been.

"You've known since this afternoon haven't you?"

"Yes Sir," the child was looking at the floor where he had been looking ever since Antonio and David had been called in from the terrace.

"And you are the only one here?"

"No Sir," he raised huge brown eyes to Antonio and then lowered them again. "There's about twenty of us here."

García did a swift calculation, around thirty were missing.

"What's your name?"

"Felipe, Sir."

"Where are they Felipe?"

"*No lo se*."

"Yes you do know. Where are they?"

"They've gone."

"I see that. Where?"

And the boy pointed down the hill from Sacromonte.

The hill from Sacromonte, except for the gypsy caves, is largely

vacant between the *reformatorio* of San Miguel and the ancient community of the Albaicín. Plenty of scrub-land, but also mature sisal, little oases of small trees and one prickly pear bush after another.

Raúl led a group of soldiers down the side of the medieval wall, crenellated like descending stair steps, between the ravine and Sacromonte. They slipped and slid, first on the dry grass that was resistant to any foothold, then on small stones that moved like gravel under their feet. No sign of any child anywhere.

Raúl was aggravated. He couldn't see the point at this stage of trying to bring in the dogs. The dog units were nowhere near, and putting out a call to civilian dog handlers was unlikely to get a quick enough result since most civilians were in the process of being evacuated. On the other hand he had been determined to lead the search party. He couldn't wait to get his hands on them all, most of all Alberto.

There was nothing. Not a noise, not a flicker anywhere. And they had already been at it an hour and half. Raúl flicked open his phone and double-checked the time with his watch. Then he decided. Missing children or no missing children, this couldn't go on any longer. Enough time had been wasted following that Cuban's psychological games. Tomorrow he felt sure Marín would have to act and allow them to move in at daylight.

If the children got caught in the crossfire, well it was their own fault. Anyway, the children were all delinquents. Did it matter? He called the search to halt. There was no more progress to be made in the dark.

In the dark he thought she was not more beautiful or less, just beautiful in a different way. Up until now it had been afternoons, albeit only two of them. But now, in the dark, O'Reilly could feel his way across her, experience the softness, plunge himself into her more fully, no thought of seeing or being seen, just immersing himself in her as far as she could take him. And she received him as if there were no end to her depths, her moistness, her HEAT.

And in the moment when he juddered to climax, more than with any other woman before, she could have had whatever she wanted from him. It was hers, for the taking.

Taking the steepest route had been Alberto's idea. Without any light, it made sense to follow the contours of the wall, especially with the uncertain sky. Anyway, he'd done it many times. Who would see them? The gypsies were always drunk, or playing their guitars wildly, as if they were drunk. The *reformatorio* staff were either always asleep or, as Lola liked to put it, *pursuing their adult interests*. Granted he'd never led an entire gang down the hillside before, but then, when before had the staff all been off-site? It was a glorious feeling.

It was a glorious feeling to take her right there and then against the wall, just as he had the first time at the *fiesta de san miguel*, only then the air had been warm and the moon bright in a cloudless sky. She could not stay angry with him for long, nor he with her.

Even when she admitted to wanting his child, despite knowing she would never name him as the father, even though he had held her face as if in a vice and tried to stare her into submission, even these moments of conflict had done nothing to dampen their desire. They had probably inflamed it.

One look across the firelight and each had found a reason to leave the music and the others and separately find their way to the wall. Then he raised up the ladder they kept concealed at the edges, hoisted himself up with it, leant down and helped her up

with one strong pull. They clambered over and then, breathless, it was up with her skirts.

It was made more glorious by the knowledge that tucked deep inside her was his child, now being bathed in the warmth of more gushing seed. God, would he ever have enough of her? Ever ever ever?

"What's that noise?" said Lola.

"Hmm." Alberto held up a hand to stop the descent.

Joaquin Montez flattened himself against Ana and the wall, slipping instantly from her sticky thighs, dropping her skirts and closing his trousers in almost one deft movement.

Alberto couldn't hear them at all anymore and wondered if the snorting and snuffling had been some animal. But Ana and Joaquin could hear them perfectly. They were far too numerous to be silent, and even if they had been, nearly thirty pairs of lungs panting in a combination of excitement and fear made a considerable noise to the ears of practised musicians.

"Who is it?" Montez leapt up the ladder, onto the wall and looked down on them.

Alberto, never one given to silence, was speechless at the sight of this handsome gypsy looming above them in the intermittent moonlight.

"It's Alberto."

"Alberto who?"

"Alberto *de la Vega*." Alberto improvised.

"And who else?" Joaquin asked, noting in astonishment the pairs of eyes looking up, and the youth of them all. "Is this some massive break out from the *reformatorio*?"

"Not exactly."

"What exactly?"

"We're going to the Alhambra."

Ana had now scrambled up beside Joaquin, and seeing the fear in some of their small faces said,

"I think you had better tell us what's going on."

"There's no more risk of fatalities or damage than with any other method." Raúl was insistent.

"Everything has changed," Antonio said flatly.

"Nothing's changed Sir," Raúl said passionately.

"Raúl, we now have thirty children missing and very likely making their way into the Alhambra as we speak," Antonio passed a weary hand across his brow. "You can't expect me to authorise a military operation until we at least have some information as to their whereabouts."

"Sir..."

"There's nothing more to say."

"Shall we at least prepare?"

"Very well," agreed Antonio. "Prepare for an assault at first light. I will give the order. Where's García?"

"García Lorca was, if not Spain's greatest poet, then the greatest of his century. That's why they talk about him all the time. There are still people alive who knew him, heard his recitals, played music with him," Reggie was in his element.

"Read all this in the guide books did you Reg?" said Daniel Goddard morosely.

"Passes the hours my dear boy and beats getting pissed all the time," Reggie said tartly.

"Like you would know," Daniel retorted. "Anyway, the booze is all gone in the *parador*. Our delightful hosts have, in their wisdom, poured it all down the drain. But," Daniel paused with a theatrical smile, "all is not lost. In the gardeners' cupboard by the *patronato*, kindly left unlocked and unattended by those same dear hosts, I came upon a saving grace. Here I have upon me a

small vial of purple liquid, which, I am reliably informed by the down-and-outs from our own fair city, our dear York, will suffice briefly, until reinforcements come," and he raised the meths above his head and then to his lips and said, "to York."

"Daniel, don't be so bloody stupid. Meths? Come on man, get a grip."

"My dear sir. A grip is what I have. This grip," and he flexed his hand, "on this charming bottle of, let's call it, the Alhambra cocktail. Let me just try a small swig." Daniel put his lips to the bottle and drank deeply. "Oh my God, he said turning misted eyes to Reggie. "Oh my God."

"Daniel, I beg of you. Stop it."

"*Daniel I beg of you stop it*," he mimicked. "Christ, you sound like my mother!" And with that he set off into the night.

Rashida helped with the meals and was satisfied that Dolores was resting once more in the *hotel america*. Mary had said that the earlier prayer gathering of the women had helped. Although Dolores had been tired out by it, she was peaceful. Rashida thought she would go and find Mary to see if her head felt any better. The brute had pulled her along by the hair and although she hadn't lost much, she had said her scalp was sore. Maybe after prayers they might walk a little in the evening air.

"Do you always wash before prayer?" Mary asked her as they meandered among the pomegranates.

"Yes. I try. It isn't always possible, but Allah will not punish anyone prevented from following Islam by circumstance. Even taking an alcoholic drink can be permissible, " Rashida answered looking at Mary from under her lashes. Non-Muslims often enjoyed finding this little fact out.

"Really?"

"Yes. Islam is very flexible you know."

"It doesn't come across like that," said Mary thoughtfully.

"No it doesn't. But then American Bible thumpers don't really express very well what Jesus Christ stood for do they?"

"True enough!" Mary had laughed.

Rashida stopped from time to time as they were walking to touch the box hedges and run her hands along the tightly woven cypress hedges.

"You love it here don't you?" Mary asked.

"Don't you?"

"Yes. It's everything I dreamed it would be, and more."

"I'll say! You didn't expect to be caught up in this mess did you?" said Rashida laughing.

"No. I mean it's more beautiful than I ever imagined. But you, for you it's more, isn't it? You know, the way you touch the plants and look at the buildings. It's like you really belong here."

"I just think, how long will this go on? Will there be an Alhambra or even a Rashida in the morning? I want to notice it, be mindful of it, every day. Mustafa, that's my husband..."

"You're married?" Mary sounded incredulous.

"Of course. What did you expect?" and when Mary didn't answer Rashida continued, "our favourite Hadiz is, *If you think tomorrow might be the Judgement Day, plant a fruit tree.* I always think that's a message of faith and hope if ever there was one."

"Do you think that is the most important thing then?" asked Mary.

"What?"

"Faith." said Mary.

"No."

"What then? Hope?"

"Yes," said Rashida

"What's the difference?"

"Faith is knowing," said Rashida definitely, "knowing, without evidence, what is true. Faith doesn't allow for doubt. But

hope, hope is a more risky business altogether. With hope you just don't know and the not knowing helps keep you alive."

They wandered in silence toward the *secano*, where the bricks of the *medina* might still have the retained heat of the day. The scent of the sun on the conifers was gone and the nets swung low across the excavations. After a while they sat on the stubby walls. The wind was chill, the clouds were moving across the moon, and Mary wrapped her scarf around herself more tightly.

"I've been pondering on poison." Rashida said aloud. "I've been watching them all. It could be lead poisoning, but it's not likely given they have moved around. Maybe mercury," she faded out, "but before I did my midwifery training, general nursing, well we did a bit on radiation sickness. I have been wondering if that could be it?"

Before Mary could answer they heard a rustling and were startled by a sonorous voice singing madly and a figure weaving through the hedges and onto the open space around the silo where Nita's body had been lowered.

"Nita my lovely," the voice sang in English. "Nita my delight. Let me warm your cold body in the heat of this night."

And the women watched in horror as Daniel Goddard leaned far over the edge of the silo and then tumbled, as if in slow motion, to the depths below.

Below the Sierra Nevada, toward Motril, the clouds had first gathered during the morning. They had been pushing in from the sea all day in a contest with the mountain air, seeing which of them might gain the advantage. Part of the rolling light and dark that had characterised the afternoon had been caused by their frolicking between themselves. Finally the clouds were becoming heavier, and the first heavy drops began to fall on the *vega*. The plain, which had been dry for so long, absorbed every drop as it hit the earth and anyone watching would have seen them disappear instantly through the dust.

Dust to dust. Ashes to ashes. Mary Stansfield wept at the side of the silo, too deep to descend, too dark to see. Of all the people she had imagined might perish since their capture, Daniel Goddard had never been one of them.

One of them had to go. Alberto knew it had to be him. But he was afraid. The rain had started and looked unlikely to stop. Lola might want to float, but if the watercourses filled to the top, they would not be able to breathe, and if the water flowed too fast they would pitch into the great reservoir sealed tight below *la plaza de las armas* and never, ever be able to get out.

"To get out they will need to stop here, if not before *calle real*, then not far into it. Certainly before the swift descent into the reservoir below the *la plaza de las armas*." Dr Jesús stabbed at the map. "Javi will agree with me, with the rain..." he gestured hopelessly.

"What's with the rain?" asked García, already afraid he knew the answer.

"The channels will fill, the water will flow fast, and without the sluices operating..." he trailed off.

"What do you mean without the sluices operating?"

"Well all over we have little sluices, here, here, here," Javi placed at least ten pencil dots on the map in the palace gardens, "this is how we water the gardens, we draw off the main water, or re-direct it if we have too much."

"Or up here," Dr Jesús joined in, "up by the *generalife*

where we have the main on-site reservoirs, we just shut down the channels and fill the reservoirs, get the pressure up and conserve water. And then of course there are the other water rights that operate."

García thought he might explode. This muddled method of gathering information was increasingly one of the things that was driving him insane. Two steps forward one step back could describe all the interrogations. What had Antonio called it, *wading through treacle*?

"Which rights are these?"

"Well people with land, you know people with fields, they can draw water off the River Darro at pre-arranged times."

"How do they do that?"

"They have sluice gates too. Everyone has a specified time when they can take water so the channel doesn't empty all at once."

"Where are these fields and these people?"

"All along the River Darro."

"What all the way back from the Alhambra to the Sierra Nevada?"

"Pretty much."

Antonio intervened, saying,

"Manuel, go find out what times and where people are irrigating. Right back as far as the source of the Darro. It's a small mercy we are not in the middle of high summer when everyone would want to irrigate. Even so, get me the names of every local authority and every water authority from here to the top of Veleta."

Veleta, although the second largest peak of the Sierra Nevada, if viewed from the city of Granada looks bigger than its sister, Mulhacén. It is an illusion. Valeta is simply nearer, sloped, rather than jutted. She catches the sun most of the day so is illuminated, while Mulhacén remains largely in the shadows. On a clear day, when the ever-increasing pollution from Granada does not either taint Veleta with a dirty orange hue, or obliterate it totally from view, she provides a dramatic backdrop to the scenes of the city and the Alhambra, grand, shiny, dominant and eternal.

Gerardo fancied he could feel the cold air coming off the snow of Veleta as he reconsidered their position. He put out his hand. Yes. He could feel it just beginning, spritz of rain. He cast his eye downward to the metropolis below. The city was growing hourly more populous and more quiet. Such an unlikely combination. And all the while he could see that his own people were failing like the light. The latest small explosion had done little to elevate their spirits. They had stopped asking him now if anyone had responded to their calls.

They looked at him with sorrow more than expectation. Under Jay's direction he had led them here, and to what? The Alhambra should have provided the platform from which at last they would be heard. It felt instead as though it might be their tomb. He thought of Mary and longed for her vitality.

"Hope is the one thing Alberto always has," said Javi, smiling fondly. "He is a natural optimist. He always thinks that something can be made to happen that will change things and make them better. He will be in already, or if not, he won't be far off it."

"OK, so how do you think they will go in?"

"I'm more interested in why they might be going there," said Manuel.

"For Agustín," stated García flatly. What people missed always astounded him. Had they not watched and listened to this fragile child? Whether his chest was puffed out, or whether he was delinquent, could they not see what was an almost palpable

longing the boy had for the old man he called Agustín?

"The old man?" said Manuel in a dismissive tone.

"Of course," said García. "He loves him."

"They'll never get in," said Raúl, leaving unsaid his real point, *if the army can't get in, then thirty kids can't.*'

"Oh yes they will," said García knowing only too well how human determination operated. There was no defence that could neutralise someone who was prepared to trade their life for a cause, or for someone they loved. Suicide bombers had demonstrated that a time or two. Alberto would probably have no sense of the trade that was at stake. All this determined little human being wanted was to be with possibly the only adult who had ever shown him personal kindness. García was in no doubt but that Alberto would get in.

"All right. Assuming they do get in, how will they do it?" asked Manuel.

"They aren't going to go in here," said Dr Jesús pointing at the effluence channel. "Alberto said yesterday it was too high up and the flow was too strong to go against. They can easily go in here at *la torre del agua*, just take the aqueduct right across the path of *cuesta de los chinos*, but they have to get there, unseen. Not easy for thirty kids."

"They'll go in through the *generalife*. Won't they?" said García quietly. "They damn well will. They'll do what he said. They won't use the old dry tunnel. He's going to float them. From here, the new pumping station. I'll bet you anything. And then they'll drop. Right here. Into the open reservoirs, the *albercones*. These square tanks right here. Right above the *generalife*. They won't have to sneak around. Look, it's obvious. All this new channelling. This stuff from the 1960s. All this that Javi talked about. All this water. Here. Running to the new car park. And then through it. All this decorative stuff..."

"All useless, silly, wasteful, stuff," muttered Dr Jesús under

his breath.

"This will get them in. To *la torre del agua*. Without even raising their heads. Lola will have them all floating. In amongst the cedars. Christ! And then here," García pointed to the path that separated *la torre del agua* from the *generalife*, "that's it. This is all they have to do. One by one. They slip across this path. Here in the shadows. Here, beneath the cypress."

"They just float on in," Dr Jesús shivered as he repeated Garciá's words.

"But he won't do it tonight." said García. "Fisher is right. The kid's street-wise. He's too smart. It's too cold. He'll be afraid of the rain. He'll wait until morning."

"Wait until morning."

"I can't. The boys." María pulled on her clothes in the dark.

"I can't either. My wife..." O'Reilly trailed off with a slight Irish brogue, "but I wanted to ask you anyway."

"Thanks."

"Thanks," said Antonio to Manuel when he handed him the list an hour later. "Good work." And then to Raúl he said, "Get your men to start ringing round."

"What, now!"

"Wake people up, it's the only way. All those sluice gates need opening up."

"Opening up my heart isn't easy María."

"I'm not asking you too."

"Yes you are. By never asking me for anything you a are

273

impelling me to give it to you!"

María leaned over and kissed O'Reilly on the forehead.

"You're a good man Eddie. You'll do the right thing."

David felt a foreboding with the rain.

Nature was the permanent wild card. One day after they had arrived in Miami, the first of the season's hurricanes had hit. One day. If they had left one day later they would never have made it. He, his brothers and sisters and parents would have been fish fodder at the bottom of the ocean.

Alberto was street-wise. But was he wise enough? If the water rose too fast, if he went in too soon...all he would have done was buy another day of delay while the army became even more determined.

An involuntary prayer escaped David's lips. His homosexual self might be *persona non grata* in the Catholic view, and even if his prayers for the Muslim Rashida were not deemed worthy of a Catholic God's intervention, surely he could raise a Catholic prayer for Alberto? García no sooner framed the thoughts than he laughed out loud at himself. *Sod any god that be*, he thought, *and let the Alhambra in her ancient majesty save them all*.

dusk

"David!" Antonio whispered into the darkness of the sleeping quarters.

García woke instantly, sat up and pulled on his sweater and trousers.

"I'm here," he said walking towards Antonio's voice.

"Come outside."

On the *terraza* once again, but well in under shelter from the rain that was now torrential, Antonio leaned on the railings as García came and stood next to him.

"Raúl is going to want to go in at first light. I want to stop him. I want to wait and see what these kids do."

When García said nothing, Antonio said,

"Well look happy," and clapped him on the back. "You've got your wish."

"I'm happy Raúl isn't going in. But I am concerned."

"Because now there are too many wild cards?"

García smiled a lop-sided smile.

"Yeah. I think there may be." Then he said, "Tell me. Viznar. Where they shot Lorca..."

Startled by the change in subject, Antonio said,

"What about it?"

"They say they put a monument there."

"Yes. Finally. They did."

"When?"

Antonio looked at García curiously. It was just like the ride from the airport. García was asking short, seemingly irrelevant questions.

"I don't know, a few years ago, 2001 or 2002 maybe."

"He was shot in 1936. Took a long time. For so great a man I mean. Don't you think?"

"Yes. Too long."

"Why do you think that was?" García asked almost conversationally, looking across the ravine at the Alhambra.

Antonio was quiet for a moment. Then he said,

"Shame. I think we felt – we feel," he corrected, then clarified, "the death of Lorca shamed us all."

For a long time, as much as three minutes, neither man spoke and then Antonio said,

"What do you think they imagine those kids are going to do when they get there?"

"Your guess is as good as mine," said García shaking his head. "I have no idea."

"I have no idea when it first started. I only know that one day the life went out of me."

"How?" Mary was very still in the crook of his arm.

"Everything was an effort. I couldn't think anymore. My arms and legs were heavy. Then I noticed everyone was like that. My sisters, my mother, all the women in my family."

"And all this?" she said gesturing toward the hole in *la torre de cautiva* just visible from *la sala de las dos hermanas*.

"We can't do this for much longer," he admitted. "But we can take out the towers one by one."

"Why don't they come to talk to you?"

"I don't know. We have been sending messages. But they are probably going to storm the place. It looks better on TV," he said cynically.

"You can't be serious!" and he moved awkwardly as she jerked with her exclamation. Mary was suddenly aware that he was uncomfortable, bony and angular, the earth was bruising him.

"Here," she said, "let me get you something soft."

"No," he said. "Don't move. You're soft. This is perfect." And he closed his eyes.

Mary lay beside him, looking out at the rain that was beating in torrents on the water of *el fuente de los leones*. It was hard to imagine that no less than three hours before she had been in despair at the side of the silo, crying over Daniel, her tears and the rain mingling together, while Rashida had tried to comfort her.

And then, as always, this man had come and found her where she should not have been. Gerardo. Gerardo. His name was Gerardo.

Rashida had explained to him how she had seen Daniel tip in. Even though they knew he must be dead, Mary still thought that perhaps there was some hope. But this man had shaken his head and Mary had known he was confirming it was useless and she had sunk to the sodden ground, not in a faint, but in a final surrender as to the ugliness of death: the babies, Nita, now Daniel. And soon, she thought, as the tears gathered, doubtless some of the older men in The Constantine Singers.

Rashida had tried to help her up but Mary made herself heavy, like she used to when she was a child and she didn't want to walk anymore and wanted to be carried. At first she was crying about Daniel and Nita. Then she was crying about the possible demise of the nine surviving members of her group. Then she was crying about every motherless child that had ever been born. Later she moved on to the starving and the dispossessed. She wanted to be left in the rain, left in the mud, left to just wreck herself in tears.

He too had tried to lift her, joining Rashida, but he barely made an impact on Rashida's efforts. And Mary made herself even heavier, and the soaking of her clothes in the downpour added more pounds. Finally he had sent Rashida to get help while she lay on the ground, the taste of the earth in her mouth and wept for the world.

"Don't cry," he had said to her over and over. "Don't cry. Don't cry," and he had stroked her hair. "I am sorry for earlier.

Sorry for hurting you. Sorry for dragging you down from the *generalife*." And she had looked up at him then and reached out a filthy arm. "I couldn't help it," he went on. "I was afraid, afraid you would ruin everything." She looked at him with a question in her eyes. *Ruin everything*? What was *everything*? She shrugged silently at him and fell back against the mud. He continued to stroke her. "Don't cry. Come with me. Come on. Get up. Come on."

And with her strength and will she had pulled herself up against him and he had guided her through the *medina*, into *calle real*, down past the *palacio de carlos V*, to the shelter of the *sala de las dos hermanas*. She had slipped on the water that dripped from her clothes onto the sleek stone flooring.

He had caught at her and held her with a steadiness that surprised him, and then he had guided her toward the pile of blankets that the women folded each morning. For now that everyone had taken refuge in the hotels, they were still stacked neatly on the side.

"Here," he had said gently. "Here. Dry yourself. Take your things off, dry yourself." And slowly he had helped her undress, wrapping the blanket around her as the garments fell to the floor.

She had watched him wring them out and string them up on the balcony of the *mirador*, beyond the first chamber, deep into the shadows, beneath the vaulted marquetry ceiling. Naked, wrapped in her blanket on the pile of folded ones, she had waited.

"Here," he had said, "give me that one. It's wet. Take another." And he watched and waited with his hand out to take the discarded cloth as she loosed it and let him have it, whilst wrapping herself self-consciously in another. He took off his own wet shirt and hung it up and she saw his back was defined by his ribs. Then he bent to release his trousers and saw her looking at him.

"Don't worry," he had then said as he slid them off. "I can't do it anymore. You're quite safe from sex with me."

And the look he gave her was so bleak she could not help herself and went to him and put her arms around him and said,

"I'm so sorry."

And her damp naked body slid on his and he had held like he would never let her go.

"Go on." Joaquin said.

"My idea is to get in," Alberto spoke in front of the huge fire. "Once we are in, we can take it from there."

Ana looked at him.

"It may be an idea to have a bit more of a plan," she said. "Maybe you could let us know you are there."

"But how will we do that?"

"And how will we know you have seen us?" asked Lola.

Joaquin leaned forward across the guitar on his lap. All thirty sets of eyes were on him as he said,

"I have an idea."

And they remained fixed on him as he laid it out.

SUNDAY

Quiero vivir en Granada
Solamente por oir
La campana de la Vela
Cuando me voy a dormir

I long to live in Granada, if only to hear the clean
Pealing of the Vela as I drift to dream
Trad.

dawn

Agustín had always told Alberto to be careful of the *patronato*. Sucking on his pipe, or bent double in his fields, he had admonished the boy to be watchful of all those *functionarios* or bureaucrats. The *new royalty*, he had called them. On days when Agustín was particularly riled he would deliver a complete tirade on the laziness of the civil servants who had jobs for life, who only worked each day until 2pm, who never worked public holidays or *festivos* and who, even when they were at work, did very little, spending more time on the telephone arranging their social lives than attending to the increasing work load.

And the boy remembered it now, rubbing his eyes and walking, away from Lola, in and among the sleeping children, prodding each of them with his foot where they slept at sixes and sevens in Agustín's porch. As they stirred he looked from Agustín's house toward the walls of the Alhambra. It was still there, red and erect.

Yet it looked tired, thought Alberto, and he thought it was odd that a building could look tired. But it did. It looked like an old man that had seen one sadness too many. The Alhambra looked like his grandfather looked when he left Alberto at the *reformatorio*. It looked like an old man who had no hopes. It looked alarmingly like Agustín.

"Ever since the governor of the Alhambra went," Agustín had told Alberto, "when I was just a boy like you, well, things have been different. Now there are always big fights about the water." One reason, Agustín told Alberto he had always kept his gloves in his pocket, was in case he ever needed them to punch up *el director*. "Because," he said, "one thing is sure, the old director wanted to get rid of us, so the new one probably will too."

"Why?"

"He doesn't like us living here on the *finca* between the *generalife* and the Alhambra." Agustín was very dismissive when he talked about such things to Alberto and Lola and always waved his hand over his head as if a Flamenco flourish would send the old director and indeed any new one, straight to hell. It was just another modulation on his theme of the THEYs of this world. "And one sure way to get rid of us," Agustín explained, "is to ensure that no-one else can cultivate this little strip of land. THEY go on and on about the Alhambra's water rights. THEY say we have none. As if water can BELONG to anyone... and any idiot knows you can't cultivate a *finca* without water."

Alberto could not imagine the *finca* without Agustín and Rosario. He could not imagine the Alhambra without them. He could not imagine life without them.

"Anyone will tell you," Agustín had said many times to Alberto, "that in the good old days, they would ring The Big Bell, *la vela*, in *la torre de la vela* and everyone would know that this was the moment to open the sluice gates and do the daily irrigation. The water was for everyone.

"Of course," he told Alberto, "the fact that we actually live on the *finca* is the real sore point. They think our house is too big and too dilapidated. They said that the last time they tried to buy it from me. That was the word they used." Agustín had been indignant, "Dilapidated! How dare they? My family have always lived here. Just like the people in the *hotel america*, or old María Santos Moreno in *calle real* who thinks she is above us all. These are our homes and have been for generations. Just because the new European State of Spain wants to tidy everything up and prissy it for the tourists, I don't see why we should all be run out of our homes. *Cuesta de los chinos* is a perfectly agreeable way to walk into town and I don't feel there is anything about my house to detract from the pleasure of it. And another thing *hijo*," he had added, "don't you forget it: if we can survive Franco, we can survive democracy, and somedays *hijo mio*, I am not sure which is the lesser evil." Then Agustín would see Alberto's look of concern and Rosario's look of alarm. Instead of labouring his views on THEY, and crushing the child's hopes, he would modify his opinions and say instead,

"The people, in the end, can always win the day. Remember that."

"And Viznar?" Alberto had asked. But Agustín had not answered but instead repeated,

"The people, in the end, can always win the day."

Alberto had looked at Agustín with total and pure admiration. *The people, in the end, can always win the day*. It sang through his soul like a mantra. It meant that anything was possible. It meant one day he might be warm. One day, so might Lola. One day... The possibilities were endless. Perhaps it was even possible that one day, even he, as one of the people, even he might *win the day*. It meant one day he might be man like Agustín, someone who too might call a boy, *hijo mio*, my son.

For Alberto, in that moment, Agustín and the Alhambra became one, Agustín was the Alhambra. It was Agustín who, on their route down the hillside from San Miguel, always fetched Alberto and Lola in for *cola cao* in winter and a cup of *gazpacho* in summer. It was Agustín who was everything that Alberto revered about the Alhambra and now, Agustín was now revered in his own right. Agustín had wisdom, warmth, generosity, ancient-ness as Lola called it, and, finally, Agustín had knowledge.

But on this night, Agustín was not at home. Alberto could tell as they had approached. There were no lights burning, no dogs barking and above all, no *chiminea* smoking and plenty of food left out uncovered. Rosario would never leave food out and uncovered. So now he knew for sure THEY had come and THEY had taken them.

Too many tears and too much excitement had exhausted Mary. She lay for a long time with her eyes wide open, staring up into

the masonry and fretwork of the ceiling, layered upon layer, she felt as though she might become lost in its tiers. This was a moment never to forget. This was a moment that even the loss of Daniel could not penetrate. If anything, his death made the moment sweeter. Next to death suddenly life was the dearest thing, even caked in tears and mud, even lost in uncertainty, even shot through with fear, in whatever form, even here, in silence and stillness.

This day before her, unknown and unknowable, would be lived and would likely have outcomes that were completely unpredictable if yesterday were anything to go by. Even this day before her was already sweet. Daniel lost his life because he had no care for it. He lost it to the deep of the silo, but he had lost it long before.

She was careful how she moved in case she disturbed Gerardo. She need not have been. He had hardly slept at all. He had spent the entire night listening to her breathing, feeling the fluttering of her heart under his hand where she had placed it beneath her shirt.

Beneath her shirt he could always just see the gold shimmer a chain and cross. When she got undressed it was the only thing she didn't take off. In the past, that would have been a turn off. He would never have felt comfortable seeing the cross with his eyes, whilst feeling something so against the cross with the rest of his body.

This time the reverse was true. He loved to see the cross on María's naked breasts when she straddled him. It was that above all else that alerted O'Reilly to the fact that this was different. That, and her connection to David García.

García leaned forward, scarcely able to believe his eyes. Picking up a pen he noted the web address, closed the webpage, and leaned back in his chair, alternately clenching and twiddling the pen between his brown fingers, twisting his ring. He stood briefly, stretched, sat again, and typed another set of key words into the computer, waited as the light from the screen played across his face and the search engine at last rested on the pages. He clicked twice, leaned forward again intently, and then scrolled down the page and then back up.

Back-up might be needed, and not just more soldiers either. Antonio was reluctant to ask lest it be interpreted as meaning that he was struggling with the command. Given that they were running on very little information, they were withstanding the strains of impotence quite well. But others might not agree.

He swung himself out of bed and ran a hand over his stubble. If he was quick he might manage to get a shower and a shave before anyone else. Whatever might be interpreted from a call for back-up, he thought as he reached for his shirt, it posed more problems because it would mean more people. It was already a strained team. Since García's young red-haired wild cards had bought him a little time, maybe he could delay just a little longer. Antonio was inclined, at least for a few more hours, to let it play.

"Let it play," Raúl grumbled to his junior, "in fact turn it up." And he turned in his cot, almost petulant, toward the wall. The news reader simply reiterated what they all knew, or what they thought they knew. Satisfied they knew nothing of note, Raúl threw his legs over the side of the cot and let the rod of the cot edge bite into his thighs. He discarded his tee shirt, dragging it up and over his head from behind his neck in one swift action. It was damp with sweat. He gave it a swift sniff, used it to wipe under his arms and threw it to one side. With his elbows on his knees he put his head in his hands.

He would be happy when this whole thing was over. It was a strain. No doubt about it. But not the strain for him that he knew it was for the others. Unlike them, he knew exactly what needed to be done. There was too much at stake NOT TO DO it. He even knew he was the man TO DO it. That was why they had appointed him. None of that was a strain.

It was the waiting that was the strain. There was the waiting for the command that would authorise them to go in and there was the waiting for García. With all that athletic yet mature male strength, and that Cubano look, García was a man worth waiting for. And Raúl was pretty sure García was a man hungry enough to explode.

The outer calm belied a furnace of need, Raúl was certain. One touch and he would bet his life the man would ignite. It wasn't possible to keep the control that García exhibited without it costing him. The sleeplessness was a key indicator, and the way he spoke. Those short staccato sentences. Then too, the twiddling of his ring, the way he gripped things: pens, chair-backs, books, door handles, even coffee cups. You could tell so much by how a man made and held a fist. And no man Raúl had ever had could keep his fist balled beyond orgasm. Raúl couldn't wait. He had to wait. He couldn't wait. He would wait. He was waiting.

He was waiting to complain at Ana as she entered his cave and turned off his radio. He turned over again and groaned. Joaquin Montez didn't remember the last time he had been awake at dawn. That is to say, the last time he had been to bed and then been awakened at dawn. He had played and danced, and a few other things besides, all through the night until dawn, but it had been years since he had actually arisen to dawn.

"Come on. Get up!" she said laughing at him. "You promised!"

"You promised us Mamá," said Chico, squeezing himself into bed next to Carmen Romero.

"I know, I know," said Carmen trying to pull the duvet up higher.

"You have to wake up," said Chico emphatically.

Carmen was quiet, wanting to tell her son that she had been awake for hours. This night had been particularly long. More full of dreams of Daniel than usual. Dancing. Dancing. Dancing. The dreams were always of dancing.

"The twins are hungry," he said stroking her arm. "Gabby is hungry. Ange is hungry."

"Aw, Chico! You didn't wake Ange up did you?"

"She says we all need to stop worrying. She says Jack will sort it out and be back soon. And we all say that we need to eat *huevos rancheros* and you promised to make it."

"Make it count Rashida," was what her childhood friend Marta had told her. "As far as we know this life is not a dress rehearsal. This is it."

It had been years since Rashida had even thought about Marta. She had read that at the moment of death one's whole life passes before one. Was she thinking about Marta today because this was the beginning of the end? On her bed in the *hotel america* she strained to hear the birds' first song, then stood and flung open the balcony to meet the dawn.

The trees between the hotel and the distant walls were lacy with new leaves. The dawn was so pristine that the trees cast no shadows. It was time for prayer. Here in the grey still moments between night and day, this was the time the spirit moved. This was the time when her communion with Allah was most acute.

She leaned on the window and saw the light stealing the dark, washing it from her sight, and gripped the frame. Mary was with her man. She was sure of it. Somewhere out there, in a monument that had seen thousands upon thousands of lovers, there were two more. She felt her pulse race and her stomach turn. She scanned the horizon and longed for Mustafa more than she dared allow.

"The end result is what matters Paula," Jack Fisher tried to reassure his wife. He went up on one elbow, pulling the sheet up over her bare shoulder, looked her in the eye and said, "The powers that be will do their best, and there is not a lot we can add to that."

"You always say that we can affect the outcome Jack."

Jack fell back on the bed recognising that this one of those little pearls of wisdom that he had dropped carelessly from time to time on front of the children to help them build their own confidence. And here it was, ready to return to him and bite him in the arse. He groaned.

"Not all things."

"I know," said Paula smiling. "I'm just rattling your chain." Then she paused and added, "But I'm scared."

He put his arm around her.

"You should be. The whole thing is scary. For everyone."

Everyone was more or less up when Manuel leaned down from his cot and reached for his bag of *pipas*. He still wasn't sure if the obsessive eating of sunflower seeds was going to save him from tobacco.

He rather feared that by giving up cigarettes, what he had avoided in lung disease, was going to be more than made up for with dental bills for gum treatment. He rubbed his jaw. The amount of lacerations he had given himself on the *pipas* shells these past few days beggared belief and hadn't made anything easier either. And for what? What did the bastards want?

"Want to look?" García said to Antonio as he approached, while still continuing to look at the computer screen.

"You look rough," Antonio said walking around behind David to look over his shoulder, and taking in García's own stubble and square eyes.

"Internet. Been on all night."

Christ, thought Antonio, does this man never quit?

"Anything interesting?" he said aloud.

"The nets. Javi said fishermen could spread them. It made me look. Here. Fishing communities in northern Spain," stated García.

"Yeah?" Antonio leaned forward.

"See," García pointed at the screen. "Cross-refer this with the World Health Organisation. Now. Have a read. There's something curious here."

morning

Rashida Santiago had completed her prayers at the open window of a bedroom in the *hotel america* and then moved into the hotel kitchen to prepare a coffee before taking it to sit very still in *el partal*.

The broken stone, the splintered wood and the torn up earth all appealed to her sense of doom. Yesterday afternoon's small explosion was just another reminder they were about to die at any moment anyway.

One man's terrorist was another man's freedom fighter. Wasn't that another thing that her tutor Marta had said? along with *where there is death there is hope*. Rashida had challenged her about that one and Marta had grinned at her and said,

"Don't you get it Shida, who would have wanted Franco forever? Or Isabella and that rat's ass Ferdinand? In the end everyone dies. Isn't that GREAT!"

The thought of it now made Rashida laugh out loud.

"Out loud," said Antonio, "read it out loud."

"'*Two years ago, el Pueblo de Conchi, a small fishing village in northern Spain, took action,*'" David García read his screen, then stopped and said as an aside, "I think what we call in the US, a class action, *against the British Fleet.*" García paused.

"The British Fleet?" Antonio repeated. "That's a very big *class action* I would say. What for?"

García scrolled down the page. The text raced by on the screen, and then he said,

"It doesn't say but it goes on and on. Essentially they made a claim. They say it has been ignored. Look here. They threaten to take steps. Any necessary to get justice." David looked up at Antonio and said, "Does this ring any bells?"

Antonio shook his head,

"Not immediately. But it might ring someone's bell. Hang

on," and he took out his mobile. "*Hijo*, it's your father. Do me a favour will ya?"

"Ya know, the minute I saw him looking up at you, trying with all his might to appear fearless and strong, I loved him," Ana said to Joaquin.

It was true. There he had been the night before, bold as brass, with all his followers pressed against the wall that stair-stepped down from the *reformatorio* almost to the River Darro itself. With his red curls and his dancing eyes she had been completely enchanted by him, so much so, Joaquin now joked that he was getting jealous.

She and Joaquin had led them off toward Joaquin's cave. They were almost there when they had heard the soldiers. They had all hit the dirt and lain close to the *chimenea* that would later hold the dancing flames that had warmed them all. Lying silent and unmoving, despite the stabs from the sisal ends, scarcely breathing, they had listened as the soldiers had finally retreated amid oaths and swearing.

Then, at last, stomachs full of *migas*, they had sat around the fire and spoken long and earnestly, their NEW PLAN erradicating their earlier fears. Joaquin had played guitar a little while Ana and some of the children cleared up and others prepared to leave. Finally Alberto had stood with all his companions to continue on to Agustín's *finca*.

"We have to see if he and Rosario are OK," he had reiterated his earlier worries. Then he had looked up at Joaquin and said, "You promise to do it?"

"I promise," Joaquin Montez had said, and smiled down at Alberto as the boy gravely shook his hand.

Alberto had then set off down the hill again with all the children, the night half gone, everyone warm and with full stomachs. The ache in Alberto's heart had lightened, for after their long talk at the fireside, Ana and Joaquin and all their cousins had agreed to do it, and he knew that they would.

They would kick off now. Bugger it. Just his luck. No sooner had Jack Fisher thought he had it cracked, and the choristers had agreed to the idea of flying home, than they had gone into solidarity mode. Suddenly no-one had anything pressing to do in York. No-one had a wife or family to get home to, and seemingly not one member of The Constantine Singers had a job, or had ever had a job, or was the least interested in ever having one again.

At first when Paula and Jack had arrived to tell them all that there was no news, everyone had seemed very conciliatory and respectful. They listened carefully to Jack and nodded at all the right moments. But within half an hour all that had changed. Jack had been politely informed that everyone had cancelled their flights. They were here and they were, they said, *staying for the duration*.

"The duration of such an illness, Mary, is hard to predict," Rashida was helping her fold the blankets. "It depends on how great the damage."

"He has almost no flesh on him Rashida. He's just a bag of bones. It's almost like they are going to poke through his skin at any moment. And..." she paused.

"And what?"

"He's..."

"Impotent, right?" Rashida supplied for her.

"Yes. How did you know?"

Rashida was quiet. Silently she revised her earlier opinions.

They were just flesh and blood, like anyone else, just trying to find a way through a life that to them was as grim as any action they might be taking. She said gently,

"It sounds like radiation sickness. It makes me think of chemotherapy and radiotherapy for cancer cases, where the body is subjected to terrible poisons and doses of radiation. The whole point is to attack the disease while maintaining the survival of the body. So people do survive. But without a proper set of medical reports, to see what levels we are talking about, well these guys, she swept her hand across the air, it's anybody's guess."

"**It's anybody's guess**. But I doubt it somehow," said Antonio. "If the children were there then I think we would have had some indication by now."

García stared at the Alhambra. Although it had poured with rain without ceasing before dawn, this morning it was as if no drop of rain had fallen. The sky was as clear as any he had ever seen, with wonderful azure Andalusian sparkle.

"And so," he said to Antonio.

"I'm holding off as long as I can David."

"Antonio!" Manuel was beside them. "That question that García raised earlier about missing explosives. I followed it up," García shot him a grateful look. "And guess what? We have an MER from the quarry above Cájar."

"Missing Explosives Report?" Antonio turned on his heel.

"They are missing a truck load of explosives." Manuel was jubilant. "Since last week. Right here, under our noses."

Antonio looked at Raúl who said,

"That's not possible. A truck? Last week? An MER would have been with us by now."

"Not necessarily," said García thoughtfully.

"Yes, necessarily," retorted Raúl. "In Spain especially. As

Fisher has said already, MER is required in Spain and Northern Ireland. In those places and only those places in the European Union, you can't move explosives from one place to another without a CATD. Every single time. One has to be issued every time," he repeated for emphasis. "There wasn't one transfer over the past six months that hasn't been delivered. We checked."

"CATD?" questioned García.

"Competent Authority Transfer Document," supplied Antonio.

"Any other country and you can get a license that lasts for as many transfers as you like within a limited period," Raúl went on, "but here, because of ETA, and in Northern Ireland because of the IRA, it's different. Nothing moves without authority. Every time. Nothing."

"Maybe it didn't move," said García quietly.

"Well something did," snapped Raúl. "A few towers have been demolished."

"Actually García's right," said Manuel consulting his notes. "In a way. It didn't move. It didn't move off site. It just moved from one storage point to another, on the same site. The shot-firer at the Cájar *canteras* rang in this morning. We sent someone to talk to him."

"Cájar? How far is that?" interrupted García.

"The other side of the Alhambra," Antonio replied. "About as close to the Alhambra as Sacromonte. It's a big local quarry, supplies the construction industry and also provides land-fill at the same time."

"The quarry is closed," Manuel continued, "because of all this," he said gesturing toward the Alhambra, "so he thought he'd go in and finish rotating the stock while it was quiet. The transfer truck had been loaded with Gelamex on Thursday to move it to the upper site for blasting on Friday. So he drove it up and started unloading. Something about the cases didn't seem right. When he

303

opened them they were full of beer."

"Beer?"

"Yeah."

Yeah. Gerardo muttered to himself, *all present and correct.*

He fingered the detonators' box carefully and then set it aside. No problem at all. His problem was Gelamex. He wasn't going to have enough to take out the *alcazaba* if he needed to, or even *la torre de la vela*. Well, not unless he scaled the walls downward and retrieved the charges from the rest of the towers.

That was impossible. Even if he could do it unseen, he could never prise them back out of the holes they'd been rammed into. The Gelamex had already deteriorated anyway. That was evident from the poor showing at *la torre de cautiva*. The sun and the damp together was reducing the life of the nitro-glycerine. As if time weren't against them enough.

"Enough!" Manuel held up his hands in mock horror. "I don't get it."

"Me neither," said García. "Can we have it slowly? How would it be?"

"Well," began Antonio, "Our man knows they are moving stock within the site."

"How would he know that?" asked García

"The same way anyone ever knows stuff," said Antonio with a shrug. "This is not New York. Granada in the end is little more than a village. Loose talk, a few beers at the local bar, someone's friend's sister's mother-in-law's brother. The usual jungle telegraph, half fact, half idle gossip.

"So then the guy brings in a beer truck to deliver. Swaps out the contents. Fills his empty cardboard outers of beer with

Gelamex. Drops the 'beer' at the Alhambra." He raised his eyes to Raúl. "How would that work? Where would they have found the time to do the swap?"

"A quarry? A beer delivery? A drop at the Alhambra? How would THAT work?" García added to the list of questions.

"We get deliveries everyday," Javi piped up. "Certainly a truck every day. Usually a medium sized one. They come mostly for the hotels. Sometimes it's a beer truck, sometimes it's soft drinks on the side. Sometimes water. Even yoghurt."

"All on the same truck?" quizzed García

"Yes."

"We are very efficient when it comes to transport," said Manuel proudly.

"Comes from having had to move everything around by mule or bicycle for too long," Javi added dourly.

"OK," Antonio drawled. "So let's imagine the quarry takes a delivery of water..."

"But the swap?" quizzed Raúl.

"Not that hard to imagine," Antonio thought out loud. "I can picture it. It's *festivales*. There's a holiday mood. Weather's warming up. We have two drivers, not one. They arrive at the *canteras*. The store is already open because the truck is in to be loaded for the transfer of Gelamex to the top site. They drive into the store to get out of the sun. Instead of unloading the water there and then, the driver leaves his mate and goes into the office with the paperwork. They have a smoke and a chat. The mate makes the swap."

"But how would they know? Too many variables."

"Not really," said Antonio thoughtfully. "This is Spain. More than that, this is Andalucía. Everyone chats. Everyone stops to chew the fat. Especially in the heat. Especially just before a big holiday like this one. It didn't have to be a plan for that day. It could have been a plan for any day. Once they had the stock they

305

simply needed to use it before it deteriorated. This was a plan for the day when it would work. I don't think that they cared if it was this week or last week or next week. As long as they had detonators, it could be anytime at all."

All of them could get through, Alberto was sure. He and Lola were the first into the *generalife*. Then Alberto had doubled back, just to test that the way was clear and to bring the rest of them. Lola sat alone, still and small and waited. She could hear a rustling close in and turned her head, hoping to see a squirrel, or one of the cats returning from feasting on the fish bones at the *mimbre restaurant* just outside the walls.

"CHhhhhhhh," she heard, and peered toward the sound. "CHhhhhhhh."

She stood and moved away from the steps to the *archivo* and toward the amphitheatre. Nothing.

Nothing. Jack Fisher checked his watch again. Nothing from the English, nothing from Sacromonte, and all quiet at the Alhambra. The hum of traffic in the city was virtually nil. The road-blocks had obviously worked.

But he could hear voices everywhere. Those who were here in the city were probably not intending to leave. He had the distinct impression that there were more people than ever. He wondered if they might be abandoning their cars and coming into the city on foot. He stepped onto the balcony, smelled coffee and the sweet aroma of fresh-fried *churros*. For some people at least, it seemed that it was business as usual.

There was nothing else for it. He left Paula a note propped on his pillow next to her and went to find the café responsible for assailing his senses. He would indulge in caffeine and the fresh fried sausage shaped dough-nuts the city was so famous for. There wasn't much chance of today's English language paper, but maybe yesterday's would still be on the stands if he could find one open. He closed the door to their room and left quietly.

Quietly, for emphasis, Manuel Pedraza said, "And there's more. Raúl says they have found the detonator stem. Well, at least one of them. He's on his way."

On his way Raúl had to think. And he had to think by himself, away from the rest of them. He diverted to the toilets, found a stall, locked the door and sat on the closed seat. They had finally picked out the detonator handles from the careful telescopic viewing of the site. Not the stems from the later explosions as far as he could tell. This one was from the very first explosion. Enough of the serial number on the stem was visible to do a search. It was now commonly known that there were no detonators missing from the *canteras* in Cájar. If they ran a search the serial number would dump him well and truly in it.

A search of the *mimbre restaurant* gardens revealed nothing other than stray cats, and Lola was pretty sure cats didn't say CHhhhhhhh. Then she heard a rustle again from beyond the bigger pines. Then she saw him. He put his fingers to his lips for her to be silent and then moved away, indicating she should follow.

"Follow-up," said Antonio Marín into the military brick of a 'phone. "Yes," he nodded into the receiver, "certainly," he paused, "certainly, when we know more," then he rang off. He turned to García. who was waiting questioningly. "I am trying to put off letting Raúl and his men go in for as long as possible." Antonio said apologetically.

"How long will that be?"

"It's not entirely my call anymore."

David's head snapped up.

"Since when?"

"Since now."

"What happened?"

"That was army big brass."

Big brass ringing, thought García. *Ringing the brick? Wasn't that Raúl's 'phone? But then, Raúl had that neat little 'phone he was fond of flipping out. Had he two 'phones?*

"Who rang who?" García asked him with a light, dangerous softness to his tone.

"They rang me."

"On that?" said García pointing to the brick.

"The official line. The number everyone has."

"Who's everyone?"

"Oh for God's sake David."

"No, no," David touched Antonio's arm. "Humour me. The official line. What's that? The brick?"

"Yes, you could call it that."

"It's Raúl's right?"

"No, it's not his! It's the operational 'phone, a military 'phone, extra battery capacity."

"And when has it been used, since, say, I arrived?"

Antonio was now looking at him curiously.

"We took the call on it when they asked for a midwife, and then nothing until about ten minutes ago."

García's mind was racing. Raúl, that first night, with his head bent over the brick when García had been unable to sleep...

I wonder... he thought.

"And so what has happened?" he asked Antonio.

"The joint forces have put us all under pressure."

"What sort of pressure?"

"Seems they want a result."

"For Chrissake Antonio, if they would just be patient they may get one."

"I know. I told them."

"What did you tell them?" Between trying to work out what Raúl had been up to, García was also terrified for a minute that Antonio had let it be known what he was recommending. Namely sending in a platoon of eight-year olds and hoping they would meet up with some women on the other side to liberate the nation's finest monument whilst the entire world watched. He put his head in his hands. Antonio bent his head to García and said, in an amused tone,

"Don't worry. I simply told them we have a plan."

"We have a plan," Joaquin Montez told the assembled musicians. "Not a great plan, and not an infallible plan." Joaquin refrained from telling them it had been hatched with an eight year old. "But we have one. So who wants to join in?"

"To join in here with blue patrol," Raúl droned on, stabbing at the map, "we need yellow patrol to scale these walls. It may be dangerous."

"It **will** be dangerous," García said clearly. "It will be dangerous. All of these towers. Every one, is laced with explosives. We know that."

"Mr García," said Raúl with a painful expression on his face. "This is a military briefing and..."

"*Captain* García to you Raúl if we are now reverting to titles," snapped Antonio.

"My point is, Antonio..."

"I know your point Raúl, I know you think this is the right way. And," Antonio held up a conciliatory hand, "you may be proven right. All I am asking for is two more hours to see what happens with the kids. Two more hours, that's all. Two more hours, to make sure we are not blowing thirty children up on international TV. Too much to ask?"

Raúl was quiet. Then he said,

"No Sir." Followed by, "Two hours then. So as there is nothing here to do, if no-one minds, I'll go and get prepared. Starting with a shower." And he left, shooting García a look.

"Look, I contacted the local paper in Navarra, near to Pueblo de Conchi. One of my friends here has a sister who's a cub reporter up there."

"And?" Antonio was impatient down the 'phone, and then instantly contrite. "Sorry *hijo*," he said to his son. "Sorry, just cut to the chase willya?"

"She says there was an action. Well not really. It was denied."

"Denied?"

"Yes. They couldn't get past the judge."

"Where? What judge?" barked Antonio.

"Couldn't get it past *la junta de navarra*. The twelfth circuit judge of Navarra county ruled it out."

"Why?"

"Apparently the basis of the action wasn't sound."

"In what way?"

"The people claimed radiation poisoning because of an alleged leak from a nuclear sub just off the coast of Pueblo de

Conchi. All the people there who fish..."

"Got really sick, really fast," Antonio supplied for his son. "And why was the action denied?"

"The judge said there wasn't enough evidence."

"Why not?" asked Antonio.

"Well, there were a couple of complications. One was that it seems the local people couldn't afford to have the specialist tests done," the younger man replied.

"And the other one?"

"It was an international issue. The sub was British. You remember the sub that ended up going for repair at Gibraltar where they have experts? Remember everyone was incensed that Gibraltar was being used for something potentially lethal and in effect on Spanish soil?"

"I think the problem is that it isn't Spanish soil," Antonio told his son dryly.

"Well you know what I think about that one," the young man said, and when his father studiedly didn't reply, he went on, "anyway, the judge seemed to think that there was no clear audit trail between the sub and these people. The judge said," and Antonio could hear his son shuffling some papers, "yes here it is, I quote, *there are protocols for actions of this magnitude and they are not within the realm of private citizens.*"

"Hence the World Health Organisation, right?"

"Seems some of the younger people in the village got up a deputation and went to Switzerland to ask for help. They went personally, but the WHO couldn't do anything."

"Why not?"

"Because they only deal directly with governments, in other words, European Union member states. Spain itself."

"Round and round," said Antonio in a tired voice. "*Hijo*?"

"*Papá*?"

"Anything about where these guys worked other than the

311

fleet? Any of them work in civil engineering? Anything like that?"

"No. No other information."

Antonio knew his son was thorough. He would have asked, and would have noted any interesting answers.

"Do you know anyone at Canal Sol, the local TV station here in Andalucía?"

Antonio could almost hear his son's grin spread across his face.

"I imagine I can find someone *Papá*. Leave it with me."

"Leave it with me Captain Marín," said O'Reilly down a terrible transatlantic line. "I am sure we can organise something."

O'Reilly put the phone down in its cradle and stared out the window at the Manhattan skyline. It was a pisser being at work on a Sunday when all he wanted to do was to be with María, but he felt he had to at least phone and find out. Now he could tell María that he done his part.

His part, he had told her, had been to organise something.

"And they believed me. So everyone in the village put their money together and we went to Switzerland. Even Dolores, who was so sick after having the first baby not long dead. Even Dolores went. She's my sister. And they just said they were sorry, they couldn't help. They were very nice about it and gave everyone coffee. But there was nothing they could do."

"This is outrageous," said Reggie when Rashida's translation reached his ears. "This is a scandal. But," and he eyeballed Gerardo, "you can't just wander the world blowing things up. God may help those who help themselves but...."

Mary sucked in her breath. This was not the moment for Reggie to start with his Christian do-good crap. Although a part of her agreed. Even so, what could people like Gerardo and Dolores do? They had tried all the proper channels, exhausted the routes open to them because they had exhausted their resources. Yet, she caught herself wondering; they had managed to get themselves some explosives. If they could afford that, then surely they could afford tests.

"So where did the explosives come from?"

"All of us. My brothers," said Gerardo sheepishly. "And my cousins, their cousins from Almería."

"So many people?"

"And a few more."

"How do they get it?"

"It's not hard if you take small stocks here and there. It's the road program," he said, half apologetically. "We have so many mountains and we are building so many roads. There is continual blasting," then he added, "it helps that Spain is the major manufacturer of explosives in Europe. Many people from our village have worked on the gangs to build the roads.

"And then on top of all this there is all the house construction. People want stone and cement and marble. There is always someone quarrying something. We have been stockpiling for a while. We got our biggest haul locally."

"But the stocks don't last do they?" Reggie looked at him shrewdly. "Ask him," he said to Mary and Rashida, "they go 'off'. Am I right?"

Mary looked at Reggie with new respect and asked,

"How would you know?"

"Civil engineer, yes?" said Gerardo in English, understanding the conversation. And when Reggie nodded Gerardo went on, "they don't last as long as I would have liked. That's why we needed a local source. We had to top up for this. Just last week."

"And the detonators?" asked Reggie knowingly.

"Ah," said Gerardo. "Now that's another story."

Story telling had always been cathartic for Agustín. It had been something to balance the sameness and smallness of his real life, something to bring drama to the mundane quality of the day after day.

It kept bright and warm the memory of the one day he had lived, but never lived right. All his life he had regretted that moment in *calle angulo*, the moment when they had come for HIM and the doors had swung open into the August heat. The day when he, eight years old, had watched the opening bars of the crime of the century as though it were some exquisite dance of death, and taken not one step toward it.

He closed his eyes. In his mind there was no forgiveness for his part in that day, no peace, no rosary to say, no happy ending. But now suddenly it seemed that after all these decades there was a chance of redemption. Lola was beside him. She had emerged from the bushes near the *mimbre restaurant*, in response to his CHhhhhhhh call, dripping wet and was telling him everything. This then was yet another such moment. This time he knew it for what it was. He looked steadily at the girl and heard the answer to a lifetime of, what had always seemed futile, prayer. He said,

"Sometimes you ask me about Viznar don't you? When I say that *the people will win the day*, sometimes you ask me about it."

Lola nodded and whispered,

"*Viznar, Viznar, so near, so far.*"

"And I know I have never answered you. But I have an answer," he cleared his throat. "Lorca would have lived, I think, if just one person in the chain from *calle angulo* to Viznar had taken one different decision."

"Just one person?" asked Lola quietly.

"I think so. Just one person. Just one different decision. Maybe even just a prayer."

314

Prayer, for Rashida, had always part of her life. Having by-passed the standard ritual for the early morning she now felt disinclined to skip the next set. Unusual circumstances might allow for unusual responses, but under a cloudless sky with no immediate pressures, there was no excuse not to face Mecca and recite.

Even so, she found herself saying the practised words but thinking of other things. Mary was one of them. Mary with her interminable questions about medical matters and about her faith. At first it felt like the familiar voyeur types she had grown up with. Kids from her school in Granada asking what they ate at home, how they slept, if they had a toilet. She used to wonder when they might ask her if her mother had two heads. But quite quickly Rashida realised that Mary was genuinely interested, and the interest was more than academic.

"So," Mary had asked her, "When you are facing Mecca what is happening?"

"What do you mean, *what is happening*?" Rashida had almost been short.

"I mean, do you feel floaty or pure or special?"

"No."

"Well what then?"

"What do you mean what then??"

"I mean you stop everything four or five times a day," said Mary seemingly oblivious to Rashida's impatience.

"Five."

"Everything comes to a halt five times a day and well, what for? What's going on?"

Rashida had never thought about it like that before. She had never asked herself what was going on. It was just something she did like eating and breathing. Dawn, mid-morning, mid-day, evening and dusk, that was what she did. Out came the prayer mat, a quick wash of all the orifices and then, genuflection.

315

Mary had just stood and continued to look at her with her wide navy-blue eyes. Rashida began, for the first time, to articulate the architecture of her faith.

"Stopping is an important part," she said haltingly to Mary. "Yes," she said with more confidence, "stopping is an important part. Prayer five times a day actually makes you stop what you are doing and do something completely different. It puts the meal you are preparing, the argument you are having, the letter you are writing, the research you are undergoing, it puts it all into perspective. It makes what is big, suddenly, not small, but smaller." Mary said nothing and continued just to watch her, so Rashida went on, "and it gives life a structure."

"Structure?"

"Yes. More than, say, Christian Sundays. Not that I would say anything against Christian Sundays..." Rashida was quick to add.

"Don't worry. I'm not that keen on Christian Sundays myself," laughed Mary.

"What I mean is the structure of Islam is not a once a week affair," Rashida rushed on, "when you pray five times a day, it's hard for your beliefs not to have an impact on your life every day. You can't store stuff up for days." Mary just looked at her. "It gives my life structure. Yes," Rashida paused, "yes. I think that's it. Like you English people might walk the dog, or even, go to the pub everyday and have a beer." Amused at her own honing in on the *haram* – the forbidden in Islam – she smiled and then asked, "do you know what I mean?"

"I mean he's here!" Lola exclaimed to Alberto.

"Shhhh."

"Alberto," Lola lowered her voice to a whisper.

"What?" Alberto was marshalling everyone toward the

cedar path between the steps to the *archivo* and *la torre de las infantas*.

"He's here!"

"Who?"

"I saw him!"

"Who? Who?"

Who? And why? David García felt confused. He twiddled his cold cup of vending machine coffee in his hands, flexing and curling his fingers. Why was Raúl fielding calls on the operational telephone and not passing on the fact that they had been received?

Was it possible that the Spanish authorities were so cold-blooded that they were actually trying to make a major incident occur? García may have said to Antonio that it played into the hands of those raising the 'war-against-terror' battle cry, but even David wasn't sure, when put to the test, if he really, really believed it.

And then there were the explosives. They might have an idea where they came from, but they still knew no more about who had taken them or why. Manuel had confirmed that in all only seven boxes had gone missing. About enough to blow maybe five towers provided the shot-firer was experienced. And this guy was. But he was also very likely to be out of ammo.

Furthermore, if García's hunch was right, and these people's actions were somehow related to the efforts of the humble citizens of Pueblo de Conchi to bring suit for radiation poisoning, then they were nothing to do with the usual ETA or Islamic suspects.

So why would Raúl care? Why would the Spanish authorities care? Why would they care enough to escalate events by refusing to respond? As he turned the ideas over in his mind he crushed his plastic coffee cup with such force the cold coffee shot up, ran down his shirt and soaked through to his skin.

Skin deep. That was all justice was. A window dressing. But these, these were the business. Gerardo always thought about the moment when he had finally received the detonators as akin to a poem conveying something in absolute terms without the precision of verbal definition, like church standing for God, or music standing for the soul. When he had finally seen them, lined up, at his disposal, when he recognised the power they represented, he felt awe flood his hopes and he had known peace for the first time in three years. These weren't detonators, they were sceptres.

Detonators were uppermost in García's mind when he arrived at his cot, discarded his shirt, snatched up a clean one and went to the showers to rinse his chest. Raúl was inside the block, half shaved, towel around his waist. García stopped in his tracks. Their eyes met in the mirror. David started to turn to retrace his steps.

"Oh come on, come on," Raúl beckoned said to García's reflection in the mirror and gave him a look, half coquette, half hard-man.

"Don't even go there Sanchez," David was surprised at the coldness in his own voice.

"You can fool all of them out there," said Raúl, continuing to talk to the mirror. "But you can't fool me Ángel David García."

David swallowed hard, finding it impossible to lower his eyes from Raul's, trying to find words, wishing to repel the advance, longing for the advance. He wanted to say something witty and light to break the moment but was afraid he might say something truly inane like *what can you mean?* Instead he said,

"I'm not about to try and fool anyone."

"Well that's good," said Raúl continuing to razor his face. "I don't think we should either of us play the other for an idiot,

318

do you? I say," said Raúl conversationally, splashing his face with water and then turning to face David full on, "I say, one touch and you'd be mine. What do you say? Shall we test it out? See who is the fool really?"

He advanced on García. David could not move.

In part, he could not move because he was too well trained. In a conflict situation, always step forward, never step back.

In part he was mesmerised by the raw animal beauty of the man. Shucked down he was everything García had known he would be, full muscled, taut with promise, a potential machine of sexual desire and satisfaction.

To say the sight of him made García ache was not to know fully the daily depth of longing that David lived with. Typically, until that moment, he himself had not even known it.

David García moved slightly forward and turned his face against Raúl's words and the bruising of his heart. In that one forward motion he had an insight into how his brand of Catholicism could eat so profoundly into the soul of a man and create a hunger for transformation so intense that it was possible to believe that raw, base sex alone could offer deliverance.

"Maybe I am the fool," he said. "But Antonio is not."

Raúl looked suddenly confused. This was not the response he expected.

"Antonio? What's Antonio got to do with this?"

"He's called hasn't he?" García spoke softly but there was menace in his voice. "The shot-firer. You have spoken to him." It was a statement not a question.

"And so what?" Raúl's eyes glinted. "Come on handsome. Come on," he beckoned at García.

David moved forward. It was hard to keep his emotion in check, a combination of out and out pulsating, electrifying, naked want and white-hot fury.

"Keeping them hanging," David continued his advance. "By

doing what? Agreeing and not delivering? What?"

"Take me down big boy. Take me down," Raúl squared up to him, running his tongue over his lips and reaching toward Garcia's naked chest at the same time.

"Don't you get it?" David stared at him, side-stepping Raúl's reach. "There are people in there who are depending on us."

"That's right big man. And they're going to get us. Not you and your clever words and ways."

Ways *and means*, thought Manuel Pedraza, trying to comfort himself with the words of his cadet training. *The Job*, they had always been told, *has many ways and means, and all of us have to play our part*. The past few days seemed to show that his part was destined to be that of a messenger and not a policeman.

He watched the fax machine spew out another page. Why they couldn't get everyone onto email was beyond him. This love affair with the fax machine was tedious to say the least.

He yawned and some shards of sunflower shells fell into the roller mechanism. He leaned forward and with a licked finger end tried to extract them before they rolled around into the paper spool. He failed, and collected the fax sheets to take to the men.

"The men can't see him because he is hidden," said Lola

"Where?"

"In the trees."

"So he is here," Alberto spoke with wonder.

"You said he would be," said Lola. "Didn't you believe it?"

"Believe it," said Manual flatly in response to voiced doubts.

"Are you sure?" Antonio raised an eyebrow at Manuel.

"That's what it says," Manuel replied, indicating the fax in Antonio's hands. "And I rang and checked, just in case it was a clerical error."

"I would say there had been an error Manuel," said Antonio sternly, "but not a clerical one."

"Is this to be kept confidential?"

"Yes. For now," Antonio turned away and then said, "Manuel, you can, however, let our people know that the trace on the detonator took us back to the military. You can tell them that much."

"That much," Raúl held up his hand, a small gap between thumb and forefinger. "That's all it would take." And he turned a bronzed and muscled back to García in a gesture of rebuke and disgust.

García swallowed hard, felt the intensity of the moment and was half afraid that Raúl might be right. But then Raúl continued conversationally, "Manuel told me all about you and your approach. Well that's New York for you. Crime capital of the world and we know why. If you aren't on the criminal payroll then you are soft on negotiating."

And with that, any desire that García may have had for him was lost.

Suddenly Raúl turned again, this time fully toward García and his hand shot out toward García's crotch. But García was too quick for him and thrust his hips back out of reach and then brought his knee up in an automatic defensive move. He only just caught the side of one of Raúl's thighs and the younger man also moved back. His eyes were glittering now. García raised his palm toward him,

"Give it up," he said to him. "Back off. I'm not some cheap whore. You are out of line. And..." he didn't finish.

Antonio's reflection was in the mirror looking at them both.

David García closed his eyes, wishing the drain would suck him into the sewers and wondering for how long the older man had been watching them.

Watching them had been like watching a dance. García was nimble, that was for sure. But it was also like watching a ceremony from a different culture. Although there were different cues for the interaction, and although García was not a willing participant, it was clear that David García knew absolutely and unerringly the moves.

Of course there had been gay affairs in the army. Antonio knew of them and on occasion had had to discipline the men involved. But he had never witnessed such a display of raw male sexuality man to man. It shook him. And it disturbed him to see García being preyed upon. Make no wonder García and Sanchez had been so abrasive with one another.

"I'll see you both in the office," he said, turned on his heel, and left them to it.

It could only make María grateful. She listened carefully to O'Reilly's soft mix of brogue and New York twang down the 'phone line. The she hung up. O'Reilly hadn't spoken to David directly but he had spoken to the Spanish officer in charge. It made her feel a bit better. Combing the news in New York, there was precious little detail about events in Spain. A few lines here and there. Not that O'Reilly had been much more informative.

The thing was, David was all she had left of Marilita, and Marilita had been the living evidence of her love for him and his for her. That she would love him always was not in doubt, but that he would live long, was. The possibility that he might die was unbearable to her.

To her it was still surprisingly quiet. Rashida expected that there might have been more hurried purpose about the day. She did not find it hard to feel sorry for them and also responsible. She might be caught up in something that was not her fault, but indirectly she and those like her were probably to blame. Someone, somewhere had made a mistake. Some naval operator had been too tired, too badly trained, too afraid to cop to their error. Whatever it was, the mistake had cost these people dearly. And while two wrongs never made a right, surely these walking cadavers all around her should at least have the promise of a comfortable downhill run to death.

Surely it was not too much to ask of a government that citizens mortally wounded by negligence be treated well. And why did there have to be the compulsion of proven blame for a government to deliver that which could readily be explained as good old fashioned charity? At the very least they should be listening.

Listening, Raúl stood before Antonio looking uncomfortable. He was finding it hard to keep eye contact with Antonio. Antonio was surprised to find himself on the brink of fury for a second time in fewer days. He was angry enough to have heard about the 'phone calls, but he was just as angry that Raúl had rattled García. This was not the place, and definitely not the time.

"So Raúl, how long have you been receiving calls from the Alhambra?"

"Since yesterday Sir."

"And so this fax here, which responds to your enquiry concerning the serial number on the detonator, which they received on FRIDAY, how would that fit into the scheme here?"

"The number on the detonator handle was visible Sir."

"Was visible on Friday?"

"Yes. On Friday."

"And you knew right away it was army and not civilian, didn't you?"

"I did."

"Yet you chose not to share this with me."

"That's correct."

"Might one know why Raúl?"

"Orders Sir."

"Orders," repeated Antonio amiably. "So let me get this straight. You have known since Friday that the army," and Antonio emphasised the word army "is completely up to its arm-pits in this. You have been getting phone calls from this guy, this so-called madman," and Antonio gestured wildly toward the Alhambra, "this shot-firer, that we are all supposedly here ranged against and for reasons, best known to yourself, you kept this from me, from all of us."

"Sir, my Commanding Officer..."

"Good God man!" Antonio's voice rang out and everyone in the building seemed to jump to attention. "I AM your Commanding Officer and this is OUR operation. Christ Almighty, has it not occurred to you that we have upwards of thirty children over there? Then there are probably three old people, maybe fifty sick people, all of whom are Spanish nationals?"

"We don't know that for certain Sir, if I may say."

"Certain? You want certain? There is no certain! On top of that, we have a woman from this city, who volunteered to go in there and help, who will be a national martyr, probably an international one as she is, quite incidentally, a Muslim. And won't all the extremists on both sides love that? And then, just to make life interesting for everyone, we have eleven UK nationals, at least ten of whom are over fifty-five. You have got me under the gun to perform a miracle in," Antonio looked at his watch, "Fifty-five minutes. Or you, under some OTHER authority, are going to go in

324

there and bomb the living daylights out of everyone. Or, as you will probably later say, cause someone else to bomb the living daylights out of everyone, just so you can't be held responsible. Well I am responsible. I am responsible for this operation, for those children, and all those people who are, for whatever reason, tangled up in something more complicated than even I know. Now, either you tell me exactly what has been going on and why, and then maybe, just maybe, we can figure this out without completely ballsing it up. Or I am going to shoot you stone dead. What do say Raúl, sound like a plan?"

García could almost not resist applauding.

afternoon

"**Applauding terror** by negotiating with terrorists is not the way forward. We will not have talks with terrorists. We will not negotiate. Terror will not be allowed to insinuate itself onto the national agenda of this country."

David García watched as more senior politicians babbled on. He thought of the coverage of wars, of hostage crises, and thought, *give me a general any day for the analysis. Politicians know as much about what is going on as my grandmother.* He sighed as the interviewer went on,

"Do you think Sir that this is a wise course of action given the situation of these people? They have tried to get support and..."

The politician leaned forward in his chair and addressed the presenter,

"Young lady. Terror is the new warfare. It is the warfare of the soul. Nations will be lost through it if they do not stand firm. The integrity of this nation shall not be besmirched by relinquishing to the power of terror."

The integrity of this nation shall not be besmirched by relinquishing to the power of terror. García repeated the words in his mind and turned down the sound only to put it up again as the camera showed streets full of people,

"The news from Granada," spoke the newsacaster, "down the hill from the Alhambra and in the city centre, is that things are hotting up. The army, who have spent the past two days evacuating the city and setting up road blocks to prevent traffic entering the city, appear to have been thwarted. People are walking into the city, along the banks of the River Genil, across the *vega*, and also slipping down through the Albaicín. Our reporter in the field today has been talking the people who seem determined to come into town and see the action..."

The camera angle changed and a microphone was thrust into the face of a young man with several face piercings,

"Well, we heard it on the news and well, we just thought we should come and see what was happening."

And then another citizen,

"Whatever happens I want to be there."

And another,

"I was married in the Alhambra. Me and my husband. So we just decided to come."

There was some more inane commentary and the news moved on to famine in part of Africa and García muted the sound again.

He could imagine how angry Raúl would be to find that people were coming in across fields and along rivers. Not only was he going to have civilians to contend with if the news was right, he was going to have more civilians than ever. Hell, Raúl would just have to live with it. Raúl. García twisted his ring on his finger and felt himself tense. The scene in the showers burned again in his memory.

And now he had been relegated by Antonio to keep watch on Canal Sol. Antonio had asked him with his usual pleasantness saying he thought there was some news that his son had been working on that might break that. But more likely Antonio wanted to separate David from Raúl, and from the action. García was, after all, he reminded himself, yet again, merely an observer. David could hardly blame Antonio. He would have done the same if the situation were reversed. What Antonio thought of David now, he could not imagine, and again he surprised himself that it even mattered.

The thing was, thought David, no matter how good you were at your job, how fine a parent, how true a friend, even how devout a Catholic, being gay always bit you back one way or another. He couldn't even think of Raúl without his stomach turning. His mother used to say, *handsome is as handsome does*. And then added to David and all his siblings, *men fall in love with their eyes and women fall in love with their ears*. So my sons, you need to learn to speak and listen well.

Raúl was as handsome as any man David had ever seen. But he wouldn't have wanted him if he were the last man in Granada, both because of who Raúl was, and also because of the shame he felt when he had seen Antonio in the mirror. David closed his eyes, as he had in that moment, as if by closing them somehow the entire scene would disappear.

He turned back to the TV, determined to push it all from his mind. *Terror as the new warfare*. What a load of trash. Terror had been around since the beginning of time. ETA was still active. The IRA was still active. The Red Army Faction was dormant but who knew when that German aberration might reassert itself, or how far it had transmuted from 1970s Germany to 1990s Afghanistan?

There was nothing new about terror. Jack Fisher had been right about that. Ask Rashida Santiago what her family knew about terror. Ask her dead parents if they thought the *integrity of the nation* might have once been *besmirched by terror*?

As for terror's power, how short were people's memories? García wasn't even proposing considering the twin towers. What about here in Granada? How long since a fairly powerful terror had hauled Lorca off to Viznar and shot him, along with hundreds and hundreds of his countrymen. And for what? Because they differed in opinion? Because they could not have all that they longed for?

Well wake up world, wake up Raúl Sanchez, García thought bitterly, *wake up Governor*, he nodded at the television, *wake up all you people on the Alhambra hill and all you people on the outside if it. Wake up. Sooner or later, whatever side you're on, you negotiate, or you die*.

"You die, Alberto, I die," Lola said to him, her eyes as round as pies, and she clasped him to her.

"Get off Lola," he said, conscious that everyone was watching them. "I'm not gonna die. Javi says the drains are open a lot of the way. I'm fast. I know the water is high. That's why you have to wait here. I am not going to plop into the sealed reservoirs at the end. Honestly. I'll be OK." He relented and gave Lola a small swift hug. "I'll let you know. Trust me."

"What shall I tell Agustín?"

"If you see him again, if he calls you with his CHhhhhhhhhh sound, tell him we have come to get him. Tell him that the gypsies and us are going to make all the others go away. Tell him he's right. People can change things. Tell him we are of the people, and that," Alberto hesitated and then said in a special voice, "*we can win the day*. Tell him to meet me at the *alcazaba*."

At the *alcazaba*. It's the only thing that makes sense," García spoke urgently in a low voice. "At last you have a means to contact them. Set it up. It's my job. I do it all the time."

"You're not authorised," said Antonio.

"Please," García stared at Antonio. "You're kidding. Right? Who cares? We are so past procedure here. Tell them I am coming. I can walk there from here. They can see me. They meet me or not. We have to try."

Try as he may, Gerardo could not dissuade Jay from the meeting. They were in too deep. And Jay had that look, the 'Jay' look, as Gerardo referred to it privately. Gerardo had known there would have to be a meeting from the moment his mobile had leapt in his pocket and he had known that Jay would have to go. Knowing Jay, nothing would change their course, but also knowing Jay, the opportunity to talk to one more person could not be passed up.

Up the ravine and to the right was the appointed place. In the end Antonio had chosen it. Not at the base of the *alcazaba*, which was visible from the city where too many people were still gathering. But to the side, within easy distance of the *reformatorio* and with clear line of sight for the marksmen.

He had put his own man on it. He had no intention of risking some trigger-happy young fellow from Raúl's brigade. His instructions had been clear: keep García in sight at all times and only take the shot if there was a threat to García's safety. Otherwise, no action. He spoke into his sleeve,

"Have you got it?"

"Roger that Sir. Got it."

"Got it," Gerardo breathed in and looked at it closely. You could not hold it in your hand. Well you could, but it was ill-advised. They were the only part of the modern arsenal that was still volatile. The heat of a man's blood could be enough to set them off. Undeniably that was part of the attraction. If you caressed them for too long, as a desperate man might, they would blow your hand off. And some. And now he only had this one left.

Left, then right again at the mine shaft. García dropped to a squat to wait.

"Wait. You are kidding me, right?" Raúl said.

"García's on his way down there now," Antonio re-affirmed.

"You let him go?" Raúl was incredulous. This was not what he had expected when Antonio had said things had moved on. "What's he going to say?"

"Well, soon we'll know."

"We'll know in a few years," Gerardo said to her as she seated herself next to him. "That's the most assurance they can give us."

"But this caper could mean you don't live to see it," she swept her arm across the wreck and ruin of their vista and across the explosives at his feet. "Or, when this is over, if you do survive it, you will go to prison. We call that in English, *Hobson's choice*."

He raised his eyebrow at her,

"Which is?"

"No choice at all."

"There are no choices here Mary," he said bitterly. "This isn't living. Holding you and barely being able to bear the weight of your head on my chest. Not being able to make love with you. Watching my sister die and all my nephews and nieces. This isn't living but it's all we have."

"We have the children to think of too. And they could be anywhere," said Antonio to Raúl who, since hearing about García, was standing as though he were a dog straining at the leash. "I've checked it through with Dr Jesús. If the children have gone in and used the water courses, there will be some indication."

There was a silence and then,

"Antonio, you should know." Raúl swallowed hard, "The military were aware that detonators had gone missing. But only recently."

"What took them so long?" Antonio asked coolly.

"It's not easy to keep track."

"Jesus, Raúl. This is the army. They keep track of when you shit." Antonio was not convinced.

"We're not that good at explosives if the truth be told Sir." Antonio raised his eyes at this while Raúl went on, "Commercial shot-firers are a lot better than our boys. They do it all the time," he added as a lame attempt at an excuse. "They have more practice."

"Doesn't explain missing detonators unaccounted for."

"The thing is Sir," since the incident in the showers Antonio noticed that Raúl had been adding a lot of *Sir* to his speech, "we issue multiple detonators at training. We expect people to get it wrong and return any that are left."

"Except this one, and a few others," said Antonio grimly, "were not returned. Am I right?"

"Something like that Sir."

"So why the big secret?" Antonio kept looking toward the Alhambra, toward where David had his *rendez-vous*.

"It was embarrassing," Raúl replied, "with the observer here."

"No," said Antonio slowly. "Nice try. I don't buy it."

"But we need to move in Sir," said Raúl. "We need to send in the troops. We do."

"First we wait. In ten minutes we'll find out."

Out of sorts with her own thoughts, Rashida sought Mary for reassurance. She was probably with Dolores, helping her with the meals, but in effect doing it all for her. She found them in *la sala de las damas* and watched as Dolores, was once again leading prayers.

"Oh blessed Virgin, send us health and send us children. We thank you Lord for our blessings and as you to forgive our sins. We ask this in your name. Let us pray."

Mary came over and stood beside Rashida.

"It doesn't do it for me," she said under her breath.

"What doesn't?"

"All this intoning the blessed Virgin crap."

Rashida looked at her sideways.

"Why not? People need their comfort, Mary."

Then she saw Dolores beckon them.

"Show us your way," Dolores said to Rashida as she approached.

"What do you mean?"

"Show us your way to pray," said Dolores. "God knows, we need all the help we can get."

"Prayer you mean?" asked Rashida.

"Yes," said Dolores and then cast her hand out toward *la sala* generally, "this is absolutely the right place. And I, we, should like to learn how you pray. Maybe with all our voices we will be heard."

As she unwound her headscarf Rashida she was aware that the call had rung out long before. She was late for mid-day prayers and early for evening. But it didn't matter. Allah, as far as she knew, didn't have a wristwatch.

She lowered herself to her knees, looked to each side and then began the ritual rolling forward. As she rocked forward from her heels and brought her forehead to the ground she felt the earth moving.

Moving through the scrub a slender figure approached, as it neared, García could make out the features, high cheek-bones, regal bearing and tall, willowy grace. García made to rise from his squat but a melodious voice told him to remain seated. Squatting opposite, a hand was put forward,

"I'm Jay and you are García, yes?" García took the hand, strong, brown and lean, warm against his own. "I hope I have not kept you waiting too long."

"It's good to meet someone at last."

Jay laughed, relaxed.

"Yes it is."

"Yes it is? That's all you have to say in your defense?" Antonio fixed Raúl with a stare.

A stare *that was steady* would be the main thing that David would say about Jay. It would be the one thing that would linger.

Jay plucked at the grass, responding to García's remark that they had a pretty big situation on their hands.

"No. This is just a small side issue," there was a movement of the head and García saw a fat plait move from the back toward the side.

"Not a small or a side issue for the people who are dying in there," García replied slowly.

"No. For them, not at all."

"So you are not one of them?"

"We are all the same people García," and Jay looked at him with patience. "These people were poisoned. But we are all poisoned, it's just theirs is more obvious and the consequences more imminent."

García was quiet. The main weapon in the negotiator's arsenal was silence...

"Ah," said Jay, with the same patient look. "The gift of the negotiator, let the perpetrator speak... And I am not kidding. It is a gift." There was more silence while Jay looked across García's shoulder to the horizon and then back at García himself. There was a clearing of the throat and then Jay said, "Here's the deal. There are fifty-three men up there, all within a few months of death. The women are already on their way out. There is no force

337

needed to take them out, and the explosives they have, well, let's just say they are past their prime. A few more bangs maybe," Jay pulled at some more grass and selected a long stalk to chew, set another toward García, "want one?"

David took it.

"So what's the point?" asked García.

"In real terms? Applying the one-hundred year rule? There is none."

"The one hundred year rule?"

"Will any of this matter in a hundred years?" David was quiet. "You know," Jay continued chattily. "There is a lot of talk about saving the planet. This action here," the grass stalk was taken out of the mouth and waved loosely toward the Alhambra, "has been a way to draw attention to, let's call it, the plight of individuals, to highlight the dangers of human activity to the seas, to the people who live from the sea, and to put values on show... an antique monument, a group of victims, to demonstrate even the values of terror, if you like."

García, waited, waited for the punch, the demand...

"And," he prompted.

"And nothing. The planet is going to be fine. The planet will survive perfectly well, with or without humankind. No-one cares about the planet, they just care about themselves." With a small sharp breath Jay moved fluidly from squat to standing. "That is all."

Jay was gone through the scrub before García himself could get to his feet.

His feet, shoulders, hands and eyes relaxed. The target was gone. He could stand down. The marksman radioed Antonio.

Antonio knew something about Raúl Sanchez's statements didn't ring true. His bullshit about an observer being present being the reason why there had been delay in passing information was nonsense. Spain was an ally to the US. And this alliance had been more significant in recent times, simply because the US had so few nations' support when it came to their analysis of the out and out war-on-terror. There was no way the simple facts concerning the provenance of a detonator would have been classified. He even doubted the explanation as to how it had been acquired in the first place.

"In the first place, it's our business, they're our mates," the red-faced Englishman stuck his finger in the other man's chest. "SO, IF YOU DON'T MIND, move forward everyone," the very Yorkshire voice sang out. "Move forward. Come on. It's no good staying in the hotel. It's all happening out here. Just shove!"

A group of middle-aged men pressed through the crowd in *la plaza nueva* far below the *alcazaba,* the fortress tower of the Alhambra, which was high above. They elbowed people out of the way who were squashed right next to them, and continued determinedly toward the River Darro. They were oblivious to the afternoon sun, sharp on their heads and shoulders. They took no notice of the troops trying to push people back onto *la plaza nueva* using crash barriers.

It was an impossible task anyway. There were simply too many bodies to fit in the space. As soldiers pushed the line back at the front, others spilled off at the sides. Then the sides were tackled and the front surged forward again. The Yorkshiremen took every advantage of the chaos. One of the men turned to Fisher and said in a plummy voice,

"Sorry PC Fisher, I know this isn't what you wanted, but if I had been in there I'd want to think there were people out here routing for me. I'd like to think that no-one would go home until this was all over. You have to keep up the morale don't you know," he gave a salute and added, "you know, morale of the troops."

"The troops move one inch before this ten minutes is up and I swear to God, Raúl, I'll kill you myself."

García stopped in the doorway and watched amazed. Either Antonio was stressing out, or the struggle between Raúl and Antonio's positions was coming to a head. Antonio had twice threatened this man. Antonio was clearly feeling the heat.

HEAT was not only not so bad after all, O'Reilly decided, in fact it was probably the one thing he had been needing in his life for a long, long time. Maybe his hatred for David García all these years had been because García had the one quality that he, O'Reilly, subconsciously knew he lacked and was so desperately hungry for.

He looked across at the pinched, sour features of his wife. *Make no wonder*, he said to himself, *when I have allowed her nothing of me for more than twenty years*.

"I've been thinking," he said to her out loud. "I've been thinking now the children are grown, we should probably get a divorce. What do you say?"

"What do you say?" Antonio had spotted García over Raúl's shoulder and strode toward him. "Tell us."

"Met them. Listened. No demands."

"What?" barked Raúl.

"The leader?" asked Antonio.

"Early thirties. Perfect Spanish. Looked like a Slav. Relaxed.

A discourse on the demise of humankind. Detail about who's inside. I have it here," he passed across the recording of the conversation. "There's nothing of value. That's it."

It was a struggle to get their old bones moving but they had to do it. They had to.

"To find out that ordinary people are unable to get, not just justice, but a fair hearing for their troubles is never good. It could be said that this doesn't happen here in Spain. We now have one of the best systems in modern democracy. As a new state we have it all mapped out and no-one need ever fear they will not be heard. Those awful days before democracy are over. Or are they...

"I am reporting from the base of the Alhambra here in Granada in our fair province of Andalucía. I have come here today, not to watch how a battle unfolds and comment on what may be the latest conquest of the Alhambra, I have come instead to tell a tale of something worrying in our fair country.

"We have a problem, it is the problem of the people of Pueblo de la Conchi, and their problem is our problem... and if you don't believe me," the reporter turned away from the camera and gestured toward the crowd behind him, "look around.

"The latest estimates say that as many as five-hundred thousand people have made their way on foot to this city over the last three days. Let me clarify that," and the reporter paused for dramatic effect, "Five hundred thousand people is half a million." Another pause and then, "Who says that people don't care about this monument, or about their country, or about each other?"

The TV, already switched on in Antonio's office, now had the volume sky high. Everyone was crowded around. Other than the presenter's voice the only other sound was the incessant chomping of Manuel on his sunflower seeds. David could see the relief flood Antonio's features and his slow smile,

"That's my boy." he said. "Well done *hijo mio*."

"Your son's behind this?" García asked.

"You bet your ass he is," said Antonio and clapped David on the back. "You bet your Cuban ass!"

And then they all turned toward the Alhambra as there rose an incessant and incredible noise.

Noise flooded the *vega*. Joaquin Montez seized his guitar.

"Come on you lot," he said to Ana, his father, uncle and all his cousins. "Come on. This is it. We're on."

On any other day García would have said that nothing could have surprised him anymore. He had already had an encounter with a terrorist that seemed more like a fire-side chat. He recognised that the siege of the Alhambra was nothing like anything he had ever known or could even understand. It followed no recognisable pattern and had no predictable manoeuvres. After the last few hours he would have said that in his life, more or less, he had seen and heard it all.

Not this sound.

"What is it?" he said to Antonio, "I've never heard anything like it."

"I have," said Antonio snatching up the binoculars. "I have. Every day of my childhood. We could hear it as far as Pinos Puente. Even the earth moved."

And he turned from the Alhambra and lowered the binoculars from his eyes and García thought he could see they were wet with tears.

"It's *la vela*," Manual Pedraza said.

"The Great Bell, David," said Antonio, "The Great Bell in *la torre de la vela*. It always rang to tell people it was the time to open the sluices and to irrigate. Once, long ago, the Alhambra's great gift to the people, to the *vega*, was its water. And someone is up there ringing *la vela*."

"And I've got a pretty good idea," García muttered to himself, "who that, doubtless small, curly-red-haired, someone might be."

"Be that as it may. The troops must go in now. They must," Raúl spoke with the urgency of a man whose case is lost.

Lost in the moment, Agustín was in his element. He was so excited he thought he might wet his pants. Rosario, with her knees as bad as ever, had made it up the first flight of stairs to the bell tower and could see *la vela*, but could go no further and was sitting looking up at them, ancient María Santos beside her, blue eyes blazing.

Agustín had felt all the excitement of a child when the first peal rolled out across the *vega* and he left Alberto hanging momentarily while he rushed to the edge and waved at his wife. He couldn't decide who had been the more pleased, he, or Alberto, when earlier they had finally found each other. The child had clung to him, dependent and vulnerable in one minute, and then, stood back, absolutely adult and controlled the next. Alberto had told Agustín in short breathy sentences that he had come to find him, that he had planned to *win the day*. And that the gypsies were going to help.

"*We will not have the great weight of regret upon us,*" he quoted Agustín's own story back at him gravely, and then added quietly, "You will see, Agustín, you will see!" Then, childlike once again, he had exclaimed to Agustín, gleeful as if in the centre of a harmless adventure, "Come on!"

And with that, the two of them had climbed to the top of *la torre de la vela*.

The boy had been too light to start with, and without Agustín to add his weight he would have struggled to get the big bell moving. But now it was swinging, as long as he could hang on. It seemed to have developed its own momentum, back and forth, as a clock pendulum, with Alberto's legs waving wildly below.

Later, when Alberto would talk about the important things that had made everything possible, he would say it was Agustín's gloves. Huge on his hands, they had kept the flesh from being chewed up on the rope as he had clenched it minute after long minute, swinging freely high above the city of Granada below.

Below, Ana didn't need binoculars. Her long sight could make out the red of his hair. He looked as wild as the flags atop the tower. One for the European Union, one for Andalucía, one for Spain, one for Granada. *Perhaps one day*, she thought to herself, *there should be a flag just for children*.

"Children," was all Dolores could say. She looked upwards and saw the boy swinging across the skyline. But the thing that really caught her attention was what she imagined were his friends scaling the stairs, swarming the platforms and rushing to the sides of *la torre de la vela*. All she could say in hushed wonder was, "children."

"Children are still priority under my command," Antonio affirmed. "Look," he made to pass Raúl his binoculars but it was unnecessary, the younger man was glued to his own. "We have to wait now," Antonio ended.

"I agree," nodded Raúl, defeated. "I agree."

"How many can you see?" asked Antonio.

"Not thirty," said Raúl glumly.

"So now what?" asked Manuel.

"We wait," said García.

"And while we are waiting," said Antonio, "we can talk about detonators and piece this whole sorry mess together."

"Together."

"Alright," said Mary in answer to Agustín's instruction. "We can do that."

And slowly, painstakingly, she encouraged her nine elderly singers to take the stairs up to the top of *la torre de la vela*.

La torre de la vela was higher than he realised. Suspended above the Darro, swinging across the crowds below, Alberto felt like a bird, and his heart soared. But not for long. His natural anxiety reasserted itself as he scanned the throng. *Were they there? Would they keep their promise? Would this just be another time when he and Lola would be left behind?*

Behind Mary and the choristers, Gerardo, weaker by far than the old Englishmen, said,

"We have to get up here where it is safe. There is no point in blowing anything now. It's over. It's only a matter of time." Jay had told him that much. "They will attack if we don't get up here. It's the most secure place and we have to let them see us. If they see us there is a chance they will send in the negotiator again. Now the bell is ringing, everyone will be looking to the tower. Let them see you are all there. Come on."

345

"They won't make it," said Mary turning, alarmed at the prospect of so many sick people climbing the stairs.

"They will," he said. "They made it this far. What's a few more stairs?"

A few more stairs and we are there," Commissioner O'Reilly said over his shoulder.

"You certainly move quickly Eddie."

"Too quickly?" he said looking at her meaningfully.

She flushed,

"I don't mean that," she said.

"I know, I was just teasing."

"I know."

"I don't want you to feel under any pressure María. Believe me, this divorce is long overdue. She agreed in a heartbeat, and I didn't see any point in hanging around. This is cheap and temporary until I get things sorted out."

"I like cheap," said María, cupping his backside as he opened the door to the apartment.

"Spoken like a true Spic," he laughed.

"Na, Eddie, a true Cubana."

"And what about temporary?" he looked at her half-serious.

"Let's see how it goes."

It goes down fast," Javi confirmed, nodding gravely.

"So, if we open all of the sluices..." Manuel began.

"...it will drop away to almost nothing within twenty minutes," Javi supplied.

"That fast?"

"Maybe faster," Javi frowned. "Until we know where the

children are, we need it to drop faster."

"Well, we have alerted all the local authorities between here and Veleta to draw off water. Not that it's necessary now," said Antonio, "Some older people will open the sluices simply because of the ringing of *la vela*."

"*La vela*. That's why," said Lola as they stood at the sides of the new water channel to the car parks and watched the level drop dramatically. "Alberto is ringing *la vela*, and everyone is stealing the water!" her eyes danced.

She could not know that the ringing of the bell was only part of it. She could have no idea that a team of soldiers had phoned every local authority between Granada and Veleta to ensure that sluices were opened all along the River Darro from the snow to the plain.

"And it means Alberto and the others are there!" cried one of them. "They got down there. They didn't catch them!"

"Shhh," Lola warned them. "They are there, but we aren't yet. Come on everyone. Are you ready? It won't be that cold, and you have to move quickly before the water is all gone. You all go first and I'll come last."

"**Last** time *la vela* rang in the middle of the day?" Antonio shook his head trying to remember so as to answer Manuel.

"Sir?" Raúl spoke. "Sir. We have to go in now."

"You do?" Antonio looked at him. "Why?"

"We need to secure the site."

"Raúl," Antonio put his arm over the younger man's shoulder and drew him away. "The site IS secure. As secure as it needs to be for now. It is swarming with children who seem to have taken control of the main tower. There is nothing to do now other than

347

wait. But you can't wait, can you?" Antonio spoke kindly, as García looked on. "You are under orders, yes? And I imagine the orders are to move in at any cost... am I right?"

"Sir?"

"The price is going to be high Raúl. You are going to have to get past me to do it," Antonio watched Raúl briefly touch his sidearm.

"And me," Manuel stepped forward. García wanted to add, *and me too*, but he felt it was too heavy handed, and, as an outsider, unwelcome. But the words weren't necessary. Raúl would know he was outmanned and out-gunned.

"But if there is something I can do," said Antonio, calmly, "some compromise, some agreement we can make here, that will save your ass, tell me now."

Raúl silently shook his head, "It's the evidence," he said at last. "It's the evidence they want destroying."

Destroying the Alhambra was one thing, taking out children wholesale was another. If ever there was a moment in his life when everything lined up and made sense, it was this one. Joaquin Montez tuned his guitar. Then, as agreed with Alberto, he stood and faced *la vela*.

"*La vela*?" When did it last ring? I can't remember," said an elderly British ex-pat who had latched on to Jack Fisher as they all listened in amazement. "I have lived here for forty years. I can't remember the last time. It will have been a long time ago."

"A long time ago." Rashida said sadly, "when the Muslims ran the city, water was freely available."

She was speaking to Dolores as they were making their way slowly upward through the *alcazaba*. The sight of the children climbing the tower had made Dolores want to go faster, but her lack of strength held her back. Rashida flanked her as they progressed inexorably toward the big bells' tower.

"Yes, but the ringing of *la vela* is to bring attention to us yes?" said Dolores with both fear and excitement. Fear as to what that attention might mean and excitement that at last something was beginning to happen on a grand scale.

"Yes, I am sure it is. But it will also bring back memories for people," Rashida said sagely.

"What do you mean?"

"When the Christians took over..."

"But Rashida that was centuries ago!"

"Yes, you're absolutely right, the same year Columbus set sail for the New World," she agreed

"Yet you talk like it was yesterday."

"History is yesterday. It just depends how much impact it has on your life," she said gravely. "You of all people know that."

"Yes." Dolores nodded, almost too weak to talk much more.

"The first thing the Christians did was build the cisterns down there." Rashida pointed down to the large area between the *alcazaba* and *el palacio de carlos V*. "They did it so they could hoard water here in the fortress and starve the town below. Granada was a truly multi-cultural city then. Jews and Christians and Muslims.

"The irony is, all of us are what we call, People of the Book. We can live in harmony. Our values are the same. We should learn that from Granada. Before Ferdinand and Isabella, we had it all. The world can have it all again. I believe that."

Dolores looked at Rashida squeezed her hand.

"We need to keep the faith Rashida, now. All of us. We need

to believe we will be OK, that everything will be OK."

"That's what we believed when Ferdinand and Isabella came. They promised when they took over that everyone would be spared. But they lied," Rashida looked at Dolores bleakly, "the Jews were the first to go. Right away, as many as twenty thousand were sent into exile, others killed, others made to convert and then killed later because no-one believed that they had truly changed their faith. And you know what?" Rashida looked at her. "It took them ten years to turn on us. You know why? The water. They couldn't operate the water system without us. We had built it and it was too complicated for them. So for me, history is today. Look at us sat here waiting to know our fate."

"But it isn't because we are of different faiths Rashida."

"Isn't it? Isn't it because these people," she pointed toward Gerardo, tucking people into the sides of the tower, "believe they have a case and those people," she indicated past the tower, "isn't it because they have a different one? In the end, isn't history just the same old story over and over? To tell you the truth, at the moment, I don't feel very different to how I imagine my ancestors felt in 1492. It may as well be now."

"Then what we need to do," said Dolores fighting for breath, "is concentrate less on what separated us then and more on what we have in common now."

"Now!" said Joaquin Montez. "Now, one, two, three..."

"Three, four, five, no, more, look! Look!" Dolores had stopped and was standing supporting herself on the railings looking away from The Great Bell, away from Alberto and his friends and back toward *calle real*. "*Madre mia*, the Virgin heard our prayers! Look Rashida, Allah was listening! Even more children! Children!

Look!"

"Look," said the children as they emerged wet from the aqueduct, pointing high toward *la torre de la vela*, past where Rashida was standing,

"Look! It's Alberto!"

And the children seemed to skate across the cistern caps toward the entrance to the *alcazaba*, upwards, bounding and leaping across the stone stairs toward Alberto swinging from *la vela*, and toward Dolores's outstretched hand.

"Hand me the other ones," said Antonio to Manuel. The younger man gave him the more powerful set of binoculars. "There are may be forty people up there, as well as the children. Maybe more. The press are all over it. The crowds are going wild. Your men can't keep them back Raúl. Look!"

"He's right," said García. "Look. On *la torre de la vela*. Look. At least forty. Maybe more. And look. Look." He indicated down the slope, toward the city, toward *la plaza nueva*. "Hundreds more. Christ, maybe thousands. Just watching."

"We have to get in there. We have to go in." Raúl sounded desperate.

"And what?" Antonio turned to him. "What? Bomb the place. Shoot everyone?" and when Raúl Sanchez didn't answer he said, "Raúl. It's a joke." But looking at Raúl's face, Antonio Marín suddenly wondered if, to the younger man, it were a joke. "Is that what you mean when you say destroy the evidence? You mean to..." but Antonio couldn't find the words and ended with, "...to do what?"

"To kill everyone?" García supplied. "Go in. But it's over. Look man. It's over. Whatever is done now," said García with resignation, "the world is watching."

"And whatever the secret," said Antonio to Raúl. "Believe me, it can't now be kept."

And when Raúl said nothing García added,

"Tell him Antonio. For God's sake. Tell him. Tell him what he has to do."

"All that's left to do now for the army, for your career Raúl, is to front up to it. All that's left that you can do is damage limitation. Nothing more."

More people pressed forward against the walls of *la torre de la vela*. The older ones clasped their hands to their ears and looked over the edge to the sea of people below. The sickest among them sat at the edges, folded up, almost like the blankets they had left in the *palacios*. The younger ones, the children, unable to see over the parapet, jumped up and down and shouted.

All around, people were in differing states of animation. Gerardo felt defeat and relief. Dolores felt deliverance. Mary felt a rising jubilance. Alberto felt the breeze on his face as he swung back and forth.

Agustín scanned the horizon where the sky met the city and drove his gaze hard to the right. He fancied he could make out the trees of *la plaza trinidad* just up from the house of the Rosales brothers. He screwed up his eyes and looked harder. With enough focus, with enough concentration, maybe he would see *calle angulo*, maybe he would be able to pinpoint the very doors through which the great man had stepped so long ago.

And then he saw Him, the widow's peak, the snappy dresser, the great dark eyes, looking up, up at the Alhambra. Lorca, so near and yet so far, the Flower of Granada, and then the great man's eyes met Agustín's in recognition. It was as if an invisible baton passed from the younger man to the older, and then the

352

poet turned to speak across his shoulder back into the Rosales house.

Agustín felt a peace come upon him. Amid the din of rejoicing, seeing the numbers of people below them pressing and thronging toward *la torre de la vela*, Agustín knew for sure that today was the day that THEY could not win. Today, no amount of fancy footwork would be able to hide the evidence.

"The evidence they want to destroy is the people themselves," Raúl spoke slowly. "They are dying anyway. All of them," he said indicating *la torre de la vela* in the distance.

"So why not finish them off?" asked García rhetorically. "That's it, right? You need to go in there. You need to get rid of them. You need to complete the job. Am I right?"

"You don't understand," retorted Raúl, failing to deny it.

"Enlighten me," Antonio interjected with exaggerated patience.

"The nuclear sub did leak," Raúl sighed. "The British never denied it. But it leaked for a reason," he paused. "At first it was said that it leaked because it had been the subject of a terrorist attack," he paused and then went on, "and everyone believed it. But then we found it wasn't terrorists at all."

"Go on." said Antonio.

Raúl sighed and continued,

"It seems like it was one of the Western powers, maybe the UK, maybe the US. Christ, maybe even Spain. It was what they call a "Munch".

"Munch?"

"Shame on you Antonio. You haven't read your Gazette recently?" said García dully. "Munch," he went on. "Short for Münchausen. Medical term. It describes a syndrome. People who pretend an injury to seek sympathy."

"In other words, creating an incident falsely, in order to incite a response," said Antonio and Raúl nodded.

"So," said García flatly, "the leak was intentional. Politicians assumed terror. Press assumed terrorists. No-one bothered to correct them."

"Yes." said Raúl.

"Why?" asked Antonio.

García was sure he knew why but felt it was not his place to answer. To him it was hardly rocket science. Budgets released to fight terror, manufacturing stepped up to feed a war effort, be it against terror or some middle eastern oil magnate, populations scared into staying home and spending in their own economy instead of someone else's. Invoke the fear of terror and everything was permissible. Killing off a few of your own that got caught in the crossfire, hell, what did it matter? People were dispensable, replaceable, just like Fisher said. Hell, there was a new one born every second.

"It suits government," said Antonio flatly, "to have the people think that terror is all around."

All around, people were pressing toward the Alhambra. Jack Fisher was struggling to keep upright with the jostling. He saw Paula a few feet away talking with some of The Constantine Singers as they pushed forward at the edge of the River Darro. He could see the beginnings of the narrow streets that climbed up toward the monument. What defined their perimeters was the mass of human bodies all surging between the buildings toward the sound of the ringing of *la vela*. Crowd control was at break point. Any moment he was afraid there would be a stampede. He looked right and left, wondering what escape routes there might be. Wherever he looked there were simply more people.

"People don't get it." said Raúl.

"Get what?" said García sharply. "That terror is all around? Well you know what? It always has been," he said, answering his own question. "And more so if you keep adding to it."

"Free nations cannot at the moment afford to have anything shed doubt on the validity of the responses to the war on terror. We have to maintain a state of alert. Terrorists are always at hand. What would you prefer García? Our forces moving and taking control of this situation, or the terrorists continuing to destroy the building?"

"It's the same thing," said David García wearily.

"You're wrong," Raúl said. "Your liberal shit is wrong. There is a threat."

"Yes there is," García. "I have never denied it."

"So what's your problem?"

"There is never only one way. To deal with a hostage situation. With any situation for that matter."

"What would you have us do García?" shouted Raúl. "Let them go on and blow everything sky high? Let them live and bring the governments into disrepute? Allow people to doubt the effort to contain the threat of terror? You must see then that people's attention has to remain focused on the threat? Surely you can see that?"

"All I can see is that none of this works," García spread his hands. "There is always someone ready to blow someone else up. Governments cannot prevent it. Force cannot prevent it. That's all I know."

"That's right," said Raúl as though he were resting his case. "And what? You think that this case is any different? You think that the fact that these people might be dying gives them special consideration?"

"I think we have to always be ready for..."

"A miracle?" snarled Raúl.

And García suddenly stared at him and said slowly, nodding,

"Maybe," he twisted his ring. "Maybe. Maybe a miracle."

"Man you are losing it," said Raúl shaking his head. "This is Granada, not Jerusalem. Not the dawn of the first millennium. This is the twenty-first century."

Twenty-first century *Granada*, thought Fisher. *Who would have thought it? So many people taking to the streets. So many ordinary people on their feet, standing together, looking to what they loved, and being seen to do so.*

"So my love," whispered Mustafa, stood at the open window of their *carmen* in the Albaicín and looking over the Darro gorge to the Alhambra. He tried to make out Rashida's turban, brightly unconventional, it was sure to stand out. "Now then my wife," he continued under his breath, "my love. You see. Miracles happen all the time."

"All the time the policy is about inventing threats?" asked Antonio. "Are there not enough real ones?"

"Look Antonio," answered Raúl earnestly, "you've served in the military. We are just the puppets of the politicians. They say jump. We jump. Right or wrong, stupid or smart, THEY decide."

"So let's have a few incidents. Right? Keep everyone interested? Remind them. Being blown up is always a possibility. Right?" David bit out.

"Look García," snapped Raúl, "it wasn't my idea to cause a nuclear sub to leak and I wasn't there to cause the leak either..."

"...but hey," said García conversationally, "since there was one, why not run with it? Eh?"

"Don't tell the public, because they might panic," Antonio was ticking off reasons on his fingers, "slap a D notice on it," he said, referring to government powers to suppress a news story. "If any victims of a leak finally come to light, ensure they disappear." He looked over at Raúl and said in a lower tone, "No wonder these people have gone to such extremes. There is no way their case can be heard. Am I right?" Raúl said nothing. Antonio then asked, "And the detonators?"

"It is an embarrassment," said Raúl. "Twelve of them. We don't know."

"Or you do know," said Antonio wearily. "Someone gave them to these poor bastards precisely so there would be an excuse to wipe them all out."

"Never!" exclaimed Raúl as the idea took hold. "Never!"

"But you can't be sure," said García steadily. "Uncertainty. The flip side of hope. The greatest psychological tool of all. Whether in their hands or in ours," he turned his back on both of them and said with finality, "I know it well. I'm a negotiator. That's the game."

Game *on*. thought Gerardo, as the true power of their position slowly dawned on him. Below them were thousands. Around him, were all ages and sizes. This was completely different to what he had expected.

He had expected a confrontation. He had expected that eventually the army would move in. He had even expected there would be death. But now these expectations had changed. Events had moved everything onto a bigger canvas, a wider platform. Antonio Marín felt a lightening of his heart. He was aware of the many below him in the city and the few on *la torre de la vela*.

Whatever happened now, since the ringing of *la vela*, it was not going to be what any of them could have imagined. How the army would move now was entirely within his gift. At last he had the upper hand. He heard them both, as if through glass, continuing their battle of words,

"The war on terror," began Raúl

"The war on terror," García drawled. "Now there's a thing. A war. Imaginative to think of that. War as a solution. Really effective. People live. Nations have no waste. Children eat well. There are no long-term consequences. Excellent idea."

"It's all very well being sarcastic García, and no," Raúl said raising his palm toward him, "please not the loss of your sainted child." García thought he heard Antonio's sharp intake of breath. "These issues are bigger than us as individuals."

"That's what they always say Raúl," García said softly with an edge of menace, "and leave my child out of it. Because, my lovely, that's what THEY always say."

"The potential loss of public confidence is enormous," said Raúl, wrong-footed by Garciá's term of endearment, rummaging for his argument.

"What about confidence in them? In the people?" Antonio came out of his reverie. "How come we cannot trust the very people we think we are protecting to devise solutions? Look at this!" he cast his hand down toward the city. "The place is full. They can't keep the people away. Look up there, on *la torre de la vela* for God's sake, ordinary people. They see. They know."

"They don't know how bad things could be," said Raúl.

"Yeah they do," said García quietly. "Half of those people have radiation poisoning. A third of them are orphans. God knows what's happened to the rest of them. Here's the thing Sanchez," he said eyeballing Raúl. "Once governments deny truth. Worse, forget what the truth is. Everyone is screwed. And you Raúl," he advanced on him, "you stand at the fulcrum. You." García came so close to Raúl that Antonio thought he might kiss him. The negotiator chameleon cupped the blond man's face in his hand and said, "All this," and with his other hand gestured to the crowd below and the crowd on *la torre de la vela*, "all this. It is colliding at your feet. Here is your other option. Like I said. There is never only one. The question for you is this. Do you take it? Do you choose *the way less travelled*?" he said. *Quoting Robert Frost now,* thought Antonio. Then García dropped his hand from Raúl's face and put his arm around his shoulder and said, "These terrorists are tired. Too sick to go on. Their hostages are tired. I just met with the person who has told us as much. Your siege is over. Nothing will be blown up now. Unless you blow it up," he said to Raúl. "I'd say it was just arrests and clean up now."

Antonio nodded in agreement, noting once more the eloquence, and said,

"Damage limitation Raúl, you can play this to your advantage. Whatever happened with detonators, with your orders, with wiping out the evidence, you can retell the tale and come up smelling like roses."

David García dropped his arm from Raúl's shoulder and said in his ear,

"A man seldom gets perfect line of sight, my lovely. It's rare to know before you act how that can make a difference. This is your moment."

"Listen," Antonio put the binoculars to his eyes, then dropped them and said, "listen. *La vela* has stopped."

Raúl was speechless, could scarcely hear, the blood was pounding so loudly in his ears. He felt the double effect of García's touch and his words. Something reversed in him. He moved from sexual predator to a desire to be worthy. Just another sort of waiting he supposed. He turned to Antonio,

"Will we go in now Sir? Time to take the sick to the hospital.

Yes?"

And at Antonio's assent he left the room.

García moved to gather up his papers.

"This operation is over I think. For me," he said stacking his files. He went toward his briefcase. Somewhere, below them, toward the Albaicín, Antonio and García heard a faint call and a trill of guitar.

"It sounds like *cante jondo,*" said Antonio. "Deep song," he added by way of explanation to García.

"I know what it is. Lorca wrote about it," said García quietly.

"And wrote for it," said Antonio. "Listen, it's getting louder."

"Louder!" shouted Ana to all the assembled crew. "Louder!" And she began to clap as Joaquin Montez threw back his head and sang. *Cante jondo.*

Cante jondo barely affected Antonio ordinarily. He could listen to it at home on CD, enjoy the perfection of the recording art, but be totally unmoved. When the live music, suspended and then lost in time, was etched forever on reflective laser sensitive plastic, something of the raw passion of it was erased. But here, performed at his feet, faltering and falling in its controlled stylised way, here with the caves barely a stone's throw down the incline, the man's voice reverberating, he thought inevitably of Lorca, and he turned to García and quoting Lorca's poem of tall towers and mysterious men. García looked at Antonio, and then to the Alhambra, while the very *duende*, the soul, of the gypsy's voice pierced him. He recalled Lorca further than Antonio was quoting, and remembered Lorca's sentiment, that *cante jondo* singers, like love, are blind. And he did not know why, but it was as if his heart, or the heart of the singer, might break.

"Break it up!" Alberto said to all the chattering children. "Listen. Joaquin is doing it. He has seen us!"

Mary was on her feet. She ran to the sides of the *alcazaba* and looked toward the sounds of the singing.

Alberto turned to her.

"Where are you from?" he asked.

"England," she said.

"Where in England?"

"York."

"Hmm. It's quite cold there yes?"

"Often."

"And floods, yes?"

"Yes," said Mary looking at him strangely. "What's going on? Who is that voice?"

"It's our friends." said Alberto. "They are singing so we know they have seen us and they will tell the authorities we are here."

Mary pushed past him and looked out but could see no-one.

"Where are they?"

"Over there," Alberto pointed.

"I can't see them," she said. Then the voice broke, it's force and volume lost by over-reaching. Alberto turned from Mary toward where he knew Joaquin would be and cried out,

"Oh no! Oh no!"

"OK. OK. I know. I know," and she turned toward The Constantine Singers and said, "on your feet men. On your feet. Over here."

Over here! Over here! I can see them now."

"Look it's Mary,"

At *la plaza nueva* another of The Constantine Singers dragged at Jack Fisher's arm and said,

"Look you can tell it's her."

"Yes," said another. "It's her red hair and she always wears that frightful scarf across her shoulders."

"Shoulders back, relax and..." Mary Stansfield raised her arms, sounded a G, and on the down beat they opened their mouths and began the first of their Lorca folk songs,

"*El caballo*....

"El Caballo..." sang twenty choristers standing at *la plaza nueva* hearing the familiar song and joining in. Around them, citizens of Andalucía, all pressing forward toward the Alhambra, didn't even turn, but instead, put their hands together to drill out the rhythm. Those who knew the words that went with the familiar tune joined in. Joaquin Montez, Ana, Fernando and their parents and cousins altered their tempo, Joaquin rested his voice and the guitars rang out from the Albaicín in rhythm and counter-rhythm. The music soared.

The music soared up past the Albaicín toward the *reformatorio* of San Miguel, to Antonio Marín, David García, Manuel Pedraza and all their staff.

Raúl Sanchez could still hear it as the trucks rolled down the hill away from the hillside of Sacromonte, away from the Albaicín and the more distant Viznar, onwards to the Alhambra.

Dr Jesús and Javi the gardener stood apart in wonder on the *terraza* and tears ran down their cheeks.

And the people of Pueblo de Conchi sat small and tired and relieved on *la torre de la vela*, while the children jumped up and down in glee.

And the people of Andalucía in *la plaza nueva,* and as far as the eye could see, clapped and stamped. They sang for the Alhambra and they sang for Granada. They sang the words of Lorca, in one voice, as only Andalusians can.

evening

If the operation had enjoyed an international flavour with the presence of Fisher and García, all of that ended once Antonio authorised the advance. From then on it was a Spanish affair. It had to be. Before darkness fell, Dr Jesús, Javi, his fellow gardeners, with help from army engineers, levered open the doors at both *la torre de las infantas* and *la torre de carril*. Once they were breached, they, the Red Cross volunteers, army soldiers, Antonio and Manuel disappeared deep into the fray.

Raúl, at last, had the chance he had been waiting for, although the mobilisation of his forces was not quite for the reasons he had hoped. Nonetheless his trucks rolled up the hill through *la puerta de las granadas*, echoing the many trucks that had rolled up there seventy years before. This time, instead of taking the living up the hill to a certain death in the cemetery, they were bringing the dying down the hill for saving.

Jack Fisher and David García watched it all from the sidelines but then followed together in the wake. For all García's declaration that his job was done, he could not bring himself to leave without seeing it for himself: a siege that had collapsed in the embrace of music.

García found it eerie to pass through the walls and into the monument. He couldn't imagine how people like Antonio or Dr Jesús, with a long acquaintance with the Alhambra, must find it. Other than the glow from bonfires there was no light. The roar of trucks pulling up the Alhambra hill remained incessant and he knew it would not be long before he would hear the humming of generators and the snapping on of flood lights, but initially, in the shadows, a chaos of people darting, shouting and swearing, filled his eyes and ears.

At *la torre de las infantas* there was a smell of splintered wood, which very briefly, had been even stronger than the aroma of the pines. Underfoot, as he and Fisher followed the route down toward *calle real*, the path was soaked. Water was overflowing all of the watercourses, washing its descent through the *secano*, past the silos and downward toward *el palacio de carlos V.*

As they approached, García felt the smoke catch at the back of his throat, and tasted the acrid spittle as his Adam's apple contracted. All too familiar was the intangible stench of fear and all too real the smell of burning. For him, they combined into a veritable cocktail of uncertainty and despair, whether his own, or universal, García could not have said. He was in no doubt that his response mirrored everything he associated with bombing of the twin towers. He was far too savvy not to have prepared for it. He knew that, as proximity to the site increased, remembrance of scenes from New York would come vividly to the fore and he had braced himself mentally for their painful onslaught.

But what caught him unawares was the exquisite quality to the pain. It was like the bittersweet sensation of pressing a bruise. He felt himself to have the merest gossamer sheath enfolding his emotion. His feelings were exposed yet contained at the same time by a web that seemed at once a protection and a revelation. It lit across his consciousness like an angel's breath, as though Marilita herself were once more in the ether, and as if he, once again, just as he had at the twin towers, was breathing deeply to suck deep into his lungs any vestige of life. Involuntarily he put his hand to his chest, his fingers splayed across his heart.

Incongruously against all of it, he could still hear singing. Some in Spanish some in English, almost anthemic across the increasing sounds of men and machines moving into position. García was barely aware of Jack peeling away toward the music, doubtless seeking his own countrymen. García stood, taking time to control his breathing.

His breathing was laboured. Surprisingly the descent from the tower had been harder than the ascent. He leaned in hard against the pomegranate tree. Gerardo knew that he could not go much further without assistance.

"Assistance is on its way," Fisher told them, trying to make out the numbers and faces in the gloom. "Mary. Mary Stansfield. Are you here?" he peered with his hand at his forehead, as if by shielding his eyes he would be able to penetrate the darkness better.

"She was a minute ago," said a voice from the darkness. "I'm Reginald Coussins," Reggie stepped forward, "Fisher! What are you doing here man?"

"I happened to be here on holiday," Fisher smiled at Reggie, trying to gauge in the poor light if he looked as strained as he sounded. "Everyone OK?"

"Yeah, we're more or less OK. But people are tired." Then he came up close to Fisher and said, "But we lost Goddard."

"What do you mean, you 'lost' him?"

"He's dead."

As Reggie Coussins related what had happened Jack Fisher could not help but think of the golden boy of his youth. He recalled the times Daniel had batted the ball in cricket well beyond anyone's capacity to retrieve it. How in turn he had fielded perfectly and then sung and played and drank at the pub afterwards, as if there was no tomorrow. And now there was no tomorrow.

What had Daniel said of him when they had spoken in The Blue Bell that fateful Sunday during the Festival of Angels? *You were a wicked batsman Fisher and one hell of a wicked drunk.* Well that was no longer true either. *The people we know in our youth*, Jack thought, *assume a connection with us far beyond most of those of adulthood.* He paused, and was about to continue in police mode, when he was aware of García at his side.

"Reggie, this is Captain García, New York Police, here on

secondment. David, Reggie Coussins from York."

"How are you doing Sir?" García asked, shaking hands.

"Reggie was just telling me they've lost a man. Daniel Goddard."

García remembered Fisher talking about Goddard and his connection to the Romero woman at El Piano. He shot Fisher a look, but was far too much of a pro to skip a beat and said to Reggie,

"I'm sorry to hear that. What happened?"

"Daniel is, well was," Reggie hesitated and then plunged on, "he took to drinking some meths and well... " he petered out.

"I knew Daniel," Fisher helped him out. "We were at school together and later, for a few years, played cricket on the same team. I know Daniel's capacity for alcohol."

"I think that was the problem," said Reggie sadly. "He didn't have any capacity for it. But you don't like to speak ill," he left out, *of the dead*, "do you?"

Listening to Fisher and Reggie, and remembering Richard, García was aware of his own lips moving in silence over Lorca's words about Death's entrance and exit. The tavern's death...

"He fell apparently," Fisher told García.

"Where?"

Reggie answered.

"He fell into one of the silos. It's where we buried the girl and her baby."

"Where?"

"Where's Lola?" said Alberto in sudden alarm. "Where's Lola?"

The singing continued and he couldn't make himself heard.

"Don't know," answered one of the wet children.

"Lola," he called, first darting through the children on *la torre de la vela*, then down the stairs, across the tops of the cisterns toward the *palacio de carlos V*. "Lola! Lola!" he ran again up to the top of the tower. "Hey," he said pulling on the arm of one of the children and stopping her clapping with the music. "Where's Lola?"

The girl looked around.

"I don't know, she went last. I haven't seen her."

Alberto dashed again, back down the tower, back across to *calle real* and stood a long time looking at the water rushing and gushing along the channel, spilling over and washing down onto the road. It was at twice the level it had been when he had made the journey.

The journey of the last three days seemed a lifetime to Gerardo. He shrunk further into the tree and watched the action around him. The vitality was almost overpowering. It made him feel even weaker, and he realised that the entire effort of capture and maintaining the Alhambra had very likely sapped the last ounce of his own life from him. He simply had no more will.

"Will you step this way gentlemen?" García said to The Constantine Singers, as he watched Jack in consultation with Antonio at the door of the *hotel america*. "It looks like we are going to use the hotel to accommodate everyone and that the heating and lighting is being restored. It's just until we get everyone processed. Step this way."

This way he had of exerting his will could not let him down now. He was determined. He sank to the ground and watched as though

371

he were in a dream.

Huge flood lights were floating on poles higher even than the posts he and the others had placed to frustrate any attempt by the authorities for an air descent. He picked out the extent of the devastation wrought over three days. The smoke was now more clearly illuminated than it had been in the moonlight and he saw for the first time how much was still smouldering.

Toward the higher trees he saw Jay raise a hand. Gerardo raised his in response and watched as the figure slid, first into the shadows, and then the trees.

At the centre of the compound swarmed uniformed men. He could see the blond head of the man apparently in charge. Suddenly it felt more important than anything to be the one who found him, and not the other way around.

"Around three hours ago," Paula Fisher said into the 'phone. "Once they could see everyone on the big tower, and the singing... my God the singing Ange, you should have heard it!" she exclaimed to her sister-in-law. "It was phenomenal. Out of this world. It was as if the whole city was singing one song. And now it's over."

"It's over," Joaquin Montez seized Ana's hand. "It's over," he repeated hoarsely. "I can't believe it. It's over."

"It's over," he said looking up at her.

"I know," Mary said.

She found she stroked the trunk of the tree as she sank to a squat at his level. *I'm becoming just like Rashida*, she thought to herself. *Always caressing the foliage...* The coral buds of the pomegranate seemed tougher under her hand than their delicate paper appearance had seemed by day. She hoped that was true for Gerardo.

He looked at her with a long appraising look and then he said,

"I need to get up and find whoever is in charge."

Mary stood, extended her hand down to him and said,

"Come on then soldier. I'll go with you. On your feet."

Feet away, Rashida Santiago composed herself. She felt she needed just a few minutes of respite before walking from one three day predicament into another new one. All the hollering around her, the movement of men and machines should have filled her with relief, instead, the action and frenetic activity just seemed like another set of crises to survive.

She knew she was in shock at last. Calm on the outside and coping during events, yet when the crisis was over, there was a collapse. And she was in it now. How close had they come to being blown away? How close was the Alhambra to being gone forever? What savagery walked the earth that could have caused so terrible an outcome? How was it that humankind could so readily be the vessel and the instrument of such destruction? Did it come with birth? That violent eruption of one body from another? For how could birth could ever be described as anything else? Whether natural, induced, Caesarean or still, the whole beginning of a life was described by blood and gore. Was this three days at the Alhambra a manifestation of all that humankind knew absolutely and from the outset? That every comfort is temporary, every breath is bought, every end is in sight?

She wanted to weep, to sleep, to go far into her heart and mind where no-one would find her. Not even Mustafa. But she knew it was a vain desire. They would come for her soon enough. Somewhere the policeman Antonio Marín had to be there, it was just a matter of time before he or one of his juniors would come to look for her.

Somewhere would be Ángel David García.

Garcia's priority had been to look for her. Once he overcame the ill effects of being plunged again into the debris of fire and explosion, that priority re-asserted itself. He had the photo of her from Fisher's incident wall firmly in his mind. He had not asked The Constantine Singers where she was, nor Jack Fisher. Somehow he wanted to keep it to himself that he was looking for her. He expressed an interest instead in Mary Stansfield who was still nowhere to be seen. It crossed Garcia's mind that the two women might even be together. He left Fisher in incident-mode again, this time, not with a room and photos to organise, but the real people themselves.

García was pretty sure that she would not have got by him. Even in the dark he could keep in his awareness a wide fan sweeping across all the activity from the left to the right. He would have seen her, felt her, known she was there.

He worked his way steadily through the crowd of Raúl's soldiers as they themselves fanned out to cover every inch, every square metre and equally to flush out the old, the injured, and the hiding. He even brushed shoulders with Raúl himself, who had flashed him a victorious smile.

He could see a crowd of children gathering just past the turnstile into *la torre de la vela*. Eventually he would make contact with Alberto, but first he needed to satisfy himself that Santiago had survived. Where could she be?

To his astonishment, he felt prayer form again in the back of his throat. *Please God let her be alive*. The lapsed Catholic, he admonished himself, does not exist. What had Richard said in one of his frequent discourses on history and religion? *You know what they say Davie; there are no atheists in the trenches.*

Then he thought he saw her. It was a woman of the right age, stooping to talk to a child, but when she turned toward García he was disappointed. Where could she be? She had to be alive. Surely. And then to one side, a little way from the epicentre of the activity he made her out.

She was standing quite still, a bright scarf around her head, her hands in her pockets, slightly slouched, just watching. She lifted her head and caught his eye. A sudden welling of what he could only have described as pure love washed through him.

Through him Carmen had finally experienced the love that people wrote poems and songs about. Ange had said it was over and Daniel would be back in York in hours, a day at most. So it was only a matter of time before The Constantine Singers would be home and she would have the chance to tell Daniel, no matter how drunk he was, or how inconsistent, that she would always love him. There was nothing like nearly losing someone to make you aware of how important they were.

They were all finally gathered in one place. Manuel thought it was like trying to herd eels. No sooner had he three or four children together than a further four or five would slip away. Finally, reluctantly, Raúl agreed to position some of his men with the children, to keep them in one place. Manuel then went with Raúl to assist with the group of weak souls he was now having force-marched toward the *hotel america*.

The *hotel america* was the better place, Antonio had decided. Although not as commodious as the *parador*, unlike the *parador*

it had manageable entrance and exit. There was no rear terrace for escape. The *hotel america* only had a small internal courtyard with two stories of hotel rooms that formed the quadrangle. They could keep the *hotel america*, and all in it, quite secure. Although, to be fair, one look at the group Manuel was shepherding toward him and he thought the likelihood of anyone moving at speed, let alone escaping, was remote.

He instructed some of Raúl's men to check through the building and to open all the rooms on the first floor. At a glance he could see that the reception area had been the site of one of the births. Crouching toward the tiled floor he could see that blood and vernix was still in evidence. He called a couple of soldiers over and told them to glove-up and clean.

He herded the sorry band into the central courtyard and turned on the flood lights. They looked small, defeated, and ill. He asked for a leader. No-one stepped forward, and as each one of them had looked around, apparently they themselves seeking sight of someone, he concluded that any leader they may have had was still at large. He left them under armed guard and returned to the entrance.

Outside, soldiers were still moving equipment and supplies. The children were either dancing around in frenetic excitement or looking ashen with tiredness.

Hunger, thought Antonio. *Nothing that a plate of food will not revive.*

"This lot need feeding," he said to one of the soldiers. "Where's your Commanding Officer?"

"Sir," a young man stepped forward.

"What have we got to feed this lot?" Antonio asked him.

"Soup Sir. And some fruit. Oranges."

"Very well. See to it will you?"

"Sir."

"Sir. Step back please," a soldier barred his way as tried to cross from the base of the *alcazaba* toward the palaces.

"Let him pass," Raúl said at his shoulder. "This is Captain García," he said and looked at García. David thought if it were possible to have a salute in a voice, maybe there had been one. He nodded at Raúl as Raúl repeated, "Let him pass."

David kept moving toward the *alcazaba* until he was standing opposite Rashida Santiago. Only then did she take her hands from her pockets and straighten up.

"Rashida Santiago," he said. "David García," and he stretched out his hand. "New York Police Department. Negotiator. US observer to this operation."

She looked at him and then said,

"That would be Ángel David García, Cubano, yes?"

And to herself she said, *Mamá he has come, Angel David.*

"Yes," he smiled at her use of his full name, remarking to himself how, in crises, the most inane of responses was commonplace.

"Thank you," she said and moved forward to kiss him on each cheek.

"It's been quite an experience," he said to her. "How are you bearing up?"

"Not bad," she said smiling softly. "Not bad," and then shifted her weight. "I had more comfort than some."

She linked his arm to walk toward the *hotel america*.

"I imagine your husband won't be far away now," he said.

"*Enshallah*," she said quietly.

"Ah yes," he said. "Your faith. It sustains you."

"All faiths do," she answered. "In whatever system of belief. If they don't, then they are not your faith."

García took her words into himself and looked at her sideways.

"It's a funny business isn't it?" he asked.

377

"What?" she said as they neared the hotel.

"Not knowing if you will survive."

"Yes. We have a saying for that, my husband and I, *If you fear tomorrow is judgement day...*"

"*...then plant a fruit tree.*" he ended for her.

She looked up at him wonderingly and said slowly, "Yes."

And in that moment she seemed so like Marilita it was all he could do not to put his arms around her. But then she did it for him, reached up and held him tight. As she did so she felt a flutter deep in her stomach. The flutter she had always dreamed of, told other women about, longed for, and never felt herself. Her babies had always miscarried before the pulse of life was palpable to her. The sickness. Now the flutter.

She pulled away and looked at him in a sort of wonder and remembered Mustafa and his frequent declaration, *miracles happen all the time*, and said again,

"Thank you," and then, "I am ready now."

"I am ready now," Gerardo told Mary, and they walked forward into the light.

The light from the massive lamps showed up the worst of the wreckage as Dr Jesús ambled slowly, trying to take in, and mentally catalogue, the damage.

It was not as bad as he had feared. The doors, forced by the army, were probably beyond repair, but he comforted himself with the knowledge that they were reproduction anyway.

The pillars, taken from *los palacios nazaríes* and erected in front of the *palacio de carlos V*, had taken some knocks when cut and dragged from the palaces, but he doubted there was much that could not be restored.

He fingered the plasterwork, the saw and axe marks where they had been hacked from the marble floors, and shook his head. But the fretting was largely intact. History had been made this weekend. These marks, adding to the many, continued the monument's existence as a living testament to the ages.

His walk through the *generalife* and down had revealed both *el partal* and *el mirador romántico* as more or less destroyed, but beyond a few infractions of the walls around *el partal,* the damage was limited. The banisters of water leading from *el mirador romántico* down to the *generalife* were miraculously intact.

As for the watercourses, they had survived worse. Once the *albercones*, the ancient Arabic reservoirs, were repaired and refilled, the water flow would rapidly return to normal.

As he headed away from the *generalife* toward the main compound, the gates were the least of his concerns. Jesús remembered the entire rebuilding of *la torre de las infantas*. Using the old bricks and the old methods of mixing mortar they had ensured that few people passing through would ever notice that it was less than a few decades old. With patience, time and a grant or two, it could all be made good.

At first he had concerns about loss of revenue from visitors, but then he realised that the magnitude of events would draw a different sort of tourist. People would come to see the result of the three-day siege. If anything they would probably have more visitors than ever before, and many would contribute extra cash to the rebuilding once they knew the extent of the problem.

Jesús sighed. Writing information sheets and leaflets, applying for grants, assessing the damage, organising the repairs: there was a lot to do. It would take a long time. But then what else did the *patronato* have to do other than painstakingly take care of things over many years?

"Years," Gerardo answered.

"Can you be more specific?" Antonio asked grimly.

"I think it was about three years ago when we first thought of it."

"And why?" Antonio pressed.

"It was our fallback position."

"Excuse me?"

"It was what we decided we could revert to if all else failed."

Antonio looked at him almost exasperated. He didn't want to spend long with him, at least not until all the easy interviews were complete, and as many people as possible had been sent on their way. But an initial discussion was essential to inform the other interviews.

"And this isn't a failure?" Antonio cast a hand toward the door of the *hotel america* as if to encompass all that lay outside of it.

"Talking to you Captain Marín," said Gerardo looking at Antonio steadily, "is the reverse. Talking to you is, in fact, an unprecedented success."

"Success," Jack Fisher said into his mobile phone to Superintendent Michael Small. "All of them are here, including Mary Stansfield."

He didn't add that it had taken him nearly forty minutes to find Mary after first meeting up with The Constantine Singers. Nor did he add that the relationship between Mary and her captors appeared to have crossed the divide, where the hostage and the hostage-taker unite. All that could wait.

"Excellent," said Small.

But what could not wait was,

"Unfortunately Mike, Daniel Goddard didn't make it."

"What do you mean?"

"I mean it seems as if he got blind drunk."

"Nothing new in that Jack."

"No, I mean actually blind drunk. They say he was drinking meths, and then he pitched himself into one of these silo things they have here. A sort of deep, deep storage well in the ground, easily a sixty-foot drop. They've recovered the body. It's definitely Goddard."

"Jesus," Fisher heard Small exhale.

"I knew Goddard," said Jack. "If it can wait, I'd like to be the one to tell his family."

"I don't think anyone will fight you for it Jack. How long before you can all get away?"

"Well, the consul has finally arrived. Some of the older ones aren't in great nick. We thought about staying another night but to be honest, I think everyone is really eager to get out and get home. She is organising some flights. It looks like she can get half of us on a ten o'clock flight into Manchester, and the other half of us on a flight at about midnight into Leeds."

"Take the Leeds flight Jack. I'll meet you there."

"There you are," García advanced on Fisher as Jack punched the completed-call button on his phone and pocketed it. "Jack, this is Rashida Santiago."

"Ms Santiago," Jack took her hand. "The Queen of Morse."

She smiled and answered,

"I never knew if you got those."

"We did," García said, "and Fisher here, he was your scribe."

"Thank you," said Rashida.

"No. Thank you," Fisher told her. "How are you?"

"I'm fine. A little," she smiled shyly at him, "I don't know, a little overwhelmed."

381

"Hardly surprising Ms Santiago. You must be eager to get home."

"That would be nice."

"When did all this lot arrive?" said García to Fisher indicating the press who were out in full force. Cameras were everywhere and there were nearly as many media vans as there were military.

"About half an hour ago," Jack replied. "Antonio didn't think he could keep them out much longer. Anyway, have you seen Marín?" said Fisher turning to him, thinking of Rashida wanting to go home and knowing full well that no-one was going to get away without Antonio's say so.

"No," said García.

"Well, he's questioning the prisoners in the *hotel america*. Obviously he needed to get away from this circus. They reckon to have rounded them all up."

"The leader there?" García asked.

"No. Not the person you saw. Seems to have disappeared. But the operations guy is here. He gave himself up."

"Yes. Sanchez told me," said David, remembering Raúl's look of unbridled triumph.

"Not Rafael I take it, or ETA," said Fisher.

"Or Islamic Jihad," said Rashida softly.

Fisher and García had the grace to nod at her. García said,

"Walked up to Raúl. Bold as brass. Introduced himself. Oddly enough the English woman was with him."

Fisher knew about Mary. Raúl had told him a good half-hour before, just when Fisher had begun to think that her body might also be at the bottom of a silo. He hadn't even begun to think about how he might de-brief her.

Best thing, in a set up like this, was to get the easy interviews out of the way. If Antonio was following the usual protocol he would be thinking the same way.

"The same way as us," the child answered Antonio's question as to how Alberto had arrived at *la vela*. She grinned up at Antonio with an impish smile.

Antonio sighed. The girl's interview was just like the interviews with Agustín and Rosario. The same as with the elderly María Santos Moreno, now back at home next door to the *hotel america*. They were matter of fact, in places repetitive, and provided only snippets of the bigger scenario.

The one diversion had been when the white-haired, blue-eyed, old woman had taken Rosario with her, insisting in a querulous tone to Agustín that his wife was exhausted and if he wanted to *carry on running around like a madman* as she put it, well, he could, but she and his good wife were going to rest and take a plate of *migas*. Whereupon Agustín stalked tight lipped from the room and was heard to mutter,

"As if a man has not enough trial with one woman telling him what to do, now I appear to have two."

Apart from Agustín's obvious pride in Alberto, and the final hours helping the child ring *la vela*, it was clear that the old people and The Constantine Singers had all more or less been swept along with events. The Constantine Singers' account sounded more boring than frightening. They had long been discharged. Except that is for Mary Stansfield, who still needed to explain herself.

As far as Antonio was concerned, he was pretty much done with the children too. Only Alberto and Lola were missing, and knowing them, they could be in Morocco by now. He ran his hands through his hair, feeling tired for the first time and barked at a young soldier at the door for a coffee. Then he said to another,

"Get some transport arranged for the children to take them to the *reformatorio* at San Miguel. Did you get them fed?"

"Soup and oranges Sir. Like we said."

Antonio raised his eyes to the door and saw García and

383

Fisher enter with Rashida Santiago.

"Ah, Ms Santiago."

"Captain."

"We owe you a great deal."

"Not really," she said. "These people are very sick. There was no way this was going to last for long."

"True," Antonio said holding her look. "But we weren't to know that without having had your help. I wonder if I might delay you a little longer? I just need to ask you some questions. Perhaps you would prefer to go upstairs. The rooms must be warmed through by now. I know I would be glad to get out of the draught from this door opening and closing every few minutes."

"Antonio," Fisher felt it was a good moment to step forward and take his leave. "Unless there is a reason not to, I'm going to take the Singers down to the city and get people organised for the trip home."

"Not at all Jack. Thanks for everything."

"The British consul is outside," Fisher said. "She will stay to assist you with any enquiries with Ms Stansfield. If I am needed, they will bring me back during the week. We have some flights booked for tonight and you have enough to do without extra people in the way."

Fisher moved toward Antonio and shook hands.

"It was a pleasure Fisher. Anytime you are in Madrid..."

Jack Fisher laughed.

"No no no. Next time I am on holiday I am going to make sure No-one knows where I am. Certainly not either of you!"

García stepped up and put out his hand.

"It was..." García looked for the word. "It was an education," he ended.

Fisher took García's hand warmly and said,

"Wasn't it just. I am wondering if I should ask you to lose my card," he clapped García on the back. "I'm only kidding; I wouldn't have missed it for anything. Maybe see you soon if I am required for a debrief and you are still here. All the best. Goodbye Ms Santiago," and Fisher walked from the hotel into *calle real*.

"Shall we go up?" Antonio indicated the stairs. "García?"

"Sure," David thought he may as well sit in on an interview Spanish style.

Room 111 was at the front of the building. The walls were warm orange tones offset by old dark Spanish furniture. García went towards the windows and looked past the heavy wooden shutters out from the front of the hotel to the street below.

There he could see the children waiting for the bus to take them to their *reformatorio*. They seemed possessed of a renewed, and still more boundless, energy. Those not running and jumping and shouting, were sat in groups, chewing on bread and oranges. The heating was certainly working well, and after the cool of the evening and the draughts of downstairs, it almost felt stuffy. He heard Rashida ask,

"May I open the window?"

And García watched as if all were in slow motion as she stood and moved toward the shutters and then flung the glass outward. *If I die*, he heard Marilita's voice, *will you leave the balcony window open for me?* It was as if his child's hand was in his and he could hear her clearly in his ear, *will you leave it open for me if I leave it open for you?*

He turned to Rashida, watching her arm rise and then fall from the latch, and in that moment he fancied he felt Marilita disengage herself from him. All that was left of his child in him seemed to move through the window toward the children below.

With that one gesture of Rashida's hand, he excused himself from the interview and took the stairs two at a time downwards and then out into the night to look for Alberto.

"Alberto said, *home is where the heart is*, yes?" Joaquin questioned Ana.

"Sí," and then added, "I told Fernando."

"And?"

"And nothing."

"Where is he?"

"Gone to get drunk I think."

"And so?"

"And so now he knows. If you mean, what happens next? I don't know."

"But at least he knows," stated Joaquin and he took Ana's hand in his and looked across at la Alhambra.

"And one day," she said to him, "you can tell this child how you helped to save his heritage."

"He may not believe me," Joaquin smiled.

"Yes he will. Because it will still be there."

"There is no guarantee Mary," said Gerardo.

"No there isn't," she said steadily.

"So?"

"So we just live today."

Then they led Gerardo away.

"They're taking me to the *comisaría* too," she shouted as the car pulled away. "I'll see you there! I will!"

"Will she still be there? Will she? Will she?" Alberto was jumping up and down in front of Raúl.

"Alberto," García said to him. "What's going on?"

"He thinks she didn't get out of the water course in time," said Raúl.

"Lola! Lola!" Alberto's plaintive voice shafted García's heart.

The child's face was stained with tears, muddy streaks across his cheeks where he had been wiping them away, over and over.

"She's not here. She must be under there!" he pointed to the raised tops of the sealed cisterns in the approach to the *alcazaba*.

"Why do you say that?" García asked, growing alarmed.

"We came down the water, like I said we would. At first, when I came, it was quite high. But I was not afraid because I knew to count the covers like Javi said, and I knew on the ninth one, after that one, that was the time I had to keep my hands along each side and then grab the handles," he made a grabbing action, "and then, when I got the handles, to push up and get out. Get out," he repeated.

"OK," said García going down on one knee and holding the boy by his shoulders. "OK. And then what?"

"I told them. I told them. I told them to wait for *la vela*. I told them when they heard *la vela* they would know I had got there, and that when they heard *la vela* the people on the *vega* would open the sluices and the water level would drop. And Marie Carmen told me it did. She said that the water did drop. But then, when I when went back to look, when I went to look when everyone was singing, it was higher than ever!" he wiped a hand across his face, looked at García and he began to cry, "Lola! Where is she? She will be so cold. So cold! It's been hours."

"Hours of waiting and wondering really," Rashida folded her hands and looked at Antonio and said, "I don't have anything to add."

"Thank you Ms Santiago," said Antonio and took her hand. "We have your details, if we need...."

"Please," she cut across him, "feel free to contact me at any time."

Time was running out. It is a well documented fact that missing children are more likely to stay missing with every moment that passes. Missing children who are lost in water courses, missing children who are lost in the dark, missing children who were last seen navigating rushing water with a level rising and falling like the sea, must be a hundred or a thousand times more likely to remain missing forever. *Think, David. Think.* García ground out to himself. There was no time to get Antonio, and anyway what did he know? *Think, David. Think.*

The old man? No. Even if he knew where Agustín was he would be the one needed for comfort, not for action. And Alberto looked up at him and saw David García's face scrunched against the effort of thinking and Alberto knew García was working hard to find a way.

And then David saw the answer, lean, aesthete, with the light of the floods glinting off his glasses.

"Allah be praised," David was amused to hear himself whisper, and then added for good measure, "Thank God for that."

"That one," barked Raúl. "That one. Pull it round, release the cable. Come on man!"

"Are you sure?" García asked his companion.

"Totally," Dr Jesús handed his glasses to Alberto, then dropped to a squat and peered at the ground, moving and scraping at the red earth. "Yes," he said. "Here. If the vehicle might just be manoeuvred a little further back this way Mr Sanchez."

Raúl barked again,

"To the rear. One metre, more, more, more. HALT."

Then Dr Jesús said,

"How many of these do you have Mr Sanchez?"

"Rocket launchers?"

"Yes.

"Another three."

"Three o'clock they reckon. Shall we go and meet them?"

Chico Romero listened to Ange ask his mother and was thrilled. There was little he liked more than a night-time adventure. Jack and Paul would be there. Gabby and the twins would definitely go if Ange was going. Mamá would see Daniel and maybe this time it would all work out.

Out in the corridor beside Room 111 of the *hotel america* she fingered the plants along the stairs and started slowly to descend them.

"Your husband is here Ms Santiago," announced a soldier coming through the door and looking up at her.

"Her chances aren't great García. You know that don't you? If she is there, she will either have drowned by now, or have hyperthermia, or both."

Raúl's pronouncement almost made García laugh out loud with caustic mirth. "Drowned AND hypothermia," he said scathingly. "How wonderful."

How wonderful *to have it at last*, O'Reilly thought. After so many years chasing it, love had finally found him. María in three days had brought him what thirty years of marriage had never achieved. There was jubilation, desire, but oddly enough, there was also a sense of peace.

Peace. That was how he would describe it to himself for the rest of his life. Alberto was the first to see her, first a crack, then half a meter. She lay there, white like alabaster, still like stone and to his practised eye, he was sure, she was cold as marble.

"More torque. More dammit," Raúl spat out. "More goddam torque."

The rocket launchers were lined up side by side stabilised to their limit, as though to withstand the launch of the four rockets they each held. Under Raúl's command the steel cables, slowly but smoothly twisted on their reels, dragging and dragging their hooks. The huge iron rings Dr Jesús had unearthed creaked and groaned under the strain of being pulled.

The giant stones, long sealed over the reservoirs at the foot of the *alcazaba*, the giant stones, long under the feet where people gathered daily, the giant stones, beneath the great square between *los palacios* and the ascent to the iconic *torre de la vela*, the giant stones slid away.

Away to the left the ambulance was waiting with its rear doors open, and Rashida saw the men raise the stretcher and shovel it in like fuel into a furnace. The boy with red curls scrambled in after it, was half hauled out, resisted, escaped, and finally was left to accompany the body. Rashida stepped back into the shadows out of respect and bumped against someone.

"Rashida Santiago," said García, ashen with the effort of helping Alberto, bone tired of the emotional cost of finding Lola and managing the aftermath.

"Captain García," she replied moving toward him. "Are you all right?"

Yes and no, he wanted to answer. *Yes* because life is beautiful. And *no* because it is too short. *Yes* because life is long, and *no* because it is ugly.

She put her hand on his arm and said,

"You look tired."

"And so do you."

"Well, I always say, *you can sleep when you're dead*."

"Yes," García was still. Then he spoke, "My daughter used to say that," and then he said, "this is for you," he took off Marilita's ring from his little finger, "it belonged to her." His voice half broke, "She said I should give it to one of life's captains. Here. Take it."

Rashida took it slowly and put it on, leant forward, embraced him one last time, and half ran toward Mustafa.

night

Jesus, thought García, imagining a dozen scenarios as he waited outside the children's ward at the Hospital Ruiz de Alda, *it doesn't bear thinking about*.

Looking into the ward he saw Lola was still sleeping. Under her bed a large pair of boots was sticking out. They twitched slightly.

Good, thought García, *finally Alberto is asleep as well.* He turned from them and leaned into the window, bracing his back on the edge where the frame turned the corner with the wall, and looked through the window into the courtyard below.

Without Dr Jesús she would have died. That much was certain. And without her own peculiar knack for survival as well. Jesús had ordered the lids of the cisterns prised off and knew exactly the weak points to apply the pressure. García vowed he would never underestimate an academic again.

The floodlights had picked her out almost instantly. She was lying on one of the narrow shelves that skirted the top of the deep reservoir. García had known then for the first time what 'blue with cold' meant. They had wrapped her in tin foil and rushed her to the hospital.

García hadn't even asked if he should go. He simply clambered into the ambulance. Alberto, almost glued to her side, had dogged every movement, and then fought to lie next to her on the gurney, desperate to keep her warm.

The hospital had paged García a good few hours later to take a 'phone call.

"How is she?" Antonio's voice rasped with tiredness down the line.

"She's gonna live," and then García had said, "and how are you? You sound like shit."

Antonio had laughed at that.

"I'm good. It's about as over as it can be now. Well my part at least. They've taken all our terrorist fishermen to San Cecilio.

The nuclear medicine department there is as good as they come in Andalucía. They look more like they're going to die than organise an attack. Gerardo is in custody. Fortunately it's no longer my problem."

"What will happen to him?"

"Hard to say. People won't take kindly to him blowing up parts of the nation's most popular monument. On the other hand, if what they say is correct and they've been poisoned by governments colluding in some attempt to heighten fear, then they may get a lot of public sympathy, especially if Gerardo gets a good PR team. You should know that García, coming from the land of PR. If he cultivates a sympathetic image he may even walk."

"And the mysterious Jay?"

"Disappeared. Gerardo won't be drawn on it. Mary Stansfield says she never met anyone answering to either that name or the description. It will be down to you to sit with a police artist and go through the mug shots."

"Joy."

"But that's another day. For now, Dr Jesús says he can fix the damage, we just witnessed the most extraordinary concert ever given, and I am more tired than words can say. I'll come pick you up."

"I'll come pick you up," Michael Small said, and then put down the 'phone.

"Who was that?" Carmen Romero asked Ange.

"Dinky." And when Carmen raised a quizzical eyebrow she said, "Superintendent Michael Small."

"Dinky?" asked Carmen.

"Slang for small," Ange explained, knowing that Carmen still struggled with colloquialisms.

"And is he?"

"Is he what?"

"Small?"

"No actually," said Ange remembering Small when he had accepted her resignation from the force. "He's quite a big bloke. He's Jack's boss. Used to be mine once. He says he will take us to the airport to meet them," she paused. "What about the kids, Carmen? Shall we take them?"

"Of course. I hope your Dinky has a big car."

"I think they're laying on a coach. They had better."

Better *late than never*, thought García as he heard the doors swing at the end of the corridor and turned to see a dishevelled Antonio carrying a small kit bag and heading straight for him.

It took David back to what seemed like a hundred years ago. Back to Richard in all his youthful beauty, back to the first and only time Richard spoke to him in Spanish, bending to him for that first kiss with the sweet taste of wine on his tongue, quoting Lorca's declaration that neither one was fit to meet the other. When the long deep kiss ended, Richard had pulled away, already half cut with an afternoon of boozing, and left David reeling, his wedding ring cutting into his hand through his fist, so great had been the tension in him.

As Antonio neared David, Lorca's remarks seemed more true to him now than ever. David could only feel his backbone half sliced by the wall as he pressed himself into it to try to block out a molten and impossible longing.

"Extra clean clothes for the 'twins'," said Antonio, walking by him and quietly depositing the kit bag near Alberto's feet. "The nuns are back and sent them down. Apparently Alberto lives in mortal fear of being too cold. Come on, we're both exhausted," he said to García, who remained immobile, "the car's waiting downstairs. Let's go back to San Miguel, pack up our personal stuff and get a few beers," and when García didn't answer, Antonio put his arm over David's shoulder and drew him off the wall, "tell me García," he said chattily, "why Lorca? What is it you like about his work so much?"

And when García found his voice,

"It eases me," was all he could manage to say.

"Say? I have no idea. All I know is that I'm not looking forward to it," said Jack Fisher to Paula at the departure gate. All the men of The Constantine Singers were seated waiting for the flight to be called, some were talking animatedly, others seemed tired. A few were humming.

"You did a great job Jack," said Paula. "All you could have done. It was a good outcome," She took his arm and looked with him out of the window.

"Not for him," he said, watching as the coffin caught the lights of the building and was loaded onto the conveyor belt into the belly of the plane.

"Daniel Goddard, Jack," Paula shook her head sadly. "He was never destined for a long life."

"Try telling Daniel's family, all the people that drink with him. Try telling Carmen Romero that."

"That's too bad," said Antonio to García barely fifteen minutes after they left the hospital as he was packing up some of the things on his desk. The drive across town had been fast and easy. Apart from the perennial bin men moving like dancers among the refuse, there was not a vehicle in sight. Antonio had ignored the no entry signs, the one way streets, even the pedestrian footways. "What day's your flight? There is a place I want to show you before you go."

"Tomorrow morning," said García. "There won't be time. This is my last day."

Antonio looked at him.

"*Último día*. Last day," he shook his head at García with a small smile."*Penúltimo día*. In proper Spanish, unlike you Cubano heathens, we never have a last day, or a last drink, above all, in Andalucía we don't. We only ever have the penultimate, the second to the last of anything that is good."

"I think I like that notion," said García, amused for a change by the homespun philosophy. He was about to say so when Antonio said,

"Besides, I spoke with your Commissioner yesterday and told him you needed some more time here."

"O'Reilly?"

"Yes."

"What did he say?" García couldn't imagine O'Reilly agreeing to him having anything beyond the most basic consideration.

"He said OK, and to tell you he had seen María a few times and she was OK too."

García stopped for a minute. O'Reilly cutting him some slack and messages through him from María. He wondered. María and O'Reilly? Was it possible?

He looked at Antonio and remembered how he had felt when Antonio had come toward him outside the children's ward. If he could fall for Antonio who was straight, and not for Raúl, who was gay, anything was possible.

Once he got back to New York he would know about María and O'Reilly soon enough.

Enough. That was all she could think. She had heard enough. Could take no more. Carmen held up her hand to try to stop Jack

from speaking. She laid her fingers across his mouth. Her son Chico came and stood very close beside her. Jack took her wrists and drew her arms to her side and then looked over her shoulder at his wife as he drew her into his arms.

"I'm sorry Carmen. I'm so sorry. I wanted to be the one to let you know."

"You know, García," Antonio said, once they were back at the *reformatorio*. He was amazingly lively, thought David, given the events of the three days and the fact that it was well into the night. It was as if the ending of it all had given him a renewed energy. "You know, I have been completely straight all my life," he said conversationally. David García looked at him, his throat suddenly dry. "And I don't imagine that will change," Antonio went on. García shrugged his shoulders, looked down studiedly and continued his own packing up, ramming his paperwork into the case, "But friendship is the one choice we make in life that is ours. We cannot choose our parents, our children, or even our lovers. All that is either pre-destined or, God help us, an emotional roller-coaster over which we have no control at all."

"True enough," García found his voice and was happy to hear that it sounded halfway normal.

"So," Antonio continued, "do you think the common love of a poet is enough upon which to base a friendship? Or, do you think David," he looked across at him, "do you think that to offer a man friendship when he wants love is like offering a man bread when he is dying of thirst?"

David García stood unnaturally still and then he said,

"I think I have never been sure if there is such a thing as completely bent or completely straight."

Antonio looked across at him surprised at the length of the sentence, but also reassured, and said,

"*A ver*? Shall we see?"

"It's your call," said García looking at him steadily.

"Then my call would be that tomorrow I show you Fuente Vaqueros, and afterwards, we impose on my cousins at Pinos Puente and let them feed us on their fabulous *terraza*, from which it is not possible to see even one inch of **la Alhambra**."

Acknowledgements

Bringing out a book that is nearly 20 years in the making and that has more than 40 voices is not unlike any big project – it involves many people all giving their creative energy.

Our incredible translators, they tell me, often together acted out the parts of characters in their front rooms in order to get the tone and cadence. Pepa Santamaría and Cristina Fernández-Figares Suso, you have been amazing, and the book, in both English and Spanish, is better because of you.

The words come through me but they take a lot of polishing and placing and correcting. Florence de Valladares, who reads equally well in English and Spanish, is a marvel, a critic and guide. I appreciate you more than I can say. Raquel Raya Porcel, you kept us going when we flagged. Thank you for that final push.

Thanks to the editors and proof-readers Mike Jackson and Rachel Davies in English and to Andrés Cárdenas and Alfredo Vázquez Pinteño in Spanish.

The cover is beautiful because of Mark Withington's artistry. Mark, thank you so much.

Much though it is nice to think of a novel as art it is still a product. It needs to be lovely in your hand. Thank you Marco Marziale.

Researching bomb-making is a questionable pursuit. I was fortunate that the North Yorkshire police knew me from Festival of Angels, both the book and York's annual event. Danny Kaye's tour through detonators, 'marzipan' and shot-blasting was invaluable. The errors, some of them deliberate, are mine.

Thanks to Prof. Mary Renfrew for so much information and insight into the work of midwives both today and in years past and to Pam Warhurst, CBE, for the *one hundred year rule*.

Thanks to our readers, Shonét Hockley, Víctor Ruida, Inocencia Prieto, Inma Marchena, Cristina Suso González, Jacinta Suso González, Pedro Santamaría Grant, José María García Candalija, Leah

Amber Jackson-Blake and to everyone in EL PIANO, staff, customers, suppliers. In particular my special thanks to Mayra Marín Salazar and Luis Castro.

Thanks to my fans...especially Patricia Neal and Vicky Harris. It takes a long time to write a book and is incredibly encouraging when people communicate their praises of work already published.

Basharat Hussein, my friend, my true friend and Robina Akhtar. Everything you taught me is here.

A book has to be talked about to be sold. In Spain this would have been impossible without Alfredo Arostegui and Inma Marchena. In the UK, Kaye Hyde and Liz Chadwick have always supported my efforts. Lucy Shepherd...a rare and valuable connection, your enthusiasm flows on and on...

Michael Pleascia, I love working with you. Thank you for all that you bring to our collaboration, for the confidence it gives me, and thanks to Ana for letting you.

Our reviewers were fearless in the face of galleys all riddled with faults. Despite their better judgement they put their names to their praises. Most of you I have not met, but I am so grateful.

Whatever writers may say about characters being fictional, they can only be informed by our experience. I am immeasurably grateful to the many Andalusians I have known whose vibrancy I hope drums through the book, in particular I acknowledge my Spanish Celt, Don Quixote de la Vega, Original Metal Fork, and last, but by no means least, Pepe López and the late, great, Inocencio Ortega.

I am privileged to know Roanne and Brenda, Lyndon and Digby, Bill and Liz, Elaina and Mike, Chris and Derek, Peggy and Alf, Robert and Antonio, Miranda and Ellen, Elaina and Mike, Pepe and Conchi, José Luis and Sacri, Sally and Drew, Arturo and Marie, Kim and Debs and the trio of Jenny, Tom and Liz, who, as examples of mutual devotion, infused many of the characters with the same.

My family: without you there would be no book.

The Alhambra

The Alhambra, the first and last words of the book, is, for any who know her, a vast site comprising fortress, palace and gardens, and deserves an ackowledgement page of her own.

I am happy that the prospect of anyone being able to capture her and hold her to ransom is hugely remote. Even so, I have taken great care to misdirect information. I know that many of the staff there are happy I have done so. This means that, while the book can be used as a guide to trace some of the footsteps of the characters around the monument, any readers who are keen to get to know the Alhambra in depth will need to go and make their own investigations.

The first draft of SONG OF GRANADA was written entirely in the Hotel America, Room 111 to be precise. It is within The Alhambra compound and forms part of the monument. The staff and family could not have looked after me better. In particular I must thank Rafael Garzón Román, Isabel Alconchel Navarro, Manuel Fernández and Ángel Fernández Ariza.

I spent hours in The Alhambra and the archives...and was even there at night and in the snow. I was allowed to go almost anywhere. The gardeners, the monument archeologist, the ticket sales staff were always fantastic. In particular I must thank Jesús Bermúdez, Martina Dobson and María Agustias García Garrido.

Finally I acknowledge all the many people who have cared for The Alhambra over the years. Finding the balance between saving everything, altering nothing, AND opening up to both public access and to change, is at the core of conservation. It is a very fine line to walk. I cannot thank enough the many unsung, unknown stewards who preserve our past, that we might learn from it, and who connect that past to our present and our future. The Alhambra stands as much as a monument to them as she does to herself.

Reading Group Guide

The points which follow are intended to help enhance your reading pleasure and provide some talking points for Anne Sikking's acclaimed novel about three dramatic days in Spain.

1. It has been suggested that The Alhambra is THE main character of SONG of GRANADA. How far do you agree? Would the story have worked just as well set in any ancient monument?

2. Anne Sikking, when interviewed, has discussed how she hoped to portray the heroism of ordinary people in SONG OF GRANADA. Do you think that heroism is a theme in the book? Has the author been successful?

3. The character Ángel David García has a particular take on terrorism and its role in modern life. Which parts of his perception do you agree with, if any?

4. The work of Federico García Lorca and the poet himself appear extensively in the book. Anne Sikking has referred to Federico García Lorca as the 'glue' that 'over-arches' the story and holds the characters together. Do you agree? How would the story be without him? What does his inclusion in the story tell us about Granada? About each of the characters?

5. It is often said that a good novel depicts conflict and resolution: man against man, main against nature, man against himself. Do you recognise these conflicts within SONG OF GRANADA? Are they satisfactorily resolved?

6. Rashida is very pro-active when events are happening during the seige, yet, when it is over, she becomes far less so. Why do you think that is?

7. Would you agree that no one action and no one person caused the outcome of the seige? How far does that reflect outcomes in real life?

8. In the book very different social groups are knitted together. Anne Sikking has spoken about the importance of 'outsiders'. How did you think that the novel developed this theme?

9. By chosing to have the action take place over three days the novel follows a classical formula. Did you notice? Does it work?

10. Critics have spoken of the novel as a work of art, as poetic. Do you agree with them? Did the style add to, or detract from, your enjoyment?

11. If the three seminal feelings in life are fear, anger and grief, did you find all three respresented in the book? Which characters expressed all of these, if any?

12. How do you think the lives of Antonio and David will develop? How would you like them to develop?

13. In some ways the book unites people who have little or nothing in common in the face of a common enemy. What would you say the enemy was? Was there more than one? And how realistic is it to think that people might unite in such a way? Are there real life examples of this?

14. The book was received by The Alhambra officials as electrifying yet distressing and security arrangments at the monument were reviewed. Can you relate from either history, or your from own experience, how reading a book has led to change?

Further reading in English:

Anything by
Federico García Lorca
Anything by
Ian Gibson
in particular his biography of Lorca
and his walking guide to Granada
Anything by
Gerald Brennan

Further reading in Spanish:

Anything by
Federico García Lorca
Anything by
Ian Gibson
in particular his biography of Lorca
and his walking guide to Granada
Anything by
Gerald Brennan
Anything by
Brígida Gallego Coín

Reading Group Notes

Also from Anne Sikking

Festival of Angels
available on KINDLE
ISBN 978-0-9563980-7-9

"With over forty characters
this is story telling on a grand scale."
YORK EVENING PRESS

"The drugs racket is just a sprinkling of angel dust
on a story which is
principally about a much deeper issue...
Of what is the Spirit made?
In this case, not of family,
religion or ethnicity,
but of trust and accident of place..."
Karen Maitland, DREAM CATCHER

"I haven't enjoyed a book so much
since I read Captain Corelli's Mandolin"
Patricia Neal, Derby

Festival of Angels

Angel time

The City of York has a heart but almost no lungs. Its green spaces are diminished, ragged at the edges, made smaller still in winter by rising water, for every year the River Ouse marks itself higher and higher on the flood defences. Groundwater seeps, more sewage than sweet. The air is dense with the odour of sugar and chocolate. It hardly moves. Under this layer of aromatic confection is the armature of air, its base molecules, the structure upon which breath rides. If it were solid it would be rock hard and rotten. Fossilised.

Except for the Minster, where the wind is outrageously behaved, the air in York is still. The plain keeps it tucked in, re-cycling the same air now as was there two millennia ago. All that ever breathed it, sang with its lift, laughed through its intake, exhaled with its power, sighed in its mercy, are joined. Through the air they share the common needle of living.

Realtime

A stone's throw from the Minster is The Quarter. This is a good name for a place that is not a whole. The irony is not lost on some of the people who live and work here. A city with two drinking establishments and one church for every day of the year has become accustomed to irony. The Minster is underpinned, quite literally, by a history of Charlemagne, Constantine, and Alcuin.

The Quarter, by contrast, is underpinned at first by a history of whoredom, of women alive with pox lifting their skirts to any punter on the street, at any time of day, in public view.

Later, The Quarter's history is of workshops, warehouses; yet more spaces that are essential but never openly displayed. Now in The Quarter there is the surface elegance of exclusive shops. There are men's suits, ladies' knickers, shoes and designer...

Also from Anne Sikking

In the Smoke
of the
Sagebrush

available on KINDLE
ISBN 978-0-9563980-4-8

"a novel about...a kind of healing...
it is the raw power of grief
that makes the book so memorable..."
Stephen Lewis, YORK PRESS

"This book has a big heart
& is full of wisdom about the human condition"
Miranda Castro, HOMEOPATH & WRITER

"Reminded me of THE BONE PEOPLE..."
Morgan Ladd, DR GOURMET

In the Smoke of the Sagebrush

"The night was black about me and terrible with swift fire,
and the sending of great voices and the roaring of the hail.
And as I cried, I begged the grandfathers to pity me
and spare me...
then we all got up
and it got dark with dust and smoke."

Black Elk
Holy man of the Oglala Sioux

They were all moving and shouting to try and be heard above the noise. There was the cracking of spark and wood and the sound of helicopters overhead. There were no sirens, but the flashing lights on the rescue vehicles seemed to make, if not a noise, then a pulse in their repetition that beat in counter-rhythm to the sound of splintering.

I stepped back and the heat subsided. I stepped forward, only one step mind you, and there was a wall of heat, just like that. A wall. My nose could be through the wall, on that side, and my cheeks on this side. My nose could feel like it was burning, and yet my cheeks were just flushed. This is the fineness of fire, its exquisite tuning.

If you were to say to people 'fire' and they didn't know it as it can be, if you were to say to them 'fire' as if you were playing a game of connection, most would answer 'heat' or 'burn' or 'flame' or 'smoke'. Some of the lateral thinkers might say 'brimstone' perhaps. Even if they did know fire a little, they would say 'choking' or 'gasping'. Few would ever say 'noise'.

But the noise, my God, the noise, it was cacophonous.

There is very little modern fiction about Granada. Most writing today focuses on times gone by, when perhaps it is thought that there was a golden age, or on a war that many are torn between remembering or forgetting.

SONG of GRANADA was a joy to write. It allowed a celebration of the modern and wonderful qualities of the city NOW, of its people and of Andalusians in general.

It was also possible to give voice to our concerns NOW. How will we care for our planet in the future? Who are life's everyday heroes? What threats do we face? A fundamental question I try to address is simple: *is being a decent human being enough to create change? And indeed what is a decent human being?*

It is often said that a writer should write what they know of the world, about how it is. Another way is to dream what the world might be and celebrate what we know we are capable of.

If any of this has been achieved in SONG of GRANADA, then this is pleasing.

Anne Sikking
Granada, 2014

Michael Plescia's series, LISTENING TO WRITERS, includes some short interviews with Anne Sikking where she talks about the writing process, Lorca and Granada. These can be seen in English & in Spanish on Youtube or by linking through

www.cancion-de-granada.com
www.annesikking.com
www.song-of-granada.com

ANNE SIKKING is a mongrel American of largely Native American descent with Dutch, Irish, Scottish and German ancestry. She has a US passport, a Bristish education and probably a 'Granainan' heart.

CRISTINA FERNÁNDEZ-FIGARES SUSO is a native born 'Granaina' who works both as a solicitor and technical translator. Since 1999 she has worked together with...

...PEPA SANTAMARÍA, who lives in Granada and has family roots there, but was brought up and educated in the UK. She works as a translator and interpeter as well as teaching English at all levels.

MARK WITHINGTON is a former cathedral stonemason and master carver who has recently returned to fine art. His paintings are the covers for the Angel Trilogy of which SONG of GRANADA is the second part.

Call for poets
Poems of the Diaspora - (working title)

Thousands of people leave their countries each week in search of work. Many find themselves at last able to use their qualifications and have employment, but far from home.

Most are experiencing their new lives with a mixture of gratitude, improved self-esteem, loss, bitterness, confusion, joy, new relationships... the list is endless.

SQUAW PIES is seeking poetry from people of WHATEVER background and nationality for a new anthology.

Selected poems will refer to themes of emigration and immigration, homeland, opportunity (equal or otherwise), national/tribal identity, frontier and personal development. Poems may refer to recent events or to historical ones, be personal, impersonal, narrative or classical. They need not say something NEW, but they must in some sense be celebratory...

All poems must be submitted in their original language AND in English. All will be published in English, AS WELL AS their original language and alphabet/script.

Poems should not be longer than 300 words.

For more information about how to submit, payment, rights and publication, see our website

www.squaw-pies.com